PRAISE FOR

PRICELESS

"The very talented Ms. Stewart is rapidly building an enviable reputation for providing readers with outstanding stories and characters that are exciting, distinctive, and highly entertaining. Four and a half stars."

—*Romantic Times*

"The best of romance and suspense. Flowing dialogue, wonderfully well-rounded and realistic characters, and beautifully descriptive passages fill the pages of *Priceless*. . . . Not to be missed."

—RomCom.com

"Ms. Stewart's storylines flow like melted chocolate."

—Writers Club Romance Group/AOL Reviews

"In the style of Nora Roberts, Stewart weaves a powerful romance with suspense for a very compelling read."

—*Under the Covers Reviews* (Manatee.com)

"An exceptionally gifted storyteller with a unique ability. . . . [Stewart has] a rare talent that places her in the company of today's best-selling romantic suspense authors."

—CompuServe Reviews

MOON DANCE

"Enchanting. . . . A story filled with surprises."
—*The Philadelphia Inquirer*

"Irresistible author Mariah Stewart rounds out her marvelous trilogy with the exciting conclusion, *Moon Dance*. Visiting with the Enright clan has been a joy from beginning to end. Four and a half stars."
—*Romantic Times*

"A fine love story that pushes the romance into the mainstream arena."
—*PaintedRock.com*

"Stewart's books, like Nora Roberts' sibling sagas . . . are about relationships. I can't think of many writers who can do this better."
—*Under the Covers Reviews* (Manatee.com)

"Filled with excitement, suspense, and a passionate love story, told by a master storyteller. A book to cherish."
—*Belles & Beaux of Romance*

"[Stewart] hits a home run out of the ballpark. . . . A delightful contemporary romance with well-developed characters, gentle humor, and a bit of suspense."
—*The Romance Reader*

WONDERFUL YOU

"A much welcomed and vastly entertaining sequel to *Devlin's Light*. You can't help but be caught up with all the sorrows, joys, and passion of this unforgettable family. Four and a half stars."

—*Romantic Times*

"*Wonderful You* is delightful—romance, laughter, suspense! Totally charming and enchanting."

—*The Philadelphia Inquirer*

"A multilayered novel that will appeal to fans of romance, mainstream fiction, and family sagas. Mariah Stewart exceeds her own high standards of excellence with a work that compares favorably with the best of Barbara Delinsky and Belva Plain."

—Harriet Klausner, Amazon.com

"Mariah Stewart writes the kind of three-dimensional, lovingly crafted novel this reader thought no longer existed."

—Writers Club Romance Group/AOL Reviews

"*Wonderful You* is simply . . . wonderful. I lived every page of this book as I read it. [Stewart] set perfect lyrics to a perfect tune and made this story sing."

—RomCom.com

"A keeper not to be missed! Outstanding! SIX BELLS!"

—*Bell, Book & Candle*

Books by Mariah Stewart

Moments in Time
A Different Light
Carolina Mist
Devlin's Light
Wonderful You
Moon Dance
Priceless
Brown-Eyed Girl

Published by POCKET BOOKS

MARIAH STEWART

BROWN-EYED GIRL

POCKET STAR BOOKS
New York   London   Toronto   Sydney   Singapore

This book is a work of fiction. Names, characters, places and incidents are products of the author's imagination or are used fictitiously. Any resemblance to actual events or locales or persons, living or dead, is entirely coincidental.

An *Original* Publication of POCKET BOOKS

A Pocket Star Book published by
POCKET BOOKS, a division of Simon & Schuster Inc.
1230 Avenue of the Americas, New York, NY 10020

ISBN: 0-671-78588-5

First Pocket Books printing April 2000

10 9 8 7 6 5 4 3 2 1

POCKET STAR BOOKS and colophon are registered trademarks of Simon & Schuster Inc.

Cover art by Vince DeVito

Printed in the U.S.A.

For our brown-eyed girls—
Susan and Mom

Grateful acknowledgments . . .

Chris Mattox, for sharing his knowledge of the prison system in general and death row in particular. Any errors are mine, not his.

Jim Silver, for the short lesson on handguns.

Lauren McKenna, who never says she *can't*.

Kate Collins, for the careful editing that has made every one of my books better, and especially for her enthusiasm for this book.

Loretta Barrett, who is teaching me to fly.

Prologue

He stood in the shadows of the trees, just beyond the shoulder of the road, watching the cars file past in the dark. The need pounding within his veins was so precise, the demands so certain, that his hands were beginning to shake. He rubbed his palms together, hoping to ease the tension, knowing that any such relief would be temporary, at best.

He whimpered imperceptibly at his pathetic plight.

If the voices had been clearer—they usually were *so* much clearer—this last-minute distress, this *chaos* would not be necessary.

What to do, what to do?

Frustrated by his lack of direction, he chewed distractedly on a gritty fingernail.

What would be the telling sign?

The voices had been dull tonight. He had heard them, but only barely. They had teased him along, taunting him, but offering no clues.

Where to look? Where to begin?

How would he know the one?

He began to sweat, the churning in his stomach growing worse for his plight and the buzzing in his head increasing with each moment that he remained indecisive.

A red car. He heard the pronouncement clearly, though it was little more than a whisper on the wind.

Tonight she'll be driving a red car.

Calming slightly now that he knew, he regained his focus, the sudden flow of strength rippling through him. Now he need only decide on where to seek her.

The all-night convenience store less than fifty yards to his left—situated just off the interstate—had served nicely in the past. He could sit in that little wooded grove at the edge of the parking lot and wait for her to come, wait all night, if necessary. He'd watch for her to pull off the highway and into one of the parking places in the lot. Then, when she went into the store to buy a pack of cigarettes or a cool drink and perhaps a snack to tide her over until she reached her destination, he'd slip from the darkness and follow, ever so nonchalantly. He'd have to be very clever, of course, to get close enough to see if she was *really* the one he'd been waiting for without calling any attention to himself.

It was always a personal challenge to see just how close he could get and still pretend not to notice her at all.

If she wasn't the one, then he'd leave and she'd be safe, at least for that night, and from him. Then he'd go back to his car and wait for the right one. Some nights he waited longer than others, but never had he waited in vain.

If she was the one, he wouldn't stare, he'd give no sign that he recognized her for who she really was. No, no, he was far too smart for that. He'd make a quick purchase and leave before she did. Once outside, he'd slip alongside her car and pretend to pick up something he'd dropped, and with the long, thin sharp blade he pulled from his boot, he'd slit her tire. Then he'd get back into his dark little nondescript car and he'd wait for her.

He'd follow her—at a distance of course—until the tire went flat. If he sliced it just right, it would hold until just about the time she reached that section where the road narrowed and the woods began in earnest. She'd be forced to pull over and within less than a minute, he'd pull over behind her.

She'd turn anxiously as she watched him approach from behind, her heart beating with uncertainty as he grew larger in her side-view mirror.

Chances were that she'd trust him. It had been his good fortune to be blessed with the face of a cherub and a most sincere smile. They almost always trusted him. Especially when he put the blinking red light on the top of his car.

He'd stride up slowly, purposefully, as if this was something he did every day, giving the appearance of searching the car with his flashlight before shining it on the flat tire.

He'd offer his help, offer her the use of his cell phone, which he'd pull out of the deep pocket of his tan shirt.

Of course, if she refused his help, or if she had her own cell phone, he'd be forced to smash out the window with the flashlight, but he hoped it wouldn't come to that. He hated to begin a relationship with violence. It threw off the rhythm and darkened his mood.

His favorite times were the ones when he'd been able to slip unnoticed into the backseat of her car while she was inside shopping. Once she resumed her journey, he'd let her drive on for a while, giving the hypnotic cadence of the journey time to lull her, and giving him time to savor the moment, to anticipate what would come. To learn the scent of her.

Perhaps she'd turn on the radio and sing along. He loved it when they did that, loved hearing the voice sing a favorite tune. Once he'd even taped it, taped her singing softly to a Fleetwood Mac song on the tiny recorder he had tucked into his jacket pocket. Later, he had taped her screams, and it had given him infinite joy to have played that tape. That the same voice could vary so had fascinated him. But he'd inadvertently erased the screaming part when he'd tried to re-record the tape so that he could listen to both her screams and her singing at the same time, an unfortunate error that still upset him to recall.

But so few women left their cars unlocked anymore—what had happened to *trust,* he lamented—that he'd been forced to come up with a different plan.

Still, the taking would be easy.

It was always so easy.

Once, of course, the voices told you how to spot the right one.

Last week, the one had blond hair. The week before, she had been wearing black boots. The clues changed constantly—who knew how many disguises she had, how many ways she knew to trick you? You had to find her, and when you did, she had to be reminded of all the times she had tricked you in the past.

And then she would have to be punished.

Again and again and again . . .

Chapter 1

The drone from the tired engine hummed through the small plane like a lullaby made weary from infinite repetition. Leah McDevitt shifted slightly in the narrow seat, clutching the worn brown leather portfolio to her chest and smiling even in her sleep. Dreaming, no doubt, of the expression on her cousin Catherine's face when she saw the article Leah would deliver for the May issue of *Trends,* the bimonthly magazine they had inherited from their uncle eight years earlier.

Pragmatic Catherine, the heir to the majority of shares as well as Uncle Harry's business sense and his position as editor-in-chief, had long since proven herself a worthy successor. Leah, having been born with a healthy dose of wanderlust and a freewheeling, creative spirit, was delighted to have been given carte blanche in the features department, where she had seemingly endless opportunities to travel, permitting her to acquire a firsthand knowledge of exotic cultures and explore new vistas, much of which would eventually grace the pages of *Trends* in one form or another.

Leah's current project, photos plus text, had taken her

on a jaunt to trace the use of tattoos—a current hot
fashion trend—through antiquity. From Egypt to Greece
to Turkey, she'd been fascinated by her finds and hoped
that her readers would be also. In a museum in Greece,
there had been fourth- and fifth-century Greek vase
paintings that depicted women with strategically placed
tattoos intended to accentuate their muscular physiques.
The designs—vines, geometrics, spirals, and animals—
were almost contemporary in nature, and she could
barely wait to see the color photos she'd taken. She'd
learned that throughout the ages, tattoos had served to
mark prisoners of war and slaves in some cultures just as
frequently as they were used as symbols of beauty and
wealth in others. The tiny tattoo of an owl on a modern
youth might be chosen to symbolize wisdom. The
ancient Athenians, however, used it to mark the fore-
heads of their prisoners of war.

Leah yawned and opened her eyes momentarily, snip-
pets of the article already floating around in her head,
eager now to get home and work her notes into their
final form before deciding on her next venture. The silver jewelry she'd seen in the marketplace in Turkey had
been lovely enough to tempt her to return, and the fab-
rics she had purchased in Bulgaria—along with the attar
of roses the country was known for—had caught and
held her imagination. Perhaps an article about Eastern
European crafts? Then again, there had been those
ancient adobes in the American southwest . . .

Leah shifted again to ease the weight on her left hip
and leaned her head against the window. They'd be in
Amsterdam soon, then on to New York. She had yet to
decide whether she'd go straight to the country house in
Connecticut—little more than a cabin, really—or to the
brownstone in Manhattan, another bequest from Uncle

Harry, she shared with Catherine. Knowing she had at least a dozen more hours before she'd have to make the decision, she covered her yawning mouth with her hand and permitted herself to drift back to sleep.

It was almost two in the morning when Leah collected her luggage and began to make her way through JFK Airport. Well rested after having spent so much of her time sleeping on the plane, she was looking forward to writing her article. Once outside, she spotted the car she'd arranged to pick her up and opted to go straight downtown to the office, rather than to the townhouse where she would more than likely awaken Catherine upon arrival.

The lobby of the narrow, weathered brick six-story Dean Building was well lit, the guard at the horseshoe-shaped front desk clearly visible from the street. The car pulled up in front, bringing the guard to the front door to investigate, one hand on his cell phone. Leah waved as she climbed out of the backseat, and, recognizing her, the guard unlocked the front door.

"I wasn't expecting anyone. It's late for anyone to be out." He said this almost accusingly, as if irritated to be taken from the warmth of the lobby on such a frigid night.

"I should have thought to call you, Frank. I'm sorry." Leah flashed him her best smile. "I'm just back from my trip and thought I'd stop in and do a little work, since I slept through most of my flight."

"I have coffee on in the kitchen," he offered as apology for having chastised her, however mildly he'd done so. After all, he did, in a manner of speaking, work, if not for her, then certainly for her family.

And he'd known all of them, from the Harry Dean who founded the magazine that over the years had become *Trends*—it had been *Milestones* back then—to Harry's children, Sally, Harry, Jr., and Anna, all gone now, Harry, Jr., having outlived Sally by a year, Anna by many more. As Harry, Jr., had no children of his own, the magazine had passed into the hands of his nieces, his only living relatives, upon his death.

This new generation was surely different, Frank shook his head imperceptibly. That a young lady would show up at a Manhattan office building in the middle of the night to work! Certainly, Leah's mother, Sally, would never have done such a thing, but then, *kids today*, he rolled his eyes.

"Coffee sounds great. I'll grab a cup on the way up. Thanks, Frank." She rolled her wheeled suitcase close to the desk. "I'll just leave this here, if you don't mind. No sense in hauling it upstairs."

"I'll take care of it for you," Frank said, tucking the suitcase closer to the area behind the desk. "It'll be right here when you want it."

Leah ducked into the small room, no larger than a closet, and helped herself to a Styrofoam cup that she filled with dark fragrant liquid. Day or night, one could always find a good cup of coffee in the lobby of the Dean Building, if one knew where to look. She sipped at it appreciatively, tucked the leather portfolio under one arm, and hoisted her travel bag over her shoulder before heading to the elevators. She touched the arrow pointing upward with her one free finger and the doors slid open immediately, as if awaiting her pleasure. Leaning forward to tap the button for the fifth floor, she caught a glimpse of herself in the mirrored wall.

In baggy khaki pants and a navy pea jacket, her dark hair tucked behind her ears and held back with a loose ribbon, her face bare of makeup, Leah looked younger than her thirty years. The large canvas travel bag over her left shoulder weighed her down, and she listed slightly to one side to compensate for its weight. She looked more like a graduate student returning from a vacation than the features editor of a popular magazine returning from a business trip.

Leah stepped off the elevator onto a well-carpeted floor and followed the silent hallway to her office. Unlocking the door and turning on the light, she sighed when she saw the mountain of mail that awaited her attention.

Well, it will all have to wait just a little longer, Leah thought as she dropped her bag on the floor and turned on her computer. Pushing the stack of envelopes aside, she pulled her notes out of the brown leather folder and spread them out upon her desk. Slipping into her chair, she toed off her shoes as she sipped pensively at her coffee, her opening line already formed and at her fingertips. She set the cup down and began to type, her thoughts clicking along as smoothly and efficiently as a commuter train. Later she would download the photos she had taken and begin the process of deciding which to use.

Three hours later, as the sun was just beginning to rise, Leah rolled her chair back from her desk and read the copy for the tenth time, changing a word here, a phrase there, also for the tenth time. Rubbing the back of her neck she decided that what she had was a good first draft. Achy and stiff from sitting so long in the same position, she rose and, after a series of stretching exercises, went into the small bathroom to the left of her office where she splashed cool water on her face. Still patting her skin dry with a pale blue towel, she rummaged in the small refrigerator near her desk in search

of a cold bottle of spring water. Finding one near the
back behind a container of long-expired peach yogurt,
she sat back down at her desk, refreshed and, she figured, good for at least another hour or so.

Leah was determined to finish the article and leave it
on Catherine's desk so that it would be there when her
cousin arrived for work. Which should be soon, she realized after glancing at her watch. Catherine was an early
riser and could be found at her desk most mornings by
seven o'clock.

*Maybe one more read-through, maybe just a little more pol-
ish*, Leah thought, hitting the print icon on her computer.

Leah preferred to do her editing on paper rather than
on the computer screen. As she stood up and leaned forward to reach the pages that slid quietly from her
printer, she knocked over the pile of mail and memos
she had previously shoved aside. Cursing softly, she
knelt down to pick them up.

Carolyn, her ever-efficient assistant, had put little
sticky notes on just about every item in the stack.

"Proofs for the beach-bum article" was printed neatly
on one. "Call Mr. Allen in production on this piece . . .
he says it's too long," read another. "This woman called
three times but wouldn't tell me what she wanted" was
noted on one of the pink telephone messages. "This is
marked *P & C*, so I didn't open it" sat upon a plain white
envelope on which her name and address were neatly
printed in blue ink.

Dropping everything else to the side of her desk, she
slipped one finger under the partially opened flap on the
back of the envelope marked personal and confidential.

"Damn," she muttered as the paper sliced into her finger, causing a thin line of red to emerge. "I hate paper
cuts."

Leah stuck the bleeding finger into her mouth and pulled the cheap white paper from the envelope, snapping it slightly to open it flat.

It took several readings before she understood the message. Even then, she did not—could not—believe what she was seeing. Her knees weak, she dropped into her chair and, with shaking hands, read it over yet again.

And then she began to cry.

"Dear Ms. McDevitt," Catherine read aloud from the letter a white-faced Leah had met her with before she'd even managed to welcome her cousin home or open her office door. *"I saw you on that television show, the one about missing persons. I know where your sister is. Does this mean I get the reward? Signed, Raymond Lambert."*

Catherine's eyes had widened with every word. Finally, she looked up at Leah and said, "It's another hoax, honey. You know it is. Just like the others have all been."

"Cath, the others weren't from Raymond Lambert."

"And you don't know that this one is." The letter rattled slightly as Catherine waved her hand. "It's possible that someone else wrote it. Anyone could use his name."

"Sure. Anyone on death row at the Robert Orville Johnson Correction Center down there in Warehamville, Texas, could be using his name."

"That's right."

"Catherine, you do know who Raymond Lambert is, don't you?"

"Yes. Of course."

One of America's most notorious serial killers, Raymond Lambert was currently on death row awaiting a lethal injection that three other states also would love to administer. Texas had earned the right, however, by virtue of the fact that they'd caught him first and tried and sentenced him even before his long trail of homicides had been unraveled.

Catherine tossed the letter onto her desk and sat down, her bottom jaw clenched.

"There's never been any connection between Melissa's disappearance and Raymond Lambert, Leah. Through all the trials, and all the hoopla over this guy, all of his confessions, he's never mentioned her name." Catherine spoke as if she was thinking aloud. "He—or someone else—is simply playing with you. Didn't the host of that television show ask you if the reward was still available?"

Leah nodded.

"And you said something like, 'The reward will stand until we find out what happened to my sister.' That's pretty much what you said, wasn't it?"

"Yes."

"Sweetie, fifty thousand dollars is a lot of money. People have told much bigger lies for a whole lot less."

Leah pulled a high-back leather chair close to her cousin's desk and sat down, her elbows resting on the highly polished desktop, and studied Catherine's finely boned face. Catherine's blue eyes had darkened and narrowed with concern, her mouth had been drawn into a tight, controlled line.

Catherine Connor had not risen to the top of her field by losing her head even under the most emotional circumstances. Calculated where Leah was spontaneous, precise where Leah might be impulsive, Catherine managed the magazine in the same manner in which she managed her life. There was no room in either for anything that wasn't concrete, factual. This letter was obviously a hoax as far as Catherine was concerned and, as such, merited no more of her time.

"What if he really knows, Cat?" Leah asked softly.

"He doesn't." Catherine rolled the letter up into a ball and tossed it in the direction of the trash can.

She missed. The paper ball rolled slightly to the left and bounced off the wall.

"Leah, I'm so sorry. God knows that I would do anything in this world to find Melissa. But I don't believe for one second that this guy is doing anything but pulling your chain. If I recall correctly, he was known to enjoy torturing people. Don't be another one of his victims, Lee."

"All these years, I've wanted to believe that she was out there, somewhere." Leah looked across the desk at Catherine with eyes that were suddenly very weary. "Everyone thinks I'm crazy to believe that she could still be alive. Maybe I am—"

"Of course you're not, sweetie," Catherine's response was quick and certain. "There are thousands of stories about people who had been missing forever showing up unexpectedly years later. As long as you and I believe she could still come home, does it matter what anyone else thinks?"

The phone buzzed rudely.

"Yes?" Catherine asked of her secretary.

"Ellen Petersen is on the line."

"Thank you." Catherine turned back to Leah, her voice softening. "I'm sorry, sweetie, I have to take this call. If I thought there was any chance that Lambert knew anything about Melissa's disappearance, I'd be on the first plane to Texas. But he doesn't. Let it go."

Leah rose without responding, pushing herself out of her chair with heavy hands and walking to the door on leaden feet. The balled-up letter lay near the door, and she bent down to pick it up.

Crushing it within her fisted hand, she returned to her office and looked out the window, her mind abuzz with a million thoughts that careened off each other like tiny bumper cars.

Finally she buzzed Carolyn.

"Carolyn, please call archives and get me everything—I mean *everything*—you can get your hands on about Raymond Lambert."

"Raymond Lambert? The serial killer Raymond Lambert?" the young woman asked uncertainly.

"Yes."

"When will you need it?"

"As soon as possible. As much as you can find, as quickly as you can get it."

"Sure thing, Leah," Carolyn replied. "I'll get right on it."

Leah released the crumpled paper from her fist and spread it out on the desk. The printing was small and precise. No superfluous curls or flourishes. Even the message was clear and to the point.

I know where your sister is. Does this mean I get the reward?

Chapter 2

$\mathscr{M}$s. McDevitt," the young FBI agent stared at Leah with patient hazel eyes and pushed a strand of light brown hair back from her forehead, "what makes you think that there's any connection between Raymond Lambert and the disappearance of your sister?"

Leah removed the crumpled letter from the folder in her briefcase.

"Since Melissa's disappearance seven years ago, I've become very active in Without a Trace," she began.

"The national organization for families of missing persons?"

"Yes." Leah nodded. "I've appeared on numerous radio and TV shows. I've also written several articles and sponsored advertisements in *Trends*—that's a magazine, it's owned by my family—"

"I'm familiar with it." The woman motioned for Leah to continue.

"About six weeks ago, I appeared on a special segment of *Newsline* with several other siblings of persons who had been missing for five years or more. There was also a private detective on the show who talked about the probability of finding anyone—dead or alive—after so long a time. About a week later, I left the country on business. I was away for almost three weeks. When I came back, this was waiting for me at my office."

Leah handed over the rumpled letter that she had retrieved from the floor of Catherine's office.

The agent, Genna Snow, leaned forward slightly to look over the document. Before she could comment, Leah handed her a second, less rumpled paper.

"And this one arrived two days ago."

Genna Snow's eyes slid from the first letter to the second.

"It appears that they could have been written by the same individual," she told Leah after long moments of study, a spare hint of the deep South clinging to her words. "The printing is identical. Uses the same sentence structure. Same direct message."

Agent Snow looked up from the letters and asked, "What would you like us to do?"

"Well, I thought . . . I mean, you're the *FBI*," Leah responded, unprepared for the question. "I assumed you'd want to know, that you would want to investigate this."

"I'll certainly discuss this with my supervisor, Ms. McDevitt, and get back to you. But I'm sure you realize that Lambert's been sentenced to death by lethal injection. In fact, assuming that his latest appeal is denied by the governor—and I have every reason to believe that it will be—Raymond Lambert will depart this earth in roughly thirty days."

Leah stared blankly at the woman sitting across from her.

"But if he's executed, I won't find out what he knows

about my sister." Leah's voice carried a breath of the panic that had just begun to rise within her.

"That's assuming that he's telling you the truth, that he's not just playing with you." Snow tapped the end of a slim black and gold pen on the folded letters as if debating. "It wouldn't be the first time, you know. Lambert is, among other things, a sadistic son of a bitch. If he had seen you on television, it wouldn't be much of a stretch for him to have sensed your pain. Raymond Lambert feeds on the pain of others. Even from his prison cell."

"But why would he lie? Why would he confess to a murder he didn't commit?"

"Ah, but he hasn't done that, has he?" The agent held the letters by their lower right corners and waved them once before setting them back down again. "He's said only that he knows where she is—no mention of whether she's dead or alive. And why? Maybe it just gives him pleasure to know that he's giving you a little hope that will, eventually, end in more sorrow. Or maybe he's simply hoping you'll use your suspicions to throw a wrench into his scheduled execution, that you'll appeal to the governor on his behalf to delay the state from carrying out the sentence until the matter has been investigated." Snow's gaze searched Leah's face. "Then again, maybe he just wants the reward."

"What would a man on death row do with fifty thousand dollars?" Leah asked.

"Good question. Especially since he has no family to leave it to." Snow shrugged, then added, "You do know, of course, that Raymond's parents and two sisters were his first victims?"

"Yes."

"Shot his father in the face with a shotgun as he came into the house one night after work. When his mother ran in from the kitchen, he shot her, too. Then he killed his fourteen-year-old sister by slicing her throat and sat on the back porch eating grapes while he waited for his other sister, who was nine, to come home from the library. After doing to her what he'd done to their sister, he chained the family dog up outside, gave it fresh food and water, set the house on fire, and drove off in the family car." Genna Snow paused and asked, "Did I mention that he was sixteen years old at the time?"

"I knew. I've done some reading—"

"Well, then you know that it was all downhill from there for little Raymond. Or uphill, depending on your point of view. He earned his nickname—"

"The Vagabond."

Snow nodded. "He was a cagey little bastard. Learned early how best to slip into an area, how to slip right out again, and how to hide his tracks. It took them years to track him down. Only caught him by accident."

"I read that he was picked up by a small-town police department for blowing a stop sign."

"And while the police officer was walking up to ask for Raymond's license and registration, he noticed a red substance dripping out from under the car. Seems Raymond had just finished stuffing his latest kill into the trunk of the car, which happened to belong to the victim. An old Chevy with lots of body cancer and a few serious holes in the undercarriage. Upon closer inspection of the red substance, the officer determined that it was dripping from a human hand that had worked its way through the larger of the holes and was dangling underneath the car. Hard to say who was more surprised, Raymond, at having been caught, or the officer who responded to the call for back-up and stood there while Raymond coolly opened the trunk."

"The articles I read all said he was very arrogant."

"More arrogant than you could possibly believe." Snow shook her head. "I took a class at the academy from one of the agents who worked the case. He said Raymond Lambert was the coldest, most arrogant son of a bitch he'd ever come across."

"What can you do to help me?" Leah asked directly.

"Well, as I said, I'll discuss it with my supervisor and see if we can reopen the file. Though it's my guess that this is a case that everyone would like to see stay closed."

"But the letters—"

Snow cut her off.

"For one thing, you don't know for certain that Lambert himself actually wrote these letters. But let's for the moment assume that he did. We would have to then move on to the fact that Lambert has not said that he killed your sister. He said only that he knows where she is. Of course, one might infer that if he knows where she is, it could be because he put her there. But he has confessed to no crime. Nor given any indication that a crime has been committed. There's not even a body that we know of at this time."

"But—"

"I understand your frustration, Ms. McDevitt, but keep in mind that Raymond Lambert is scheduled to be executed in a little over one month, and there are a hell of a lot of folks who won't be happy to have anything delay that. Now, I will run fingerprints on these and match them against the ones we have on file for Lambert. At least then we'll know if he actually wrote these. There is always the chance, you know, that another inmate saw the same television show and thought maybe they'd best get your attention by signing the name of someone notorious."

"Do you think that's the case?"

"I don't know. But you need to realize that it's a possibility."

"I appreciate that, thank you." Leah tried to smile but found she could not. "And if Lambert's fingerprints are on there, if he really did write the letters—"

"Then we'll see what we can do about having the case reopened. Now, I see he's a bit annoyed with you for not having answered his initial letter." She pointed to the second letter. "Perhaps you might want to consider responding. Maybe drop him a note. See what information you can get out of him. Of course, that's strictly up to you."

"What would you do, if Melissa were your sister?"

Genna Snow paused, taken off guard.

"Very honestly?" she asked, meeting Leah's eyes fully and holding her gaze steadily for the first time since the meeting had begun.

Leah nodded.

"My approach might be a bit different than what I might recommend for someone else," the agent hedged.

"Tell me."

"I'd do exactly what you're doing."

"And what else?"

"Well, I guess I'd find out what I had to do to schedule an appointment with Lambert and I'd make a little trip to Texas. Have a little sit-down with him, face to face, and see what I could get out of him. And I'd find out what he really wants. Maybe it is the reward, who knows? Maybe he figures to buy a few last favors on this earth while he still has a little time left."

"Could you help me do that? Help me get in to see him?"

"Do you think you could look into the face of the man

who may have brutalized your sister—Lambert never killed anyone he didn't brutalize first—and have a rational conversation with him about where he left her body, and then hand over money for the privilege of having had to listen to it all? Do you understand how difficult that would be?"

"It can't be any more difficult than what I've already gone through."

"You might be very wrong about that. For any information he gives you, he'll exact a price."

"For years, Agent Snow, I believed that Melissa was still alive. I read newspapers from every major city in the country, looking for some small mention of a young woman being found, maybe wandering without identity. I followed up on every lead. I called every institution I could think of—hospitals and prisons and mental institutions—on the chance that some bizarre thing might have happened. Maybe a seizure, an accident, had caused her to lose her memory—any off-the-wall thing you could dream up. For a while I even imagined some freak scenario where she was railroaded by some redneck cop in some backwater town for God knew what and ended up in some forgotten prison someplace like you see in those awful B movies from the seventies. Anything could have happened to her. She had to be somewhere. Missing, yes, but still, *somewhere*, alive. I never could bring myself to believe that she was not alive. It felt like a betrayal to give up on her. Besides, it was too terrible to be true. For seven years, I have held on to the scrap of a chance that she was somewhere and just couldn't get home. I considered every possible scenario other than alien abduction. Though I admit, in moments of weakness, that, too, crossed my mind."

Leah swallowed the hard lump that rested painfully in

the middle of her throat, took a deep breath, and continued very slowly. "I think I've just been fooling myself for a very long time."

"It's not so unusual to want to hold out hope for the best, Ms. McDevitt. Especially when no body has ever been found," Genna Snow said gently.

"Thank you for not making me feel like a total idiot. It's amazing what you will allow yourself to believe, when you feel you have to." Leah's mouth tightened slightly at one corner. "If nothing else, these letters have forced me to face the truth. It's just been too hard to even consider that she could be dead. My sister was all I had left of my immediate family."

"I understand. I'm sorry."

"Agent Snow, I think it's a possibility that my sister could have been murdered by Raymond Lambert and that her remains are hidden someplace where they haven't been found."

"And you think that Raymond Lambert will tell you where they are?"

"Right now, he's the only show in town. And yes, to answer your previous question," Leah looked levelly at the agent, "I do believe I can sit across from him and converse rationally if it means I will be able to find out what happened to my sister. All I really want right now is to locate her remains and bring them back and bury them with our parents. I do not believe there is anything I would not do to accomplish that. I owe it to my parents. I owe it to her."

"And if it turns out that Lambert's lying?"

"Then I'll be no worse off than I was before I received those letters, will I?"

Genna Snow nodded slowly and said, "Give me a few days to check out the prints and talk to my supervisor.

Let's find out if Lambert is in fact your correspondent. Then you can decide what you want to do."

Leah wrote down a series of phone numbers on the back of one of her business cards and slid it across the desk.

"I can be reached at this number anytime—it's my cell phone. Most weekends, I'm at the Connecticut number. Come Mondays, I'm back in New York. You can reach me at the office or at my home. My assistant's name is Carolyn and she always knows where I am or how to get in touch with me, if for whatever reason you can't get me at one of the other numbers. And you can always leave a message on the answering machine at my home number." She said as she stood up, "I'll wait to hear from you."

"Did anyone besides yourself handle these?" Genna tapped the top letter with the handsome black pen.

"Only my cousin Catherine, but I doubt that the FBI would have her prints on file. She's hardly the criminal type."

"Well, then, there should be only one set of prints that will match what we already have on record. I'll be in touch soon." Snow stood and stretched out her hand to Leah. "In the meantime, you might want to give serious consideration to whether you really want to meet Raymond Lambert face to face."

"I've waited seven years to find out what happened to my sister. I'd sit down face to face with the devil himself if I thought that would give me what I want."

"And what is that, Ms. McDevitt?"

"I want Melissa to be at peace. I want all of us, finally, to be at peace."

"You may find some things you wish you hadn't learned, hear some things you wish you hadn't heard.

Lambert won't be easy on you. He'll want to hurt you, want to tell you everything that he did to her. He'll relish every second that he gets to relive her torture and her death. He'll want you to suffer, and he'll love it, love savoring your pain. He'll spare you nothing."

"I understand," Leah said. "Thank you."

Leah smiled.

"I think that you think it could be him," Leah couldn't resist saying it out loud. "I think that *you* think he could have done it."

"I never said that—"

"No. No, you did not."

"What he's doing to you . . . it's not without precedents," the agent conceded carefully. "He has bargained in a similar manner before, with other families. *'I'll tell you where to find your loved one if you do something for me.'*"

"And did they? Find their loved one?"

"I believe they did, in at least several cases that I know of. But all of this was years ago. There hasn't been a peep out of Lambert in at least five years. He's been a model prisoner, as a matter of fact. But I do believe that there were a few who found what they were looking for."

"That's encouraging."

"Don't get your hopes up just yet. We still don't know for certain that it's Raymond."

Genna Snow stepped through the doorway of Leah's office and walked down the hall toward the elevators without a backwards glance.

Oh, but we do know that it could be, Leah watched from her doorway, *and that's more than I ever had to hold on to in the past.*

As the doors opened and Genna Snow stepped inside the narrow car, Leah couldn't help but wonder who the others had been who had bargained with the devil they knew as Raymond Lambert, and what price he had exacted for his sad and terrible secrets.

The drive from Leah's townhouse in New York to the old cabin in the Connecticut countryside was a pleasant one, once you got out of the city, off of Interstate 95, and headed north on the back roads along the Connecticut River. Wide and shallow, with picturesque towns dotting its banks, the river split the state in two as it flowed south toward Long Island Sound. The cabin, which despite its improvements and modernizations over the years had retained a somewhat rustic air, sat a mile outside the town of Bannock, population 1717, which fluctuated depending on the season and who was home from college when the heads were counted.

The old cabin had been built by the first McDevitt to have come south from Boston to clear virgin land and raise his family in this farmers' paradise. Over the years, tobacco had been added as a cash crop, and it had brought a goodly amount of cash into the family coffers. Soon a new, larger home was built, with a large barn to house the family's horses and a second one to shelter the cows and sheep. It wasn't long before the McDevitt family was firmly ensconced in the social and political scene of the growing town. For several generations, the old cabin had been all but forgotten, until Leah's grandfather decided to restore it as a weekend getaway, a place of peace and solitude to share with his new bride. In time, the farm had been sold off, all but the cabin, which had passed to Leah's father, then to Leah and Melissa upon their father's death. The deed still bore both the names of John McDevitt's two daughters.

Used as a weekend retreat for the family, there was no place on the face of the earth that held as many happy memories for Leah. She had temporarily moved there after Melissa's disappearance, where she waited impatiently for her sister's return. After several long, agonizing weeks had passed with no word from Melissa, Leah found that she could not bear the silence, the emptiness. Locking the cabin door behind her, she went back to the house in New York that she and Melissa shared with Catherine, and it was several years before she was able to venture back to Bannock. Only the ninetieth birthday of a much-loved neighbor had brought her to the cabin's door. Finding the windows covered with ivy reminded her of a children's nursery rhyme, one where a beautiful princess was kept captive inside a castle covered just so. Leah spent the next several weekends clearing away the vines, having the heating system updated, and painting the interior. It had been therapeutic for her and had helped pass many hours. The cabin would be ready for Melissa when she came back.

It was the only place where Leah felt truly at home. As much as she enjoyed living in the brownstone, with its sleek furnishings and contemporary artwork, it was increasingly more reflective of Catherine's taste than of Leah's. Since Melissa's disappearance, Leah had spent less and less time there, and Catherine had spent more and more. It was natural that the house would seem most like the home of the person who cared for it on a day-to-day basis.

Not that Leah blamed Catherine, she conceded as she drove the last short bit of paved road to the cabin. After all, it *has* been seven years, and she, Leah, spent so much time traveling for work. Bit by bit, Melissa's personal belongings had been packed away and stored in the attic. No one had ever suggested that they be disposed of, and Leah wondered now, in light of the communication from Raymond Lambert, what to do with Melissa's things.

She was still thinking about it—wondering how one gathered the strength to choose what to keep, what to give away, what to throw away—when she pulled up to the cabin, and was pleased to find that a driveway of sorts had been shoveled through the hard-packed snow. She parked carefully between the tidy and pristine four-foot-high white piles that lined the makeshift drive on either side.

Mr. Calhoun must have made a visit this week, she thought as she turned off the car and made a mental note to call the kindly neighbor who kept a watchful eye on the property during Leah's absences and whose wife kept the place dusted and vacuumed and who stocked the refrigerator with Leah's favorite foods when she knew in advance that Leah would be there on any given weekend.

Swinging her weekend bag over her shoulder, Leah dropped the keys in her pocket while she gathered a bag of groceries from the backseat. The recent snowfall had sent drifts across the narrow front porch to rest against the door and she cleared a path with her boots, all the while balancing her burdens. Once inside, she dumped her belongings onto the floor and slid out of her boots, then, holding them over the threshold, slapped them against each other to knock off the loose snow before closing the door behind her. Carrying the wet boots, she passed through the quiet rooms, pausing to inch the thermostat up to seventy-five degrees before turning on a light in the kitchen and placing the boots on a mat inside the back door.

Leah flicked on the lamp that sat on a small table in the great room, with its stone wall and a two-sided fireplace that opened on the other side to the kitchen. Wood was stacked neatly, cut to fit by Mr. Calhoun last fall and brought in by Leah before she left the cabin for her last business trip. She paused to place several pieces in a stack on the grate, opened the flue, then balling up newspaper from a basket just to the side of the hearth, she knelt and proceeded to build a fire. The cabin felt cold, empty, and damp, and she was shivering—had been since she'd first opened the door, she realized.

The fire caught the dry wood and began to crackle, sending pleasant fingers of warm air to circulate throughout the room. Satisfied that the fire would burn and hold well, Leah stood up and brushed a spot of ash off one knee, then stopped and looked around curiously. While all looked exactly the same as it had on her last visit, she had the vague feeling that someone had been there, had touched the room with their presence.

Leah went to the piano in the corner and stared at the photographs that marched across the polished top. All seemed to be exactly as she remembered.

The piano had been a fixture in the cabin for years, a gift from Leah's father to her mother, when young Sally Dean McDevitt—the quintessential city girl—had lamented that there was nothing to do so far from Manhattan. The following week he had had the piano delivered and began work on the deck that still stood off the kitchen. To his wife's protests that she did not play the piano, John McDevitt replied that she would learn from Mrs. Owens in Bannock. The deck, to which several large, cushy lounges had been delivered, were for relaxing, reading, and watching their daughters play in the stream that cut across the back of the property. Sally McDevitt would say in later years that those two gifts, her piano and her deck, were the most precious gifts she had ever received, because they reminded her—the consummate businesswoman—of the simple joys in life, of the beauty of the hours spent with her beloved husband and children.

Leah had never learned to play well, but Melissa had a true musical gift. Even now, Leah could close her eyes and see Melissa, seated ramrod straight on the piano bench, her feet dangling above the pedals, her head bent over the keys as she played a piece that sounded so complex to Leah that it made her head spin just thinking about the effort it would take to learn to play it. And sometimes in the evenings, Melissa and their mother would sit side by side, perfectly in sync as they played their favorites together. Leah would sit next to her father on the sofa, her head on his shoulder, and drifted slowly off to sleep, wishing that she too could play the way Missy played. That someday, she too could make her parents' faces glow with pride, the way Missy did.

Missy. Even now, it was difficult for Leah to speak aloud the childhood name she'd given her sister.

Missy, the living doll who had come to stay when Leah was five years old. Who, after the deaths of their parents, less than two years apart, had been Leah's only stability in an unstable world.

Missy.

Leah's fingers drifted toward the piano top, reaching for a favorite photo. Leah and Missy in a canoe on the lake nearby in Bannock. At fifteen, Leah had worn her dark hair in a sleek ponytail. Ten at the time, Missy had worn braids. They had had such a wonderful time together that summer, exploring the woods around the cabin, walking or riding bikes into town for ice cream or to go to the small library.

And there were so many others. Missy and Leah playing along the creek. Leah swinging Missy on the big wooden swing that their father had hung from a high branch in the tall maple at the back of the property and that could, with sufficient push of the swinger, propel the swingee out over the creek. A proud almost six-year-old Leah with the pudgy, not quite one-year-old Missy on her lap. Missy, years later, seated at this same piano, looking pleased with herself as she had just finished playing a complicated piece; their mother in the background, beaming and applauding proudly.

The piano had not been touched for years, but Leah couldn't bring herself to get rid of it. When Melissa came back, she would expect her piano to be waiting for her. She would want to play.

Leah returned the photo to its place with the others. For years, she had taken solace in them, pictures of those happy children, the products of a happy marriage, a happy home.

All gone now, all but Leah.

The fire crackled loudly and Leah bent to rearrange the wood, feeling lonelier than she had since Melissa had first disappeared.

Tears stung bitterly in the corners of Leah's eyes. She'd always clung to the hope that Melissa would come back, a victim of amnesia. Of white slavers. Of any improbable scenario other than the unspeakable, the unimaginable.

And yet the unspeakable had been spoken, the unimaginable imagined. Once reality had managed to sneak past Leah's defenses, the truth was boldly, glaringly obvious.

Melissa was, in fact, dead. Not missing. Not kidnapped. Not wandering the halls of a hospital trying to recall her name.

Dead.

Had been dead all these years Leah had spent hiring private detectives and consulting with psychics and praying.

One by one the detectives had been fired, the psychics had been vague, and the prayers unanswered.

And all that time, Melissa's bones waited in some unknown place, her spirit—where?

Did it matter to the dead where their remains lay? Leah wondered. She had to think that it did.

Leah carefully piled two more logs on the fire, then wrapped herself in an afghan and curled up in the oversized plaid chair to watch the flames, thinking about Missy being dead.

How had it happened? Had she been shot? Stabbed? Strangled? Leah shivered at the possibilities.

Leah's readings about Raymond Lambert had taught her that he was an opportunist, one who on occasion would grab his victims at random. His primary criteria seemed to be that they appeared to be someone who belonged someplace—no misfits for him!—and that they be easy to take. Lambert, for the most part, was not a stalker. More often than not, he'd simply grab whoever had been unfortunate enough to cross his path when his murderous urges struck—and they'd struck often.

Complicating matters, as far as the law enforcement community was concerned, was the fact that Lambert had no favorite weapon, no ritual means of dispatching of his victims. He'd use whatever was handy and would find the most ingenious means of torturing with whatever killing tool was within his reach. Identifying and catching Raymond Lambert had been a nightmare, in more ways than one, because he had no discernible agenda, no set MO. He was everywhere and he was nowhere.

Where had he found Missy? What tool had he used to hurt her, to take her life?

Leah twisted uneasily and tightened the afghan around herself, pushing thoughts of Lambert aside, wanting none of him here, in her sanctuary. She tried to see instead her mother's face, but she had a hard time calling it up. How would her mother have coped, had she been alive when Melissa had disappeared? Would she have recognized the truth sooner than Leah had? Would Melissa's fate have been easier to accept if the rest of the family had been intact, instead of having already gone to their own sad graves?

Leah closed her eyes and soon drifted off to sleep.

The sunlight dancing off the ripples of cool, clear water was bright enough to blind her. Leah strode through the grass to the stream that ran behind the cabin, and there she watched the water stutter around the rocks, her eyes seeking the small fish that darted so quickly from shadow to shadow. Leaning closer, she discovered not one, but two reflections in the water. Startled, she looked up to see Missy sitting on the opposite side of the stream, stringing a handful of cornflowers into a chain.

"You'll never catch them," Missy was saying. "They'll always be too quick for you."

"I've caught them with my hands plenty of times before," Leah reminded her.

"Maybe when you were young and quick. You're not so young now, Leah. Nor near as quick as you were back then. When you were ten, you could run like the wind. I always tried to catch up, but you were always bigger and faster." Missy sighed and dropped blue petals into the water, which had suddenly begun to rise and surge like a swift river.

"Where are you, Missy?" Leah asked.

Melissa's eyes widened slightly, as if surprised by the question. "Why, I'm just waiting, Lee."

"But, where—?"

"Where I've been. I want to come home, Leah." Melissa's voice raised slightly, not in a whine, but a quiet plea. "I want to come back here, to the cabin."

"I'll find you, Missy. I promise. I'll . . ."

But Melissa was gone, gone from the grassy spot where she'd sat, her reflection gone from the water. Only the chain of blue flowers, drifting rapidly downstream, remained, and even they were beyond Leah's reach now.

Leah woke with a start, drenched with sweat, her face wet with tears. It had been years since she had seen her sister's face so clearly, even in a dream.

"I *will* find you, Missy," Leah said softly to the ghost her memories had conjured up. "One way or another, I'll find you and I'll bring you home."

It had been almost six days since Leah had first met with Genna Snow, six days she'd spent debating what she should do. Long enough.

Tomorrow morning, first thing, she would call Agent Snow and find out the results of the fingerprint comparison. If in fact the prints had been Lambert's, she'd find out what she needed to do to arrange a meeting with Raymond Lambert. Then she'd go there, to his prison, and she would look him in the face and listen to his horrible tale and permit him any twisted satisfaction he'd derive from the telling of it, if, in the end, it would mean she could bring Missy home and lay her to rest.

Chapter 3

Ethan Sanger stepped from the raw cold of a mid-March morning into the small shed off the kitchen and found it only slightly warmer than outside. Slapping his gloved hands together and shaking the snow from the hat that had covered his dark hair, he pushed open the kitchen door, and glanced at the stove upon which a pot of oatmeal boiled in a frenzy of beige bubbles. Dieter, their aging German shepherd, a heap of dark fur upon the light wooden floor, thumped his tail in glad welcome. Ethan thanked him by pausing briefly to scratch the dog behind his graying ears.

"You're out early," Ethan's father, Tom, said as he pitched a handful of raisins into the pot.

"Kelly McKinley went into labor just around midnight last night. Bob called to see if I could plow them out to the highway so that he could drive her to the hospital."

"And you're just getting back now?" Tom glanced at the round, wood-trimmed Seth Thomas clock that hung on the wall. It was twenty past six.

"There was a tree down across the road. I had to stop,

hook it up to the back of the truck, haul it off to the side of the road, and unhook it again. Took a little time."

"Hmmph."

"What's that *hmmph* for?"

"Nothin'. Just hmmph." Tom reached past Ethan to give a quick stir to his breakfast. The oatmeal was clinging to the sides of the pan like paste to the fingers of a first grader.

"Damn," he muttered as he tried to scrape the sides before the oatmeal burned.

He glanced over at his son, who had turned on the television and settled on one of those early morning news shows.

"Did you want some of this?" Tom asked, the pan in one hand, a large wooden spoon in the other.

Ethan shook his head. "No, thanks."

"You'd be fixin' eggs then, this morning, I suppose," Tom commented.

"I already ate." Ethan's attention was on the figures chatting amicably on the small TV screen.

"Oh? And when might that have been?" his father asked casually.

"Earlier, at McKinley's."

"Couldn't have been much of an emergency, if they stopped for breakfast."

"They didn't stop. I stopped back at the house after I finished plowing the road clear down to the highway. Kelly's sister Candace is staying with the two little ones, while Kelly is in the hospital. She offered to make breakfast for me when I'd finished up. I was cold and hungry and accepted the offer graciously," Ethan said flatly without turning around.

"Oh." Tom's face brightened. "Isn't Candace the sister with the great legs?"

"Yes. And no, I didn't ask her out."

"Hmmph" was Tom's only comment.

Ethan knew that, eventually, there'd be more.

"It wouldn't have hurt, you know," Tom stated after a few moments of silence had passed.

"What wouldn't have hurt?"

"Asking Kelly's sister out. You could have offered to take her out to dinner, sort of to repay her for the breakfast."

"I said thank you. Just like Mom taught me. And I don't have time to take her out. I'm leaving for Bangor this afternoon."

"What's in Bangor?"

"I have to meet a client in the morning. Don't want to take a chance that the weather might turn."

"Bangor." Tom said thoughtfully, "I suppose you'll be taking a day or so to visit with your cousin Cal."

"I suppose I will not."

"Why's that?"

"Because every time I stop to see Cal, his wife tries to set me up with one of her friends, that's why."

"A little female companionship never hurt, Ethan."

"If I want female companionship, I'll pay for it," Ethan replied dryly.

"You can get all kinds of STDs that way, Dad."

Ethan's daughter, Holly, stood in the doorway, her blond hair mussed from sleep, her arms crossed over her chest. She wore a heavy fleece robe of blue and white plaid and thickly padded light blue slippers.

"STDs?" Ethan's eyebrows raised almost to his hairline.

"Sexually transmitted diseases," Holly told him as she crossed the room and lifted the lid on the oatmeal. "Is some of this for me, Grampa?"

"If you want it," Tom told her.

"I know what STD stands for," Ethan informed her, mildly amused in spite of himself. "I was just wondering how you know."

Holly rolled her eyes to the heavens.

"Dad, I'm almost *fourteen*," she said, as if that was explanation enough.

"And . . . ?" Her father motioned her to continue.

"And it's the type of thing you have to know about."

Ethan looked at his father accusingly.

"She's being home-schooled, Ethan, she's not being prepared to enter a convent," Tom said calmly as he poured two cups of coffee and handed one to his son. "We are required by law to follow the normal curriculum that is taught to every other eighth grader in the state of Maine."

"And how exactly do sexually transmitted diseases fit into the curriculum?"

"Health," his father said succinctly.

Ethan grunted softly.

"If it was up to you, I wouldn't know anything about sex," Holly remarked.

"Apparently, if it was up to your grandfather, *The Kinsey Report* would be on your reading list."

"Dad, I'm not a baby."

"No, you're not *a* baby. But you're *my* baby. No matter how old you get, you'll always be my baby."

Holly ignored her father's comment, which would have any other occasion been met with a scowl and a roll of the eyes. Today, she had something more important on her mind.

"Does this mean I have to be home-schooled for high school, too? Can't I go to school in town?"

Ethan's jaw tightened. "We'll see."

"That means no. You always say *we'll see* when what you really mean is *no*. Why don't you just come out and say *no?*"

Ethan opened the refrigerator door and hunted for the half-and-half.

"You are so unreasonable," Holly was just winding up, her adolescent indignation beginning to kick in. "You can't keep me in this damned lodge forever, Dad."

"No. Not forever. And don't swear."

"Dad, I want to go to high school in Arlenville in September. You told me you'd think about it. You promised."

Ethan squirmed uncomfortably. Yes, he had promised he'd think about it, but that was last year, when high school still seemed so far away.

"Maybe next—" he began, and she cut him off.

"No, Dad. Not next year. September. I want to start high school with everyone else in my class." Holly glared, then repeated firmly, "*This year*," before stomping out of the room.

The only sound was the scraping of Holly's slippered feet on the uncarpeted steps as she fled to the haven of her room on the second floor.

Finally, Tom cleared his throat and said, "She's right, you know. And you *do* know it, Ethan, no point in tryin' to pretend otherwise. She'll be fourteen in a few months. You can't keep her here forever."

Ethan did not reply.

"Listen to me, son. She can stay with the Mattersons—"

"She's too young to live away from home."

"An hour away, Ethan. She's not too young for that. Holly's growing up. She needs to be with kids her own age. You want to be a hermit, hide away back here in the woods, that's fine. That's your choice, your life. But you don't have the right to do that to your daughter."

"She's all I have, Dad. I have to keep her safe."

"Not at the price you're making her pay," Tom's voice softened. "A smart, spirited girl like Holly needs to have a pack of friends. She needs to be with other kids, havin' fun, being young, not stuck up here in the middle of nowhere with an old man and a father who comes and goes several times every month. Hell, Ethan, if it wasn't for her friendship with Chrissie Matterson and the summer campers, she'd hardly ever see kids her own age. It's not healthy for her. It's not right."

"I don't want her living with strangers."

"The Mattersons are not strangers. We've known them forever. Of course, you could always rent a house in town, but then again, that would mean you'd have to socialize every now and then. Might even have to speak to the neighbors on a regular basis."

"I'll think about it."

Ethan pushed his chair back from the table abruptly and went into the shed at the back of the kitchen, pulled on his jacket, and buttoned it even as he opened the back door, grabbing a shovel as he passed through.

The truth was that he *had* thought about it, and he wasn't happy with his own inevitable conclusions.

Once outside, Ethan began to clear a path from the house back to the barn. Holly would be wanting to feed her goats before she began her lessons that day, and Tom was just too old to be lifting this much snow.

It took almost thirty minutes of hard shoveling, and it wasn't long before Ethan's back, arm, and shoulder muscles began to burn, and sweat glistened on his forehead.

His father was right. Of course, he was right. Holly

was right. Intellectually, Ethan knew that his daughter needed the companionship of her peers, needed the social interaction if ever she was to develop into a well balanced, whole person.

Besides, Ethan reminded himself, Holly was growing into a young woman. What could he or his father possibly teach her about *that?* How could she learn all she would need to know?

And yet, in the depths of his soul, Ethan feared for her, deeply and truly. How could he protect her from the world if she was *in* it?

Every time Ethan looked at Holly, he saw her mother's face. When Libby Sanger had been taken from them so tragically, Holly had been barely four years old. After he'd lost his wife, Ethan had retreated to White Bear Springs, the sporting camp in the Maine woods owned by his father, and sought refuge for his daughter as well as for his own wounded soul. He had never left.

Ethan leaned on the shovel and exhaled, his breath frosting clearly in the dense morning air.

He was being unreasonable. Unfair. Unrealistic.

All her life Holly had been home-schooled because, six months out of the year, the weather could keep one landlocked for weeks. Driving down to town—to Arlenville—every day was out of the question, especially in the winter months when storms could rise up unexpectedly. When Holly had been younger, it had been okay, even practical. Not great, but okay.

It was no longer okay.

Holly deserved better. She deserved the nights out at the movies, the dances, the sleepovers with her girlfriends—all the group activities she had been denied.

Ethan didn't like it. Wished it didn't have to happen. But Holly was growing up, and there was nothing he could do to stop it. He had to love her enough to start to let her go, even if only this much.

He'd shoveled his way to the barn, the path no wider than the blade of the shovel, its course slightly ragged owing to his lack of concentration, but it would do. He leaned the shovel up against the side of the barn and turned, prepared to unlock the door, when he saw his daughter marching toward him, her stride determined, her sense of justice intact, her fight renewed. Her indignation wrapped around her as tightly as the scarf she wore around her neck. Holly was a child who had always known exactly what she wanted and who had long since discovered that, when dealing with her father, logic was the surest route to success.

Ethan smiled in spite of himself.

"Daddy," she said as she approached, her blue eyes flashing, her jaw squared just as his own did when he was busy digging in his heels.

Ethan held up both hands in a gesture of surrender.

"You can go, Hol."

Holly stopped in midstride, her eyes narrowing suspiciously.

"Go where?"

"To high school next year in Arlenville."

"Really?" she asked cautiously.

"Really."

"Oh, Daddy!" Holly pounced, throwing her arms around his neck so that he could swing her around, just as he had when she was a small girl. Her words poured out in a rush. "Thank you! Thank you! Can I stay with Chrissie? Mrs. Matterson said it would be fine, there's an extra bedroom on the third floor—"

"I haven't decided how we'll do this. We'll take it one step at a time."

"Oh! I can't wait to call Chrissie!" Holly beamed, her joy embarrassing Ethan to his very soul. He'd known she'd wanted this, but had no idea just how much it meant to her. "Will you play baseball with me this summer? Help me to get my swing down? I want to try out for softball next year. And maybe could I go to soccer camp this summer? I've always wanted to play on a team."

"Yes, I'll help you work on your swing. And yes, we can look into soccer camp. But right now, there are five hungry little goats inside waiting for their breakfast."

"Daddy, you are amazing." Holly kissed his cheek.

"Sweetheart, I'm sorry for . . . for . . ." Ethan struggled for the words.

"I know that you worry about me because you love me so much, Daddy. I understand all that. It's because of what happened to Mom." Holly's smile faded slightly and an old sadness touched her eyes. "But you know, if Gramma and Grampa had kept Mom locked away in the woods, she'd never have met you. And there would be no *me* to worry about."

"How did you get to be so smart?" Ethan asked, a lump in his throat.

"Must have been the home-schooling." She grinned, the light coming back into her smile. "All that one-on-one attention . . ."

Holly danced into the barn, calling her goats by name, leaving Ethan feeling sad and a little frightened, and infinitely older than his thirty-five years.

There were forces beyond the woods that he would not be able to control, forces that he didn't understand, forces that could take you to the far side of your faith, to places where even prayer could not reach.

How, Ethan wondered, could he protect Holly if she

was someplace else? How could he trust her safety to strangers who had no understanding of how cunning those forces could be?

How could he explain to her that he'd looked into the eyes and soul of a beast without a soul, that he knew with certainty that evil walked this earth in forms the average person could never suspect? That unwanted glimpse into the darkness had shown Ethan more than he had ever wanted to know of hell, had changed him for all time. Ethan could never go back to the man he'd been before the beast had grabbed him by the throat and forced him to *look*, and to listen.

But it was too late to question what he'd done, he'd given her his promise. Ethan had never willingly broken a promise to Holly, and he knew he could not break this one.

Sighing uneasily, Ethan turned back to the house, using the shovel as a sort of walking stick while he prayed that he would never have cause to regret this first bit of freedom Holly had won.

The road leading from White Bear Springs Camp down to what passed for highway in this part of Maine had been plowed two cars wide, one side when Ethan went down to McKinley's in the middle of the night, the other when he came back at dawn. Not that there was much need for a two-lane road, there being a mere half-dozen or so inhabitants in this stretch of woods, but it pleased Ethan for some reason to see the wide road looming ahead of him as he came through the trees. He slowed slightly as he passed the McKinley place. There were lights on in the kitchen, and as he passed, he saw a shadow move across one of the front windows. Candace, probably, having heard the Jeep's approach, likely pausing to take a look to see who was passing by so late in the afternoon.

Candace really was a nice woman, Ethan admitted. She taught third grade in Arlenville, in the very school system Holly had begged to attend. And she was pretty enough, Candace was, with light brown hair and a pleasant smile. She did have nice legs, as his father had reminded him. What would it have hurt if Ethan had stayed a little longer this morning, to have given himself a chance to get to know her a little?

He just hadn't had much to say to her, that's all. She was nice and she was pleasant and attractive, but there just hadn't been a spark. Ethan couldn't remember the last time he'd felt a real spark between himself and a woman. It wasn't that there hadn't been women. There just hadn't been any he'd especially cared about.

Since Libby's death, and all that followed in its aftermath, Ethan had felt little connection to anyone except his immediate family. Everyone had told him he had to get on with his life, and he was trying to, as best he could. It just wasn't as easy as it sounded. The nightmare had been too terrible, and it had lasted far too long.

The thought had occurred to Ethan that perhaps things might be different, once the beast had passed from this earth.

The Jeep jerked slightly as it left the unpaved road and entered the highway at an oblique angle. Ethan slowed to avoid skidding into the opposing lane compliments of a patch of black ice. Not that there was anything in the opposing lane, of course. Not at four o'clock on a Tuesday afternoon on the main road—the only road—into Arlenville. It would be a straight run into town, and Ethan would make a quick stop to pick up a package that UPS, not willing to drive so far back into the woods at this time of the year, had left for him at Grand's General Store. Next he'd pick up the mail at the post office, then drive on down to Bangor.

Maybe I should have called Cal, Ethan thought.

And it wasn't that Ethan didn't *like* Sharon, Cal's wife. It was just that even the most casual visit with them turned into an opportunity for Sharon to play matchmaker. Over the past eighteen months, Ethan had met every available female who had ever passed through Sharon's life. Last time it had been the daughter of a woman Sharon bowled with. The time before that, it had been a single mom from one of the kids' play groups. To be fair to Sharon, none of the women she'd foisted upon him had been obnoxious or unpleasant. And to be totally truthful, they'd each been fairly attractive, in their own respective ways. It had just become increasingly difficult for Ethan to get around the barriers he'd been forced to erect to maintain his sanity. He knew it was time—past time—to take them down. He just didn't know where to begin.

Ethan reached for his car phone and debated whether to dial Cal's office number. He would arrive in Bangor in plenty of time to meet Cal for dinner. With any luck, Sharon wouldn't have enough time to call up one of the troops. On the other hand, maybe he should have dinner in the hotel while he looked over the materials his client had sent him.

As a private investigator specializing in arson investigation, Ethan only took several big cases each year. The rest of his time was spent at camp, making off-season repairs on the cabins and the docks and leading hiking, hunting, and fishing parties into the Maine woods in the summer. There were several insurance companies that sought

Ethan out when they suspected but had been unable to prove arson when a property burned under suspicious circumstances. Having written the definitive tome on arson investigation some years ago, Ethan was still recognized as the expert to call on when all else failed.

The current case involved a medical center that had burned to the ground in the middle of the night. The owner was the prime suspect, but his wife swore he had never left the house after an early dinner, and a neighbor who'd walked the floors all night with her new baby had testified that the owner's cars were visible in the driveway that night. The police had done a good job investigating, and while they had concluded arson, they were unable to find the smoking gun—or in this case, Ethan corrected himself, the lit match. Ethan's job would be to investigate the property owners, their finances, and their personal lives to determine where their motive might lie, and then to report his findings to the insurance company, which would then determine whether or not to honor the claim.

Maybe he'd give Cal a call from the hotel, maybe see about hooking up with him tomorrow, after he met with his client. Chances were that he'd be leaving town for a few days to conduct an on-site investigation, if he agreed to take the job, which he most likely would do. This particular client was an old-time insurance manager who had given Ethan his first big case years ago, and he only came to Ethan when he was truly desperate.

The sun was already beginning to settle beyond the white birches that rose above the snow on one side of the road. Behind their gray-white trunks, a seemingly endless forest of pine darkened the landscape. As he approached the town limits, Ethan came upon a pond where young skaters, released from the confines of their classrooms for the day, had pushed aside the snow with wide brooms and now spun across the ice in chains and in pairs.

Ethan slowed to a stop to permit a group of young girls to file across the road to the spot where another group awaited them. They were all similarly bundled against the cold, in their parkas and hats and scarves and heavy gloves, their skates tied together and tossed jauntily over their shoulders, and they shrieked to one another merrily as the two groups joined. Ethan couldn't help but wonder if his daughter would be a part of this same crowd this time next year—they all looked about Holly's age.

He waited, almost protectively, till the last one had safely crossed.

"Thanks, mister!" this last young straggler called to him, waving and smiling over her shoulder before she, like the others, disappeared onto the darkened path that led down to the pond.

Ethan sat a moment or two longer than necessary, picturing Holly among the carefree crowd that would be sitting on fallen logs at the edge of the pond, lacing on their skates. Holly could skate like the wind. In his mind's eye he saw her taking her place on the whip that was forming, could almost see her eager face, hear her happy laughter as she set the pace for the other skaters. And Holly would be the one to set the pace, Ethan felt pretty confident of that. She wasn't cut out to be a follower.

It was, Ethan conceded, high time that Holly was given her chance to lead. With a silent salute to the girls on the pond, Ethan hit the accelerator and headed toward Bangor.

$\mathcal{M}$uch of what Leah would later recall of her arrival at the Robert Orville Johnson Correctional Center seemed to be wrapped in a haze of barbed wire and underscored with the scent of pine disinfectant.

Once inside the prison proper, Leah walked down one long, wide, brightly lit yet eerily quiet hallway after another, accompanied by a tall guard with thin lips, a tight drawl, and very bad skin. The floor was scuffed gray and white vinyl tile, the walls a pale tannish-yellow that had taken on a sallow tone over the years.

The guard spoke to Leah once, when she'd nearly walked past the doorway of the room they'd set aside for her use at the request of someone highly placed within the prison who'd been contacted by a personal friend from the FBI. The room into which Leah was directed was a narrow rectangle, windowless, the same jaundiced shade of tan as the hall. There was no carpet, nothing in the room other than a long, wide wooden desk, the center of which was positioned so that half sat on either side of a Plexiglas wall that divided the room and that would prevent physical contact between visitor and the visited. Two worn and weary straight-back chairs sat on either side of the desk. As she approached, Leah could see a veil of screening set in the Plexiglas.

Just like on TV, she could not help but think.

"It's still not too late to change your mind," Leah heard the guard say, his voice suggesting that she might be wise to do exactly that.

"Thank you, but I'm here now," she told him as she sat down. She hesitated momentarily, then asked, "What happens next?"

"If you're ready, I'll tell them to bring him out."

The guard—J. Wilbers according to the name on the hard plastic tag pinned to his shirt's breast pocket—nodded to his right. Though why she'd want to see Lambert was beyond him. This one was the fourth visitor the famous killer had had this month, last week had been that lawyer lady from Los Angeles. Why so many good-looking women would come to see this monster was anybody's guess. He—J. Wilbers—had never understood it himself.

"I'm ready." Leah leveled her chin and her gaze and sat up just a little straighter on the hard chair.

Ready as I will ever be.

Leah's eyes were fixed on the door at the back of the small room, beyond the screen where the empty chair awaited its occupant. Her heart pounded loudly, her breath came unevenly, but she wanted to watch him walk into the room, wanted to watch him as he watched her. Wanted to learn all she could from his body language. And she wanted to do it all without blinking.

For Missy's sake, I will look him in the eye and I will not be intimidated.

The door opened, and a pleasant looking, handsome blond man peeked into the room almost playfully.

"Leah?" he asked brightly.

She nodded slowly and squared her shoulders just a tiny bit more.

"I'm so glad you came," he said as he strode to her, smiling, his movements swift and deliberate. He had something folded in the crook of his left arm, and he placed it on his lap as he sat down.

Leah squinted slightly, as if her field of vision had narrowed and shrunk with each step he took in her direction. She'd seen his photo a hundred times, and so his handsome face, his blue eyes and soft cheeks, came as no surprise to her. She'd not, however, been prepared for the misplaced air of boyish innocence that seemed to surround him. The contrast between image and reality was ghoulish, in its way, and it turned her stomach.

Leah fought to keep her breakfast down and willed herself not to blink—not even when he spoke her name in such soft, intimate terms, as if addressing an old friend. Someone with whom he shared a history.

Leah swallowed, refusing to acknowledge that, like it or not, there was in fact something shared between them.

"Leah. It's good to meet you." He spoke as if they were exchanging pleasantries at a cocktail party.

The hairs on the back of Leah's neck stood up, and she had the feeling that something without legs had just slithered across her skin. She felt her hands begin to shake and she clasped them together to keep him from knowing how unnerved she was by his apparent normalness.

Ray Lambert could have been the man who had held the lobby door for her that morning as she left the hotel for her drive to the prison. He could have been the man who sat next to her on the plane flying down from New York, or the man she bumped into at the dry cleaners yesterday morning on her way into the office.

Totally, utterly, terrifyingly normal.

And so good looking, with his wavy blond hair and clear blue eyes that now assessed her even as she stared at him.

The thought that someone who looked so sane could have committed such unspeakable atrocities stunned her.

Another wave of nausea washed over her, and Leah fought it back. She had this one chance. She could not back away from it—or from him.

"So." He clapped his palms together lightly. "How was your trip?"

"Fine." Leah's voice sounded weaker, more uncertain, than she wanted, and so she forced herself to add something to her response, if for no other reason than to prove to herself she could be steady, she could take charge, could address the demon without faltering. "My flight was straight through so there were no delays."

"Good, good. That's a lovely pendant, by the way." Lambert nodded at the amethyst that hung from a thin gold chain around her neck. "One of my sisters had one very similar. Of course, hers wasn't real."

"Was she wearing it when you slit her throat?" Leah asked coolly.

Lambert's eyebrows rose slightly, though whether in surprise or amusement, Leah wasn't quite sure.

"I brought something to show you," he told her, smoothly ignoring her remark, and for a moment, Leah was almost frightened by the possibilities. She was relieved when he held up a hardcover book.

The Vagabond Killer was scrawled in lurid red across a white cover.

"This book was written about me," he announced with no small amount of pride. "The author is a well-known private investigator. Have you read it?"

Leah shook her head, no.

Lambert held up the dust jacket so that she could see the author's picture, and she viewed it curiously. The author—identified in the brief blurb as Ethan J. Sanger of White Bear Springs Camp in the state of Maine—had a face that might have been described as handsome had his eyes not been so darkly cold, his mouth so tightly drawn.

"Why," Leah wondered aloud, "would anyone want to write a book about you?"

"Oh, any number of reasons," Lambert said, amused once again. "Mr. Sanger had his, as I recall."

Stroking the spine of the book as if it were a pet cat, Lambert leaned forward and made a show of looking at Leah's hands.

"The last lady who came to see me had little American flags painted on the tips of her fingernails. Little red, white, and blue flags, partially unfurled." He tapped one finger on the top of the desk that sat between them. "When she was here at Christmas, she had little sprigs of holly painted on them. No little flags for Leah McDevitt, I see. Not your style, eh? Even if you hadn't bitten your nails down to the quick."

When she did not respond, he grinned and added, "Of course, the other lady was a member of one of those ACLU-type organizations that is determined to protect my civil rights from violation. But now you, Leah McDevitt," he leaned forward and lowered his voice, "something tells me not to expect to see you out there with the protesters at the prison gates the night they strap me down on the gurney."

"You're assuming I believe in the death penalty."

"And could there be a chance you do not?" He sat back in his seat, his hands folded neatly and patiently upon the desk, watching her face.

Refusing to let him see anything of herself, to give him anything of herself, Leah shrugged and said, with as much nonchalance as she could muster, "What I think about the death penalty or anything else is none of your business. I'm not your friend, and I'm not here to make small talk or to entertain you. I'm here for one reason, Lambert, just one."

"Ah, yes. Sweet Melissa." He taunted her with a half-smile that spoke of intimacies she could not permit herself to even imagine.

"Don't even speak her name." In spite of her resolve, Leah's facade began to crumble more quickly than she could repair it, and she hissed at him without even realizing that she was doing so.

"How can we then discuss the *situation,* if I am not to speak her name?"

Lambert was still smiling. At that moment, Leah wanted more than anything in the world to slap that smile from his face with one well-aimed, open-palmed smack. She'd never hit anyone once she'd passed through the terrible twos, had never believed that violence solved anything. Yet right at that moment, an open shot to Lambert's baby-face held more appeal than anything else she could think of.

"You're thinking of how good it would feel to hurt me," he commented softly, matter-of-factly, as if he could read her mind.

"Yes. Actually, I am," she replied calmly.

"How would you do it?" he asked. "Would you use a weapon?"

He leaned a little closer and asked, "And when would you stop? When I started to bleed? When I started to scream? When I lost consciousness? Perhaps when I stopped breathing?"

Leah pushed her chair back abruptly, sickened by his attempts to suck her into what to him was surely sport.

Raymond Lambert smiled with great satisfaction and said, "Some places you'd rather not go, Leah? Afraid you'll find out we've more in common than—"

"We have nothing in common!" Leah started to stand up.

"Oh, but we do. We have some*one* in common."

Leah froze and stopped caring if it gave Lambert pleasure to see her pain.

He motioned for her to sit down, and she did, slowly, her hatred of him at that moment building almost uncontrollably.

"That's a lovely jacket, by the way." Lambert slipped back into pleasantries. "That shade of blue suits you. Is that a new cut this year? Few of the women who visit me dress as well as you do."

He regarded her silence for a long moment.

"I can see that you're surprised that women voluntarily come to see me. It would shock you to know how many fans I have. How many marriage proposals I've received. How many visitors I've had lately." He chuckled and shook his head. "No accounting for taste, is there, Leah?"

"Obviously not," Leah snapped, recoiling at the thought of a woman seeking out the likes of Raymond Lambert for any purpose. Even her own. "Just being in your company makes me sick."

"Ah, Leah, I enjoy the plucky spirit that you hide under that cool manner. I wouldn't have expected that of you. It pleases me."

"I couldn't care less about what pleases you or what pisses you off. You told me you knew where my sister is. We can talk about that, or we don't have to talk at all."

"Now, Leah, calm down." Lambert's tone was soothing, hypnotic. "You're tense. Are you thirsty? I can ask the guard to bring you something cold if you—"

"Stop it!" Leah slapped her right hand palm down upon the desk with such force that the reverberations rippled along the length of her arm. "Everyone tried to tell me you'd play with me, but I thought since you were the one who initiated this contact in the first place, that you'd tend to business and be done with it. I can see I gave you more credit than you deserve."

Leah rose from the chair and grabbed her leather bag from where she'd dropped it on the floor, angrier than she'd been in years and muttering as she turned to leave, "I'm wasting my time with you. This is nothing more than a sick game as far as you're concerned. I'm not going to play anymore."

"Why do you suppose your sister wore brown contact lenses?" he asked softly, stopping her in her tracks less than halfway to the door.

"What?" She half-turned toward him.

"I mean, she had blue eyes, right? Why did she wear brown contact lenses?"

In that moment, for Leah, the world had stopped.

"Curious, don't you think?" Lambert continued. "Then again, I'm sure that you know why, but it was sure a surprise when one popped right out and just sat there on her cheek like a mole. Now, who would have suspected, blue eyes under those brown contact lenses."

Leah had turned fully to face him.

"I see I have your attention now."

"Where is she?" Leah whispered in a voice that was close to breaking.

"Why did she wear brown contact lenses?" Lambert repeated his question.

"Melissa had one blue eye and one brown. She had two sets of colored contacts, one blue, one brown. Sometimes she'd wear one, sometimes the other."

"So sometimes she'd have two blue eyes, sometimes brown?"

"Yes."

"Pity she chose the wrong ones that one time. Most unfortunate." He shook his head slowly. "A fatal choice, it would seem—"

"What?"

"It's of no consequence now." He waved her question away.

"Where is she?" Leah asked again.

"First things first. Sit down, Leah. I believe we've a bit of business to conduct." Lambert pointed to the chair and said, "Let's chat about the reward."

"I'd rather stand."

"I'd rather you sat." He watched her face carefully.

Leah sighed and sat down.

"Now. About the reward—"

Leah shook her head. "Not until I find Melissa."

"No. What guarantee do I have that you'll pay up, once you have what you want?"

"What guarantee do I have that you'll tell me the truth if I pay the reward first?"

"Hmmmm. We have what I believe is called a Mexican standoff. Ever wonder why they call such situations—"

"No," Leah cut him off, refusing to be lured back into unnecessary conversation. "Half now, half after I find my sister."

Lambert considered.

"But first you have to give me some information."

"What kind of information?" Lambert's eyes narrowed.

"A general idea of where she is would do."

"Upstate Pennsylvania, the western end, near Lake Erie and the New York border."

"Anyone who saw me on *Newsline* would know where she was last seen. You'll have to do better than that." Leah dismissed him coolly. "Be more specific."

Melissa, on her way home from Ohio State University for the summer, had dropped off her roommate in a town called Meadville, just south of Erie, and not far from New York. Missy had last been seen about ten miles over the New York border, at a gas station where she'd stopped to fill up and to make that last call home. It had been around eight-thirty at night, and Melissa had left a message on the answering machine at the townhouse in Manhattan that she thought she'd drive straight through. It was conceivable that she'd met up with her killer there, and he'd taken her over the New York border back into Pennsylvania.

"There are some very remote areas up there, you know. Miles of trails through the mountains, miles of dense woods. Some of the towns are little more than a crossroads. I guess that's why the Amish have settled there. Large tracts of open land, little outside influence to corrupt their young."

Leah wet her lips and swallowed hard.

"Are you telling me that Missy is in a wooded area near one of those little towns? Near one of the Amish settlements?"

"You asked me for some general information. Some good-faith information, as it were. Well, you have it. That's all you're getting for now."

"I'll have half the money wired to you when I get home." Leah stood on unsteady legs.

"Send it to my attorney, Robert Miller, in Houston. He'll get word to me as soon as the money arrives."

"You'll call me immediately after you've been notified that the money has been received and you'll tell me exactly where to find her. After she's been found, you'll get the balance."

"And I can rest assured that you will honor your debt?"

"I'm giving you my word. You'll just have to trust me."

"Would you extend such trust to me?"

"No," Leah answered without hesitation.

Lambert laughed out loud.

"I agree to your terms."

Leah signaled her readiness to leave to the guard who waited in the hallway beyond the door, his arms folded across his chest, as he watched a wall-mounted television.

"By the way," Leah said as she turned toward Lambert. "What would a dead man do with fifty thousand dollars?"

Lambert stood and smiled that enigmatic smile once again.

"We all have our secrets, Leah. Even the dead are permitted to keep theirs . . ."

Chapter 5

*C*atherine was sitting at the highly polished ebony dining table methodically sorting through a pile of mail when Leah arrived at the townhouse. It was almost ten o'clock at night, Leah's flight having been delayed due to a thunderstorm.

Looking up as Leah dropped her flight bag in the entry and began to unbutton her jacket, Catherine noted, "You look like you've been through the wringer."

"Hello to you, too, Cat," Leah responded dryly.

"I'm sorry, Leah. That was a bit abrupt." Catherine pushed her chair back from the table and met her cousin with a hug as she climbed the two steps up from the foyer. "How was your trip? How are you?"

"I'm exhausted. I haven't eaten since early this morning and I feel soiled and violated just from breathing the same air that Raymond Lambert breathed." Leah rubbed at her temples, trying to rub away the tension that had been building for two days and had yet to leave.

"I can't believe you actually sat down and talked to that monster, Leah. I told you that I didn't think it was a good idea."

"I'd never be able to live with myself if I hadn't followed up, Cat. He's as close to being a lead as we've ever had. And in a few short weeks, this narrow window of opportunity will have closed. No one expects the governor to grant a stay of execution." Leah kicked off her shoes. "Shit. I'd inject him myself if they'd let me."

"Did you make a deal?"

"With Lambert? Yes." Leah nodded. "Half the reward money now, half later. When we find her."

"If you find her."

Leah followed the hallway into the kitchen without comment. She filled a copper kettle with water and set it on the stove, then searched through an assortment of tea bags in a canister of dark green glass.

Hearing Catherine behind her in the doorway, Leah asked "Tea?" as she placed a navy blue mug emblazoned with the magazine's logo on the counter. Her hand reached back into the cupboard, pausing on a second mug.

"Sure. Thanks. See if there's any chamomile."

"That's what I'm having, too," Leah told her, striving for some sense of normalcy, of routine, that would assure her that now that she was home, life could somehow be right again.

Catherine opened the refrigerator and looked for the small bowl holding the lemon she'd sliced earlier in the week, when she and Leah had settled in for tea as they sometimes did at the end of a long or trying day. "Do you want to talk about it?"

"Do I want to talk about how repugnant it was to sit there and let this madman play head games with me? No. No, I do not." Leah leaned back against the counter, her arms crossed protectively across her chest. "It was every bit as nasty as the FBI agent told me to expect, though not in the way I expected. The agent, Genna Snow, made me think it would be a lot more gruesome than it really was."

"She called earlier, by the way," Catherine interrupted Leah.

"She did? Genna Snow called?"

"She wanted to know if you were home yet. I told her I didn't expect you until later because of the flight delay. She wants you to call her in the morning."

"I'll do that. Right after I have Lambert's first installment wired to his attorney's office."

"Leah, are you sure you don't want to tell me about it?" Catherine asked.

"Catherine, *being* there was one thing. I mean, the Robert Orville Johnson Correctional Center is big and it's quiet and you can only imagine what goes on there at night." She enunciated the name of the prison, as if it was too important a name for so mean an institution.

Leah's eyes narrowed and focused on a distant point, as if remembering something from a dream. "But Lambert is your worst nightmare. He looks like the boy next door, all grown up. The *incongruity* of it—"

"A homicidal maniac should look like a homicidal maniac."

"He shouldn't look like a choirboy. It's grotesque, Cat. Someone so evil, looking so pure." Leah hunched her shoulders, as if shivering.

"You know, I recall seeing pictures of him in the newspapers right after his arrest and later during his trial." Catherine turned off the wailing teapot and poured boiling water into the two mugs. "And I remember the news media talking about that contrast, about how young and innocent he looked. How the prosecutor was afraid that the jury would be swayed by his appearance."

"Fortunately, the jury wasn't fooled."

"Sweetie, you look just terrible, after all this. You know, it's not too late to call this off. You don't have to go along with it. If Melissa really is . . . gone, well, that could just open the door for other issues that need to be dealt with. Other heartbreaks. Other decisions." Catherine spoke softly, as if she would be the one to make those decisions and wasn't certain that she was up to it.

"This may be my only chance to find the truth, Cat. I can't let it slip away."

They sipped their tea in silence, each thinking her own thoughts.

"It's in his eyes, though," Leah finally said. "Regardless of how normal he looks, when you get close enough to him, you can see it in his eyes."

"What did you see, Leah?" Catherine asked, her eyes narrowing.

"The fires of hell, Cat."

A bone-weary Leah picked up her mug and leaned over to kiss her cousin on the cheek before heading off toward the steps leading to the second floor.

"I swear, when I looked into his eyes, I could see the fires of hell."

Leah waited on hold for nearly ten minutes before Genna Snow picked up the line.

"Leah? I'm so sorry," the FBI agent apologized. "I simply could not get off that last call. If I'd realized I was going to be so long, I could have called you back."

"It's okay. I didn't mind." Leah got up from her desk and stretched the phone cord as she reached to close her office door. "I didn't get in till late last night, but Catherine said you wanted me to call. Which I would have done anyway."

"I just wanted to make certain that you're all right."

"I'm fine. I mean, once I got past the reality of the situation, I was fine." Leah doodled with a red-ink pen on the cover of a notebook. "I do want to thank you for whatever strings you pulled to help to set up the meeting with Lambert. For getting me in there as quickly as you did."

"I'm glad I could help. Do you feel like telling me how things went?"

"It was every bit as uncomfortable a meeting as you thought it might be, but worth every minute."

"Did he give you any information about your sister?"

"He told me the general area in which he says he left her body. A somewhat remote area in upstate Pennsylvania."

"Did it ring true? Could the information he gave you fit?"

"Missy was on her way home from college for the summer when she disappeared. Her roommate lived in northwestern Pennsylvania. It's certainly conceivable."

"Where in Pennsylvania?"

"Someplace around Erie. Do you know the area?"

"I spent some time there as a girl." Genna cleared her throat, then said, "I apologize. I interrupted your story, which is much more pertinent than mine. Please. What else did he tell you?"

"Lambert said he met up with Melissa over the New York state line and made her drive back into PA. I looked up a map of Pennsylvania on the Internet this morning. The places he mentioned are right in line with the area Missy would have traveled through. In a few more hours, I should have an exact location."

"How's that?"

"I made a deal with Lambert. I agreed to wire half the

reward money to his attorney today. Once Lambert receives word that the money is there, he's going to call me and give me the exact location. When I find Melissa, I'll wire the rest of the money."

There was a pause, a few beats longer than necessary.

"Genna?" Leah asked.

"Sorry, Leah. It's just so wrong to have to pay a murderer to find his victim."

"I have to get past that," Leah told her. "The important thing is Missy, not the money. I couldn't care less about the money, if it leads me to my sister's . . . to my sister."

"I understand." Genna paused, a slight hesitation in her voice, then asked, "He didn't make any statements about what actually happened to her, did he?"

"You mean did he confess? Did he say he stabbed her or shot her? No. No, there was no confession, if that's what you're asking. And I had tried to prepare myself for the worst, to have to hear every grisly detail. I was surprised, frankly, when he didn't do that." Leah paused for a moment, then added, "But there's no doubt in my mind that it was him. He knew about her eyes."

"What about her eyes?"

"Missy had a blue eye and a brown one. She had different colored contact lenses. So sometimes she'd be blue eyed, sometimes brown, depending on her mood. Lambert mentioned that a brown lens had popped out and her eye had been blue. He thought that was really significant somehow. He even said something about her choice of contact lenses having been a fatal one. That it was a shame that she'd worn the brown ones that night. Something like that."

"Odd," the agent murmured. "What an odd comment for him to have made."

"Why?"

"Because it implies that her eye color had something to do with her being selected as a victim."

"Don't serial killers do that? Don't they have specific agendas? An MO?"

"Some might. But understand, a killer's MO is what he has to do to carry out his crime. It's learned behavior that lets him accomplish the murder. Let's take an easy example. He might learn quite by accident that a lot of potential victims—say young, single women—live in a particular apartment complex. Maybe he observes that certain doors or windows always seem to be open. Maybe it's a door into a basement area where the laundry facilities are. Once inside the building, he can pick and choose where he wants to go. Maybe he'll knock on a door and tell the young woman he's there to deliver flowers. Once she opens the door, he's in."

"That's his MO."

"Yes. It's what he does to make the crime happen. But this eye-color thing, that's totally different. That speaks to something else. That could be part of his signature. And in Lambert's case, I don't recall that his signature had anything to do with the color of his victims' eyes."

"I don't understand."

"A killer's signature and his MO are two different things. While his MO is his means of committing his crime, his signature is what he has to do to fill the void inside himself. It's what he has to do to satisfy himself, to fulfill himself. It's part of why he kills in the first place."

"And Lambert's signature?"

"For starters, he cut off the fingertips of his victims so that it would take longer to identify them. A very large part of the thrill for him was the pain he could inflict even after the act of killing was over. It's very common for serial killers to prey on hookers, for example. They're easy to lure away and many of them are on their own. They're easy marks. But Raymond always selected women who looked as if they came from somewhere. Women who were alone but who looked as if they had people who cared for them. Women with families who took care of them. Families who would be frantic if they were missing. Families who would mourn. There wasn't a loser or a loner among them."

"More bang for the buck," Leah muttered.

"Put crudely, yes. You know, after he was caught, he told the investigators that he'd been at the funerals of every one of his victims except for the last, when he'd been caught. Dressed quietly, of course, never calling attention to himself. Always signed a different name on the register. But he was always there. Feeding off the grief of the families and loved ones. Reliving, no doubt, the actual killing right there in the midst of the mourning. He said at his trial that sometimes he even stood by the coffin and imaged himself killing her all over again."

"That's disgusting."

"Absolutely. I never came across a killer as heartless as Raymond Lambert. He gets off on suffering. He feeds on pain, physical and emotional. He tortured his victims, and then he tortured their families. That's his signature. That's what he needs to accomplish. That's what fulfills him emotionally."

There was a long and telling silence while each of the women contemplated the monster that was Raymond Lambert.

"Anyway, the comment about the eyes just doesn't seem to match, old Ray being an equal opportunity sadist," Genna said. "But I could be wrong. There's probably lots of stuff tucked along those twisted little paths inside that twisted brain of his that no one's uncovered. That's just a walk I never really wanted to take."

"It makes my skin crawl just to think about having met him face to face."

"Well, that's over now. And hopefully, before the day has ended, we'll know exactly where to look for your sister. Give me a call as soon as you hear from him, and we'll get the wheels in motion to begin the search."

"That's wonderful of you. I can't thank you enough."

"Well, once we know where to look, I think we can get the state police to move pretty quickly. Give me a call once you hear from Lambert, and we'll get started."

"I don't know how to thank you."

"You just did," Genna said as she hung up.

Leah spent the rest of the day pacing, watching the clock. She had called her bank to have the money wired as promised, but was told that—it being Friday—the money would probably not arrive until Monday afternoon. Her banker promised that she'd tend to it as soon as possible.

At 3:10 the phone rang, and Leah pounced on it like a cat on a mouse.

"Leah, do you have a television there in your office?" It was Genna Snow. She sounded frazzled.

"No, I—"

"Then you don't know. Shit," Genna cursed softly.

"What—?"

"I hate to be the one to have to tell you this. It's such a damned lousy twist of fate . . ."

A chill ran the length of Leah's spine, and the hairs on her arms raised as if touched by static.

"What, Genna? What's happened?"

"Raymond Lambert was killed by another inmate about two hours ago in the prison infirmary. He was strangled. They just released the news. I'm sorry, Leah," Genna told her. "I'm so damned sorry."

For some seconds the world seemed to stop, and Leah's senses seemed to shut down. No light, no sound, nothing penetrated the wall of disbelief that surrounded her at that moment.

And then the wall crumbled, and she began to scream.

"No! No! He can't be dead! He didn't tell me! He didn't tell me!" Leah sobbed. "He was supposed to tell me *where!*"

Chapter 6

$\mathcal{I}$t had been several days before Leah could
face much of anything outside the cabin in the
Connecticut countryside where she'd gone to mourn the
loss of her sister all over again. Feeling beaten up and
then let down by the fates, she'd sought solitude and
relief from the emotional roller coaster she'd been on for
the past several weeks.

Leah's first contact with the outside world had been
with her bank, which she'd called to cancel the transfer
of money she'd requested be wired earlier. After all, it
had been a down payment on a deal that would never go
through.

Her second call was to Genna Snow.

"I need to know if Lambert was telling the truth,"
Leah told her. "I was hoping you'd let me impose on you
just this one last time to help me form a plan. I'm just
not sure where to go from here."

"I've been thinking about that myself," Genna said.
"There are a few things I can do. I can call the law
enforcement agencies in northern PA and see if there
are any unsolved murders or unidentified bodies dating

back a few years. And I can also speak with the agent who interviewed Lambert when he was first arrested. He was the only person Lambert would meet with initially. He happens to be on a leave of absence right now."

"Do you think he would help? Even if the FBI doesn't want to reopen the case now that Lambert is dead?"

"Maybe. If I ask him nicely." Genna paused, then said, "I'm thinking that the first thing we need to determine is where Lambert was at the time of your sister's disappearance. If we can establish that he was definitely someplace else at the time, then we'll at least know that he was lying."

"And I'll be right back where I was before he sent me that first letter," Leah said softly.

"But if Lambert told the agent—his name is John Mancini—that he was in the area when your sister disappeared, well, maybe we'll have something to go on. It won't hurt to ask."

"You said this agent is not active right now. Do you know how to contact him?"

Genna smiled wryly to herself. Oh, yes. She knew how to contact John Mancini. The only problem would be in getting up her nerve to make that first phone call six months after he'd walked away from the agency, and out of Genna's life.

"I can find him," Genna told Leah. "You'll be at this number for a while?"

"Yes. My cousin convinced me to take the week off. She thought I needed a few days to myself."

"Well, I totally agree with her. You've been through a lot. I hope you have some good books to read."

"I was planning a drive into town this afternoon. I'll hit the bookstore, the grocery story, and stock up on some videos. Lots of escapism and self-indulgence."

"Does chocolate do it for you?"

"Ummm, no, but chamomile tea and coconut cake does."

"That's an odd combination, but if it works for you, I say go for it," Genna laughed. "I'll get back to you in a few days."

The narrow back road leading from the McDevitt cabin into Bannock was slick with mud following a week's thaw, but Leah drove its winding length slowly, guiding her Explorer carefully around the twists and turns. It took her almost twenty minutes to arrive at the intersection of Long and Street roads, where she found a parking spot and began her errands. At Dillard's Market she bought a week's worth of groceries and at Campbell's she rented an armful of videos. Leah's last stop was at the Book Nook for some reading material, where she gathered a few romances, a few mysteries, the latest best-sellers by her favorite authors.

Once back at the cabin, Leah arranged the stack of books on the ottoman that sat at the foot of the chair near the fireplace, piled the videos on top of the VCR, and arranged the purchased ingredients for her favorite coconut cake on the counter. She would bake first, start a book while the cake was in the oven, then read for the rest of the day. Maybe even the rest of the week, if she felt like it. She hadn't taken real time off to just relax in over a year, and she was, she admitted, long overdue.

She'd just finished frosting the cake and had settled back in to chapter four of a novel featuring a fast-talking bounty hunter when the phone rang.

"Leah, it's Genna. I have John Mancini on the line." Genna sounded a bit tense, her voice clipped and efficient.

"John Mancini here, Ms. McDevitt," a resonant male voice greeted her solemnly.

"Thank you for talking to me, Agent Mancini. And thank you, Genna, for moving so quickly on this. I didn't expect to hear from you for a few days."

"I guess we just got lucky," she said, a thin note of sarcasm underscoring her words. "In any event, we've been discussing your experience with Raymond Lambert."

"Let me first express my sympathy, Ms. McDevitt, on the loss of your sister as well as on the present situation. If I'd known you were dealing with Lambert, perhaps I could have helped somehow."

"There really wasn't much time to think about bringing other people into this, it all happened so quickly. Agent Mancini, Genna has told me that you spent a great deal of time with Lambert after his arrest."

"John will do," he told her. "And yes, I spent weeks with Lambert. For reasons known only to him, he had decided that I was the only law enforcement agent he'd speak with. I believe I heard every gruesome detail about every one of his events—he referred to his killings as *events*—but I don't remember him ever mentioning being in Pennsylvania. I don't recall that he'd gone farther north than Tennessee, so I'm curious that he's alluded to having been active in another part of the country. Most of the crimes he confessed to, those he'd been convicted of, were in the southwest, particularly Texas and Oklahoma. He said he liked the way the small towns down there did their funerals, the 'sendoffs,' he called them. There'd be lots of people in the crowd of mourners, and it was easy for him to mill about."

"Genna mentioned that he liked to go to the funerals—"

"Oh, yes, that was all part of it for old Ray, you know. He told me that, once he realized how much fun funerals could be, he had to reevaluate his methods. He started to take great care not to damage the face of his victims, so that they'd look good for their send-off. And there'd be a better chance of an open coffin if the face was not bruised. Lambert often repeated the sentiment that he loved those small-town funerals, because after the services in the churchyard, they'd sometimes have a luncheon in the church hall—'Man, those church ladies sure can cook,' he'd say."

"John," Genna said softly, a verbal tap on the shoulder.

"I'm sorry. I just thought you should know just how far he went with his victims. Attending their funerals became part of it."

"I thought police always watched funerals to see who showed up. That it was not uncommon for the killer to be among the mourners," Leah said.

"That's true. In Lambert's case, though, no one knew what he looked like. None of his victims had lived to identify him, so the police didn't know who they were looking for. And keep in mind, too, that he rarely killed more than once in the same community."

"You said that he never mentioned being in Pennsylvania."

"That's correct. And looking back over the crimes he confessed to, there'd have only been a week or so when he could have encountered your sister in May of ninety-three. We know that he'd killed Marlene Baker on the twelfth of May outside of San Antonio. Her services were held on the sixteenth. Lambert bragged about having attended. Your sister disappeared on what day?"

"The twenty-fifth."

"Nine days later. And we have him admitting to having

killed Lynn Taylor—still in Texas—on June first. Not impossible, but to tell you the truth, it just doesn't fit."

"Will you explain to Leah why not?" Genna asked.

"Lambert had already killed twenty-seven women across Texas and Oklahoma in a three-month period—he'd kill more before he was caught. He'd said several times that it was so easy to find a victim down there, as easy as picking apples from a tree. So why would he drive north—to an unfamiliar area—pick up your sister in New York, drive her into PA to kill her, then hide her body in this wilderness area that Genna has described, then turn right around and drive back to Texas where he'd kill again on the first of June? What would motivate him to do that? And Lambert was, by his own admission, a lazy coot. He liked the familiar, the easy. Killing in Pennsylvania would have been far too risky. He doesn't know the terrain. And Genna said that you had the impression that he was hinting that the body was left in the woods. He'd have had to carry her if he'd killed her elsewhere. How tall was your sister?"

"Melissa was about five feet eight or nine. She weighed maybe one thirty-five," Leah told him.

"Well, you saw Lambert. Maybe five feet ten, one hundred sixty-five pounds at the most. I don't see him lugging her body around."

"Maybe he made her walk there and then he killed her," Leah suggested.

"I just don't see it," Mancini repeated. "He committed almost every one of his murders in the victim's car or near her home. Traipsing through the wilderness just doesn't fit his MO."

"So what you're saying is you don't think Raymond Lambert killed my sister."

"I'm saying I'd be damned surprised if he had. By May of ninety-three, he'd already killed close to thirty women using the same successful method, all in the same part of the country. Why would he change his routine for that one killing and only that one killing? It just makes no sense. So, I'd have to say that I find it very hard to believe that Raymond Lambert killed your sister, Ms. McDevitt." John Mancini paused, then added, "I'm sorry. I know it would have been easier on you to have known. I just can't tell you that I believe he could have done this. I just don't believe it was him."

"Then why did he even contact me in the first place?" Leah's voice rose slightly in frustration.

"I wish I had an answer for that, Ms. McDevitt, but I don't have a clue. I'm sorry."

"I appreciate that. Thank you. And thank you for your time. For your insights," Leah sighed.

"You're welcome. I'm sorry I couldn't be of help," Mancini said. "Genna—"

"Thank you, John." Genna Snow was tautly professional once again. "I owe you one."

"You owe me more than one as I remember, but we'll let it go for now," he said just before he hung up.

"Genna, are you there?" Leah asked after a long silence.

"Yes, I'm here." Genna blew out a long breath and said, "I'm sorry that John wasn't able to shed much light on the situation."

"I think he called it the way he saw it."

"He always does," Genna muttered.

Leah paused. "Would it be rude to say that I detected a bit of an undercurrent between the two of you?"

"Suffice it to say that we have a history. I've moved on."

"I'm sorry."

"So was I, but that's life," Genna said tersely, then

softened and said, "I don't know what to say, Leah. I wish we'd been able to come up with something a little more definitive."

"Oh, but everything Mancini said made sense. And I suppose when you look at the total picture, I have to agree that it just doesn't seem plausible that he killed Melissa."

"It doesn't seem likely," Genna agreed.

"But Genna," Leah asked, "how could he have known about her eyes?"

"I don't know. That's the only piece that doesn't fit. I'd told John about it and he said it could have been something he'd heard from another inmate. I can ask my contact at the prison if there were any inmates Lambert spent time with over the years and see if any of them fit the profile. Other than that, I don't know where to tell you to go from here. I have made calls into several agencies along the New York–Pennsylvania border. I'll certainly let you know when I hear back from them, but I just don't know where else to steer you or who else you could talk to. I'm afraid that I can't think of anyone that Lambert talked to as much as he talked to John," Genna said. Then she repeated once again, "I'm so sorry, Leah."

"I appreciate all that you've done. Thanks again, Genna," Leah said as she hung up.

Leah sat drumming her fingers on the arm of the overstuffed chair for a long minute, then rose and went to her briefcase and pulled out a pen and a notepad. She made notes from the conversation that had just concluded, Mancini's comments and the facts she already had at hand, to compare with the comments Lambert had made to her.

Mancini was right. There were holes everywhere.

But the question nagged at her. How did Lambert

know about Missy's eyes? And was there reason to believe that Lambert had in fact told Mancini everything? Was there any reason to believe that a killer as cunning and resourceful as Lambert would have limited his killing to one section of the country? And if it had served his warped sensibilities not to tell anyone about them, who's to say it didn't happen?

She wished she'd known more about him before she'd met with him. She could have asked other questions if she'd been better prepared. As it was, she now had more questions than answers, and no one to turn to.

Leah sipped her now-cold tea and leaned back against the chair cushions, wishing she could go back to that day. Thinking of what she'd do differently, if she could just live that one day over . . .

She closed her eyes and could see so clearly Lambert walking toward her in the small visiting room at the prison. Sitting down at the table across from her with the book on his lap.

Leah's eyes flew open. The book.

The Vagabond Killer. By . . . someone, she couldn't remember his name. All she recalled of the author was his dark hair and dark, angry eyes. And that he lived in a place called White Bear Springs Camp in Maine. This she remembered because as a young girl she had attended a summer camp with the same name in western Massachusetts. But what was his name?

Leah looked through her newly purchased books for the bookmark she'd picked up while in the Book Nook that afternoon. Hadn't the bookmark listed both the address and the phone number of the store? It did. She reached for the phone and dialed the number. When the clerk answered, she asked if they had a copy of *The Vagabond Killer.*

She waited on hold for better than five minutes to learn that not only did they *not* have the book, but it was out of print.

Leah hung up, then hooked her laptop computer up to the phone line. Once on the Internet, she hit every one of the on-line bookstores seeking a copy of *The Vagabond Killer*.

There was not a copy to be found.

But, from the listings, she now knew the name of the author. Ethan J. Sanger.

Ethan J. Sanger of White Bear Springs Camp, Maine.

She took one last chance and clicked on an icon for out-of-print and hard-to-find books.

Bingo.

She dialed the phone number given for the bookstore in Rhode Island that claimed to have a copy and made arrangements for the book to be shipped to her overnight.

She hung up the phone and leaned back in her chair. In less than twenty-four hours, she'd have it in her hands.

The Vagabond Killer. The story of Raymond Lambert, the man who may or may not have murdered her sister.

Once the book arrived, Leah spent a full day reading Lambert's own rambling account of how he had brutally, cruelly, and gleefully dispatched a total of forty-nine women from this life into the next. She turned the pages quickly, passing the photographs of his victims, trying to ignore their faces, the alphabetical listing of their names—from Jennifer Allen, a University of Texas sophomore who had had the world by the tail that summer, to Elizabeth West, a married attorney from Atlanta and mother of a small child—a sad memorial. The more Leah read, the more she found it impossible to not look upon the smiling, happy faces of the pretty young women whose paths had not yet crossed Raymond Lambert's. Some married, with children or without, some single, mostly well-educated and attractive women, and all from good and loving families.

Nauseated, Leah read his descriptions of how he had caught the attention of each one of them, how he had gotten them alone, how he had done what he'd wanted, how he'd disposed of them once he was finished. And how he had so often stood among the mourners and soaked in their grief and their pain like a sponge. The story was told in the first person and, judging from the way Lambert skipped around, it appeared there'd been little editing, almost as if the material had been taken right from a tape recorder, maybe, or possibly from notes.

Leah could not help but wonder what kind of a man could sit and listen to Lambert's musings, could feed this diabolical ego for the sake of his own financial gain?

What kind of a man was Ethan Sanger, that he could have come that close to so much suffering, then turn the story loose on the buying public who, for $22, could enter into Raymond Lambert's world?

Leah turned the book over and looked at Ethan Sanger's face. The chin slightly squared, the dark hair curled slightly over his collar, the eyes filled with turbulence.

Had what he'd heard from Lambert been responsible for the darkness or had he brought his own demons along for the ride?

A sudden chill caught Leah off guard, and she shivered and put the book aside. It was too ugly to read all in one sitting. She'd take a walk, then maybe slip a movie into the VCR. Something light and humorous, she thought.

But later, while watching a favorite romantic comedy, she found it frivolous in contrast to what she'd been reading. Unable to concentrate, not getting the jokes in so dark a frame of mind, she turned off the VCR and picked up the notes she'd made earlier while reading Sanger's book. Scanning her pages, she discovered one important thing.

There was still a slight gap in Lambert's activities between mid-May and the beginning of June.

Leah rose and paced, slapping the notebook against the side of her leg from time to time. As she paced, her thoughts began to race.

John Mancini had not been the only person Lambert had spilled his story to, after all.

As a journalist, Leah knew that often all of the information gathered on a topic was not used. Sometimes facts fell by the wayside or were not considered important enough to become part of the finished article or were cut by an editor's pencil.

Where, she wondered, might Ethan Sanger's notes be? And would he be willing to share them with her?

There was only one way to find out.

Leah picked up the phone and dialed the number for information.

"I'd like the number for White Bear Springs Camp in Maine, please. No, I don't know what town that's near. Yes, thank you."

The operator was back in a flash with the number.

"Yes, thank you. Yes, I have it. Oh—that was what town? Arlenville? Thank you. Yes, automatic dial would be fine."

On the fourth ring, a man answered, his voice deep and rich and sleepy. Leah glanced at the clock on the wall. It was almost midnight.

"I'm sorry," she heard herself say, "I didn't realize it was so late."

"Who were you calling?" he asked.

"I wanted to speak with Ethan Sanger."

"You got him."

"Mr. Sanger, you don't know me. My name is Leah McDevitt. I was hoping you could help me."

"What can I do for you, Ms. McDevitt?"

"I read your book, *The Vagabond Killer,* and I was wondering if by any chance you still had any of your notes. If perhaps you might let me . . ." Leah's words came out in a rush, not nearly the way she'd intended.

"Is this some kind of a sick joke?" Ethan Sanger's voice had gone cold and flat.

"No, no. You see, I met with Lambert last week, before he died—"

"That's nothing I'd brag about, miss. And if you're calling to tell me that Lambert had parting words for me, keep them to yourself. I'm not interested."

"Wait! No, there're no parting words. Actually, that's why I needed to speak to you. He was supposed to give me information about a murder he claims to have committed—well, actually, he didn't come right out and say he killed her, and I can't find anything to substantiate it but I was hoping that you could help me. That you'd talk to me about Lambert and the information he gave you. That maybe there were some notes—"

"It's all in the book."

"But this *isn't* in the book, that's my point. Look, I won't take much of your time—"

"You won't take any of my time, Ms. McDevitt. I don't talk about Raymond Lambert. Period. Not to you. Not to anyone."

"But, you see, he claims that he . . . hello?" Leah paused and heard only a dial tone.

Ethan Sanger had hung up on her.

Leah returned the phone to its cradle softly, fighting the urge to throw it across the room in utter frustration, and began, once again, to pace.

Fine, then. If Ethan Sanger wouldn't talk to her on the phone, he'd talk to her in person. He'd have to, if she was there, right in his face.

And surely, once he heard about Melissa, he'd understand, maybe he'd let her look at his notes, if he still had them.

As Leah saw it, he wouldn't have much choice, because she didn't intend to leave White Bear Springs Camp until Ethan Sanger shared what he knew about Raymond Lambert.

Chapter 7

*E*arly the next morning, Leah tossed her carefully packed bags into the back of the Explorer and checked to make sure she had all of her supplies for the trip. Through the years, she'd driven through enough New England winters to know that she'd need to be prepared in the event she become lost or stranded on unfamiliar roads or had to wait out a sudden storm. Some snacks and a Thermos of coffee that could be refilled at convenience markets along the way. A flashlight with extra batteries. A blanket. The map she'd printed off her laptop the night before, along with the step-by-step directions that would take her from her front door to the front door of White Bear Springs Camp, which was, according to the Internet, 4.2 miles up an unpaved road, twelve miles outside of Arlenville, Maine, where winter still held all in its grip.

She tucked her portable phone—its battery fully charged—and a stack of CDs into her leather bag, pulled on her boots, and stopped to turn down the thermostat, then paused thoughtfully. What had she forgotten? Leaving the door slightly ajar, she went back into the cabin, lifted a photo of Melissa from the piano, and slipped it into her pocket. Ethan Sanger might say no to Leah, but who could turn her away after one look at Melissa's sweet face?

The drive through Connecticut into western Massachusetts was the easiest part of her journey. The day started off sunny, traffic was light, and the roads were well cleared of the previous week's snow. It wasn't until she got into New Hampshire where the wind picked up and the skies threatened that she decided she'd stop early for the night rather than run the risk of driving through the weather that was likely to come.

Leah considered herself fortunate to have found a small motel just off the highway that had a restaurant attached. Over a dinner prepared, then served, by the same woman who had earlier checked her into her room, Leah reread the information she'd printed out about White Bear Springs Camp from the on-line vacation site.

Built in 1905 as a logging camp, its present owner was one Thomas E. Sanger—noted to be a former college English professor who had inherited the camp from his father back in the sixties—White Bear Springs offered several types of accommodations, from rooms in the lodge to individual cabins located on the lake or in the woods. Guests were asked to specify which they preferred at the time the reservations were made. The bold print alerted potential campers to the fact that only the lakefront cabins boasted indoor plumbing. Those opting to stay deeper in the woods would have outhouse facilities only.

Two floors of guest rooms were available in the lodge, and the main dining room served the entire camp all three meals from May through October. However, from late June through August, guests could take their meals at one of the tables on the screened porch that wrapped around two sides of the lodge and faced the lake.

There were clay tennis courts and a mowed field for softball and playground equipment for the little ones. College students served as camp counselors and provided arts and crafts instruction and games in the afternoons. There were horseshoes and volleyball and walking trails, swimming and boating, as well as the gently sloping sandy stretch of beach that led down to the water's edge—a short stretch of beach, it was noted, but beach nonetheless. Fishing received an "excellent" rating, and it was noted that the camp owners strongly encouraged "catch and release." Special winter accommodations were available for snowmobiling, ice fishing, or cross-country skiing.

All in all—the outhouses aside—Leah thought White Bear Springs sounded like quite a place.

With luck, she thought as she drained the last bit of after-dinner coffee from a heavy white cup, by this time tomorrow she'd be able to judge for herself whether or not the camp was as interesting in person as its on-line hype. And if the fates were truly smiling, she would find Ethan Sanger as accommodating as the lodge.

By seven the next morning, Leah had checked out of her beige and orange motel room and had finished breakfast at the small restaurant, and was, once again, on the road, heading north. The early clouds lingered, casting a haze over the distant hills to her left and the small towns off the highway on her right. The sun had emerged enough by nine to burn off the worst of it, but by noon the sky had darkened once again, threatening snow. She stopped to fill up the Explorer just outside of Kittery, just over the New Hampshire border into Maine.

"How far ya' goin'?" a young man clad in wool jacket, cap, scarf, and gloves asked as he cleaned her windshield.

"Arlenville. Northwest of Bangor," she replied.

"Bangor's only 'bout a hundred eighty miles." He nodded knowingly. "Take you a couple a hours, depending on weather." He paused to study the sky. "You should make it before the storm hits, 'long as you don't stop to sightsee too much on the way."

"No time for sight-seeing this time around," Leah told him.

"Been to Kittery?" the young man asked.

"No." Leah counted out the proper number of bills to pay for the gas. "Maybe on the way back."

"Pretty harbor. Pretty town, even in the dead of winter, if you like old houses. Looks better in the summer, though."

"I'll keep that in mind." She smiled back and started up the engine, gave a half-wave to the friendly fellow, and pulled back onto the highway.

Interstate 95 would take her north to Bangor, where she'd pick up Route 15 northwest out of the city. Then she'd follow 15 to Route 11 straight on in to Arlenville's Main Street, which she'd take to Randall's Mill Road, which was, the Internet directions had assured, just past Grand's General Store. Leah had read the directions so many times she knew them by heart. It all sounded easy enough on paper, but who knew what the terrain was like, or how much snow the Maine skies had dumped into the area over the past few months?

Well, she mused as she slipped a CD into the player built into the dash, if she got stuck, she could always call and see if the charter plane was picking up passengers this week. Of course, the information she'd gathered on the camp indicated that the small plane was available from May through October only, but perhaps Mr. Sanger would be feeling charitable and would send the plane to rescue her.

Fat chance, she grimaced, wondering if Sanger was in fact the pilot of the camp's purported plane, and what he would do if she called him for help.

More likely than not, he'd be just as pleased to let her sit roadside until the spring thaw.

Best not to need rescue from any quarter, Leah told herself. Determined to beat the coming storm to her destination, she hit the accelerator and headed north to Bangor.

The afternoon sun was shielded by a pale haze by the time Leah passed through Arlenville, Maine. The small town was much as she had pictured it in her mind, from the wide streets and the well-kept old houses to the brick school and the town square. Right past Grand's General Store was the sign for Randall's Mill Road, just as the on-line travelogue had promised. And six miles farther down that same road was the fork with the red flashing light where she was to stay to the right and watch for the sign for White Bear Springs one-half-mile ahead. At the sign, she turned on to an unmarked road, which was, she suspected, dirt under the hard-packed snow. Barely wide enough for two cars, the road wound upwards through the woods—4.3 miles through the woods, according to her directions—to the camp's parking area.

Thank God for four-wheel drive.

Leah leaned forward, trying to keep her eyes focused on the road and her wheels aligned with the tracks of the last vehicle to have come this way. She passed one house, a compact affair nestled in a clearing, and noted its distance from the road. A possible port in the approaching storm should she manage somehow to get lost between here and there, she thought as the first tiny flakes began to dot her windshield. She turned on her wipers and hoped that she'd make it to the camp before the snow began to fall in earnest.

Aware of the dangers of skidding on the slick surface, Leah turned off the music to better concentrate on maintaining a steady path. The forest was so deep and dark that Leah suspected that if one were to pass beyond the sentinel firs that lined the road, one would enter a shadowy, mysterious place. The thought sent a shiver up her spine and brought forth a rush of remembered images from childhood stories. The Beast had lived in such woods, had he not? As had the witch in "Hansel and Gretel." And that wily Rumpelstiltskin.

Then again, she forced a lighter note, there had been those dwarves . . .

By the time Leah reached the clearing and the sign for the camp, her palms were sweating inside her gloves and her head was pounding. She parked the Explorer along the fence and exhaled a grateful breath that she'd made it all the way up the slippery slope without skidding into the woods where she was certain she'd have been lost until the next hardy soul ventured up the hill, and who could know when that might be?

Gathering up her leather bag, Leah opened the driver's side door, and hopped out, landing in six inches of fresh snow and a stillness that surrounded her like an all-encompassing cloud. That the woods were endless had been a given. That the quiet would be equally so had come as a surprise. There was nothing, nothing to be heard, other than the wind shuffling through the tops of the pines far overhead. It was, Leah thought, the loneliest sound she'd ever heard.

And despite all her travels to remote places that were, more often than not, no more than specks on a map, Leah had never felt more alone than she did at that moment. Other than that one sign, there was nothing to indicate that there was shelter close by. There were no other cars parked in the clearing, no footprints to follow through the snow.

For the first time it occurred to Leah that a stranger to these woods would be in serious trouble if there was no sanctuary from the cold. What would she do if Ethan Sanger refused to admit her? If there was no one at the lodge when she arrived?

Her step faltered slightly as she considered her situation. But there, up above the trees, wasn't that smoke she saw curling skyward? Surely someone was there. And just as surely, even the brusque Ethan Sanger wouldn't turn someone away in the midst of a storm.

Would he?

Leah hoisted the leather bag higher up onto her shoulder and promptly tripped over the sign that stuck up just above the snow and pointed the way to the lodge.

Following the sign led her down a winding path of sorts, where the snow was trampled and slick underfoot. An icy glaze had settled over the surface, where the sun had earlier melted the snow, then the drop in temperature had frozen it over again. Leah took her time, trying to negotiate the slight downward incline without falling flat on her face.

Leah's first view of White Bear Camp took her breath away. The lodge itself sat to the right of a clearing, bathed in a faint light. Beyond was a lake, now frozen over, rimmed with several small cabins that were set against trees that had shed their leaves months ago. Bare now against the winter winds, the branches of the oaks and maples reached upwards like grasping fingers, making the nearby pines, their arms heavy with snow, appear overdressed.

All was white, except for the trees and the occasional darting cardinal. And around all wrapped a quiet as dense and sturdy as the surrounding woods.

Until she drew closer to the lodge and heard the music from within. Someone was playing the piano and singing a spirited albeit off-key rendition of "Oklahoma!" The sound and the song were so unexpected, so incongruous to the austere surroundings, Leah found herself grinning as she paused on the top step. At least someone was home.

Leah knocked on the door once, waited for a moment before knocking again. When there was no answer, she realized that the music was drowning out the sound of her knocks, and she paused to debate whether or not to just walk in. Before she could decide, the door swung open and she was met by a jolly-looking man with white hair and a mustache, dressed in a red plaid flannel shirt and well-worn tan corduroy pants, accompanied by a German shepherd that looked to be, in dog years, nearly as old as the man.

"Come in, come in," the man said as he pulled a pipe from his mouth with one hand and extended the other in Leah's direction. "Don't stand out there in the cold."

Doing as she was told, Leah allowed herself to be led into the wide foyer lit only by a small but bright lamp that stood precariously on the narrow top of a roll-top desk piled with papers. The walls were lined with a dizzying array of framed photographs and along one wall stood a long wooden bench that appeared to have served time in a previous life as a church pew. The dog stood by politely wagging his tail, waiting for her to notice him.

"Was wonderin' who'd be makin' their way up here so late in the day, what with a storm comin'," the man said as he drew Leah in and closed the door behind her.

"How did you know—" Leah began, puzzled that he seemed to be expecting her.

"That someone was coming?" He chuckled. "Bob McKinley—you passed his place down near the bottom of the hill—called to say there was a red car headin' up toward camp and were we expectin' anyone. We weren't, but I thought to keep a lookout, just the same, bein' as there's no place else to go once you pass McKinley's. Nothin' else up here but an old loggers' camp about two miles to the west. Didn't see anyone headin' on up there in the kind of weather we're in for, so I figured someone'd be stopping here."

He paused as if awaiting Leah's explanation.

"I . . . well, I was headed here, actually." Leah pulled off her knitted hat and her gloves and yielded to the temptation to pet the dog.

"We don't get much trade this time of year," the man said as he crossed his arms over his chest. Though cheerful and friendly, he was obviously waiting for an explanation.

Before she could offer one, Leah realized that the music had stopped and that a young girl now stood in the doorway staring at her. The girl was elfin, with clear blue eyes and pale blond hair, a child's mouth in a face that was made-up and almost, but not quite yet, a woman's. Leah guessed her to be about fifteen, give or take a year or two. The makeup made it hard to tell for sure. Leah guessed the girl had whiled away some time that afternoon experimenting in front of a mirror with brown eye shadow and peach blush.

"Are you the piano player?" Leah asked.

"Yes." The girl nodded.

"That was great." Leah smiled. "I could hear you from the trail on my way up from the parking lot. A Broadway tune was about the last thing I expected to hear up here in the woods."

"Well, you're unexpected, too," the girl told her bluntly.

"I guess I am." Leah colored slightly under the girl's candor. "I should introduce myself. I'm Leah McDevitt."

"Tom Sanger." The man stepped forward. "This is my granddaughter, Holly. You've already met Dieter." He pointed to the dog who thumped his tail on the floor upon hearing his name mentioned.

"Hello, Holly," Leah said to the girl before turning back to Tom. "I'm sorry that I didn't call before I came up. But actually, I was looking for Ethan Sanger."

"I'm afraid you've missed him by a day—had you made that call, you'd have saved yourself a trip. Ethan—he's my son, Holly's father—left yesterday morning on some business. Now, are you a friend of his?"

"Well, no, not exactly . . ." Leah wasn't sure how best to respond. It hadn't occurred to her that he wouldn't be there, that she'd have to explain herself to anyone other than Ethan.

"Then I suppose you work for one of those insurance companies he consults for."

"No, no. I work for a magazine and I—"

"Which magazine?" The girl's interest had been aroused.

"It's called *Trends*," Leah told her.

"I've seen *Trends*." Holly nodded. "My friend Chrissie's mother has a subscription and we look at it sometimes. It always has neat stories and pictures about foreign places."

"Thank you." Leah smiled, pleased. "Those would have been mine."

"No way."

Leah nodded.

"Did you really go to all those places?"

"Yes. One of the things I do is travel to out-of-the-way places that people might otherwise not hear about and write stories about what's there and why it's worth a visit."

"Did you do the one about the merry-go-round in France?" Holly stepped closer.

Leah paused for a moment, trying to recall the article Holly referred to.

"The carousel in Avignon. Yes. That was one of the last articles I wrote on a well-known spot. Since then, I've focused on more obscure places." Leah smiled. "You have an excellent memory."

"Did you take all the pictures too?"

"Yes. And I'm so flattered that you read that article and remembered it."

"I didn't exactly read the article," Holly grinned, "but I liked the pictures of the horses, so Mrs. Matterson let me cut them out of her magazine. I still have them up on my wall by my desk."

"Well, thank you. That could very possibly be the best compliment anyone has ever given me." Leah grinned, enormously pleased. "Maybe when I get back to New York, I could send you copies of the original photographs, if you'd like."

"That's so nice of you. Thank you."

"You're welcome." Leah smiled as Holly turned on her toes—clad though they were in heavy leather shoes—and spun toward the steps leading to the second floor, where she was undoubtedly headed to her room and, Leah guessed, a telephone.

"You've made a friend," Tom observed.

"Good." Leah smiled. While the girl was charming in her own right, she was also the daughter of the man Leah had come to see. Knowing that she wasn't likely to find a friend in the father, having the daughter on her side couldn't hurt.

"I apologize for not having called," Leah said. "I should have checked to see if you had a room available."

"Oh, we have lots of available rooms," Tom told her, a twinkle in his eyes. "As a matter of fact, seein' as how camp doesn't open until late April, we're *all* vacancies. Of course, sometimes Ethan does take hunting or fishing parties out in the winter and late spring—and we get the occasional group that wants to ice skate or ski, but for the most part, we don't take guests until late spring. But of course, under the circumstances, you're welcome for as long as you like."

"The circumstances?" Leah's eyebrows knit together, thinking he referred to the impending storm.

"Well, now, don't think I haven't already figured out what you're up to." Tom winked.

"You have?" Leah blanched. How could he possibly . . . ?

"You're doing an article on Maine sporting camps and you're here to do your research," Tom announced.

"Ah . . . well, actually . . ." Leah hesitated. Tom Sanger had been so welcoming, so amicable, that she hated to out-and-out lie.

"And of course, you'd pick White Bear because we are year-round residents here—so many camps are vacant till the season, though I expect you know that if you've done your homework—and because we do offer some winter activities, which most camps don't." Tom sucked on his pipe and looked pleased, his blue eyes sparkling.

"Well, it's about time someone did a little something on the sporting camps up here in the Maine woods. We're an American tradition, you know . . . of course you would know that."

"I did read that." Leah nodded, deciding that if she needed a reason to be here, to stay here until Ethan came back, she'd just been handed a dandy. "But why don't you tell me in your own words what it's like to run a camp like this—"

"How 'bout I put some coffee on while Holly shows you to your room, and then we can sit by the fire and chat and you can ask your questions and take your notes?" Tom beamed.

"An excellent idea." Leah patted him on the arm. "I left my bags in the car, though. I'll just run back out and get them."

"Holly, open up the Rose Room for our guest and put some fresh sheets on the bed," Tom called up the steps to his granddaughter as Leah headed back out the heavy front door.

The wind had picked up and Leah had to duck her head to avoid the small sharp pellets of icy snow that peppered her face as she traveled back up the path to her car. Dieter had followed her from the lodge and had taken off. Every once in a while, she'd see a dark flash dart through the trees as he raced with more agility than she'd thought possible for an old dog. *Maybe he finds the cold, brisk air invigorating,* she mused, *while some of us only find it cold.*

The sun was totally lost now behind thick clouds, and the darkness seemed to deepen with every third step she took. She paused at the end of the path and looked off toward the woods to her far right. The spruce overhead were tall and dark against the last remaining minutes of the afternoon light. The scent of the impending storm, its icy crispness mixed with that of evergreen, swirled around her. Leah had never had so acute an awareness of isolation, of winter, and she wondered just how bad the storm would be, heralded as it was by the overwhelming sense of cold that ate right into her bones.

Cold or guilt, Leah chided herself as she stepped into the clearing.

Tom and Holly were both so open and friendly and obviously pleased to have company, Leah felt a certain discomfort knowing she was being less than honest with them. She hadn't been prepared to deal with anyone but Ethan, and the extent of that "plan" had been to basically throw herself on his mercy. It had simply not occurred to her that he wouldn't be there.

And frankly, given Ethan's reaction to Raymond Lambert's name, she hadn't wanted to press her luck with Tom, regardless of how welcoming and friendly he seemed. If she'd told Tom the truth about her visit, might he not react as Ethan had? Might not this last door slam in her face?

Leah just couldn't run the risk of being shut out, now that she was this close to the reluctant Mr. Sanger.

The reluctant though very *handsome* Mr. Sanger, Leah reminded herself. She had not failed to notice the photographs on the wall behind the desk in the foyer. It had taken her a few moments to realize that the smiling, dark-haired man in the photos with Holly was in fact the same man whose scowling, surly face graced the back of the dust jacket of *The Vagabond Killer.* The photos in the lodge were of a man with an easy smile and warm eyes who carried his daughter on his back while crossing a stream; who sat on the edge of a catamaran and grinned easily at the photographer; who had been caught napping in a hammock, his young child sleeping in the crook of his arm. The Ethan Sanger of White Bear Springs appeared to be a good-natured fellow who enjoyed the out-of-doors and loved his daughter.

The Ethan Sanger of *The Vagabond Killer* looked like a man who enjoyed, well, Leah was hard pressed to think of much that *that* man might enjoy.

And as for love, well, the Ethan Sanger depicted on the book cover looked more like a man who was filled with darker emotions.

Leah paused at the back of her vehicle, wondering which face she'd be looking into when Ethan Sanger arrived back at White Bear Springs Camp and found her there.

And what of Mrs. Sanger, it occurred to Leah to wonder as she pulled her bag from the open back of the Explorer. There'd been no mention of her. Could Leah assume that she had accompanied her husband on his business trip? And once they returned, might she prove to be an ally when she learned of Leah's quest? Would she be sympathetic to the situation, perhaps even take Leah's part in convincing Ethan to talk about Raymond Lambert? Or would she, too, insist on sending Leah away?

As she trudged back to the lodge through a driving wind that sang shrilly through the treetops, Leah couldn't help but wonder if, in Ethan Sanger's wife, she'd find a benevolent spirit. And, if she did, would it be enough to prompt Ethan to talk about Raymond Lambert?

$\mathscr{A}$s quickly as the storm had blown in, it blew back out again, dumping less than a foot of snow overnight and leaving in its wake branches from a white birch that had been snapped and scattered across a clearing like so many enormous toothpicks.

Awake at dawn, Leah pushed aside the window curtains to watch the new snow puff past in wild swirls driven by a smart wind that caused some of the white stuff to stick to the glass. Leah had to slide the window up and brush away several inches of snow to see what had been left behind by the storm. There, from her vantage on the second floor, she could see the lake, frozen hard in the dead of winter, the sun glistening off its icy surface and the windows of the sturdy cabins that stood nearby. Animal tracks—deer perhaps—crisscrossed in the snow beneath the window to form a dark X in an otherwise pristine landscape. Leah had never seen a whiter white than the snow that had fallen on White Bear Springs Camp on that late winter morning.

At seven o'clock, Leah joined Tom and Holly for breakfast, sampling Tom's oatmeal—which he served hot with raisins—and two cups of wonderfully fragrant coffee. Sitting at the kitchen table with the elder Mr. Sanger and the delightfully chatty Holly, listening to their banter and their easy laughter, Leah felt more relaxed than she had since her return from Turkey when her life had been turned inside out.

From Tom, Leah learned about the camps and the people who run them, about the guests who came back every year—many of them the grandchildren and great-grandchildren of those first guests to frequent the camp back in 1905 after that first Thomas Sanger had won the whole parcel in a poker game. Back then, the camp had been little more than a deserted logging camp with five cabins. That Tom had enlisted the help of his brothers and a few cousins to build the lodge and spiff up the cabins for a sporting camp, then the rage of city folks clear on down to Philadelphia.

"Why, at the time my grandfather took possession of this land, there were over three hundred sporting camps in operation up here in Maine. Now, you have to understand that such camps were, and are, unique to the state of Maine. These camps are not just hunting and fishing lodges, though we do our share of that. These were built as refuges in the wilderness where city dwellers could get away from the pollution and the crowds and the summer heat, where they could take part in the wholesome activities offered by so bucolic a setting. Canoeing, hiking, sailing . . . why, whole trainloads of vacationers would travel up from the industrial cities of the East for a family vacation." Tom had paused and puffed on his pipe before adding, "I've always thought it a bit ironic, though, that the trains that carried the city dwellers up here to the woods were powered by steam created by burnin' trees from those very woods they set such store by, and that many of those travelers who could afford to escape the cities were the very folks who owned the factories that were causin' the pollution they were fleeing from. Why, I can remember when—"

"Umm, Grampa, I hate to interrupt, but I have to feed my goats now," Holly said as she pushed her chair away from the table and gathered her breakfast dishes.

"Oh. Of course." Tom nodded after glancing at the clock. "They'll be waiting for you, for sure. Now, Leah, as I was saying—"

"Grampa, I thought maybe Leah might like to walk down to the barn with me." Holly turned to Leah with eager eyes and asked, "Would you like to see my goats? I have five."

Turning toward Tom, who was obviously enjoying his narrative, Leah hesitated.

"Oh, by all means." Tom nodded. "Leah should see the goats. We have the whole day to chat. Leave the dishes, ladies, I'll take care of them. And dress warmly, Leah. The wind can cut you to the bone. Do you have a scarf with you? I didn't see that you were wearing one yesterday when you arrived."

"Actually, no, I don't have one with me. But my jacket has a hood—"

"Hood, smood. You will need something warm around your neck, the way that wind is blowin'. Holly," Tom called to his granddaughter, who had gone into the back shed in search of her boots, "bring Leah a scarf. There are several hanging by the back door."

Holly appeared in the doorway, a length of red, white, and blue plaid in her hand.

"Grampa's right. The wind is pretty bitter. Here, take this one." Holly tossed the plaid scarf in Leah's direction. "It's my dad's. He won't mind."

"Pretty plaid," Leah noted. "Thank you."

"I bought it for him for Christmas a few years ago. Well, actually, Grampa bought it, but I picked it out. 'Member, Grampa?"

"I do indeed. Picked it from the L.L. Bean catalog. Holly thought all you did was call in the order and they delivered right away. Spent hours peering out that front window watching for a truck that said L.L. Bean to pull up."

Holly laughed. "Well, you said that ordering from a catalog was just like buying from the store, except you didn't have to go to the store to get your stuff, they brought it to you after you called for it."

Leah smiled and wrapped the scarf around her neck. It was soft and warm and carried a faint but stirring trace of aftershave or men's cologne. How might Ethan Sanger feel, she wondered as she zipped up the front of her parka, if he knew that she, a stranger and an unwelcome one at that, was wearing his Christmas scarf and becoming more familiar with such intimate details than might be deemed proper?

Fifteen minutes later, Leah found herself with shovel in hand, following Holly down a path that they were clearing through the snow as they went.

"It's been a long time since I shoveled so much snow," Leah gasped as they neared the barn. "I'd forgotten just how hard it is."

"Oh, you don't have to do any more," Holly assured her. "We can just have a single-width path from here."

"What, give up before I reach the end? Ha!" Leah slid the shovel back into the snow. "Never let it be said that Leah McDevitt was bested by a . . . how old are you, Holly?"

"I'm almost fourteen. But I'm mature for my age, don't you think?"

Leah smiled to herself, remembering a time in her own life when it had seemed to take forever to grow up, when "she's so mature for her age" was a compliment of the very highest order.

"Yes. I was thinking that perhaps you were closer to sixteen."

"Really?" Holly turned to face her, obviously well pleased.

"Really," Leah assured her.

"I think it's because I'm with adults most of the time." Holly nodded.

"You have no brothers or sisters?" Leah asked. "It's just your parents and your grandfather and you here?"

"I'm an only child. And it's just me and my dad and my grampa. My mother died when I was little."

"Holly, I had no idea. I'm so sorry." Leah laid a hand on the girl's arm, as if to comfort.

"Me too. I wish she hadn't died. I wish I had known her. I wish I could remember her," Holly said wistfully, "but I don't."

Holly paused, then brightened slightly. "I have lots of pictures of her, though. I have some in my room. She was real pretty."

"I'm sure she was, Holly," Leah said softly.

"And she must have been smart. She was a lawyer. And she must have been a lot of fun because we have lots of pictures of her and my dad laughing. Anyway," Holly put the topic of her mother aside abruptly, "I think spending so much time with grown-ups—I mean, *adults*—is why I'm so mature."

"Aren't there any other kids your age up here?"

"Around camp? Nah. There's only one other family on the hill, down there right past the main road," Holly pointed somewhere past Leah's head, "and they have little kids. They have a new baby. My dad drove them to the hospital because his Jeep has a plow on the front of it and he could get through the snow."

"Then I guess you get to babysit."

"Not much. There's not much to do out here, so people don't go out much like people who live in town do. Usually when Kelly and Bob—they're our neighbors—go out, Kelly's sister, Candace, comes to stay with the little ones. Like she did when Kelly went into the hospital to have the new baby. Grampa and I think that Candace has the hots for my dad . . ."

Having reached the barn, Holly leaned her shovel up against its weathered side.

"And she probably does. My dad is a fox." Holly paused with her hand on the barn door and asked, "Are you married?"

"Me? No."

Holly pushed the door open, grinning as she processed this information.

The low greeting from the goats increased in volume as Leah followed Holly into the dimly lit barn.

"Hello, babies!" Holly called, inciting a flurry of activity from within the wide pen that ran along half of one wall. "Good morning, sunshines!"

Holly grabbed a bucket and lifted the lid off a large metal bin.

"We have to keep their feed covered because we get mice here in the barn and I don't want mice eating their food. Not that the mice don't skulk around the feed dishes at night . . ." She scooped tan-colored feed into the bucket with a sort of spatula. "Then again, we have four barn cats, and the mice have to take their chances with them."

"Are you hungry, babies?" Holly cooed to her charges as

she dragged the bucket to the gate that led into the large stall. "How's your back leg this morning, Pookie?" she asked as she swung the gate open and slipped through.

The goats gathered around Holly, nudging her with noses, eager for both food and attention. She filled the low trough and stepped back to allow the goats to feed.

"Goat chow. That's what we feed them," Holly announced to Leah. "You can come in. They won't hurt you, you know."

Leah smiled and leaned against the side of the stall. "I thought I'd wait until they finished their breakfast."

"They don't mind. They're really friendly. Pookie is the baby. She was born last year. She has a twisted leg, see there?" Holly pointed to the small black and white goat, whose left rear leg hung three inches above the ground. "We think her mom—that would be Polly, the black one on the end with the white star on her face—stepped on her after she was born. Not on purpose, though. She wouldn't have done it on purpose. It would have been an accident, if that's what happened. She's really a good mother."

Holly watched the goats eat for a second or two, and before Leah could comment on Polly's maternal instincts, Holly verbally sped past her.

"I hope my grampa wasn't boring you, rambling on about the camp. He could talk all day about this place. And don't even ask him about the old days." Holly rolled her eyes to the heavens.

Leah laughed.

"I wasn't bored. I think your grandfather is justifiably proud of the camp and his efforts to not only preserve it, but to share it. It's a lovely, wonderful, peaceful place."

"Oh, it's peaceful, all right." Holly frowned. "We've got all the peace and quiet you could ever ask for."

"I guess for someone your age, a little goes a long way."

Holly rolled her eyes again.

"Camp is fun in the summer, when all the people come and there's so much to do. But the rest of the year, it's the most boring place on the planet."

"But surely, at school—"

"I've been home-schooled all my life," Holly told her, then added proudly, "But I'm going to the district high school down in Arlenville next year. I'm going to live with my friend Chrissie and her family."

"I take it there're no school buses up this way?" Leah leaned down to scratch the nose of a curious goat who, having finished its meal, was ready to investigate the visitor.

"No. The weather is just too unpredictable from about November right on through to the end of March. So you either live in town during the school year or you home-school. That's about it."

"And your father has been tutoring you?"

"No. My grandpa. He knows everything. He used to teach at a college. My dad travels sometimes on business, but my grandpa's just about always here. He loves this place so much." Holly knelt to pet the small goat she called Pookie. "I love it too, it's not that I don't. I just don't want to be here all the time. Sometimes my dad lets me go into town for a weekend and I stay with Chrissie, so I know a lot of the kids I'll be going to school with. And living in town will be so fun. It wasn't easy, talking my dad into it, though."

"Oh?"

"If my dad could keep me here forever, he would," Holly assured her, then softened and added, "I understand why he is the way he is. It's because of what happened to my mom."

And what, Leah wanted to ask, was that?

Instead, she just said, "Well, I think parents always feel they have to protect their children as best they can."

"I know. I love him anyway. And it doesn't matter now, since I get to go in September. Dad promised to help me work on my swing. You know, for softball. Do you play softball, Leah?"

"No. Sorry."

"How 'bout tennis?" Holly followed one of the goats to the water trough. With the heel of her hand, she broke through the thin sheet of ice that had formed atop the water.

"A little. I'm afraid my athletic pursuits are pretty much limited to the gym I belong to in the city."

"That's okay. You take great pictures." Holly stepped back through the gate and closed it behind her.

"Who will take care of your goats when you go to school in town next year?" Leah asked as they stepped back outside.

"Dad, probably. It'll give him something to do."

"I thought you said he traveled on business." Leah held the door against the wind as Holly slid the latch over.

"Only when he wants to."

"That's a nice job to have," Leah mused, "working only when you want to, staying home when it pleases you."

"My dad does special consulting for insurance companies. He's a fire expert. The rest of the time, he works here at camp. There's always a lot to do, even in the winter, and my grampa can't do as much as he used to do. And besides," she added, "my dad doesn't like to leave for too long."

"I might have some trouble leaving this place, too, if I lived here."

"It's not that so much." Holly shook her head. "He just doesn't like to leave me alone. Because of my mom dying."

"I can understand that. I'm sure he misses her."

"It's a little more complicated than that," Holly told her before turning her attention back to her goats. "Be good babies. If the wind dies down later, I'll let you go outside for a while. Right now I think it's still too cold for you guys."

Holly leaned over the rail and scratched a brown and white goat behind the ears.

"Ready?" She turned to Leah. "I could show you around camp a little, if you like."

"Don't you have lessons this morning?"

"Oh. Right. Well, after lessons. We have snow-shoes . . . have you ever walked in snowshoes before?"

"Yes. I spend a lot of time in the country in winter. In Connecticut. We get lots of snow there, too." Leah stepped through the barn door that Holly held open for her, squinting as her eyes struggled momentarily to adjust to the bright sun that shone off the snow.

"Well, you're welcome to use a pair if you just want to walk around camp. Don't go beyond the edge of the woods, though. It's easy to get turned around even when you know where you are. If the wind blows snow over your tracks, you might have a problem finding your way out," Holly told her. Then, looking beyond Leah, she pointed upwards and said, "Look, a bald eagle! That's the third one I've seen in the past two weeks!"

"How do you know that you haven't seen the same bird three times?" Leah asked.

"Because they're not the same size. This one is the youngest. Maybe it's last year's baby eagle."

They paused and looked skyward, shielding their eyes

from the glare to watch the immense bird soar toward the lake. Leah tried to remember the last time she had paused for such a sight.

"Oh, and look there, by those small pines." Holly motioned to her. "Rabbit tracks, see? They're the ones that look like little snowshoes. And the tracks behind it are fox. I hope the bunny outran the fox again today."

"The fox has to eat too," Leah commented.

"Well, he can eat something else. Like . . . barn mice," Holly pronounced. "Where do you live?"

"I live in New York."

"In the city?"

Leah nodded. "Manhattan."

"Wow. I never met anyone who lived in Manhattan before. The Millers, who stay with us every summer, are from New York, but they live in Brooklyn."

"Brooklyn's nice," Leah said.

"But Manhattan is . . . it's what you think of when you think of New York. I heard there was a great school there for art."

"There are several." Leah nodded. "Are you interested in going to art school?"

"I want to be a designer."

"Of . . . ?"

"Clothes. I want to have my own studio and my own fashion shows and have famous people come and buy and wear what I design." Holly's face colored a bit. "I have tons of sketches."

"Maybe while I'm here, you could show me. If you want to, that is," Leah hastened to add.

"They're probably not as style-y as what you see in New York."

"There's always room for something fresh," Leah told her as they reached the back of the house.

"Holly, it's time for your lessons." Tom met them at the back door. To Leah he said, "Nippy, isn't it? Bet you're glad for that scarf."

"I was, thank you." Leah unwound the length of plaid wool from around her neck, immediately missing its warmth. And, she realized, its scent. She touched her neck with her fingers, wondering if her skin had retained any of the woodsy fragrance. No, she realized, it was gone with the scarf that was now hanging back in its place by the back door.

"Leah, if you'll excuse us for a time, Holly needs to get started."

"Oh, Grampa. Can't we skip lessons just for one day?" Holly asked.

"No need to," Leah told her. "I wanted to go up to my room and make some notes before I forget what I saw this morning."

"For your article?" Tom asked.

"Yes. For my article." Leah smiled.

And there would be an article, Leah decided. The land was so unspoiled, so beautiful, so natural, that she could not wait to call Catherine to let her know that she was in Maine working on a story and would be back soon, weather and story—and Ethan Sanger—permitting.

Leah sat at the small pine desk near a window in her room and jotted down impressions, sights and sounds and scents. She looked out the window and watched as clouds covered the sun, watched the shadows fall and retreat, fall and retreat. Inspired, Leah grabbed her gloves, hat, and camera, anxious to see if she could capture the essence of the landscape on film. At the back door she pulled her boots back on, then paused before slipping into her jacket. Taking the plaid scarf from its hook, she wound it gently around her neck, catching the faint scent as she did so.

Beyond the door, the handsome lodge lay half in sun, half in shade for one long minute, and Leah occupied herself with seeking the perfect shot. First from one angle, then another, in full sun, in full shade, then in partial light, Leah shot frame after frame.

Then she turned her attention to the woods.

How to capture the essence of the Maine woods?

Leah spent the better part of the next hour trying to balance the light and shadow, the straight lines of the trees and the softness of clouds above and beyond. By the time she was loading her camera with the last roll of film she had in her pockets, she realized her hands and feet were getting numb. She'd finish these last few frames, then head back to the lodge.

Later in the evening, Leah sat near the fire in a cozy wing chair and discussed the direction of her story with Tom, grateful that the cover she'd invented to get herself into the lodge was no longer a fabrication. Tom and Holly both had been so charming, so amiable, that Leah couldn't help but feel pangs of remorse at having deceived them.

At least now, it's true, Leah reminded herself. *There will be an article in* Trends. *I have every right to be here.*

She smiled across the room at Tom as if to convince herself.

And with any luck, Ethan would see it exactly that way when he finally showed up.

Chapter 9

"Which color do you like better?" Holly stood before Leah's chair and held up two jars of nail polish—one cobalt blue, one mint green—for Leah's inspection.

"Ummm, tough choice." Leah appeared to consider them equally. "Maybe the blue. It matches your eyes."

"Would you let me paint your nails sometime?" Holly asked tentatively.

"Oh, sure." Leah offered her hands for Holly's inspection. "Though I'm afraid they're a bit stubby right now. I haven't had much time for manicures lately."

"I've never had one. Not a real one, anyway. Sometimes when I'm at Chrissie's and some of her friends from school come over, we all do each other's nails."

"I think that's how I learned to paint nails," Leah told her.

"Do you know how to French-braid hair?"

"Yes. I am quite good at it, actually. Or at least, I used to be."

"Would you do mine?" Holly asked nonchalantly, as if

it didn't matter much to her if Leah did, or didn't, braid her hair.

"Holly, don't bother Leah. She's working on her notes." Tom looked up from his book.

"Oh, I don't mind. And besides, I've done all I'm going to do tonight, anyway. Bring that stool over here, Holly, and sit in front of me."

"I'll get my hair brush," Holly leaped from the sofa and bounded toward the front hall, "and I'll be right back."

Leah smiled and craned her neck to watch Holly take the steps two at a time.

"You don't have to, you know," Tom told Leah. "I don't want you to feel that she's being a pest."

"Not at all." Leah shook her head. "Holly's delightful. Besides, it isn't often I have the company of teenage girls. It's fun to know they still do the things my friends and I did when we were her age."

"Well, she doesn't have much female companionship, you know. Bein' here all the time with just her dad and me. That bein' said, I still wouldn't want you to feel she's takin' advantage."

"I don't. I'm enjoying her company, too."

"It's been hard on Holly, you know, growin' up without her mother." Tom folded his book over, using the fingers of one hand to mark his place, the other hand dropping down to pet Dieter. "Libby's death changed all our lives."

"A death in the family always does," Leah said softly.

"Here's my brush. And a few hairpins." Holly appeared in a blur, entering the room, pulling the stool over in front of Leah's chair, and sitting, seemingly all in one motion.

"Well, then, let's see if I'm still as good at this as I used to be."

They sat in silence for a few long, comfortable moments, Leah brushing and braiding long strands of Holly's honey-blond hair, Tom occasionally glancing up from his page to watch. Holly was clearly content with Leah's attention. It had been so long since his granddaughter had been the recipient of such special treatment, Tom thought sadly. He hoped she wouldn't suffer for lack of it, once Leah left.

Though Leah *did* need more information for her article, Tom reasoned. And Lord knows he could tell her everything she needed to know. It could take a while.

Tom liked the young woman. Leah brought something to the lodge and to their lives, something vital and colorful that had been sadly lacking over the last few years. This afternoon he had heard Leah and Holly laughing together in the kitchen. The sound of their shared feminine laughter had touched Tom in a way he could not explain.

"Grampa, I said, the phone's ringing. Could you please answer it?" Holly was waving a hand to get his attention.

"What? Oh, yes. Right."

Holly giggled and whispered, "I think Grampa's having a senior moment."

Leah laughed. "I think he was just daydreaming. Maybe thinking about the book he's reading."

"Do you do that when you read?" Holly asked.

"Sometimes."

"What do you daydream about?"

"Oh, sometimes I'll stop and think about the scene I've just read. Sometimes things that I read spark a memory of a place I've been, or make me think about places I'm planning to go to . . . hold still, Holly, I need to secure this section—"

"Do you French-braid your own hair?"

"Not usually."

"Where'd you learn to do it so well?"

"I used to braid my little sister's hair. Just like this."

"How old is your sister?"

Leah was silent for a long minute, then said, "She died several years ago."

Holly turned quickly in her seat. "I'm so sorry, Leah."

"So was I."

"I'll bet you still miss her."

"I do. Every day."

Holly appeared to be about to ask yet another question when Tom appeared in the doorway.

"That was your father, Holly. He'll be home tomorrow, probably in the morning."

"Oh, great! Did you tell him about Leah?"

Tom paused slightly, then said, "No. I didn't."

"Why not?" Holly asked quizzically.

"It just slipped my mind. We didn't speak for very long," Tom told her, knowing that wasn't the whole truth.

Actually, Tom had been about to tell Ethan about their visitor, but for some reason, he'd hesitated, not knowing quite why but feeling a definite compulsion to omit that little bit of information. And so he simply hadn't mentioned it.

Oh, well, no harm, no foul, Tom told himself as he opened the front door and stepped out onto the porch to grab another log or two for the fire. Ethan would be home tomorrow. He'd meet Leah soon enough.

Tom couldn't help but smile somewhat hopefully as he leaned down to pick a piece of cut wood from the pile. Ethan had been alone for long enough. Tom couldn't wait to see what his son would think of their pretty guest.

*   *   *

"Her name is what?" Ethan turned slowly to his father as he plopped a large pile of mail, picked up that morning at the post office in Arlenville, in the middle of the kitchen table.

The name had struck an irritating chord.

"Leah. Leah McDevitt," Tom repeated.

"How long has she been here?" Ethan said through clenched jaws.

Tom watched his son's face as Ethan stared out the window, searching the landscape, no doubt, for his daughter and the woman who, his father told him, had gone down toward the lake over an hour ago.

"She arrived three days ago. She's—"

"Why didn't you tell me she was here?" Ethan asked.

"I didn't think to," Tom replied somewhat archly. "Last night was the first time you called home all week, and we didn't stay on the phone very long."

"Long enough for you to tell me you had a visitor."

"What difference does it make? Leah is a writer. We've had writers here before. She's doing a magazine article on Maine sporting camps, and she chose White Bear Springs for the article," Tom told Ethan proudly.

"Well, that's original, I'll have to give her that," Ethan muttered.

"What?"

"I said, that's a clever cover." Ethan turned away from the window.

"Cover?" Tom's eyes narrowed. "What are you talking about?"

"Miss Leah may be a writer, but she's not writing any article about White Bear Springs," Ethan said dryly. "My guess is that she's working on a book about Raymond Lambert."

"Raymond . . ." Tom appeared stunned. "Why would you think—?"

"Because she called me the night before I left and asked me if she could look at any notes I might have taken while I was working on *The Vagabond Killer*. It was within days of Lambert being killed."

"Now, what would Leah want with—"

"My guess is that now that Lambert's gone, she's planning on rehashing the story and making a few bucks on it." Ethan walked to the counter and peered into the coffeepot. It was empty, further darkening his mood. "Why else would anyone be interested in Lambert, all these years later?"

"I don't understand why she would lie." Tom shook his head slowly, stunned by the news. "Why she wouldn't have just told me the truth when she got here."

"Probably because I told her that I don't have anything to say about Lambert, and that I wouldn't discuss him with her or with anyone else." Ethan rinsed out the coffeepot, then turned to look at his father. "You look upset."

"I am upset. I like Leah. A lot. So does Holly. They've spent a lot of time together this week, and Holly will be—"

"She hasn't been asking Holly about Libby, has she?" Ethan's fingers gripped the handle of the coffeepot as the thought occurred to him that perhaps, not getting any information from him, Leah had spent the last three days pumping his daughter for information of the most personal kind. "If she's upset Holly, I'll—"

"Ethan, calm down. As far as I know, Libby's name only came up once since Leah got here, and I was the one who brought it up." Tom paused, still confused at having learned the young woman he'd grown so fond of in so short a time might not be who she claimed to be.

"What did you say? What did you tell her?"

"Only that things haven't been the same for any of us since Holly's mother died."

"And she said—?" Ethan waited for Tom to continue.

"That death had a way of doing that. Of changing the lives of those left behind. Or something to that effect."

Ethan stared at his father, then turned at the sound of footsteps on the back steps. Footsteps and laughter.

The back door swung open and a giggling Holly was followed by a giggling woman and Dieter, whose tongue was lolling half out of his mouth.

The first thing Ethan noticed about their visitor was that her eyes were the color of melted chocolate. The second was that her face, flushed with the last cold breath of winter, had a natural beauty.

The third was that she was wearing his favorite scarf.

"Daddy!" Holly exclaimed. "You're back!"

Holly kicked off her snowy boots in record speed and jumped into her father's arms.

"Hello, pumpkin." Ethan kissed Holly's cheek, and looked beyond her to the woman who stood in the doorway.

"Daddy, this is Leah. She's writing an article about our camp for a magazine called *Trends*. She's taken tons of pictures this week, and I'm in some of them, so my picture could be in this famous magazine. Is that the *coolest* thing you ever heard?"

"It's right up there." Ethan's gaze never wavered. Neither did Leah's.

"Hello, Ethan Sanger." Leah extended a deliberate right hand in his direction.

Just as deliberately, he chose to pretend not to see it.

Instead, Ethan swung his daughter around, effectively averting Leah's gaze, which he had found to be unexpectedly direct and wholly unapologetic. For reasons he could not name, it unnerved him, and he chose to distract himself since he was having a hard time ignoring it altogether.

"Dad, Leah said hello." Holly would not permit her father to slip off the hook.

"Hello, Leah," Ethan said without looking at the unwanted visitor.

Holly stared at her father. While not the world's most outgoing guy, she'd never, ever known him to be rude.

Under his daughter's scrutiny, Ethan bristled. That Holly and Leah had forged some sort of bond was apparent. That Holly would be devastated to learn that Leah had no more interest in her than the man in the moon was even more obvious. Holly had been beaming when she'd all but fallen through the back door, weak from laughter, her eyes shining. It was a look Ethan had seen Holly share mostly with her girlfriends these days, though on occasion, she still reserved a little of that happy exuberance for her father. To see Holly so happy in the company of someone who would only bring her sadness once her true purpose was revealed, so trusting of someone who could not be trusted, made Ethan's blood boil. Holly was an open, loving child. It appeared to Ethan that Leah had taken advantage of Holly's sweet nature to get to him. It was all he could do not to lift Leah bodily and toss her out the back door into the snow.

Such action on his part, Ethan knew, would only upset Holly, who'd be upset enough when she realized that Leah had come to the lodge under false pretenses. Rather than confront Leah in front of Holly, Ethan touched his daughter's cheek with the tips of his fingers and said, "I think Leah and I should take a few minutes to get acquainted, Holly. Would you make some coffee for us and bring it into the den?"

"Leah likes tea in the afternoon," Holly told him.

"Well, then, Leah can have tea, and I'll have my usual coffee."

With his right hand, Ethan reached out and gripped Leah's left elbow with enough pressure to let her know that he remembered her name, and knew why she was there, and that he wasn't going to let her get away with trying to charm information out of his family behind his back.

"I think that's a fine idea, Ethan. I've been looking forward to meeting you," Leah told him, refusing to flinch from his touch or his gaze, neither of which held a trace of welcome.

Tom took a step forward, about to speak, his face lined with concern.

"Dad, why don't you tend to the fire in the front room for a few minutes?" Ethan said firmly.

Without waiting for his father's response, Ethan steered Leah through the door and down the hall, not speaking until he'd reached the den and closed the door behind them.

"I will give you forty-five seconds to tell me why I should not drop-kick your ass from here back to wherever it was you came from," Ethan said, his anger just beginning to surface.

"Ethan, I understand how you must feel—"

"You couldn't possibly," he said coldly.

"But if you'd let me explain—"

"I can't think of one good reason why I should."

"You know, it's really hard for me to understand how such a rude, closed-minded man could have such a charming father and such a wonderful, totally delightful child."

"Don't bring Holly into this." He turned on her, his eyes flashing with parental concern. "Although I suppose you already have by pretending to be her friend."

"*Pretending?*" Leah's own ire began to rise. "That remark insults Holly as much as it insults me. No one would have to *pretend* to like her. Why, she's smart, she's responsible, she's fun, she's—"

"Thank you," he said dryly. "We both agree she's exceptional. That's not going to win you a second more of my time. I really resent what you've done. Your deception aside, I told you I would not discuss Raymond Lambert and I meant it. For you to sneak into my home behind my back, weasel your way into my family's good graces—"

"Wait a minute. I never set out to deceive anyone," Leah's voice edged up defensively. "When I decided to come here to see you in person, I had no idea you wouldn't be here. How would I have known that? But after I arrived and your father asked me what I did and I told him, he just sort of assumed I was here to do an article about the camp. And it took me less than twenty-four hours to realize that it was actually a great idea. This area is a natural for the type of article I do. It's unspoiled, it's beautiful—"

"How long have you been rehearsing this?"

"I'm going to pretend that you didn't say that. Because regardless of what you think, this article will be a great one, and it will run in my magazine. The only way to prove that I'm telling the truth about that is to send you a copy when the issue comes out . . . I'm targeting the July issue, by the way."

"Well, I hope you got all the pictures you need, because you won't have time to take any more. I'd like you to leave within the hour."

"I don't think you're being fair."

"You coming here under false pretenses wasn't fair."

"I did not come here under false pretenses. I came to see you, to talk to you. I believe that you might have information that I desperately need."

"Oh, so you can write the definitive book on Raymond Lambert? Now that he's been offed, you think someone should cash in and it might as well be you?"

"What the hell are you talking about?" Leah's hands flew to her hips.

"I'm talking about the book I suspect you're planning on writing about Raymond Lambert and his victims."

"And what makes you think that I'm writing a book?"

"Why else would you want access to my notes? And for the record, there are no notes of any conversations that I ever had with him."

"No notes?" Leah seemed to blanch. "None?"

"No."

"But . . . how did you write the book if you took no notes?"

"I tape recorded our conversations and turned the tapes over to the publisher."

"The tapes, then. If I could just listen—"

"No."

"Ethan, please. You're my last hope."

"No."

"But . . . you don't understand." Leah's eyes teared and her bottom lip began to shake.

"Nice touch, the quivering lip. But the answer is still no. I'm afraid you'll have to rely on newspapers and the information in my book as reference for your own. But I warn you, don't plagiarize from me. Plagiarism is still a crime, you know. Nothing would please me more than to bring charges against you."

"The newspapers didn't tell me what I needed. And I read your book twice. It didn't help, either." Leah's voice had dropped to a whisper. "I was hoping your notes could tell me—"

"Tell you what?" Ethan's eyes narrowed.

"Where he left my sister's body." Large tears rolled openly down Leah's cheeks and she made no effort to hide them, as if she was unaware of them.

The silence in the room was overwhelming.

"What was your sister's name?" Ethan asked, a note of caution in his voice.

"Melissa McDevitt."

"I sat with Lambert for weeks on end. He told me about every killing in great detail. He never mentioned your sister's name. And trust me, I remember every single one of them. I'd have remembered hers as well. I'm afraid you'll have to do better than that, though I admit it's a very clever ruse."

"It's not a ruse."

"Tell me, then, why you think Lambert killed your sister. And why you waited until after he'd been killed to start looking for her."

"I didn't know—"

"Where did this killing take place?"

"In upstate western Pennsylvania."

"You should have done your homework a little better, Leah. Lambert's kills were strictly through the south and the southwest."

Leah sighed heavily. "Would you please listen to me for one minute? And if at the end of that minute you still don't believe me, I'll leave."

Ethan glanced at his watch.

"Talk fast."

"Seven years ago, my sister was on her way home from college for the summer. She'd just finished her freshman year at Ohio State."

"When was this?"

"May twenty-fifth, nineteen ninety-three. She was dropping her roommate off in a small town outside of Erie, not far from the New York border."

Ethan shook his head.

"By his own admission, on the twelfth of May, nineteen ninety-three, Lambert was in Texas—outside of San Antonio—where he killed a young woman named Marlene Baker."

"He had plenty of time to travel from Texas to Pennsylvania. His next documented killing was on June first. He'd have had time enough," Leah insisted.

"What makes you so sure that it was Lambert?"

"Because he told me he did."

"Lambert told you he killed your sister in Pennsylvania on May twenty-fifth, nineteen ninety-three?"

"He didn't exactly come out and say that he did it, but he certainly led me to believe that he did."

"Why didn't he tell me about her? He took such great pleasure in telling me everything about every murder he committed. Why would he omit only her?"

"I don't know. And you don't know that he did tell you about all of his victims. You only know what he chose to tell you. Maybe you just don't remember."

"I remember everything. And your minute is up."

"You used up half of it with your questions. Please just hear my story."

Ethan sighed heavily and leaned back against the edge of the desk, his arms crossed over his chest. He might as well let her get it over with. The sooner she told her story, the sooner she would leave. He motioned for her to start.

"A few weeks before he was killed, Lambert sent a letter to me at my office. At the magazine."

"What did the letter say? How did he know where you worked?"

"If you'd stop interrupting me, I'd tell you."

"Daddy?" Holly called from outside the door. "Could you let me in? I have your coffee."

Still eyeing Leah suspiciously as he crossed the carpet and opened the door, Ethan took the tray from Holly's hands.

"Thank you, Holly. But if you wouldn't mind, Leah and I are having a discussion right now."

Holly peeked into the room and glanced uncertainly from Ethan to Leah. The tension was as dense as the fog that was beginning to settle over the lake.

"I promise, we're almost done," Ethan told her.

"But . . ." Holly looked at Leah curiously.

Holly had wanted her father to like Leah, but she hadn't expected him to lock himself away with her like this. And there was something in their faces. Both of them were tense and uneasy, not exactly the reaction Holly had secretly hoped her father and her new friend would have to each other.

"Five more minutes, Holly," Leah said softly. There was a sadness in her eyes Holly had not seen before.

Holly nodded uncertainly and backed out into the hall and closed the door behind her, not at all liking whatever was going on in there.

"Thank you," Leah told him.

"Finish your story." Ethan sat the tray between them and motioned for Leah to help herself.

"Where was I?" she asked.

"Lambert sent you a letter."

"Right. I found it when I came back to the office after being out of the States on assignment for a few weeks. It was in a stack of mail that my assistant left on my desk. At first I thought it was a hoax."

"What did it say?"

"It said, 'I know where your sister is. Does this mean I get the reward?' "

"Reward?"

"When Missy disappeared, we—my cousin and I—posted a fifty thousand dollar reward for information about her disappearance. There were a lot of false trails over the years, but the reward money has remained in escrow."

"You never gave up?"

"No. I never did. I always believed . . ." Leah bit her bottom lip. "Well, it doesn't matter what I believed. Suffice it to say that I always believed the reward would be paid out."

"How did Lambert know about the reward?"

"Shortly before I left on my trip, I was on a television show with the siblings of others who had disappeared and never been found. I was asked if the reward still stood and I said it would until Missy was found, one way or another. That anyone having information should contact me in care of *Trends*. I gave the address."

"And shortly after that, you got a letter from Lambert."

"Two. Two letters. I was out of the country when the first one came, and I guess he was annoyed that I didn't answer him, so he sent a second."

Ethan appeared to digest this for a long moment, then asked, "What did you do with the letters?"

"I gave them to the FBI."

"Who did you speak with?"

"Genna Snow. She put me in touch with John Mancini, the agent who had interviewed Lambert after his arrest."

"I remember him well." Ethan nodded. "But what happened to the letters?"

"She kept them to compare the handwriting to Lambert's and to check for his fingerprints. She was going to look into reopening his case if the prints matched, but of course, Lambert was killed and that was the end of that."

"So that was it? You turned over the notes and waited to hear from the FBI?"

"Not exactly. I went to see Lambert in prison. Genna—Agent Snow helped me to get in to see him."

"What did he say? He must have wanted something from you."

"He wanted the reward money."

"And in return, he'd tell you where your sister's body was?" Ethan's jaw tightened.

"Yes. How did you know?"

"A good guess," Ethan said without emotion. "And you paid him?"

"Half. I was in the process of wiring half to his attorney as we had agreed when he was killed. I canceled the transfer. He had, however, already given me a general idea of where Missy was. Not exactly where, but what part of the state, what it was near."

"But not enough information for you to find her?"

"No. He was killed the day after I was there."

"Is this the truth? All of it?" Ethan looked suddenly very weary, and very sad.

"Yes. It's the truth. And frankly, I couldn't make up something like this. It would hurt too much. I've missed my sister every day she's been gone. I've never stopped missing her for a minute. I'd have done anything to find her—"

"This must be very hard on your parents."

"We lost them both in a car accident a few years before Missy died. She was all I had left of my immediate family. There is no way you could ever understand what I have gone through, all these years."

"Oh, I think I could," Ethan said grimly.

Leah looked at the man who slumped back against the big wooden desk halfway across the room.

"Raymond Lambert killed my wife. The price for her body was the book."

Leah's throat constricted so tightly that for a moment she could not even breathe.

"He made you sit and listen . . . before he . . ." A wave of nausea hit Leah strongly and unexpectedly.

"Yes," Ethan whispered.

"I'm sorry. I had no idea. I'm so sorry." A shaking Leah pointed to a partially opened door on the right. "Is that a bathroom?"

Ethan nodded.

"Excuse me," she told him, "but I think I'm going to be very sick."

Chapter 10

I'm sorry," Leah told him as she emerged, still shaken, from the bathroom several long minutes later, her face white, her eyes almost wild.

Ethan handed her the glass of water that he'd brought from the kitchen where he'd fled after Leah had closed the bathroom door behind her. Stunned by the depth of her reaction, Ethan had done the only thing he could think of to do. He removed himself from the situation for as long as he had an excuse to do so.

"I'm sorry, too," Ethan told her. "I apologize for the things I said to you. I didn't realize . . . I had no idea about your sister."

"Apology accepted." Leah took the glass and raised it to her lips, her hands still shaking as she sipped at the cold water. "I wasn't aware that your wife . . . that is, I didn't see her name on the list of victims in your book."

"She went by her maiden name. Elizabeth West."

"The attorney from Atlanta," Leah recalled out loud the last of the entries on the list at the beginning of the book.

*   *   *

"Yes." Ethan nodded.

Leah sat the half-empty glass on the tray where her tea remained untouched, and asked, "Are you going to help me? Will you let me listen to Lambert's tapes?"

"Tell me what it is you hope to learn," Ethan said, hoping to win some time. He simply hadn't been prepared for the possibility of hearing that voice again. Not now. Maybe not ever. He needed time to think this over.

"I want to know if he made any mention of a trip to Pennsylvania in May of nineteen ninety-three. I want to know if he could have been telling the truth about my sister."

"Leah, I honestly don't recall Lambert talking about any activity farther north than Tennessee."

"Maybe it just didn't seem important at the time. Maybe it was something he hadn't elaborated on. Who knows why it might have slipped your mind?" Leah began to pace slowly the narrow width of the room. "Or why he chose not to tell you. Maybe that was just one more of his sly little games."

"I haven't forgotten a word he said, Leah. If you had heard him, talking about what he'd done . . . well, chances are you'd never forget, either." Ethan watched her slim form, in black leggings and a tunic knitted from heathered wool, walk back and forth, her feet in thick woolen socks, as casual as if she belonged there. "Maybe Lambert was just playing a game with you."

"Oh, he was." Leah stopped right in front of Ethan. "Not giving me all the information at once was part of it."

"Have you considered that maybe Lambert had overheard another inmate talking about killing your sister? Maybe it was all just a hoax."

"I did think about that. I just have this feeling . . . and

besides, he knew about her eyes, Ethan," Leah told him, explaining that Lambert had known that Melissa had worn colored contact lenses. "Lambert said the brown lens had popped out. That's not the type of thing one makes up."

"He could have overheard that from someone else. Maybe the real killer is someone he knew in prison."

"With fifty thousand dollars at stake, why didn't the real killer collect the reward?"

"Any number of reasons. Supposing he was in prison for another crime. Why would he volunteer information about a murder he'd not even been connected to?" Ethan paused, then asked, "You did get your money back, didn't you?"

"Yes. I canceled the transaction before it was completed. Though I really would have liked to have known what he was planning to do with all that money." She smiled wryly. "Maybe he was going to give it to his favorite charity."

"Lambert was his own favorite charity," Ethan told her.

"I'd rather have paid out all of it—every last dime—and found Missy."

"I understand," Ethan said softly.

And he did understand, all too well, the feeling of *not knowing where*.

Ethan had lived on the brink of that uncertainty, that emptiness, for almost four agonizing years, years when he'd begun every day with the prayer that today would be the day they'd find his wife, days that would end with the agony of one more prayer unanswered. He'd been on the most intimate of terms with that bottomless fear from the moment he realized that Libby was missing, until the day he'd dug where Lambert had instructed him to dig and found what remained of her buried beneath a dense layer of decayed leaves and dark earth in the hills outside of Austin.

Ethan shook off the feeling of desperation that washed over him whenever he looked back on that time—months and years—he'd spent adrift in a sea of grief and helplessness and guilt. He pushed it all back into that place inside himself where he'd kept it locked away in its wretchedness and slammed the door on it all, all the while looking out the window and wishing fervently that Leah McDevitt had never come to White Bear Springs, that she had never learned his name.

"Will you help me?" Leah asked again.

"I don't know," Ethan told her frankly, his mouth going dry.

"May I ask why? I've already told you the truth. I'm not writing a book. I swear it."

"I believe you. It isn't that."

"Then what?"

"I just don't know that you could deal with it. The tapes are graphic, Leah, worse than anything you could ever imagine."

"I understand that. I'll be all right with it."

"I don't know that I will." Ethan spoke softly, and it was then that Leah realized how painful this must be for the man who had once had to negotiate his own pact with Lambert.

"I don't know why you'd have to. I could just borrow the tapes. You wouldn't have to deal with them yourself."

Ethan shook his head.

"It isn't quite that simple. There are dozens of tapes. On some, you can hear his answers, but not my questions. In places, he rambles back and forth, jumping from one victim to another, then back again. I knew who he was referring to, but you most likely would not. Handing over the box of tapes and sending you alone into Raymond Lambert's psyche would be like putting you in a canoe and sending you down the Amazon River with no guide and nothing with which to defend yourself. There are some places that no one should go alone, Leah. I'm afraid this is one of them."

"Ethan, I am sorry to have brought all of this back. If there was any other way—"

"I just need some time to think this over." Ethan smiled sadly, and added, "And it's never really gone away, you know."

"I do know. I think about Missy every day. You must do the same. Especially since you have Holly."

Ethan nodded. "I think it's worse for her. I knew how wonderful Libby was. Holly never got to find out."

"Ethan?" Tom knocked on the door and called tentatively.

"Come on in, Dad," Ethan told him.

Tom opened the door and leaned in. Holly peeked over his shoulder.

"You two just about ready for dinner?" asked Tom, who, Ethan knew, must have been dying of curiosity to know what had been going on behind that door for so long.

"Yes, Tom, if you and Holly still want me to stay after you hear what I have to say." Leah took a deep breath. "I haven't been honest with you. I didn't come here with the intention of writing an article about the camp. I came to see Ethan about Raymond Lambert. When I got here and found that Ethan was away for a few days, I needed an excuse to stay until he returned. At first, after you brought it up, Tom, an article about Maine sporting camps seemed like as good a reason as any to be here. It didn't take long for me to realize that it was a great idea. And that I'd be hard-pressed to find a more beautiful setting than White Bear Springs. I'm sorry that I didn't tell you the truth." Leah looked directly at Tom and added, "I needed an excuse to wait for Ethan, and you gave me one."

Leah glanced at Holly, whose jaw had squared angrily and whose eyes had begun to smolder.

"You lied to us," Holly accused.

"Yes. I did," Leah told her. "And I'm sorry that, at the time, I felt I had to do that. But I didn't deceive you about the article. It's almost completed, and it will run this summer. I've already discussed it with the editor, and she's as enthusiastic about it as I am." Leah took a deep breath. "But it wasn't why I came in the first place."

"I don't understand why you had to lie about coming to see my father." Holly's adolescent indignation was just warming up.

"Because I needed information from him and when I got here and found him gone, I needed a reason to wait around."

"Why didn't you just call him?"

"I did call, but the information I was looking for wasn't something that he felt like talking about at the time."

"What information?" Holly persisted.

"I thought your father might have some information that could help me find my sister."

Holly hesitated for a second, then asked cautiously, "Your sister that died?"

"Yes."

"Why would my father know anything about your sister?"

"Folks, I think we need to move this discussion into the dining room," Tom finally spoke up. "Dinner is ready, and it sounds like this story will be a long one. I don't want my pot roast turning to shoe leather."

Tom held the door open in such a way that clearly announced that he expected all of them to march through it. "Leah, Holly and I offered you our friendship from the minute you stepped through our front door. Now, I've always believed that friendships built on lies weren't worth havin', but I'm willing to listen to your explanation of what was more important than the truth. Could be that you were justified in keepin' that truth to yourself for a while. Either way, you'll have plenty of time to tell your story."

Leah nodded and followed a silent, sulking Holly into the dining room. Ethan would forgive her for blindsiding him, and Tom, being a rational man, would surely understand the reason for her deception. Holly's teenage sense of fair play had been violated, however, and her sensitivities might be more deeply offended than the others'.

And up until the moment she had seen the hurt on Holly's face, Leah hadn't realized just how much the young girl's forgiveness mattered. She and Holly had forged a fast friendship these past few days, and Leah knew that if she was to salvage that friendship, her explanation was going to have to be a damned good one. Determined to give it her best shot, Leah sat on the chair Ethan held out for her and glanced to the end of the table where Tom was taking his place. She hoped that tonight, as he had every night, he'd be saying grace before the meal. Leah figured she needed all the help she could get.

* * *

A thumping in the hallway outside his bedroom woke Ethan at dawn the next morning. It took him a moment to place the sound: Dieter's tail slapping happily against the floorboards. Ethan raised himself up on one elbow and wondered what had awakened the dog. He glanced at the small alarm clock next to his bed. Five-thirty. Early even for Tom on the off season.

With a sigh, Ethan folded his arms behind his head while his brain picked up where it had left off before he fell asleep the night before.

On the one hand, Leah needed his help. While Ethan personally did not believe that Raymond Lambert had killed Melissa McDevitt, he appreciated the fact that this would have to be proven to Leah before she could accept it. And he of all people understood why she wanted so desperately to believe that Lambert had killed her sister. Knowing *who* would be closure, that, while not complete, would at least be something. Some knowledge. Some truth. In situations like this, some truth, however thin, was better than nothing at all. Leah was entitled to know.

Unfortunately, the only chance Leah might have to find that truth might be hidden in Ethan's notes.

And despite his assertion to the contrary, of course Ethan had taken notes.

As odious an exercise as it had been, Ethan had written down almost every word Raymond Lambert had spoken during those hellish months. The discipline of keeping the pen on the paper had kept him focused and sane. Without that focus, he'd have leapt through the screen that separated him from his wife's killer, and he'd have broken Lambert's neck with his bare hands. Pure and simple. He'd have snapped it with as much ease as he'd have snapped a twig and with as much regret.

And then, of course, he'd have been arrested and he'd be the one in prison, and Holly would have been effectively orphaned by Raymond Lambert. Ethan recalled having wondered at the time if anyone would have wanted to write a book about him if he'd killed Lambert while researching the book on the Vagabond Killer.

The notes were contained in a pile of stenographer's pads, not numbered, which meant that anyone seeking to plow through them would have to read them all first to put them in order. It was one of the reasons why he'd lied to Leah about not having them. It was knowing that he'd have to look through them, to sort through and order the chaos that had been Lambert's mind—and thereby relive it all again—that had kept Ethan from telling the truth about the notes. The pain had been so perfectly complete the first time, the grief and the anger so dense with emotion and hatred, that Ethan was afraid to take a second look. How many times, he wondered, could you have your beating heart removed and still survive?

Why, his inner voice demanded of him, *would you even consider risking so much for the sake of a stranger?*

You owe her nothing, the voice droned on. *You don't seek out strangers and ask them—expect them—to put themselves in a position where they could bleed to death. And isn't that what Leah has done?*

Only for him, Ethan knew, the bleeding would be of the bits and pieces of his sanity that he'd managed to hold on to, those last remnants that had not been eaten by guilt or devoured by grief. There had been times over the past few years when Ethan had questioned whether even those pieces that he'd managed to save were worth salvaging.

Ethan knew what the answer would have been if it hadn't been for Holly.

If not for Holly, Ethan might have taken that last plunge into welcomed numbness and been free of the nightmares, but having lost her mother, Holly needed her father more than ever. And there was Tom to consider as well, Ethan knew. Tom, who would never understand the desire to just pass from this world. Knowing that inflicting pain on others to be free of pain yourself was an act of selfishness he could not commit, Ethan had made a life of sorts here in the woods, helping his father with the camp and raising his daughter the best he could, passing time and marking the seasons. In the winter Ethan chopped wood and led hunting and ice-fishing groups. In the spring he made repairs to whatever in the camp had been damaged by the harsh Maine winter, and in summer he brought guests in by charter plane and helped his father run the camp. In the fall, there were hunters almost every weekend, and there was the next winter to prepare for.

Somehow, Ethan had managed to place himself squarely on this treadmill and never permitted himself to fall off, much like a tightrope walker whose very existence depended on his ability to put one foot in front of the other without fail.

This had been Ethan's life since Libby's death, the only variation he permitted being the arson investigations. The sameness of the years didn't scare Ethan. As long as he stayed exactly where he was, continued to do exactly what he'd been doing, Ethan knew that his life would always be the same. Looking ahead into that sameness didn't scare him nearly as much as looking back did.

And he well may have chosen to continue on making his way across that dark abyss on that same thin wire if Leah McDevitt hadn't turned up and charmed her way past Tom and Holly while Ethan's back was turned.

Charmed her way past Ethan, as well.

He wanted to refuse her request and mean it, send her on her way so he could return to the prickly little cocoon he'd made for himself. At the same time, her dilemma, so like his own had once been, had muddied the waters, making it impossible for him to say no and harder still to say yes.

In his heart, Ethan knew that no one should be forced to endure the kind of pain that Lambert had inflicted. And while he strongly believed that Lambert had lied to Leah, that his and Melissa McDevitt's paths had never crossed, he felt the victim's family was entitled to know the truth. That truth might be found in his notes. While not putting an end to her search to find her sister, it would at least prove to her that her sister's killer was still out there.

A sad truth, Ethan sighed. A terrible truth. But it may well be the only truth Leah finds. Wasn't that better than to be caught in the tangle of *maybe*s that Lambert had trapped her in?

And yet the thought of going into the attic, finding the box, and opening the lid on what lay within . . . Ethan just didn't know if he was strong enough. How much, he wondered, should one be expected to sacrifice for a stranger?

Dieter's barking outside brought Ethan from his warm bed and to the window. In the pale first light of dawn, he could see Leah taking small, cautious steps on the path that had iced up overnight. Happy to be outside, happy to have a companion at so early an hour, Dieter raced around Leah in ever-widening circles, barking at her to chase him, to join in the game. Hoisting her bags a little higher onto her shoulder, Leah leaned over to pat the outside of one leg with a mittened hand. Dieter came to her as bidden, his dark tail wagging, his long pink tongue lolling out of one side of his mouth. Ethan watched as the dog shimmied submissively and Leah stopped to pet Dieter's head and to scratch behind his ear.

It occurred to Ethan that Leah was leaving, with no one to see her off.but an aging German shepherd.

Ethan dressed as quickly as he could. By the time he reached the back door, the sun was creaking up over the trees, spreading light and painting shadowy reflections across the lake and the edge of the woods. Ethan hurried to the parking area—trying to look as if he wasn't hurrying at all—and arrived as Leah was tossing her bags in the back of her Explorer. The engine was running and the defrosters were all on, but there was still a layer of snow and ice encrusting the windows.

"Let me give you a hand there," he said, startling her.

"I'm okay," Leah replied. "I only have a few windows to scrape."

Ethan took the long-handled scraper from her hands. "Did you have breakfast yet?"

She shook her head.

"Not even coffee?"

"I didn't want to disturb anyone."

"Why don't you run back to the lodge and put a pot of coffee on? Maybe grab yourself some toast. This will take a few minutes. It's snowed at least once since you got here."

She took longer to debate than he'd have thought necessary.

"This is really nice of you," she said.

"I'm a nice guy sometimes."

"Apparently."

She turned and started toward the cabin, then

paused, turned, and walked back to him, stripping the plaid scarf—his scarf—from her neck.

"You'll need this more than I will," she said, tossing it to him. "I wasn't going to take it with me, by the way. I was only borrowing it while I cleaned off the car."

"Thanks." He caught it and wrapped it around his neck with one hand.

It took Ethan almost thirty minutes to clean the last bits of stubborn ice from the Explorer. He looked up as he finished the last window and saw Leah walking toward him. She had a silver Thermos in one hand and, in the other, a ceramic mug from which steam rose in a long thick stream.

"I thought you might be ready for this," she said as she handed him the mug.

"Thank you, I am." He took the mug in both hands and held it close to his face as if to thaw his cheeks and chin.

"Your dad made it, and some extra for my Thermos. I'm glad I went back in and had the chance to say goodbye to him. To thank him for everything. He's been wonderful. He and Holly both."

"Aren't you going to say goodbye to her?" he asked as if it had just occurred to him. "To Holly?"

"I did. Inside. She wanted to walk out with me, but she's coming down with a cold, so I told her to stay inside." Leah paused, then added, "I believe I'm going to miss her."

"Did you tell her that?"

"Yes. She even gave me a hug."

Ethan nodded. "Then I guess you've been forgiven."

"I hope so. I've grown very fond of Holly." Leah opened the driver's side door and placed the Thermos on the front passenger seat. "Actually, I was hoping that before I left, you'd tell me that you changed your mind about the tapes."

"I still don't know." Ethan shook his head. "I'll call you."

"Ah, now there's a line I've heard before." She smiled as she got into the car. "Somehow I'd expected something a little more original from you."

Ethan laughed and closed her car door for her and waited while the window slid down halfway. "I will be in touch, Leah. I'm not sure when. But as soon as I know, you'll know. I promise."

"Thank you. I know none of this has been easy for you. I'm sorry if I caused you any heartache by coming here. If I'd known about your wife . . ." She paused, not sure of what she'd have done differently.

"You would have come anyway," Ethan said softly.

She considered this for a long moment then said, "Probably. I'm just flat out of options. You were my only hope, Ethan. You still are."

"I'll call you," he repeated before she could ask again.

"Tell Holly I'll put the photos I promised her into the mail as soon as I get into the office. She'll know which ones."

Ethan nodded and stepped aside as she put the car in drive and made a wide U-turn in the parking lot. He followed the car's tracks in the snow without realizing he was doing so, until he found himself at the top of the hill, watching the red Explorer make its way down the mild slope. Even after it disappeared behind the first sharp bend he remained standing still, his hands thrust into the deep pockets of his jacket. The wind rustled softly around him, causing the carelessly wrapped scarf, alive now with her perfume, to flap slightly toward his face. He inhaled sharply and deeply, as if holding some small part of her there at White Bear Springs.

Ethan walked back to the lodge in a concerned fog. There was almost too much to think about.

Holly met her father at the back door.

"Is she gone?" Holly's question was punctuated by a sneeze.

"Yes. She said to tell you that she'll mail your pictures as soon as she gets back to New York."

"Why did you let her leave?" Holly searched in the pockets of her robe for a tissue.

"There was no letting or not letting. Leah had accomplished her purpose in coming here and she was ready to leave. I couldn't have stopped her."

"Yes, you could. She left because you wouldn't help her."

"Did Leah tell you that?"

"No. She said she had to leave on Sunday night for work. Something in Arizona. But she would have stayed at least a few more days if you'd have said you would help her, I know she would have." Holly looked totally exasperated. "I just don't understand why you won't help her."

"I don't know that I won't, Holly. I just need some time to think things through."

"Maybe by the time Leah gets back from Arizona you'll know?"

"Maybe."

"I hope so. I want her to come back. It was fun having her here." Holly sneezed again.

"I take it you've forgiven her for not telling you the truth about why she came here."

"Leah told me about her sister. Even before you came back. I know she loved her very much, Dad." Holly broke into a coughing spell. "She's been missing her for a real long time. It hurts her."

"Why don't you go on back up to bed and I'll bring you some hot lemonade," Tom said in the doorway.

"What about my studies?" Holly sniffed and searched the pantry for a new box of tissues.

"Looks like you're going to have a sick day. But that means you stay in bed and rest up. Take vitamins. Drink lots of fluids." Tom brushed Holly's hair back from her face. "You feel a little feverish. Take two aspirin before you get into bed."

"Okay, Grampa." Holly shuffled off to retrieve the aspirin.

"So. Our friend has gone, has she?" Tom said as he prepared a second pot of coffee, most of the previous pot having gone into Leah's Thermos.

Ethan nodded.

"This must have been very hard for you, son, don't think that I don't appreciate just how hard. And I'm sorry. If I'd known you'd already spoken to Leah, that you'd already turned down her request, I'd not have encouraged her to stay the week."

"Did you? Encourage her?"

Tom nodded.

"She and Holly seemed to take to each other right away. It seemed like a good thing, for Holly, that is. Having Leah pay attention to her. Braidin' her hair and doin' each other's nails. Girl things. Didn't seem any harm to it."

"There was no harm, Dad." Ethan patted his father's shoulder, knowing that his father was right, that Holly had loved the attention. He'd seen for himself just how much last night, after dinner, when they'd sat in front of the fire and Holly took a place on the floor by Leah's feet. Leah brushed out Holly's hair and twisted it into some fancy kind of braid. The look on Holly's face had been sheer bliss.

"I'll just run down to the barn and feed Holly's goats

for her." Ethan pulled his gloves back on and headed out the back door.

No harm but to you, son, Tom thought as he watched Ethan trudge down the path Holly and Leah had shoveled a few days earlier. *Maybe if you open up to it, deal with it, once and for all, maybe you'll find a way to be free of it. Maybe by helping Leah, you'll help yourself move past it.*

And it's long past the time for you to be free of it, son. Long past . . .

$\mathcal{L}$eah stood on the hard-packed floor of the canyon and looked up at the sheer, red cliffs that stretched skyward. Though not quite ten-thirty in the morning, the sun had already warmed things up quite a bit here in the northeastern corner of Arizona where she'd come to photograph the ruins of the ancient village that nestled in the walls of the Canyon de Chelly National Monument.

Her Navajo guide had arranged for her to meet with local artisans and photograph their work. Pottery, alive with the colors of the desert, and jewelry, heavy with turquoise, would make a stunning cover for the September issue of *Trends*. Leah couldn't wait to get back to New York and show Catherine.

Leah removed her hat and fanned herself with it. Had it really only been less than a week ago that she'd been bundled from head to toe against the brisk Maine wind? She opened the cargo area of the rented Jeep, flipped the lid off the cooler, and removed two bottles of water, one of which she tossed to Paul, her guide. She leaned back against the side of the vehicle and took a long hard drink.

I wonder how Holly's cold is. How Tom is doing in his search for student camp counselors for the summer. I wonder if Ethan's come to a decision about the tapes.

After four days in the Arizona sun, Leah had more than enough for her article and, thanks to Paul's intimate knowledge of the region and its artisans, some wonderful photographs. Now that the first part of her work had been completed, she was eager to finish the job. She signaled to Paul that she was ready to pack up the campsite and leave for the hotel. For the past three nights, Leah had lain awake in her sleeping bag in her tent, there on the canyon floor, listening to the wind tell tales of long-gone peoples in long-stilled voices. She couldn't wait to get to the hotel where she'd outline her article and begin the rough draft.

Grateful for the cool comfort of her room once she'd checked in, Leah tossed her camera bag onto the bed and reached for the phone. She dialed her own private line at the office and waited for Carolyn to answer.

"Leah McDevitt's office." Carolyn was all crisp efficiency this morning.

"Hi. It's me. What's cookin'?" Leah asked.

"Not a whole lot. Catherine's been out of town for a few days, so it's been pretty quiet with neither of you around to stir things up."

"Where's Catherine?" Leah asked, unable to recall if her cousin had mentioned an upcoming trip. Then again, hardly a week went by without Catherine going out of town for something.

"I don't remember that I heard where, but I can find out, if you like."

"Don't bother. It's not important. I'll catch up with her over the weekend. What mail came in? Are there any messages? Calls I need to return?"

Carolyn put the phone on hold while she went into Leah's office and gathered the mail and phone messages. Leah had stretched across the bed on her stomach, a pen in one hand and a pad of paper in the other to jot down any important numbers Carolyn might read off to her. Leah was doodling when she heard Carolyn say, "You had a call from an Ethan Sanger—"

"What did he say?" Leah was suddenly all ears. "Did he leave a message?"

"Only to tell you that he called."

"When?"

"Late yesterday afternoon."

Leah tapped the pencil on the pad. When she left White Bear Springs, she had mentioned to Ethan that she thought she'd be back in her office by Wednesday. She hadn't expected to be gone the extra day, and she certainly hadn't expected to hear from him so soon.

"Did he leave a number?"

"No. He just said to let you know that he called." Carolyn read off the rest of Leah's messages, then asked, "Anything else?"

"Just that if Ethan calls again, please tell him to call me at home on Friday night, or at the cabin on Saturday. I haven't decided yet when I'll drive up. And thanks, Carolyn. I'll see you on Monday."

Leah sat up and tried to picture Ethan making the call. Which phone had he used? Probably the one in the front hall, she thought. And what had he been calling to tell her? That he'd had a change of heart? That he'd be sending her the tapes? Or that he'd thought it over and just couldn't bring himself to even touch them?

Either way, Leah thought, someone would suffer.

How terrible it would be for Ethan to have to listen to that madman Lambert discuss how he'd killed the woman Ethan loved. The thought of it made Leah's head swim. How terrible for Leah if what she needed to know was in fact on those tapes, and the information was denied to her.

As much as Leah wanted to listen to the tapes, as much as she needed to *know*, she knew she couldn't blame Ethan if he said no. How much he must have endured, the first time he'd heard Lambert's story. Why would he want to put himself through the agony of hearing it all again? Leah doubted she could bear it. But he had promised to consider it, and Leah was grateful to him for that.

Dropping her jeans and long-sleeved cotton shirt on the bathroom floor, Leah turned on the shower, anxious to wash off the desert grit before turning on her laptop. She thought of Tom, kindly Tom, and of how he had so graciously taken her in and treated her like a member of the family. While she washed her hair, she thought of Holly, and how eager she had been to offer her friendship, to share her little world with Leah. Leah turned off the water and stepped out of the shower, wrapping a towel around herself and thinking about Ethan, how the first thing she'd noticed about him when she'd come into the kitchen that day was that his gray eyes had been less cold and brooding than haunted.

Though Lord knows the man has his reasons to brood.

Just the memory of that moment when she realized the terrible price Lambert had made Ethan pay so that his wife could rest in peace caused Leah's knees to quake and her head to pound. It was as if she had felt the emotions that Ethan must have suffered, and in a way, she had felt that same pain, that rage, that helplessness. How, she wondered as she drew a brush through her long dark hair, could anyone go through that and come out unscarred?

Leah turned on the blow dryer and wondered what Ethan had been like before his wife had been murdered. Holly had mentioned that she had pictures of her parents laughing together, and Leah had tried to envision Ethan laughing, his eyes dancing with mirth, but could not, any more than she could imagine his eyes without that turbulence that he hid with so calm an outward demeanor.

As she snapped off the bathroom light, Leah wondered what it would take to chase the shadows from Ethan's dark eyes and make him laugh again, what it would take to bring joy back into his life, to make him whole again.

The first thing Leah noticed when she entered the silent cabin was the light blinking on her answering machine. She pulled the door closed behind her, kicked up the thermostat, and dropped her bags on the floor as she made her way to the phone and hit the message button. Three hang-ups. She glanced at her watch. It was almost eleven.

Dragging her bags into her bedroom, she turned on the light. Coming from the heat of the Arizona desert to the cold of an early spring evening in New England had left her chilled. She wanted a hot shower and a snack. Crossing the hall into the bathroom, she turned on the hot water and let the room fill with steam. She showered quickly and slid into the huge old flannel robe that she'd had since college. It was frayed at the sleeves and the colors of the plaid had faded, but she couldn't bear to part with it. Her mother had bought it for her on the last Christmas before her death, and Leah still took great comfort from wearing it.

She turned off the bathroom light and searched in her

closet for her slippers. Not finding them, she frowned. Where could she have put them? She looked under the bed, under the chair. She found them next to the dresser on the floor, in a corner. When had she left them there? She shook her head as she slipped her feet into them, recalling distinctly taking them off and tossing them into the closet on the morning of her last visit. How had they gotten back out of the closet and into the corner?

Mrs. Calhoun had probably taken them out to vacuum the closet floor and forgotten about them. That was the only explanation. Leah flicked off the bedroom light and went in search of a snack, reminding herself that she should stop by the Calhouns' and drop off a check for their services—both in and outside of the cabin—before she left for New York.

The unexpected and shrill ring of the phone caused her to jump nearly out of those same slippers she'd just spent five minutes searching for. She reached the living room on the third ring and lifted the phone to her ear.

"Hello?" she said without a trace of her usual grace. Who would be calling her so late at night?

The caller hung up.

"Arrgghh!" she growled. "There oughta be a law!"

Turning on the kitchen light, Leah rummaged in the refrigerator. Mrs. Calhoun had done her part to assure that Leah would not fade away, having stocked the shelves with cartons of milk and orange juice, Leah's favorite yogurt, and the makings of a fine salad. She opened the freezer and poked around, in search of something more satisfying than healthy. Ah, yes, there on the second shelf. Come out and play, Sara Lee.

While defrosting the chocolate cake, she poured a glass of milk and took it into the living room. Placing it on the small table next to the sofa, Leah turned on the television. The microwave beeped from the kitchen. Sara Lee was ready to join the party. Leah sliced off a wedge of cake and slid it onto a plate, then grabbed a fork from the drawer and a napkin from the counter. Sitting back on the sofa, she channel surfed while she munched cake and drank milk.

Glenn Ford in *Cimarron*. That's about as classic a movie as you can find. Leah settled back into the cushions and drew her feet up under her. On the screen, Ford was talking to his oldest son. Leah wondered who the actor was who played the son. There'd be a good bit of trivia for you, she thought, reminding herself to check the credits at the end of the movie. A commercial came on and she flipped to the next channel, where a music video featured discordant voices and gyrating bodies. She flipped back to *Cimarron* and reached behind her for the knitted afghan that she kept over the back of the sofa and draped it around herself.

Leah watched a few more minutes of television before giving in to the need for sleep. She sighed and took her empty plate and glass into the kitchen and sat both on the counter. She'd deal with them in the morning. Walking back into the living room, she paused in the doorway, staring at the piano. What was different?

And then she remembered.

Before she had locked the door behind her on that day she left for Maine, she'd taken a photo of Missy, lifted it from right there in the front row of photos that marched across the piano, leaving a space between the photos on either side. But from the doorway, she could see that there was no empty space on the piano top, though the photo was still in her bag.

Leah stepped closer. All the photos seemed to have been rearranged somehow, though she could not remember exactly what order they'd been in. She stared, frowning, trying to come up with a logical explanation. Perhaps she'd only thought she'd left a space. Maybe she'd unconsciously moved another picture forward and simply forgot about it in her hurry to get to Maine. Or perhaps Mrs. Calhoun rearranged things on the piano as well, though she'd never done such a thing before.

Leah stepped closer and ran her finger through the thin layer of dust on top of the piano and smiled wryly. *Looks like Mrs. Calhoun spent more time rearranging than dusting.*

Maybe she got to looking at the pictures of the family, of Mom and Dad and me and Missy, and got all nostalgic. After all, Mrs. Calhoun, well into her seventies now, had known her parents, had known them all. Several times over the past few years, Leah had suggested that she could handle keeping the small cabin clean herself, but Mrs. Calhoun wouldn't hear of it, so Leah had just left the arrangements as they had always been. Once each week, Mrs. Calhoun would come and dust and straighten up and do whatever needed to be done, while Mr. Calhoun took care of anything that needed tending to outside, stacking firewood or clearing snow or cutting grass. Then, when they'd both finished up, they'd get back into their old blue Buick and head back to their snug little ranch house on the outskirts of town.

Leah glanced around the room, trying to decide if anything else looked disturbed, but nothing did. She turned off the television just as the credits began to run and snapped off the lights. After checking the lock on the front door, she walked down the quiet hall to her room.

Leah got into her bed, the warm flannel sheets as welcoming as a hug, and snuggled down under the down comforter, seeking sleep, but a thought niggled at the back of her mind. What had she forgotten?

Oh, yes, the name of the actor who played Glenn Ford's son. Next time, she told herself as she drifted off to sleep. I'll remember to watch for that next time . . .

The early morning air was brisk and refreshing and just breathing it in from the deck inspired Leah to get an early start. By nine she was already at work on her article, her notes spread out across the wide hassock that sat at the foot of her favorite chair. She stacked wood in the fireplace and made a nice little fire that lent its warmth to the room and added an extra touch of coziness. The day passed quickly, with few interruptions, and she worked right through until three o'clock.

Startled to see that so much of the day had passed, Leah ate a late lunch while reading over the first draft of her article. While good, she thought it did not adequately portray the way the desert sun touched the cliffs, nor the overwhelming sense of history that passed through her while standing in the shadows of the villages that were built more than a thousand years before Christ was born. She put her plate aside and went back to work. It would be close to midnight before she finished and, satisfied with her work, allowed herself to go to bed.

The insistent ringing of the phone jarred her awake, and, half-asleep, Leah found her way into the kitchen to answer it.

"Leah?"

"Yes?" She yawned.

"Leah, it's Ethan."

"Oh. Ethan." Her eyes were fully opened now, and it took but a second for her to realize that her pulse rate had quickened at the sound of his voice. She felt the color creep up from her neck to her face and wondered if it counted as *blushing* if no one could see it.

"How are you, Ethan?"

"Great. You?"

"Fine. How's your dad? And Holly? How is her cold?"

"Everyone's fine. Holly's cold is gone, and she's feeling particularly well right now. She's been invited to a school dance for incoming freshmen so she's spent the past few days discussing dresses with her friends. It's apparently a big event in Arlenville."

"Oh, my." Leah couldn't help but smile, Ethan sounded so . . . fatherly. "That is something."

"Yes, it is that."

"When's the big day?"

"Not for a few more weeks. She's already quite excited, though."

"I'm sure she is. Please tell her for me that I hope she has a great time."

"I'll do that."

An awkward silence hung between them. Finally, Ethan said, "Leah, I've been thinking about . . . well, about your problem. I mean, the situation."

"Yes." Leah's throat constricted in anticipation.

"I know how difficult things have been for you, not knowing where your sister has been all these years. I think you're an amazing woman, to persevere all this time. I totally appreciate what you've gone through."

"But . . ." Leah waited for the other shoe to drop.

"No buts," he told her. "I just can't come up with a good enough reason to turn you down, Leah. You deserve whatever closure you can find. So, I guess the question is, when would you like to start?"

Leah softly exhaled a breath she wasn't aware of holding.

"You'll help me? You'll let me listen to the tapes?"

"Yes. And we'll go over the notes as well."

"You told me you had no notes," Leah reminded him.

"I didn't tell you the truth about that. Actually, I have several notebooks filled with observations I made of Lambert's mannerisms and facial expressions as he discussed different . . . details of his exploits. Unfortunately, the notebooks are in no real order and in some places my handwriting is poor to the point of being nearly illegible. It will take some time to put them in order to go along with the corresponding tapes."

"Ethan, I don't know what to say. I can't thank you enough."

"Just say thank you, and remember that there may be nothing here that helps you. There's a very good chance that you might invest weeks of your time only to discover, in the end, that you're no closer to finding your sister than you were before you started."

"I'll take that chance. Gladly. It's the only one I have."

"Well, I guess we just need to decide when you want to start."

"I'd like to start right now, this minute, but I know that's not practical." She thought about her upcoming schedule. "How about next weekend? Would you be free then?"

"I have to meet an old colleague in Boston on Tuesday to go over a case I handled for him last year that's going to trial on Wednesday. I'm supposed to testify as his expert witness, but I should be finished by Friday morning."

"Great. Would you like me to meet you at camp?"

Ethan hesitated, then said, "Actually, I think I'd rather do this someplace else, if at all possible. I'd prefer not to expose Holly to it."

"I agree. We can do it here. At my cabin. There's a guest room you're welcome to stay in."

"That sounds ideal. Let me find a pen and you can give me directions." He put the phone down but was back in seconds. "Shoot."

She gave him directions from Boston, and when he'd finished writing them down, he said, "I'll see you on Friday. Probably around seven."

"That's wonderful. I can't thank you enough, Ethan. I can't begin to tell you how grateful I am."

"I just hope that something good comes of this for you," he told her softly. Then, barely taking a breath, he said, "There's someone here who's dying to talk to you."

Leah smiled, knowing who that someone was.

"Leah? Oh, Leah, the most amazing thing has happened! Remember I told you about Kevin—he's that guy who lives across the street from Chrissie—he is sooo cool. Anyway, he called me. He asked me if I was going to this big dance at the high school. It's special, for incoming freshmen?" Holly's voice had taken on an upwards tilt at the end of her sentence, suggestive of a question, that seemed to be standard young adult cadence these days.

"And you told him yes, of course?" Leah smiled, in her mind's eye trying to picture Holly's face, flushed with excitement. She wished for a fleeting second that she was there, at the lodge, at that moment to share Holly's joy.

"Of course. Oh, and we're going shopping for a dress tomorrow. Me and Chrissie and her mom. Chrissie's going to the dance, too. I am so excited I can hardly stand it. Can you come that weekend? Could you do my hair like you did that one night? With the curls down the side?"

"Oh. I don't know." Leah paused, uncertain how to respond. "I'm not sure what I'll be doing. I may have to do something for work. But if I can be there, I will."

"Promise?"

"I promise I will if I can."

"Great. Thanks! Here's Dad."

"Close the door on your way out, honey," Ethan addressed Holly as he took the phone back, before returning his attention to Leah and saying, "You are welcome to come that weekend, you know. I don't want you to think that I don't want you to come back, because of what I said about not playing the tapes here. I think that Holly really liked having you around."

"I miss her too. I told her I'd think about it. A lot depends on what we learn from the tapes. I'd hate to commit myself to anything else right now," Leah said, wondering what details—legal and emotional and logistical—there might be to deal with if indeed they found Missy.

"Yes. Right. Well, I guess I'll see you on Friday."

"Fine. I'll look for you around seven."

"Do you have a tape player?"

"Yes."

"Good. Well, I'll see you then."

"Bye."

Leah stood holding the phone, listening to the dial tone, sorry that the connection had been broken. But she'd see him on Friday night. Friday! She'd have Mrs. Calhoun come in this week and clean the guest room, put new sheets on the bed for Ethan. Maybe pick up an order at the market for her on Thursday. Eggs and bacon and bread, since Ethan liked a big breakfast. Tom had told her that. And cream for his coffee. Leah had noticed at dinner that Ethan liked his coffee light . . .

Leah picked up the phone and dialed the Calhouns' number, which was written on the list posted on a sticky note by the wall phone in the kitchen. There was no answer, but then again, it was still Sunday morning.

Leah hung up and looked for a piece of paper upon which to write a short note to Mrs. Calhoun telling her what she'd need for the weekend. Rummaging in her purse, she found her checkbook. Tallying up what she owed the Calhouns for the month, adding to it money for the items she was asking Mrs. C. to pick up, Leah wrote a check and stuck it and the note inside a white envelope. She'd drop the check off on her way out of town, which, she figured, should be soon. Now that she had had time to unwind from her trip, she was anxious to develop the photographs and see what she had that might be suitable for the cover.

Forty minutes later, Leah was pulling into the driveway of the Calhouns' white-sided ranch house, which sat back from the road on several acres. Parking the Explorer next to the elderly couple's Buick, she opened the driver's side door and hopped down, her feet making a crunching sound on the unshoveled snow.

Mr. Calhoun must be getting lazy in his old age. Leah smiled to herself. *He's always been so meticulous about cleaning away the snow from the drive and the walk before it could ice up.*

As she approached the front porch, a few hopeful birds gathered at a nearby feeder and scrambled anxiously for the remaining seeds. From under a sprawling yew, a yowling cat appeared, complaining loudly to Leah about something or other.

"What's the matter, Tink?" she asked, recognizing the Calhouns' old tabby. "Did you get locked out?"

The cat whipped around Leah's legs in an agitated frenzy as if relating a terrible tale of woe. As Leah drew closer to the front door, the cat ran to it, standing up on its hind legs as if to show Leah where the doorknob was.

"All right, Tink. Just a minute." Leah knocked on the door, then leaned over to pet the cat. When there was no answer, she knocked again, then tried the doorbell several times before looking down at the obviously befuddled feline and saying, "I don't think they're home, Tink."

Leah looked back over to the driveway. That was definitely the Calhouns' car parked there next to hers. Maybe someone had picked them up and taken them someplace. She glanced at her watch. It was barely noon. They probably got a ride to church that morning with someone else. Maybe they stayed in town and had lunch at that new restaurant that everyone in the market was talking about a few weeks ago. Hadn't they said that on Sundays seniors' meals were half price up till three in the afternoon?

Leah nodded to herself. That would surely be it. She slipped her envelope through the mail slot and turned back to her car.

Odd that they would leave Tink out when they were going out, though. Of course, maybe the cat had taken himself for a little walk and hadn't returned home before his owners had to leave.

Satisfied that the Calhouns would be back in plenty of time to bring in the cat before the temperatures dropped, Leah backed out of the driveway and headed home, trying not to think about Ethan and his tapes and notes and what she might find there. Or about the weekend she'd be spending with him in her cabin.

Oh, what the hell, she mused, thinking that there'd been little enough in her life worth fantasizing about these past few months. And Ethan most certainly was fantasy-fodder of the first order.

Then Leah reminded herself of the reason for his visit and her spirit sobered.

Wasn't it just her luck to have a weekend to spend alone in a remote cabin with a handsome, sensitive man—and have the entire weekend center around a serial killer.

Chapter 12

$\mathcal{D}$uring most of the drive from Manhattan to Connecticut, Leah had tried to convince herself that the heady excitement that had been growing inside her all week was because of the tapes and the notes and the thought that maybe she'd soon find something that would link Lambert to Melissa. Only in her deepest, most secret heart of hearts did she permit herself to admit that it was as much the bearer of the tapes as the tapes themselves that made her heart beat a little faster every time she thought about Friday.

Okay, she finally acknowledged on her drive to the cabin on Friday afternoon, *so Ethan really is something to write home about. He's deep and he's sensitive and he's got a great smile when he uses it. And yes, he has great shoulders.*

She paused and reflected for a moment.

Okay, so all of him looked pretty good. I've always been a sucker for flannel shirts and well-worn jeans.

But—reality check here—he's also a man who hasn't recovered from the loss of his wife. He must have loved her deeply, to still mourn her after all these years. So you have to ask yourself, what kind of a crazy woman would even think twice about a man who's in love with his deceased wife—deceased being an important word here. How in the hell can you compete with a dead woman?

You can't, Leah sighed. *Better just to take the friendship that's offered and let it be.*

She was still debating the likelihood of wanting to maintain a friendship-only relationship with the only man in the past three years who'd really set her heart thumping when she turned onto Waverly Road, the road that led to Bannock. Almost before she realized it, she was passing the Calhoun house. Slowing down, she saw that the lights had not been turned on and the car had not moved. *They must have gone away for a few days,* she thought.

Leah frowned. If the Calhouns had gone out of town, that meant that there most likely would be a number of things to do once she reached the cabin. Like make up the guest room and make a run to the market. She stepped on the gas, hoping to get to the cabin with enough time to do a few chores before Ethan arrived.

But even as she slowed down to make the turn into her drive, she realized that she was already too late. Ethan's dark blue Jeep was parked at the edge of the clearing across the road from the cabin. He stepped out of the car and waved when he saw her approach.

Leah couldn't help but wonder if his heart had lurched inside his chest the way hers did, just at the sight of him. She wondered what he might say if she ever had the nerve to ask.

She waved back and pulled into the drive.

"Hi. You're early."

"Am I?" He smiled and her heart flipped over.

Oh, no, she silently whined as she put her window up.

I can't be mooning over this man. Please, Lord, don't let me moon over this man . . .

"The trial was over sooner than I'd expected, and the traffic was unusually light coming out of Boston, so I made it here in record time," he was saying as he opened her car door. "I hope it's okay."

"Oh. It's fine. Early is fine." She nodded, managing to avoid jumping into him as she jumped out of the Explorer.

"How are you?" he asked, taking her arm and holding it for a long minute. "Are you sure you're ready to do this?"

"Absolutely." She nodded, the warmth of his hand seeming to soak right through the sleeve of her heavy sweater.

Remember why he's here. Focus on that, for crying out loud, she commanded herself.

"Do you need a hand with your things?" he asked.

When she shook her head no, he crossed the road again and grabbed a nylon travel bag and a box from the backseat of the Jeep and met her on the front porch as she was about to unlock the door.

"It's beautiful here," he said.

"Thank you. It's the only place where I feel sane sometimes." Leah pushed open the door and stood back to allow Ethan to enter. "I all but lived here for a while after Missy disappeared. I thought if she came looking for me, that she'd come here. But after a while, when she didn't come back, I found it too depressing to be here alone. It's just been the past few years that I've been able to spend time here again."

"I appreciate the fact that you're willing to share it with me," Ethan said as he stepped inside the cabin.

"I appreciate what you're willing to share with me,"

she told him, "so I suppose that puts us on equal footing."

She turned on the hall light and slid the thermostat up several degrees.

"It will take a few minutes for the heat to come up to temperature," she said, "so you might want to keep your jacket on for a while."

"Compared to the weather we had in Maine earlier this week, this is downright temperate."

Leah laughed. "I guess we get spring a little earlier than you do."

"Everyone gets spring a little earlier than we do." He grinned, then asked, "You do have a fireplace?"

Leah nodded her head in the direction of the living room. "In there."

"How 'bout if I build a fire?"

"That would be wonderful. Nothing takes the chill off the room faster."

"What should I do with this?" He held up the nylon bag.

"I'll put it in your room while you build that fire." She swung the bag over her shoulder. "I'll be right back."

And at least I'll get a chance to see if Mrs. Calhoun changed the sheets and put out some blankets and . . .

Leah stood in the doorway, her shoulders slumped. Mrs. Calhoun obviously hadn't been there at all. There were no sheets on the bed and nothing to cover the bare mattress but an old quilt folded over the bottom half.

Mildly annoyed, Leah proceeded to the linen closet where she found flannel sheets and a blanket. The fledgling spring had brought warmer days, and the heavier comforters would not be needed. She took advantage of the time Ethan was spending making the fire to make up his bed.

"I could have done that," Ethan said from the door.

"The housekeeper was supposed to have done it," she

told him, "but I guess she had other plans this week. I guess I'd better check the refrigerator. I dropped off a list of things I wanted her to pick up, but maybe she missed that too. We may have to make a run to the market if we're to have any dinner tonight."

"Why don't we just have dinner out?" he asked. "I'm sure there must be a restaurant close by, even in so bucolic a village as Bannock."

"There's the Bannock Inn," Leah stopped to consider. "But we'll still need things from the market."

"We'll stop at the market after dinner."

"It closes at six." Leah glanced at her watch. "We'll have to stop on the way to the inn."

"Guess it's a good thing I didn't get that fire started after all."

"You didn't?"

"Couldn't find anything to use as kindling. I did bring some wood in from the deck. After I stood and watched the sun set behind those trees out back. That's a beautiful view you have back there."

He was so close, less than a foot away, close enough for her to see the flecks of gold in his eyes, which somehow didn't appear as dark as she'd thought they were. He was still wearing his down jacket and the plaid scarf. She wondered if the scent of his cologne still clung to it.

But of course it would, she was thinking. Because he's obviously been wearing it and . . .

"Leah, I said your phone is ringing."

"Oh. Sorry." She shook her head as if to shake away those dangerous thoughts and went into the kitchen to answer the phone.

"Hello?" She opened the refrigerator and looked in, just in case Mrs. Calhoun had gotten some of it right.

She opened a carton of milk and sniffed.

"Ugh." Her nose wrinkled at the acrid smell. "Hello? Is anyone there?"

She emptied the milk carton down the drain, running the hot water to clear out the clumps.

"Another hang-up," she told Ethan when he appeared in the doorway.

"Do you get a lot of those?"

"Lately, a few. Probably some bored local kids sitting around after school, eating pizza and picking numbers at random from the phone book."

"You have a listed number?"

"Sure. Why?"

"I thought a lot of women who lived by themselves kept their numbers unlisted."

"Actually, it's still listed under my dad's name. I never changed it. But it's the only McDevitt in the county book, so I guess it wouldn't be too hard to figure out it was me."

He'd drifted closer to her than he'd intended, and once he'd realized just how close he was, he took a step or two backwards, which placed him in the foyer.

Feeling a bit foolish, he tried to cover up by saying, "That's a really handsome piano."

"That was my mother's. A gift from my father to make the country hours more civilized. My mother was definitely a city mouse," she explained as she followed him into the living room, giving no sign that she'd noticed his awkward retreat from the small kitchen space. "He always said he'd had to bribe her to come to the cabin at first, but then she'd learned to love it so much that he'd have to bribe her to leave on Sunday nights."

Leah touched the end of the piano fondly.

"We all loved it here, back then. It was always just the four of us, my parents and my sister and me."

"Do you play?"

"No." She shook her head. "I never had the patience to learn. Missy played, though. She was incredibly talented. My parents were so proud of her, of her ability to play some of the pieces she'd learned by heart." Leah smiled at him from across the back of the piano. "Missy was good at pretty much everything."

"And Leah?"

"Was okay at most things."

"A jack of all trades?"

"Master of none," she finished the phrase.

He lifted the cover and hit a few keys.

"It's probably terribly out of tune," Leah noted.

"A little. How long since it's been played?"

"Since Missy . . ." Her words caught in her throat unexpectedly. "I always thought it would be terrible if she came back and found her piano gone. She'd have known that I'd given up."

They stood in awkward silence, Ethan understanding perfectly her need to preserve what she could, that if her sister had returned, Leah would have been able to say, See, I never lost faith. I knew you'd come home.

But of course, she hadn't, and wouldn't.

"I guess we should be leaving for Bannock if we're going to stop at the market before we have dinner." Leah turned her back on the piano and switched on a small table lamp. The day was rapidly fading, and the room had fallen to shadows. "Ready?"

Ethan nodded and closed the cover over the keys.

Noticing the gentle manner with which he did so, Leah asked, "Do you play?"

"Yes. At least, I used to." He smiled. "I tinkered more than played."

"Feel free to tinker while you're here." She smiled back. "I'll just get my jacket . . ."

As she turned, she noticed the red light blinking on her answering machine. She hit the message button as she walked past to pick up the jacket she'd earlier draped over one end of the sofa.

Two more hang-ups, no messages.

"The locals kids must be really bored," Ethan noted with a nod toward the machine.

"It could be those annoying solicitation calls, too. They never leave a message." Leah shrugged into her jacket. "I get them all the time in New York. Newspapers, mortgage companies, basement waterproofers—"

"Fuel oil companies, roofing and siding . . ." he added as he followed her through the front door.

"You get those at camp?" she asked, locking the door behind them.

"Sure." He nodded, then paused on the front porch. "Want me to drive?"

"I can drive. I know the way. You just might want to pull your Jeep off the road a little more. Not that we get that much traffic back here, but the road is narrow and with the icy patches, you could be asking for trouble to leave it there overnight."

"How 'bout I leave it behind those trees?"

"That's fine."

Leah backed out of her driveway and waited while Ethan moved his car. She unlocked the passenger side door as he approached.

"It's pretty well hidden there," Ethan said as he climbed into the Explorer. "One might think you were hiding the fact that you had a visitor."

"Well, taking you into town will take care of that, won't it?" She grinned.

"Nosey neighbors up here?"

"Not really." Leah shook her head. "Not many neighbors at all. The Millers live about a mile up the road, but they're on the other side of the hill, so I never even see the lights from their house. They're the closest. Then as we get nearer to town, there are a few houses, like the Calhouns', and a few old farms. Like there."

She pointed off to the right.

"That's the Michaels' farm. In another life, it was the McDevitt farm. It was sold off after my grandfather's death. My family only kept the cabin. And down there, over those hills, is the village." She slowed up for the stop sign at the T intersection, but did not stop. "Most of the properties up here have been in the same families for generations."

"Is that because no one wants to move out, or because no one wants to move in?"

Leah laughed. "A bit of both, I would guess. There's not a whole lot to do up here, even in town. There's an old movie theater that's been here since the fifties, a library, and a bowling alley. That's pretty much it for recreation, other than church socials. There's a general store, a drugstore, a coffee shop, and the inn. That's pretty much Bannock."

She slowed the car almost to a stop and peered past Ethan toward a dark and solitary house hunkered behind some pines off to the right. The only light came from a lamppost at the end of a long, wide drive that led to a one-story garage that stood just slightly behind the house.

Even in the dark, Ethan could see her frown. He turned to look at the house.

"Is there a problem?" he asked.

"I don't know. Probably not." She stepped lightly on the gas pedal and continued down the road, still moving somewhat slowly, as if uncertain.

"Whose house is that?"

"The Calhouns'. Mrs. C. has been our housekeeper for about a million years. Mr. C. takes care of the grounds, shovels snow from the drive and the porch and the deck, keeps us in firewood, that sort of thing. I'd left her a note last week, asking her to do a few things in the cabin for me, but as you saw, she hasn't been there." She glanced in her rearview mirror at the house, which was growing smaller in the distance. "And the house is still dark. It doesn't appear that anyone has been there since last weekend when I stopped. There was no one home then, either."

"They probably took a mid-winter vacation."

"You know, you could be right. They usually do take a week or two every winter to visit one of Mr. Calhoun's cousins in Florida. I don't remember that they'd taken that trip yet this year."

With one last glance in the rearview mirror, the Calhoun place lost to the night, Leah continued on into the village of Bannock, determined to get to the market before Mr. Howard turned off the lights and hung the *Sorry, we're closed* sign on the door.

"I guess the Yankee pot roast is always a safe bet." Ethan scanned both sides of the menu that the middle-aged waitress had handed him just minutes before.

"The New England boiled dinner is another favorite."

"What are you getting?"

"I think a fowl something."

"A foul something?" Ethan wrinkled his nose.

"Fowl. Turkey or chicken or pheasant," Leah laughed.

"A good choice." The waitress returned to their table with a basket of warm rolls and a crock of butter. "The Cornish hens are one of the specials. Local hens, by the way."

"Sold." Ethan closed the menu.

"Me, too," Leah nodded.

"You won't be sorry," the waitress said with a wink and took their menus.

Ethan looked around the small, dimly lit dining room.

"These low ceilings always make me feel like ducking," he noted. "Do you suppose people really were that much shorter two hundred years ago?"

"Maybe they made the ceilings lower to conserve on lumber," Leah suggested. "The low ceiling aside, it's a pretty room, don't you think?"

Ethan nodded. "It reminds me of an inn not too far outside of Bangor. I think it has the same wallpaper."

"I suppose two hundred years ago, the selections of furniture and wallpaper might have been limited. It would probably be fairly common to find similar furnishings in buildings from the same era." Leah played with a spoon and averted her eyes from Ethan's and wished that they'd driven out to the highway to have dinner in one of the small places—a truckstop or a pizza place or any fast food restaurant—anyplace that was devoid of atmosphere.

Particularly of the romantic atmosphere that pervaded the Bannock Inn.

The room in which they sat had a huge walk-in fireplace that, combined with the low ceiling and candlelight, lent an air of intimacy. It was, Leah had long ago concluded, a room made for marriage proposals and declarations of undying love, for celebrating life's milestones. She sighed, wishing she'd remembered this before they'd walked through the wide front door into the cheery foyer with the guest book and flowers and the bowl of creamy mints wrapped in colored cellophane.

"Tired?" Ethan asked, mistaking her sigh for a sign of fatigue.

"What? Oh, yes, I suppose. A little." She tried to brighten. "I spent a lot of time at the office this week, trying to catch up after my trip. I didn't want to bring any work with me this weekend."

"Do you generally do that? Work on the weekends?"

"Usually."

"You sound like a person who probably doesn't take many long vacations."

"I guess I've never taken a really long vacation. I travel so much for my job that I don't want to travel when I have time off. And because I get to go to all the places that intrigue me personally for the magazine, there's little point in taking vacations when I'm not working, if you follow."

"What do you do to unwind?"

"Unwind?" She raised an eyebrow, as if considering an unfamiliar concept. "I guess that's why I come to the cabin most weekends."

"What do you do, besides work, when you're here? Do you entertain? Sleep? Read novels? Watch television?"

"Usually I just work on an article. I write or outline or try to come up with a place we haven't been to before that I think our readers might like."

"When do you go out?"

"Mostly during the week. I go to the theater in the city, or to dinner, or to galleries. The usual. Sometimes Catherine and I attend events for the magazine. And I go to the gym to work out. I'm into weight training right now." She flexed her right arm as if showing off her muscles.

"Catherine is . . . ?"

"Oh. My cousin. She's the editor in chief at *Trends*. We share the house and the magazine. The house had been Uncle Harry's, but he left it to Catherine when he died. And he left the magazine to the three of us. Catherine and Missy and me."

"So the two of you—you and Catherine—own the magazine outright?"

"Catherine's share is slightly larger than Missy's and mine. Our great-grandfather, Harry Dean, founded the magazine. When he died, he left it to his son, also Harry, and his two daughters. Sally, who was Missy's and my mother, and Anna, Catherine's mother. Anna died when Catherine was ten. Uncle Harry raised her. He inherited Anna's stock, and later my mother's, when she died. Then, when Uncle Harry died about eight years ago, he left forty percent of the stock to Catherine, and thirty percent each to Missy and to me."

"What happened to Melissa's shares?"

"Oh. Nothing. They're still just there in trust for her. If she's really . . . well, I would inherit her shares, I suppose, since we had reciprocal wills." Leah frowned. "But Catherine runs the magazine. Nothing could change that. *Trends* is Catherine's whole life. I certainly have no desire to run it. I enjoy my little piece of it, but I wouldn't want Catherine's job."

"Here you go, folks." The waitress appeared with their salads. "I forgot to ask what dressing you'd prefer, so I brought you a little of each."

She moved the candles slightly to one side and set a small silver tray of dressing samples on the white linen cloth.

They helped themselves to salad dressing and munched an assortment of spring greens for a moment or two before Leah asked, "What about you?"

"What about me.what?"

"Where do you go on vacation? What do you do with your spare time?"

Ethan shrugged. "I don't generally take vacations. We're busy pretty much all year round. Camp is open from the end of May through September, though we always have some open weekends for hunters in October and November, and sometimes ice fishers in the winter."

"There are always the islands in the winter months."

"I don't care much for the heat," he said, then looked up at her when he realized how curt his answer sounded. "I guess there are cold weather people and warm weather people. Coming from Maine, I guess I just prefer the cold."

Leah merely nodded, not wanting to mention the fact that she knew from Holly that Ethan had lived all his married life in Georgia—hardly a cool clime. He'd only returned to Maine after Libby's death.

"I love anyplace tropical," Leah told him. "I love beaches and warm, clear water and brightly colored fish and birds and snorkeling and water skiing."

"Sounds like you should be living in the Bahamas instead of Manhattan," he observed.

"It would take something really special to make me give up New York. I love the city. And I love being able to get away to the country on the weekends. Besides, so much of my travel takes me to tropical places. I figure I have the best of everything."

Their dinner was served, and as the piano player began to play right then, conversation was kept to a minimum for the rest of the evening, which was, Leah thought, probably for the best. There had been too much getting-to-know-you talk, as if this was a date rather than just a means of sharing a necessary meal. For the second time in less than an hour, she wished she'd thought things through a little better before suggesting the Bannock Inn.

The piano player was into his second set of romantic ballads when the check came and Ethan insisted on picking it up. They drove back to the cabin through a moonless night on deserted roads.

The cabin was so quiet when they went inside that Leah thought even their breathing seemed to echo.

"You still up for that fire?" Ethan asked.

Suddenly the thought of listening to Raymond Lambert's voice at this hour of the night spooked her.

"Actually, I think I'd like to turn in and get an early start tomorrow," she said. "You're welcome to stay up, of course. There's a television and some CDs, if you'd like to listen to music—"

"Thanks, but I think your idea of getting an early start tomorrow is a good one." He handed her his jacket, which she hung next to hers in the small closet in the foyer.

"Let me just check the back door and I'll show you to your room."

"I remember." He smiled. "The first door, just right down this little hallway, right?"

"Right."

"I'll see you in the morning, then." He seemed to hesitate slightly.

Leah nodded. "See you in the morning. And thanks."

He half turned toward her.

"For dinner."

"My pleasure," he replied, meaning it.

And it had been a pleasure, Ethan thought as he closed the bedroom door. The ambiance of the old inn had been warm and relaxed and comfortable, almost familiar. The food had been delicious, and the company charming. Ethan smiled to himself as he undressed in the small guest room. That was the second time that word had come to mind when he thought of Leah. Well, she did have a certain charm. It had been damned difficult to keep from staring at her across the small table tonight at dinner. The candlelight had played up the subtle red highlights in her hair and the warmth of her eyes and accentuated the fineness of her cheekbones and the gentle curve of her generous mouth.

Leah's mouth . . .

It had been a long time since Ethan had noticed such things about a woman. Or wondered what she was thinking. Or what she tasted like.

Careful, bud, he told himself as he sat on the side of the bed. *She came to you for help. Nothing more. Tomorrow you'll lead her into a world where the perverted was the norm. She may well hate you after she's heard it all, hate you for bringing this foul beast into her home, hate you for taking her to the places she's going to go. After tomorrow, there may be no more sweet smiles, and the light in those dark eyes may go out. She may never forgive you for what she might hear, because if she hears the worst about her sister, there's a chance that she'll never be the same again. After tomorrow, once the tape is turned on and that voice begins to speak . . .*

Ethan turned out the light, and in the dark he saw her face, her dark, pretty eyes that sparkled when she laughed, her pretty mouth that curved up just the slightest bit on one side, the way she rested her elbow on the very edge of the table, and leaned her chin in her palm and tilted her head a little while she listened to you speak. The way the candlelight had played across the delicate planes of her face . . .

The irony was not lost on Ethan, that what he and Leah would share over the next few weeks could very well result in her never wanting to see him again.

Strange, he thought as he stared into the darkness, that the only woman he'd been drawn to in four years was the one woman who he might end up alienating beyond redemption.

Once the tape was turned on, and that voice began to speak . . .

Chapter 13

. . . *A*nd the funny thing was, she just didn't get it at first. I mean, I think she thought I was playing some funky little love game with her."

The chuckle that followed sent a chill up Leah's spine and caused the hairs on the back of her neck to stand straight up. From the moment she'd sat down across from Ethan and he had turned on the first tape, her stomach had been in the tightest of knots and her hands had not stopped shaking.

She and Ethan had not made eye contact since Lambert's voice had first drifted forth from the small plastic machine that sat between the two of them on the trestle table Leah used for dining in a corner of the great room. Lambert spoke almost melodramatically, as if for effect, and in great detail about where he'd been and what he'd done and who he'd done it to, animated in the way a younger man might describe his sexual conquests to his fraternity brothers. Lambert's detachment from the torment he'd inflicted, his relish at relating all the gruesome details, his joking about what this victim said or that one did, had a surreal quality that left Leah unnerved and repelled.

She could barely imagine what it might be doing to Ethan.

Ethan had hardly moved a muscle since the tape had been turned on earlier that morning. He and Leah had risen about the same time, spent an hour or so making breakfast and chatting over coffee, but their conversation was the nervous, distracted sort of patter that people make while on their way to the doctor's office for a dreaded diagnosis. When Leah had finally suggested that they take their coffee into the great room, it was with that same reluctance.

Leah had placed the small tape recorder in the center of the trestle table, which overlooked the back of the property, rather than on the coffee table or in the kitchen, so that Ethan would have a place to turn to if he needed a calming view or something to gaze upon that could, for a moment, let his mind escape from the ugliness that would spew forth and surround him. Leah would, herself, seek the solace of the late winter scene that spread out serenely on the other side of the window nearly as many times as Ethan would before the day ended.

Lambert's voice droned on and on throughout the morning, the tape occasionally silent while Ethan asked a question in the background.

"I'm sorry, Ethan," Leah whispered, "what did you just ask him?"

Ethan cleared his throat.

"I asked him if he was still talking about Joann Stivens there, in that last part. I believe he answered by nodding."

"And that was in—"

"The Austin area."

Leah nodded and fell silent as Lambert began to speak again.

"Now, did I tell you about her funeral? Damn, I never did see such a sight." On the tape, Lambert whistled long and low, and slipped into a modified Texas drawl. "Oooh, baby, the whole town was there. I did tell you, did I not, that her old man was some kind of bigwig down there? Well, he was. The coffin was polished walnut—so shiny I could see my face in it—and lined in pale pink satin. Don't that sound pretty? And there were pink and white flowers everywhere. And after the services—after the burial and all that at the cemetery—everyone was invited back to their house for a big catered luncheon. I never did see such a spread—"

"He went there? To her house?" Leah gasped.

An expressionless Ethan nodded. "Keep listening. It gets worse."

". . . course I didn't know which room was hers, so I had to sort of pop open this door and that. Well, what do you suppose I found behind door number three? Can you guess, now, Ethan?" Lambert was taunting him here.

"No. No, Raymond, I have no idea what was behind door number three." Ethan's voice was flat, emotionless, exhausted.

"Why, Joann's little sister . . . she couldn't have been more than fifteen or so. Sitting on her pretty pink bed, crying her baby blue eyes out. Damn, if it wasn't all I could do not to do her right there. I thought about it, I gotta tell you the truth—that's what this book is all about, right? The truth?—but a few of her friends came in and the moment was gone and I just went about my business."

Leah stopped the tape with shaking fingers.

"Let me get this straight. Lambert not only went to this girl's funeral, but he went back to the house with the other mourners for a luncheon, during the course of which he considered killing her little sister? Did I understand that correctly?"

"You got it."

"What does he mean, he went about his business?"

Ethan turned the tape back on.

". . . and I did eventually find her room and I left her glasses right there on her bedside table, right on top of the book she'd last been reading. Nice touch, don't you think?" Lambert began to giggle. "And whoa! You shoulda seen the newspapers when the glasses were found, just the next day! Well, they figured out right quick that I'd been in the house. And after I was caught, of course, the other sister and her friends talked about seeing me, I'd been as close to them as I am to you. What a stir that did cause, I gotta tell you, Ethan. It really was soooo funny. Of course, hardly anyone else saw the humor in the situation."

"Who else could think something like that is funny?" Leah said angrily, turning off the tape with a snap.

"Other like-minded souls."

"Do you really think there are others like that?" She pointed to the tape.

"Oh, sure." Ethan nodded slowly. "Most serial killers are never caught. They move around. They change their MO. They die before they're arrested. Lambert didn't invent this game, Leah. He's just another player."

"He's even sicker than I thought."

Ethan shook his head. "Lambert wasn't sick. He was evil. There's a difference. Someone who is sick doesn't realize what he's doing. Lambert knew, planned, reveled in his killings. Reveled in the pain he caused the victim's family. I think he took every bit as much pleasure from making me listen to all this as he did from strangling Libby."

"Ethan, I am so sorry. I hate that you are going through this." Leah reached across the small table and took one of his hands in hers. "If there was any other way—"

"I know," he said simply, "but it doesn't appear that there is. Let's keep going."

Ethan hit the play button and the room was once again filled with the voice Leah was learning to dread.

"Now, did I tell you about Penny Gaines? I met up with her down in Galveston. Pretty Penny. Bright and shiny as her name. Her old man owned a bunch of pharmacies, her old lady liked to hold court at the country club . . ."

And on, and on. How Penny Gaines had first come to his attention while he was parking cars at the country club. How he had watched her long enough to know her routine. How one day he saw his chance when she came to the club alone and he parked her car. He'd driven it to the far end of the lot, then climbed into the back when his shift was over and waited for her.

From Penny Gaines to Ellie Henderson to Lindy Philips, so passed the morning. Finally, Leah turned off the tape and said, "You look like you could use a break."

Ethan nodded.

"How 'bout lunch, then a walk?" She stood and stretched the kinks out.

"How 'bout a walk, then lunch?" Ethan stood and did the same.

"You're on."

"Road or field?" Leah asked as she locked the door behind her.

"What?" Ethan asked, as if just tuning back in.

"Do you want to stick to the road, or would you rather walk across the field?"

"Field, I guess. I can always see what's down the road later."

"This way, then." She motioned for him to follow her across the road to the field beyond.

They passed behind the area where his car was parked, and as they reached the top of a slight hill, Ethan paused and filled his lungs with the fresh cool air, as if by taking in the new, he could expel the old, along with the demons that had seemed to seep beneath his skin. His eyes held the same haunted look Leah had seen when she'd first met him, when he'd first told her that his connection was much like her own, only so much more intimate.

It nearly broke Leah's heart to see him so, making no effort to hide his pain and his vulnerability from her, and she reached out a hand to offer solace. He took it, his long fingers wrapping around her smaller ones, and wordlessly they walked down the incline and across the field.

Much of the snow that had fallen the previous weeks had melted, turning the plowed ridges into sharp mounds with muddy sides. Their boots sank into the mud, making sluicing sounds as they walked. The sun at midpoint in the sky spoke of noon, a fact she hadn't noticed on any of the cabin's clocks. The morning had passed in a fog of inestimable sadness as the voice described acts committed without pity, without conscience, without mercy. The very telling had fouled the air, had fouled the minds and senses of those who had listened, and it helped to breathe clean air and see the trees and shrubs in bud, to see the freshness of spring as it spread out before them. Early spring flowers—crocuses and snowdrops—patterned the sides of the fields, and the colors were welcome after a bleak morning. It wasn't until she and Ethan began to walk, putting some space between themselves and the voice, that she realized she'd been biting the inside of her lip on one side so much that it had bled. Touching her tongue to it as they walked without speaking through the Connecticut countryside, she tasted the remnants of her own blood and wondered how long it had been bleeding.

Ethan stopped midway across the field and watched a flock of birds pass over on their way to a nearby tree where each took its place on this branch or that. A hawk that had been riding a thermal began a lazy descent in wide circles, still high above the tree but drifting ever closer. The birds gathered on the tree branches began to flutter slightly, the hawk's proximity not going unnoticed.

"If they all stay where they are, they'll all be safe," Ethan observed. "He can't take them all on. But if one gets nervous and tries to flee on its own, he's lunch."

They watched as the birds huddled closer together.

Ethan tugged at Leah's hand and said, "I've had my fill of predatory behavior for one day. Let's not hang around to see if any of those birds gets antsy enough to try to make a run for it."

Leah nodded, thinking to mention that the hawk stalked and hunted for survival, that there was nothing evil in his intentions toward the birds—though the birds would surely debate that if they could—but she said nothing.

The morning had been more stressful than she realized, and when they reached the end of the field, she took the lead down the paved road into the small crossroads town that lay ahead. They walked in silence, their hands still locked together, as if together they could walk off what they'd heard. When they reached the outskirts of the small village, Ethan stopped to read the sign.

"Welcome to Danner. Established seventeen-oh-three." He turned to Leah. "Do you suppose Danner has a place to buy lunch?"

"It has a small deli that makes sandwiches."

"Let's stop there and pick up something, then head on back."

"Good idea. If memory serves, they make a mean honey maple turkey and coleslaw on a big fluffy roll."

"Sounds good. Lead the way."

The deli was only two short blocks in on the narrow street that served as the main road of Danner. A bell over the door announced their arrival, and while Ethan ordered sandwiches, Leah poked through the magazines and the short selection of paperback books. When she arrived with the local newspaper in hand at the counter where the old cash register sat, she realized she had not a penny on her. Ethan took the paper and added a bag of potato chips to the pile, and was eyeing a display of commercially baked brownies wrapped in cellophane when Leah leaned over and whispered, "If it's brownies you're craving, you should know that I make a kickin' brownie."

Ethan smiled for the first time that day and squeezed her shoulder.

"I will hold you to that."

Leah thanked the woman behind the counter by name as they gathered their purchases and prepared to leave, standing aside while the next batch of shoppers filed in through the narrow door and greeted Leah and Ethan.

"Friendly place," Ethan observed as they strolled past the few storefronts that made up the shopping district.

"All these little towns are pretty much the same up here," Leah said with a nod. "Most of the residents have connections to the area that go back several hundred years. Over the years you just get to know who people are. My great-great-grandfather was a farmer up here. My great-great-grandmother sold her eggs in that store we just came out of. Sold them to the great-grandmother of the woman who was on the cash register, I might add."

"So your roots really are pretty deep here."

"About as deep as you can get." Leah walked a little faster to keep up with Ethan, who had quickened his pace. "Besides the fact that my ancestors settled here when it really was nothing more than wilderness. I spent some of my happiest days here with my parents and my sister. I feel very much connected to this place, to our cabin. I'll never sell it. Never. It's my home, my sanctuary, more than any place on earth."

"That's how I feel about our camp. I grew up there, spent so much of my life there. It's where I belong."

"I thought Holly said you'd lived for a time in Atlanta."

"We did. Libby was from Georgia. She grew up there, and wanted to move back there. She wanted to practice law in the firm that had been founded by her great-grandfather. For a while, she did. The only time she left was to go to college in Texas."

"Did you like living in the South?" Leah asked as they fell into a steady pace along the tree-lined road.

"Yes. For the most part. I missed Maine, though. When Libby . . . when she died, I sold the house and packed up Holly and headed north. I couldn't wait to get home."

"Are Libby's parents still in Georgia?"

"Yes. Holly goes down twice every year to stay with them for a few days. She's the youngest grandchild, and their only granddaughter. They need to know her. And she needs to know them. It's painful for them, though, and it seems that, the older Holly gets, the more difficult it is for them to spend time with her."

"She must remind them of their daughter."

"She reminds them that their daughter is gone."

"It can't be easy for them, either."

"It hasn't been."

"Have you stayed close with them? With Libby's family?"

Ethan shook his head. "They've never forgiven me for meeting with Lambert, for writing the book."

"But surely they understand why you did it?"

"They think I did it for the money." Ethan blew out a long breath. "As if I wanted a dime from that project. Every dollar went to a women's shelter outside of Austin."

Leah stepped back, pulling Ethan with her, as a dark car rounded the curve just a little faster than was necessary.

"Didn't you tell them about Lambert's deal, that you only did it so that their daughter . . . her body . . . could be located?"

"Yes, but then, anyone who wanted to know what had happened to her . . . what had been done to her . . . could know."

"I don't understand."

"They felt that it was somehow shameful, what had happened. They were embarrassed that their friends knew just what Lambert had done to her. Somehow they felt shamed by the indignities their daughter had suffered." Ethan's jaw tightened and his eyes narrowed. "They felt she would have been better off lost someplace, her reputation unsullied, than to have everyone in Georgia—everyone in the damned country—know that she'd been raped and strangled."

"I'm so sorry, Ethan." Leah took his arm and slowed her steps. "I just can't think of another thing to say to you. After listening to those tapes this morning, I can only begin to understand what you must have gone through back then, just to return Libby to them. And to have her parents turn on you . . . it must have been very, very hard to take."

"It was. But I didn't do it for them. Hell, I didn't do it for myself. I did it for Libby, and for Holly. So that she would never be haunted by not knowing. So that when she got older and wanted to visit her mother's grave, she could do that."

"Where is she buried?"

"In Georgia. In her family's plot. Holly makes her grandparents take her there every time she visits them. She takes flowers and stories that she's written and reads them to Libby. It's her only connection. She never knew her mother, not really."

"That's so sad, Ethan."

"Raymond Lambert spread sadness wherever he went. Libby wasn't the only one we located through the tapes."

"What do you mean?"

"There were others, other women, who he'd admitted killing, whose bodies hadn't been found. He wasn't convicted of those murders, because there had been no bodies, but he confessed to them. Through comments he made on the tapes, the FBI was able to locate several bodies that wouldn't have been found otherwise. It was worth it to have found Libby, but finding the others was an unexpected bonus."

"Was he later convicted of those murders too?"

"No, since he'd confessed, there was only a trial for sentencing. That was the only chance the families of the victims had to face him, but at least they knew their wife or daughter's killer had been brought to justice. It's little enough consolation, I assure you, but for some of us, it was all we had."

"Genna Snow had told me there had been others who had been contacted as I had been. Others who had been found—"

"I still don't believe Raymond Lambert ever laid eyes on your sister."

"Then why are you doing this? Why are you putting yourself through this?"

"Because you have to know. I can tell you what I think, but until you check this out for yourself, you'll always wonder. And there's always the chance that I'm wrong. That maybe he did make some mention of a trip up north that I just don't remember. I don't think so, but as long as there's that bit of doubt, you'll always wonder. After all you've been through, I couldn't turn you away."

"You wanted to, though."

"Yes. I wanted to. I tried to."

"Has it been as difficult as you were afraid it would be?"

"We haven't come to the hard part yet."

Leah did not know what to say, so she said nothing, merely scuffed the toes of her boots through the dirty slush on the side of the road. His willingness to relive his own nightmare to help banish hers was the sort of gift for which there could never be adequate thanks, and it occurred to Leah that she'd never known a more self-less human being. The knowledge that Ethan had willingly endured this for her sake humbled her, and she took his hand again as they started back across the field, to the cabin, and to the rest of the tapes.

The late afternoon sun had started to disappear behind the clouds as one after another of the tapes had given up their dreadful secrets. Leah had been astounded at the number of women Lambert had abducted—none of whom had ever escaped—and at the variety of ways in which they had met their fates.

At one point she had stopped the tape and shook her head and said, "This is all making my head spin. It's like it isn't even real at this point."

"That's exactly the feeling I had, when he was relating these things to me." Ethan drew a hand through the tumble of dark hair that had slumped onto his forehead. "It was all so surreal that my mind could not believe that it could be true."

"Do you want to stop for the day?"

Ethan hesitated, then shook his head.

"Let's finish up this batch of tapes today, then maybe tomorrow we'll work on the notes for a change of pace."

"I think I want to get something to drink while I have the chance. What about you? What can I get you? Coffee? Tea?"

"Ice water would be fine."

Later, looking back on that moment, Leah realized that his voice had been flat and his eyes had grown clouded. It wasn't until she had turned the tape on that she understood that Ethan had known what was imminent, and that the clouds had gathered in apprehension, in dread of what was coming.

"Now, here's the moment you've been waiting for, Ethan. You want to know about Libby, don't you?"

"I want you to tell me where she is, Lambert."

"Ah, but I want to tell you how she got there. You need to know, Ethan. A husband should know who's been where he's been, if you know what I mean—"

"Oh, God, Ethan . . ." Leah's eyes filled with tears. "We don't have to listen to this."

Her hand reached for the off button, but he stopped her. Their fingers entwined as if to anchor one another, as if to present a united front against the evil that they were about to share.

"I saw her walking through the airport, distracted, not paying attention. I hadn't been looking for anyone that day, I feel you should know that, but there she was. I picked her out the minute she stepped through the gate. One look at her, and I didn't see anyone else, if you know what I mean. Well, of course you do. I imagine it was the same for you, wasn't it, the first time you saw her? What a looker! Anyway, I followed her, watched her as she waited for her luggage. She bumped into me. Never said excuse me. Just bumped into me with her elbow and looked right through me as if I wasn't worth noticing. Well, I made her notice me. Before the day was over, I made her notice me good. Ethan, look at me . . . you're not looking at me."

Mumbled words in the background.

"You really have to know this. Because in a way, what happened next was your fault. She shouldn't have been wandering around that airport alone, Ethan. A good-lookin' woman like that should never travel alone. She's just asking for trouble." Lambert paused to inhale smoke from his cigarette and blew it out again. "So I figured, what the hell, let's see if she's meeting anyone. She wasn't. So I followed her to her rental car. She never saw it coming. She leaned down to unlock the door to place her luggage in the backseat, and hey, there I was! She didn't want to come with me, at first, but I was able to manage to persuade her to let me come along with her. She drove, by the way. I made her unbutton her blouse so that I could touch her while she was driving. I wanted her to touch me, too, but she wouldn't. Bitch! As if she was too good to put her hands on . . ."

"No more." Leah snapped off the tape. "No more."

She got out of her seat and kneeled in front of Ethan, wiped the tears from his face with her fingers.

"I can't do this to you," Leah said, oblivious to her own tears. "Whatever else is on that tape, it isn't worth what it's doing to you."

She stood and gathered his still frame to her and held him until both their tears had stopped.

"He's right. She wasn't supposed to be alone." Ethan's voice was flat and distant. "I was supposed to have gone with her to her reunion that weekend. But I didn't really want to go and she didn't force it. We canceled my ticket at the last minute and Libby went alone. I drove her to the airport that morning, and by seven o'clock that night, she was dead. I never saw her alive again."

"Ethan, you couldn't have changed what happened."

"Of course I could have. It's just like he said. He hadn't been looking for anyone, but there she was. Alone. Easy pickins."

"He was playing with you, don't you see? If he'd wanted her, he'd have found a way to get to her. Haven't you been listening to him? Libby was one of the few victims he took when she was alone. How many times over the past hours did we hear him brag about how he cut his victim from the herd? Ethan, haven't you been listening?"

He pushed her back gently to give himself room to stand up.

"Leah, I could have stopped him. Libby would be alive today if—"

"No. No, Ethan. He's convinced you of that and I'd bet my life that he took enormous pleasure from knowing that you believed him. But didn't you hear what he said? *He picked her out in the crowd right away. She was the only one he saw.*" Leah shook her head slowly.

"Ethan, he was lying when he said he wasn't looking for anyone that day. Why else would he have been at the airport, if not to look for a victim?"

Ethan turned to stare at her, but did not speak.

"He stalked her the way he stalked all the others. If you had been there, he would have made you part of the game. He'd have waited for that moment when you turned your back. He wanted her, Ethan. He would have had her, one way or another. Whether you'd been there or not, he'd have found a way to get to her. Just like he found a way to get to all the others. Convincing you that you could have prevented it somehow was just part of his game, Ethan. It simply made you another player. He made you doubt, then he played on your guilt, don't you see? And by doing so, you became another of his victims."

Ethan turned his back and walked into the kitchen. Leah heard the sliding of the glass doors, felt the rush of cool air, heard his footfall on the steps that led from the deck. From the window, she could see him cross the grassy slope that led down to the stream, swollen now with the melting snow of March, but she did not follow.

Ethan needed to deal with old demons now. Leah wasn't sure how long it would take, but she knew that when he was finished, he'd be back. She unplugged the tape player and stacked the tapes on the windowsill, and went into the kitchen to do the only thing she could think of to do.

She baked brownies.

Chapter 14

*I*t was almost an hour before Ethan came back into the cabin. By then, the sun had set and his body was visibly shivering, though not, Leah suspected, from the chill in the air.

Leah led him by the hand into the living room, sat him down in front of the fire, and wrapped him in a blanket. She served him the soup they'd bought the night before at the market in Bannock. She made him tea laced with honey and sat it on the table next to his chair. As she turned to leave, his fingers closed over her wrist.

"Don't go," he said, his voice stronger than she'd expected it to be. "Just sit with me for a few minutes, if you don't mind."

"I don't mind." Leah sat on the hassock at the foot of his chair.

"I apologize for being such a lousy guest."

"I'll let you make it up to me some other weekend."

Ethan smiled a weak half smile.

"Actually, I feel I'm the one who owes the apology," she told him. "If I'd thought this through better, if I hadn't been so single-minded, I'd have had a better appreciation for what this would do to you."

"It hasn't done anything to me, except maybe open my eyes."

She turned to look at him. Ethan leaned forward, the afghan falling from his shoulders.

"We're always so quick to grab at the guilt, aren't we? You for 'making me listen' to Lambert's tapes. Me for Libby's death. Why is that, do you suppose?"

"I don't know," she told him honestly.

"Why do we allow ourselves to believe that it all starts and ends with *us*? That *we* are somehow at the heart of every turn of events, of every tragedy, everyone else's fate?" Ethan stared into the fire. "It's like parents not being able to resist wondering where they've gone wrong when their kid gets in trouble. Maybe it's not *us*. Maybe it's another force altogether. Maybe it has nothing to do with us and everything to do with *them*."

"You mean maybe it has more to do with Libby and Ray Lambert and less to do with you? That maybe you weren't part of the equation until he made you believe that you were?"

"Something like that, I guess."

"I read someplace about survivors' guilt. That if there are five people in an accident and only two survive, that those two people feel guilty about having lived while the other three died." Leah drew her legs up under her. "I think maybe that's what you feel, or a variation on that same theme. Maybe Lambert just used that and took it one level deeper."

"Do you ever feel that way, about your sister?"

"You mean, do I ever wonder, why her and not me?" Ethan nodded.

"Every day. After all, she was the smart one. The

prodigy. The beauty *and* the brain. The girl who could do everything."

"Did that bother you?"

"You mean, when she was alive?"

"Yes."

"Sometimes. I guess it's hard to grow up in the shadow of your younger sister."

"Did you ever wish she would just go away?"

"I can remember watching our parents' faces while Missy played the piano. They were just always so damned proud of her. So, yeah. There were times when I wished she'd disappear. I don't think that's abnormal among siblings, though, to wish at times that the other would just go away."

"And when she did, did you feel responsible?"

Leah hesitated, thinking it through.

"Maybe on some level. And maybe there was a time that I believed that if I'd insisted that Missy fly home, or if I'd driven out to get her, nothing would have happened to her."

Leah got up and moved the screen away from the fireplace, then poked at the burning logs to arrange them.

"Did you feel that way, about your wife? Were there times you wished she'd go away?" Leah asked without turning around, not wanting to see his face.

"I'm sure there were times when I could have used some breathing room. I'm sure Libby could have, as well. Every marriage has its ups and downs. But no, I never wished she would leave."

"Are you still in love with her?" The words fell from Leah's mouth even as she tried to stop them.

Leah's face flushed, and she hoped that when she finally found the nerve to turn around, he'd think the high color was due to the fire. She concentrated her attention on stacking another log and getting its position on the top of the stack just exactly right.

Seemingly preoccupied, she waited, but still no answer came.

When she finally turned around, Ethan was gone.

Somehow, she wasn't surprised.

Leah pulled the hassock closer to the fire to ward off the sudden chill. It had been an exhausting day, mentally and emotionally, for her as well as for Ethan. Now that the day was over, she felt that, together, they'd traveled a dangerous trail through a strange landscape and both had somehow managed to survive. But at what cost, she wondered.

Are you still in love with her?

She shouldn't have asked. She should have forced the words back down her throat and refused to let them pass her lips.

Leah sat back on the hassock and stared at her stockinged feet. It was a question that had haunted her from the day she'd first looked into Ethan's troubled dark eyes.

The question hung in the air. She wondered if she'd ever know the answer.

The smell of coffee brewing, wonderfully rich and aromatic, managed to drift through Leah's closed bedroom door. She was half out of bed before she'd even opened her eyes. She pulled on sweatpants and an old sweatshirt and thick socks and padded down the hallway on soft feet seeking the source of the heavenly scent.

"Coffee," she muttered as she reached the kitchen door. "I smell coffee."

Ethan handed her a mug. "I found the coffee in the freezer and didn't think you'd mind."

"Mind?" She sipped gratefully from the mug. "Oh, it's wonderful. Thank you."

"You made the brownies," he told her. "Coffee was the least I could do."

"Oh, you found them."

"Yes, and they're delicious. Would you like one?" He held up the plate upon which he'd neatly stacked the cut brownies.

"For breakfast?"

"Considered by some to be the true breakfast of champions."

Leah laughed.

"I think I'll stick with something with a little more protein, like scrambled eggs."

She turned and opened the refrigerator door, pausing with her hand over the egg tray.

"Did you want some eggs with those brownies?"

"Are you crazy? And ruin a perfectly good sugar rush?"

He made toast for her while she stood at the stove, stirring her eggs.

"Are you in a hurry this morning?" she asked.

"Actually, I am."

"You know, you don't have to wait with me while I eat," she told him.

Ethan put his plate down on the counter.

"Why wouldn't I wait for you?"

"I mean, you can leave. You don't have to stay and watch me eat. I'll understand."

"What is it that you understand, Leah?" Ethan asked softly.

"Well, that after yesterday, you've probably had enough. I don't blame you. It's okay."

"You think I want to leave now, because yesterday was tough?"

Leah nodded.

"Actually, last night was tougher."

"I understand, Ethan."

Ethan smiled. "I don't think you do."

"Am I missing something here?" she asked.

Ethan stood behind her, his hands on her shoulders, his thumbs exploring the spots where stress had forced her muscles into tight bunches.

"I had hours to myself last night, hours I spent thinking about things I'd spent years pushing to the farthest reaches of my mind. It was a long time coming, frankly. For so long, I'd done everything I could to avoid thinking about what happened. I was so afraid of what I'd feel. So afraid that it would hurt too much."

"It did hurt you," she said simply.

"Yes, it did. And I survived. It didn't crush me and it didn't kill me and I'm still reasonably sane."

" 'Present fears are less than horrible imaginings.' "

Ethan's fingers stilled, momentarily, on her spine.

"It's from *Macbeth*," Leah told him.

"Well, I suppose that sums it up well enough. But once you've faced your fear, it loses its power. And I have to thank you for that. I'd never have faced it on my own," Ethan said softly. "Maybe now that I have, I can begin to move away from it. In any event, I can't go back to where I was before we played the tapes, you know. So we just have to keep moving ahead with it. You've helped me to find my truth, Leah. I'll try to help you find yours."

Leah turned down the flame under the frying pan and turned around, looking up, her eyes questioning his.

"You were absolutely right about Lambert playing with my head. I, of all people, knew exactly what games he played with every one of his victims, with their families. Whatever made me think he'd ask only that I write his book for him? Maybe the book was of less consequence than knowing that he'd made me believe I could have stopped him. That I was, therefore, somewhat responsible for what he'd done to my wife. Which is irrational, at best, I realize that. But for many years, I believed that had I been there, I could have saved her." Ethan paused, his hands lingering on Leah's shoulders. "I came out and played the tape over again late last night."

Leah turned and looked up at him. "Why didn't you come wake me up? I could have—"

"No. I should have done this a long time ago. It was the first time I really heard what he was saying." Ethan's thumbs touched the sides of her face, and a tingle began to crawl the length of her spine. "You were absolutely right. Lambert wanted Libby. He'd have done anything he had to do to have her. I doubt there was anything I could have done to stop him. It must have delighted him to know that he made me believe I could have made a difference."

The thought of Ethan sitting alone in the dark, listening to Lambert ramble on about what he'd done to Libby, brought back the memory of her unanswered question, and Leah felt the flush creep up her neck all over again.

As if reading her mind, Ethan said softly, "I want you to know that there will always be a place inside me for Libby. I loved her, Leah, and I had a child with her. I'll never forget her, and how much we loved each other. But I'm not *in love* with her memory."

Leah put her hands on his chest and he caught her wrists.

"I didn't answer you last night because I needed to think it through myself, so that when I answered you, you'd know it was the truth. So that we'd both know the truth. And for now, we'll leave it at that. We've a long way to go yet, to put the past in order." He caressed her fingers gently. "Anyway, it's been a hell of a weekend, and we've farther to go down this dark road with Lambert if we're to find out what happened to Melissa. But I promise you, I will do my best to help you to find out what happened to your sister. And then . . . well, then we'll see where we go from there."

"Well, I was thinking too," she told him, measuring her words carefully—oh so hard to do when he was standing so close to her. "You're probably right, you know. Lambert probably never met my sister. The FBI agent, John Mancini, told me the same thing. Maybe we should just stop—"

"No." Ethan shook his head, knowing what she was going to say. "No, we're not going to skip the rest of the tapes, and we're not going to bypass the notes. We're going to find the truth, Leah. One way or another, we're going to find the truth. Now, bring that plate of brownies into the living room, and I'll bring the coffeepot. We might as well get on with it."

Hours later, half of the tapes having been listened to, there was still no mention of a trip to Pennsylvania. By four o'clock that afternoon, with a full box of notes yet to be gone through, Leah suggested that they call it a weekend.

"You have a long drive," she reminded Ethan, reluctant as she was to see him leave.

"So do you," he told her.

"I'm used to it."

"Maybe we should get together again next weekend," he said, pointing to the box holding the notebooks. "We never even got to them."

"Fine with me," Leah agreed.

"Same time, same place?"

Leah nodded. "All right."

"Good. Then it's settled. I'll just get my things together."

Leah wrapped the rest of the brownies while he packed his belongings and carried the box containing the tapes and the notebooks to his Jeep. She was filling a Thermos with fresh coffee when he came into the kitchen to say goodbye.

"Ah, that's nice," he said, smiling, and she noticed that the darkness had gone from his eyes. "Thank you, Leah. That's thoughtful of you."

"It's the least I can do." She handed him the Thermos. "I'll walk out with you."

"The wind has picked up," he told her. "You'll need your jacket."

She could feel his eyes on her as she walked to the closet and slid the heavy parka from its hanger.

"Ready?" she asked, and he nodded.

Ethan held the door for her and took her hand as they crossed the road to the little clearing where he'd parked his Jeep.

"Are you traveling this week?" he asked.

"No. I'm in New York all week. Catherine and I have a business dinner on Tuesday, and a gallery opening to attend on Thursday afternoon."

"Sounds very corporate."

Leah laughed, and the sound flowed through him like church bells.

"Actually, it will be a very light week," she told him.

"Good. Then you'll be all rested up for Friday."

"Yes. I suppose I will be."

Ethan leaned down and met Leah's lips with his own, softly at first, then with a hint of demand she had not expected. Her arms entwined around his neck and drew him closer, deeper, her mouth opening to his tongue as it sought more of her and she gave, gladly, whatever he wished to take. His mouth drifted to the side of her face, soft kisses trailed to her chin. He held her close to him, rubbing the side of her face with his own. He cupped her chin in one hand and gazed down into her eyes, as if searching for something he'd lost. He kissed her at each temple, then once more on the mouth, a nerve-shattering, muscle-melting kiss that turned her inside out.

"I'll call you," Ethan whispered in her ear as he pulled away from her.

Leah nodded, unable to speak.

Ethan got into the Jeep and rolled down the window, suddenly uncomfortable leaving while she was there alone, though he could not say why. "Will you be leaving soon?"

"Yes, I expect within the next ten or fifteen minutes." She stepped back from the car as he began to back up. "Give Holly a hug for me."

"I will."

"And your dad," she called after him.

"Okay." He waved out the window and started to pull out of the parking space, then stopped.

She walked over to the driver's side window.

"Did you forget something?" She leaned toward the open window.

"Yes." His arm reached out for hers and drew her close. He kissed her lips and looked deeply into her eyes for a long moment. "You're cold. Go inside and lock the door."

"We've never paid much attention to locking our doors up here. There's never been anyone to lock out, but I have to admit that listening to the tapes has spooked me." She held his hand between both of hers. "I'm thinking I should pay more attention to whether I really have or haven't locked the door."

"What do you mean?"

"Oh, just that when we went out yesterday, I could have sworn I had locked the door behind us."

"And . . . ?"

"And, when we came back, it was unlocked."

"It was?" Ethan frowned.

Leah nodded. "I'm sure I just don't remember what I did, is all."

"On second thought," he said, turning off his engine, "let's just go back inside and close off the lights and get your things. I don't think I want to leave you here alone."

"Ethan, that's silly. I stay here alone all the time. You don't have to wait for me."

"For some reason," Ethan got out of the Jeep and looked around, feeling a bit spooked himself, "all of a sudden, I just feel as if I do . . ."

Ethan spent most of the drive back to Maine playing CDs and singing along. He didn't mind driving at night. The traffic was lighter than during the day, and besides, there seemed to be so much to think about that he hardly realized the same CD—an old Traffic album that had been rereleased—had played over and over all the way from Connecticut to Concord, New Hampshire, where he stopped to get a snack and stretch his legs. He replaced the CD with Pink Floyd's *The Wall* and settled back for the ride.

He turned up the volume when he realized the steady stream of voices in his head was beginning to get to him.

Lambert's voice. Leah's.

Libby's.

Ethan hadn't heard Libby's voice in years.

He sighed heavily, trying to sort out the rest of it.

The hours he and Leah had spent listening to the tapes had been grueling for both of them, there was no getting around that. But somehow, he felt cleansed, lighter, as if a burden had been lifted.

Well, perhaps it had been. Thanks to Leah.

And didn't it all somehow come back to Leah?

Ethan had not wanted to become involved in this mess, had given himself every possible excuse he could think of that would relieve him from having to go through with this. As terrible as her own ordeal had been, she was, after all, a stranger. But there had been something about her that had endeared her first to his father, then to his daughter, and Ethan had known there'd be no looking either of them in the eye if he turned her down. He figured he'd just do what he had to do and be done with it. If nothing else, it was making him a hero in his daughter's eyes.

Dad, her sister is out there somewhere . . . , Holly had pleaded.

In the end, he had given in, as he figured he would, telling himself it was for Holly's sake. Even then he knew he was lying to himself.

Even when he saw Leah's face every time he closed his eyes.

Even when he heard her voice on the phone and her gratitude caused his own words to catch in his throat.

Even when he opened the car door for her and she all but fell into his arms.

But everything changed when he kissed her.

He hadn't meant to do that.

He'd tried his damnedest to ignore her on a personal level while trying to convince himself that he was only working with her to resolve a problem. That once she'd heard the tapes and come to the conclusion that Lambert had in fact been toying with her, Ethan would pack up his notes and his tapes and they'd shake hands before returning to their own little lives.

He knew now there wasn't a snowball's chance in hell of that happening.

Not after spending hours watching the play of light and shadow across that finely expressive face. Not after seeing all the conflicting emotions, humor and sadness, change her eyes from warm dreamy chestnut to deepest brown in the space of a minute. Not after being close enough to catch her scent, to bask in her smiles, to track her tears. Not after tasting her and feeling her arms close around him.

All in all, it had been a pretty intense weekend.

Ethan had never expected there to be another woman in his life who would attract him so totally on so many levels.

He also knew that until this entire matter was resolved, there'd be no peace for either of them. With Leah's help, he'd put his most tormenting demons behind him. He could do no less for her. And once they'd gone as far as they could go to find Melissa, perhaps then they could get on with their own lives. Maybe even together.

The Jeep turned almost by itself onto the old logging road leading up to White Bear Springs Camp. The night was very still and cold, the stars crowding into the midnight sky. He parked the Jeep where Leah's Explorer had sat and gathered his gear. He slung his bag over one shoulder and paused, looking up. Out of habit, his eyes found the spot where Holly, at six, had declared Libby's star to be shining.

"Is heaven in the sky, Daddy?" Holly had asked.

"Well, I don't know that anyone knows for sure where

heaven is," Ethan had told her, "but some people think it's up there someplace."

"Then if Mommy is in the sky, can she look down on me, from a star?"

"I suppose that—"

"That's her star right there!" Holly had exclaimed excitedly. "It winked at me! That's Mommy, shining and blinking at me!"

Ethan had been too choked up to speak, and so had not replied. But Holly had looked for that star in every night sky since. And often, Ethan had, too.

Now he stood, looking up, and finding the star, thought maybe it was, in fact, winking at him. Wherever Libby was, on a star or not, Ethan hoped she had forgiven him, as he was beginning to forgive himself.

The cold night air closed in, borne on a breeze that swept through the pines.

She's not a replacement for you, Lib. You had your own place, and nothing can ever change that. But she's making a place for herself. And I guess maybe it's time. I'm hoping you're happy enough where you are, that it'll be okay with you. I'll never forget you, Lib, but she's moving into my heart, and somehow, it just feels right.

Ethan stood for a minute longer, looking up, feeling as if he was saying goodbye and meaning it for the first time. As he started to turn away, a flash of light moved overhead, and he laughed as the shooting star danced across the sky.

"You always did have a flair for the dramatic, Lib," Ethan said aloud to the night.

He traversed the frozen turf to the front door, entered so quietly that even Dieter, sound asleep in front of the long-extinguished fire, did not stir. Ethan paused in the hallway, then found his way in the dark to the kitchen for a snack after the long drive. He dropped his bag onto a chair and placed the box of tapes and notebooks on the table. He checked the cookie jar and found it filled with Holly's favorite spice cookies, and he smiled. She must have made them for him as a welcome home. In the morning, she'd want to hear all about his weekend. How was Leah and what was her house like? Did she ask about Holly?

The top shelf of the refrigerator held several cartons of milk, and Ethan took one out and filled a glass. Idly, he flipped open the box he'd brought in with him from the car as he munched.

Maybe he'd go through the tapes during the week—he could face that now—and see if there was anything in them that Leah should know about.

The notebooks were neatly stacked in the box, but the tapes, which he was certain he'd placed on top, were not there.

Could they have fallen out of the box in the back of the Jeep?

With the lid closed over as it had been? Unlikely.

Ethan could have sworn that he'd put the tapes in the box. He remembered putting them in there. Could swear he remembered hearing them slide around inside the box as he slid the box across the backseat when he'd loaded up the car to leave that afternoon.

Well, he was wrong, he told himself as he closed the box over and tucked it under his arm. *But no matter,* he thought. *I'll be at the cabin again on Friday. With Leah.*

It occurred to Ethan as he closed up the kitchen that he'd not had anything to look forward to in a long time. It felt better than he'd remembered. He planned to savor every bit of the anticipation.

On Friday, he'd see Leah again. At that particular moment, little else mattered.

$\mathcal{T}$he chatter that drifted through the narrow gallery was becoming more and more dense as the minutes passed and other invitees began to filter in. The art wasn't particularly arresting, to Leah's way of thinking, and she wondered how long protocol would require her presence. She looked around, smiled at this one and that as she sought to locate Catherine in the milling crowd.

Leah found her cousin at the center of a small, fashionable-looking group, none, however, more chic than Catherine. To Leah, even when they were children, Catherine had seemed worldly somehow, grown up in ways that Leah could never quite put her finger on. There were many times throughout the years when Leah had had to remind herself that Catherine was only five years older than she herself was. Of course, growing up under Uncle Harry's roof, in his care and in his world, would make anyone mature beyond their years, Leah rationalized. Uncle Harry had been the epitome of sophistication, and he had shared that sophisticated life style with his orphaned niece from the time she had lost her mother until Uncle Harry's own death just six months before Melissa's disappearance. There had been, Leah reflected, an inordinate amount of sorrow in a very short time.

Especially for Catherine, Leah thought.

Catherine, who had never known her father, her parents having divorced before she was born, had lost her mother, then Leah's parents, Uncle Harry, and her beloved cousin Melissa. Catherine had mourned Uncle Harry the most, Leah recalled, though it had been said by some that she had moved into his office with perhaps a little more speed and zeal than might have been appropriate. But then again, *some*one had to run *Trends*. It went without saying that it would be Catherine.

"Come here, sweetie, and let me introduce you to the man responsible for all this." Catherine waved her arm grandly, a twitch at the corner of her mouth. "Leah, this is Armand. Armand, my darling cousin, Leah McDevitt."

Armand kissed Leah's hand and told her how delighted he was that she'd accompanied Catherine and was there anything in particular she liked?

Leah had replied that she hadn't as yet had an opportunity to take it all in and tried to ignore the faint trace of Jersey City under Armand's French accent.

"Catherine, if I might have a word with you . . . ?" Leah asked.

"Of course, sweetie." Catherine smiled at Armand and excused herself. Taking Leah by the arm and guiding her to the front of the gallery.

"Honestly, Catherine, I don't know how you can keep a straight face sometimes," Leah chided her.

Catherine laughed. "All for the magazine, my dear. The owner of this gallery is a big advertiser. She's supported *Trends* for years. Armand is her latest find. I have to stay for a bit longer, but you, of course, do not. As a matter of fact, why not leave for the cabin now?"

"Now?" Leah considered the possibility, then dismissed it. "I'll wait until tomorrow. I still have to pack, fill the car with gas—"

"What do you need besides blue jeans and a sweatshirt or two and a toothbrush?" Catherine drew her slim cell phone from her handsome black leather bag and dialed. "Jerry? Catherine Connor. Leah's thinking about driving to the cabin tonight. Any chance you could put some gas in her car and get it ready to go? You're a dear. Thanks."

Catherine turned to Leah and said, "Done," as she slipped the phone back into her purse. "The garage will have your car ready in fifteen minutes."

"But—"

"I insist. You've been working hard for months and it's good for you to get away. If you leave early enough, you'll arrive in time to build a lovely fire and watch the news."

"Thank you." Leah kissed Catherine on the cheek. "I guess I will."

But when Leah arrived home, there was a stack of mail to go through. A letter from an old college friend to read. And she remembered she'd meant to call Genna Snow.

It was almost seven when Leah dialed Genna's number.

"You're there late," Leah said. "I thought I'd get voice-mail."

"Actually, I'm just wrapping up a case and thought I'd stay and get this report done. What's going on?"

"I spent last weekend listening to tapes that Ethan Sanger made when he was writing his book about Raymond Lambert."

"What kind of tapes?"

"The interviews that Ethan had with Lambert."

"About Lambert's kills?"

"Yes."

Genna exhaled loudly.

"That must have been some pretty rough going."

"It was. It was terrible. It makes you question everything you always believed about the innate goodness of man. If in fact you ever believed such a thing."

"Did you learn anything about your sister?"

"No. But we haven't listened to all the tapes yet. And frankly, I'm wondering if maybe John Mancini might have been right. It's beginning to look doubtful that Lambert ever did meet Melissa. It doesn't seem that he was too keen to travel very far."

"I'll let him know that. I'm sure he'll be interested," Genna said. "He'll be coming back from his leave soon. I expect I'll see him in another week or so."

"Oh?"

"I suppose he's put behind him . . . whatever it was that he needed to," Genna told her. "But back to the tapes. Tell me everything . . ."

Leah did, from the first reaction to that soft, animated voice with its slow drawl, to the start of the tape whereon Lambert began to talk about Libby Sanger.

"You know, I knew there was something about that whole Sanger thing that rang a distant bell. I'd lost sight of the fact that Sanger's wife had been a victim. I wasn't with the agency during the trial, so I guess I never had the full picture. How terrible for him."

"It was pretty bad."

"And how kind of him to do this with you."

"Very kind," Leah agreed softly. "He's an exceptional man."

I see, Genna thought.

"So. Where are you now with this project?" Genna asked.

"I'm meeting Ethan at the cabin again this weekend. Tomorrow night. We'll listen to the rest of the tapes and go through the notes . . ." She hesitated.

"But . . . ?"

"But I just don't think it's there."

"Then why continue?"

"Because if I don't, I'll always wonder. And I guess I'm hoping that he'll say something that will give me a name to follow up on. Lambert had to have had contact with the person who killed Melissa. He knew about her contact lenses. Someone had to have told him that."

"You're reminding me to follow up with the law enforcement agencies in western Pennsylvania that I called a few weeks ago. I'm afraid I got distracted by another case I've been working on. But I will make a few calls and see if we can track down any unidentified bodies that may have been found over the past few years." She paused and spoke as if to herself, "John might even want to spend a little time on it."

"I don't want to put anyone out—" Leah protested.

"I'll just mention it to him. It'll be his choice. But it will keep him busy until he comes back to work and they assign him to something else. The Lambert investigation was his, you know. He may want to putter with this as well, since there may be a tie-in here somewhere."

"I just wish I knew how."

"John may be able to help figure that out."

"Give him my number at the cabin," Leah suggested, "in case he wants to call."

"I'll do that. You keep in touch, hear?" Once again, Leah thought she detected a faint trace of the gentle South in Genna's voice before she hung up the phone.

Leah settled back into the big, overstuffed chair and stared at the ceiling, her mind taking her back to the moment when Ethan had kissed her on Sunday, a moment she'd relived so many times over the past week that she knew the script by heart. She sighed. Ethan had kissed her exactly the way she'd always dreamed of being kissed. She closed her eyes, feeling his mouth on hers, first so tender, then asking, seeking, then demanding . . .

"Leah, I thought you had left for the cabin." Catherine stood in the doorway.

"Oh. I was. I planned to." Leah yawned. "But I had a phone call to make, and I guess I made the mistake of getting way too comfy while I chatted. I guess I didn't realize how tired I was."

"Are you still planning on driving up tonight?"

"No. It's almost, what is that, nine?" Leah squinted tired eyes at the clock on the bedside table eight feet away.

"Well, I do think it would have been nice for you to have the extra day there by yourself." Catherine shrugged. "And we did call the garage and have them ready your car."

"I'll pick it up in the morning. I doubt anyone at Jerry's will notice. I'm just too tired. I haven't slept well this week."

"All that immersion in those nasty tapes, I'm not surprised. All that talk about stalking and killing women . . . it must have been brutal."

"It was worse for Ethan than it was for me."

"Ah, yes. Ethan, whose wife was killed by Raymond Lambert. Sweetie, you don't have a *thing* going with this fellow, do you?"

"Not yet. But I'd be lying if I said I didn't want to."

"Take some advice, sweetie. Wrap up your business and move on. A man whose wife was killed like that will never get over her. In his mind, she'll always be the perfect wife. Sort of absence makes the heart grow fonder, taken to a whole new level. You can't compete with a dead woman, Leah."

"That's exactly what I thought, at first. Now I'm not so sure that I have to."

"Trust me. Finish it up and send him on his way."

"We'll see," Leah said, knowing full well that sending Ethan packing was the last thing on her mind.

"Take it very slowly, then." Catherine walked the length of the room to Leah's chair, and leaned over to kiss her on the cheek. "And get a good night's sleep. I have an early meeting tomorrow, so I probably won't see you until Sunday. What time do you expect to arrive home?"

"I don't really have any plans right now. Early evening, I would guess."

"I'll see you then." Catherine patted Leah on the head and made her way toward the door. She was almost there when Leah called to her.

"I love you, Cat."

Catherine turned, a look of surprise on her porcelain face, and stared down the length of the room, to where her younger cousin lay curled up in the big chair.

"Why, I love you, too, Leah."

With a snap of the overhead light, Catherine disappeared into the dark hallway beyond Leah's room.

Ethan was sitting on the front steps of the cabin when Leah arrived late Friday afternoon. His forearms were resting on his thighs, his hands wrapped around a cardboard cup of coffee bearing the name of a convenience store about ten miles north of Hartford.

"That coffee must be mighty cold by now," she said by way of a greeting as she dragged her bags from the back of her car.

"It's getting colder by the minute."

Leah laughed.

"We can fix that." She swung her nylon bag to the ground and went through the keys on her key ring for the front door key.

"I'll do that," Ethan told her, taking the key from her, his fingers lingering on her own for just a second before standing up and unlocking the door.

"Thanks," she told him as she entered the cabin, pausing, as always, to turn the thermostat up and drop her bags. "I have some bags of groceries in the car. I stopped at the market on the way through Bannock."

"I'll get them," Ethan told her.

"Great. I'll put the coffee on. It'll take the cabin a while to warm up, and as cold as it is in here . . ."

Her voice faded behind him as Ethan went out to the Explorer, gathered the grocery bags, and hoisted them into one arm, locking both cars before returning to the cabin. He stepped into the kitchen, where Leah stood, still as a stone, staring at a box that sat on the kitchen table.

"Leah?" he asked as he placed the bags on the counter. "Leah? Are you all right?"

"It's Missy's," she told him in a flat voice. "Missy's wallet."

She clutched something dark blue to her chest with both hands.

"Missy's wallet?" he repeated.

"It was in the box. There. On the table." She pointed at it as if confused. "Where would Missy's wallet come from?"

"Are you sure it's hers?" He stepped closer and peered over her shoulder.

She handed him the dark blue leather wallet.

"Open it," she told him.

"It's her driver's license," he observed.

"It's her wallet. I bought it for her for Christmas that last year," Leah's voice began to rise.

"Where did it come from?"

"From the box," she said impatiently. "The box was on the table when I came into the kitchen."

"How did it get there?" Ethan frowned, turning the box to look at the front of it.

"I don't know how it got there," Leah snapped.

"Leah, the door was locked. We just unlocked it, remember? You gave me the key, and I unlocked the door. Who else has a key, Leah?"

"Only the Calhouns." She paused to consider this, then said, "Of course. They must be back from their trip."

"Call them," Ethan said. "Ask them if they know where it came from. There's no name or address on it, Leah, so someone must have dropped it off. Maybe they saw who it was."

Leah reached for the phone and hit speed dial. The number rang and rang.

"There's no answer. Maybe they took a walk. Sometimes, when it's nice, they even walk up here." As if in a daze, Leah walked out of the room and down the hall. "I'll bet Mrs. Calhoun found the note I left a few weeks ago and came over during the week."

She reappeared a moment later, frowning.

"She didn't change the bed linens." Leah opened the refrigerator door. "And it doesn't look as if she picked up anything at the store, either."

"Leah, I think you need to call the police."

"I think you're exactly right." Leah hit speed dial again.

While Leah spoke with the local chief of police, Ethan put the groceries away and started a pot of coffee.

"They're sending a car over. The police . . ." Leah was beginning to sound as unsteady as she looked.

"Go sit down," Ethan told her. "You're white as a sheet."

"I'll build a fire."

"I'll do that. You just sit here."

"I'm not used to being waited on."

"Good. Then you'll appreciate it. Sit."

"The coffee's done," she said a few minutes later from the doorway.

"So's the fire." He turned, frowning, his eyes sweeping the room once, twice.

"What?" she asked.

"The tapes aren't here." Ethan frowned.

"Of course they're not. You took them with you on Sunday. You put them in the box with the notebooks."

"I thought I had, but when I got home, they weren't there."

"But I saw you . . ." Leah turned her head at the sound of the car pulling up out front. "It looks like Bannock's finest have arrived."

Leah stood in the doorway of the cabin, holding the door open for the young police chief who'd won the job after the previous chief had retired last November. Leah had met him several times, twice at the market in the village. Tonight he looked as casual as he had then. Off duty or on, Darren Hunter had a relaxed way about him. And why not? The only crime he'd been called on to investigate since taking the job was the theft of Billy Johnson's Christmas bicycle by a jealous fifth-grade classmate. It was a testament to the safety of the streets of Bannock that just about any unusual call would send the chief of police out to investigate.

"Miss McDevitt." The young man stood on the narrow porch. "You called about a missing wallet—"

"Come in, please."

Chief Hunter motioned to another officer outside to remain with the car and turned to enter the house.

"It's in here, Chief." Leah showed him into the kitchen. "Ethan . . . Chief Hunter, this is my friend, Ethan Sanger. Ethan thought we shouldn't handle it."

"I don't understand. I thought the report said the wallet was missing."

"No, no." Leah shook her head, then stopped. "Well, it was missing. It belonged to my sister—"

"Who is where?"

"Missing. The wallet belonged to my sister who's missing."

"How long has she been missing?"

"Almost seven years."

"Seven years?" the young man repeated.

"Yes."

The officer nodded. It was all coming back to him. He'd been a boy when Melissa McDevitt had disappeared, but he recalled hearing the story.

"Refresh my memory." He took the chair at the table that Ethan held out for him, and Leah gave him the abbreviated version of Melissa's disappearance, the contact weeks ago by Raymond Lambert, her meeting with him, his sudden death, her efforts since then to find out if Lambert had been telling the truth.

All of which had led her to this night, and the wallet that someone had left on her kitchen table.

"How did this person get in?" Hunter asked. "Who else has a key?"

"Mr. and Mrs. Calhoun. They sort of look after things here for me while I'm working. I tried to call them but there's no answer." Leah paused, then frowned. "Actually, I haven't been able to get in touch with them for the past few weeks. I thought they might have taken a winter vacation, but they must be back now. I mean, if they were here to unlock the door and bring in the package, that means they're back, right?"

Hunter stood up and walked to the front door.

"My folks have a condo down in Tampa. They leave in November and don't show their faces back up here until May . . . hey, Henry?" he called to the officer who waited outside. "Give Bobby a call on the radio and ask him to drive down to the Calhoun place and just check to see that they're okay, would you?"

He came back into the kitchen.

"An officer will check in on the Calhouns. Now," he sat back down in the chair and tucked his long legs beneath the table, "has anything been taken?"

"Taken from where?" Leah asked.

"From here. Your house. Did the person who left the wallet take anything while he or she was here?"

"I . . . I didn't think to check. But there's not much here. A television, VCR, stereo . . ." Leah disappeared into the living room, "some CDs . . ."

She looked around the room.

"Everything's in place, Chief."

"How about jewelry—"

"I don't keep anything here," she said, shaking her head.

"So there's been no sign that anyone's been here, except for the wallet in the box."

Leah hesitated, then said, "This could be reaching, now, but a few weeks ago, when I came into the cabin, I almost felt that someone had been here."

"You didn't tell me that." Ethan stood, scowling, his hands on his hips.

"It was right before I drove up to Maine to see you

that first time," she told him. "I suppose I just forgot about it. But Ethan, there were your tapes—"

"What tapes are they?" Hunter asked, and when Leah had told him, he exclaimed, "You had interviews with *Raymond Lambert* on tape?"

"Yes. And Ethan put them into *that* box." Leah pointed to the box that sat on the table. "I saw him do it. He folded over the top, just like you see it there, and put the box on the backseat of his car."

"When did you discover them missing?" the officer asked Ethan.

"When I arrived home the next day."

"You drove all night?"

Ethan nodded.

"Make any stops on the way?"

"Several."

"Leave the car unlocked?"

"No. I'm positive of that."

"At some point, between the time you took that box out of here, and the time you took it into the house, the car must have been unlocked and unattended," Hunter told him.

Ethan shook his head. "No, I'm certain—"

"Ethan, you did leave the car unlocked, remember, when you helped me bring my things out? We closed up the cabin together."

"That's right. I did. I left the car at the edge of the clearing across the drive," Ethan said with a nod.

"Someone could have taken them from the box then."

"It was maybe only fifteen minutes." Ethan frowned.

"More than enough time to rob your car," the officer reminded him. "Did you see anyone around last weekend, notice any cars?"

Leah and Ethan both shook their heads.

"Was anything else missing?" Hunter asked.

"Not a thing."

"Why would someone take the tapes and leave the box?"

"What else was in the box?"

"Notebooks. Notes I made of my conversations with Lambert."

"How heavy was it? Heavy enough that you might need two hands to carry it?"

"What are you getting at?"

"Well, you said no other cars went by. It's kind of far from town for someone to have walked out here, and you don't have any close neighbors. So it makes me think it could have been a kid on a bike. Passing by, saw the car, it was unlocked, stopped to take a look. Saw the box, opened it up and saw the tapes, maybe thought he'd found a stash of music tapes and stuck 'em in his pockets to listen to when he got home."

"If he did, he got one hell of a nasty surprise when he turned the tape player on," Ethan told him.

It was then that Leah noticed the red light blinking on her answering machine. She rose and pushed the button.

Three hang-ups, then Catherine's voice.

"Just wanted to make sure that you arrived safely and that all is well. Good luck this weekend. I'll be in touch."

"Who's that?" the officer asked.

"My cousin, Catherine. I live with her in New York."

"She didn't come with you this weekend?"

"She rarely does. Catherine doesn't like the country," Leah explained.

"And the hang-up calls?"

"I get them all the time. At least, I have for the past few weeks," she said.

"Well, I think I want to have the cabin dusted for fingerprints, along with the wallet and the box, which I'll have to take down to the station. If you would both stop down, we'll take your prints, too, just so's we know who's who."

"We'll come now." Leah nodded. "I want to get to the bottom of this."

"Good. The sooner the better. And we'll see what a trace on the phone line brings up."

Ethan grabbed his jacket and Leah's from the back of the sofa and tossed hers to her.

Leah grabbed her purse and addressed the police chief. "Shall we follow you to the police station?"

"That's fine." He preceded her through the front door.

Leah paused to lock the door behind her, and Ethan tried the doorknob.

"Just testing," he told her.

"It's locked," she told him as they walked to the car.

"It was locked last week when we left, too," he said as he guided her across the road to the Jeep. "It bothers me to know that someone was so close last weekend. Close enough to steal the tapes from the car. Closer still this week to get inside the cabin and leave the wallet."

He unlocked the passenger side and Leah climbed in. As he got in behind the wheel, Leah said thoughtfully, "But if it was just a kid who took the tapes, as Chief Hunter thinks, then it wasn't necessarily the same person."

"It wasn't a kid who lifted those tapes, Leah. And Chief Hunter, nice as he is, probably has about as much experience investigating break-ins as my daughter Holly has."

"Bannock isn't a high-crime area," Leah agreed.

She was staring out the window at the trees lining the road as they passed by in the dark.

"Are you all right?" he asked.

"I think so. It was such a shock, seeing Melissa's wallet . . ." She shivered back into her seat.

"When we're done with the Boy Scouts here, I think you need to call your friend at the FBI."

"Genna? Why?"

"Because sooner or later, we've got to figure out how that wallet came to be in your house. Who left it there? How did they come by your sister's wallet?"

"Well, someone could have found it—"

"If they did, it must have been a while ago. The leather was in good shape, and there were no leaves or dirt. That wallet has not been exposed to the elements for the past seven years, you can be sure of that."

"Maybe they found it a long time ago—"

"And just decided to return it now? And how would some random person know to bring the wallet here? I didn't notice anything in that wallet that had this address in it. The address on the license was in New York."

"Maybe it was . . ." Leah looked confused. "I don't know, Ethan. I can't think of anything else."

Good, he thought. *Then you haven't come up with the only thing that makes sense to me.*

Ethan was debating whether or not to share his theory with her when the police car they'd been following took off like a shot, the twirling overhead lights making strange shadows on the trees on either side of the road.

"Wonder what brought that on?" Leah frowned.

"Maybe he's testing his new V-8 engine," Ethan said dryly.

But minutes later, when Ethan caught up with the car, it was parked at the edge of the Calhouns' front lawn, the lights still whirling and bouncing off the side of the white ranch house.

"Pull in," Leah told Ethan. "Something must be wrong."

Ethan pulled over behind the police car and Leah jumped out. She began to walk rapidly toward the front door, where the chief of police stood huddled with his two officers.

"I'm sorry, Miss McDevitt," the chief said, "but I'm going to have to ask you to wait in your car. Better yet, go on back to your cabin, and we'll—"

An ambulance drove onto the lawn. Several attendants hopped out and ran to the house.

"Inside?" a paramedic asked.

"This way," Chief Hunter told them, "but I don't think there's anything for you to do here."

The two attendants, the chief, and a second officer disappeared into the Calhouns' house.

"What's happened to Mr. and Mrs. Calhoun?" Leah asked warily.

"We're not really sure," the young officer replied, somewhat unsteadily, Ethan thought.

"I want to go in and—"

"No. No, you don't." The officer stopped her gently before she reached the door.

"But Mr. and Mrs. Calhoun—"

"Please wait in your car, like the chief asked you to do. This is a crime scene, ma'am."

"A crime," Leah said, puzzled. "What crime?"

"Appears to be a double homicide."

Chapter 16

*E*than couldn't decide who was more shaken by the discovery of the Calhouns' bodies, Leah, who had known the benign couple since childhood, or the young police officer who had found them and who now sat in the backseat of the police car, his face frozen in a horrified mask.

Leah sat similarly in a distressed sort of stupor in the front seat of Ethan's Jeep until, at long last, a visibly shaken Chief Hunter approached the car.

"I'm sorry that you folks had to be here for this," he said, his face ashen as he leaned in the window. "I've never seen anything like this. Things like this just don't happen in Bannock."

"Have they been there . . . for a while?" Leah asked.

"Ten days, maybe a couple of weeks. But we'll know more after the medical examiner gets here."

Leah turned to Ethan, her eyes wide. "My God, the day I dropped off the note, they could have been lying there, dying. If I had done something . . ."

Before Ethan could reply, Chief Hunter interrupted her.

"No, no you couldn't have. There was nothing that anyone could have done. They were dead when he . . . when whoever . . . was finished with them. There's nothing that anyone could have done to have saved either one of them. Except the killer himself." He took off his cap and ran his fingers through light brown hair. "I'm thinking about calling in the FBI here. We're just not equipped to handle an investigation like this. Whoever killed these folks took his sweet time doing it." He shook his head. "I can't for the life of me imagine why he did what he did—"

"Chief, what do you want us to do at this point?"

"Well, for starters, I was wondering if Miss McDevitt would know of the next of kin? If there's someone we need to notify, we'd like to do that as soon as possible." The chief leaned against the side of the Jeep as if grateful for the support.

"No children, but there were several cousins, and I think a few nieces and nephews. I never heard them speak of anyone else," Leah said softly. "But you might ask Reverend Fuller at the Presbyterian church in town. That was their church. He might know."

"Okay. I'll have someone stop by there first thing in the morning. Now, I can't help but think there's a connection between what happened at your place and this murder. First of all, the timing. You know what it's like up here. Two bicycles missing over the course of a summer represents a crime wave. To have something like this happen at the same time your sister's wallet shows up after . . . what was it, five years?"

"Seven."

"After seven years, your sister's wallet is left inside your house. The only people who have a key—other than yourself—are murdered. I'm no genius, but I'd have to be pretty dense not to look for a connection. So what I'm getting at here is that we need to locate the Calhouns' key to your front door. Any idea where they kept it?"

"There's a hook near the back door. They always left the key hanging there."

"You've seen it?"

"Sure. Many times. I often dropped off a check for their services when I was up here. Sometimes Mrs. C. would invite me in for tea and, if I had time, I'd spend an hour or so just chatting."

"Would you know if anything was missing from the house?"

"I don't know. I never paid much attention to what they had or didn't have. I do know the key should be near the back door," she told him. "And their cat, Tink, should be around someplace."

"A big tabby? Black markings on his face?"

Leah nodded.

"That bugger shot right past us when we opened the door. Right to the kitchen and to its food bowl."

"Poor thing, he must be starving. Having to fend for himself must have been tough on him. He's a pretty pampered kitty. Mrs. C. doted on him. I wonder how he managed to survive out here all this time."

"Well, we don't know that he's had to."

"What do you mean?" Ethan asked.

"Well, it appears that our killer may have holed up here for more than a few days, judging by the number of dishes that are piled in the sink and pots and pans on the stove top. Looks like the cat's been fed within the past few days, anyway."

"You think this person killed the Calhouns, then stayed in their house and ate their food?" Leah asked.

"And apparently fed their cat while he was at it." Hunter nodded. "My guess is that the cat could have gotten out within the past day or two, when our man left. Now," he asked, "can you wait just another minute while I run in and check for that key?"

Leah nodded to the chief, then after he'd walked away, turned to Ethan and said, "I can't believe this is happening. The Calhouns are wonderful, sweet people, Ethan. This never should have happened."

She turned to look back at the house.

"One of the things I've always loved about Bannock, about my cabin, is that it always seemed so far removed from all the madness that seems to happen everywhere else. I always felt so completely safe here. I don't think I'll ever feel that way again. Not after this . . ."

Ethan took her hands between his own and attempted to rub the chill from them, knowing that it was more than just the cool evening temperature that had robbed her of warmth.

"And the thought that that person could have been in *my* cabin. Has a key to *my* home . . ." She shivered.

"We're going to have to find a place to stay tonight," Ethan told her, and she looked up at him, as if considering this. "For one thing, your cabin may be part of the crime scene. They're going to have to do more than check for fingerprints."

She frowned. "What do you mean?"

"Trace fibers. Perhaps blood. If the person who killed the Calhouns was in your cabin, he'd have left fibers. Maybe hair. The police are going to need to check for these things."

"Is there a chance that it's just a coincidence? That maybe it's not the same person?" Leah stared out the window.

When Ethan did not respond, Leah turned to look at him across the distance of the front seat.

"You don't think it was, do you? A coincidence?"

He shook his head. "No."

"Actually, neither do I. I just can't stand the thought of that person being in my house. Of touching my things. Of touching . . ." She froze.

"Go on, say it."

"Do you think he's the one?" Leah said slowly. "The one who killed Missy?"

Ethan tapped silent fingers on the steering wheel. He'd wondered how long it would take before the thought occurred to her, since it had already occurred to him.

"I think it's possible. I don't know how else he would have come by that wallet."

"Maybe he found it." She looked at Ethan, whose dark eyes were hidden by the shadows in the car. "We already pretty much ruled that out, though, didn't we?"

"We could be wrong, but I don't think we are."

"Would he have been a friend of Lambert's? Lambert would have had to have known him, wouldn't he? To know about Missy's eyes?"

"That's a reasonable guess."

"Why now?" she asked softly. "Why now, after all these years?"

"Maybe he wants you to know that he's out there."

"Why?"

"I don't know. But the chief was right when he said you have to consider the timing. Maybe it all goes back to the reward."

"Why didn't he claim the reward himself? Why have Lambert do it?"

"Too risky. There'd be too many questions. He'd have

to explain how he knows what he knows. Lambert, on the other hand, had nothing to lose. He was already on death row with no chance of appeal. Who better to step up to claim the cash?"

"Why not sooner, though? Why wait all this time?"

"I have no idea. But I think you need to talk to your friend at the FBI. I think that you need to be in a safe place for a while."

"If he's after money, he's not likely to do me any harm," she said. "Who would he collect from if something happened to me?"

"That may be a bit of an assumption," Ethan told her. "You don't know who he is or what he's after."

They were both still sitting in silence, pondering the possibilities, when Chief Hunter came through the front door and walked toward the Jeep. Leah rolled the window down as he approached.

"There's no key ring to be found. Can you describe what kind of key ring it was on in case we come across other keys in the house?" he asked.

"It's not difficult to pick out," Leah told him. "It's a small white cardboard disk with a metal ring around it. It's clearly marked, 'McDevitt Cabin.'"

The chief blew out an exasperated stream of air that puffed white in the cool evening air.

"Of course, Mr. Calhoun might have it in his jacket pocket," Leah suggested. "You might look there."

Ignoring her comment, Chief Hunter leaned into the car and said, "The medical examiner just arrived. Why don't you folks find a place to spend the night, then come into the station in the morning and we'll take your prints then. I don't have anyone to spare to dust your cabin now, anyway. I suspect we'll be here for the rest of the night and then some. There's a motel about eight miles down the road. You can stop at the cabin and get your things, but I'm asking you not to go into any area that you weren't in earlier today, and only take out what you brought with you. I'll have a car follow you."

"I don't think that's necessary." Ethan shook his head.

"Do you have a gun with you, Mr. Sanger?" the chief asked.

"No."

"I'd feel a whole lot better if someone went along who did. What he did to those poor people . . ." the chief nodded toward the Calhoun house. "Anyway, I'd planned to post someone at the cabin to make sure that no one else gets inside and contaminates the scene. I'd feel a whole lot better if he went with you now. We don't know who we're looking for, or where he is."

Chief Hunter slapped the side of the car lightly with his open palm.

"Just come by in the morning to give your statements and your prints. There's nothing for you to do here tonight."

With that, Hunter walked away, muttering into the night, knowing that, for him, the night had just begun.

The first thing Ethan noticed when they entered the motel room was that it had been freshly painted with a dull shade of tan that made the old brown carpet appear even older and browner. But it was warm and had two big beds—as Ethan had requested—and would serve for one night.

Ethan hoped that, by this time tomorrow night, they'd be in Maine or on their way. He had a very bad feeling about everything that was going on, and he could not get Leah out of Bannock and to someplace *truly* safe soon enough.

"Which bed do you want?" he asked.

Leah shrugged her indifference at the same time she flopped onto the one nearest to her. She closed her eyes and drew her legs up. Ethan dropped their bags on the floor and removed his jacket, then sat on the edge of Leah's bed to help her to remove hers.

"Can I get you anything?" Ethan asked after he'd hung up both jackets in the small closet.

Leah shook her head. "I'm fine. Thank you."

Ethan leaned over her to kiss her cheek, and it was then he realized that she had begun to shake all over.

"Oh, you're fine, are you?" he muttered, stripping the blanket from the other bed and tucking it around her.

When Leah opened her eyes, and he saw they were wide with fear and with sorrow, Ethan got under the blanket and drew her close, seeking to both comfort and warm her, knowing that the chill was too deep for mere blankets to banish. More than an hour had passed before her breathing told him that she'd fallen asleep. He slipped his arm out from under her head slowly, so as not to rob her of whatever rest she might get this night. He leaned up on one elbow and gazed down upon her face, studied it until he knew every line and every freckle. And still he watched, wanting more than anything to cup that face in his hands and kiss those softly parted lips until she forgot her own name, to touch that sweet body and feel that silken skin beneath his hands. Ethan wondered if he'd ever wanted a woman more than he wanted Leah at that moment and came to the conclusion that if he had to think that hard about it, the answer was probably no.

As quietly as he could, Ethan slid away from her sleeping form until he could stand up without jostling her. He turned off the lights except for the dim lamp near the bathroom door and sat down in the chair next to the bed. He'd sit there all night, watching her, guarding her, if it meant that she would be safe. Tomorrow they'd go to the police station and give their statements and fingerprints, and then they'd leave for White Bear Springs. It was the only place Ethan could think of where this evil could not reach her. Something evil had stolen someone precious from him once before, and it had almost destroyed him. It wasn't going to happen again.

By noon the following day, local and national press had gathered at the small brick building that served as the Bannock Police Station, making it all but impossible for anyone to enter or exit without detection. Ethan and Leah arrived before the reporters, and their meeting with a bleary-eyed and weary Chief Hunter lasted the better part of the morning. As he had mentioned he might do the night before, the chief had called for assistance from the FBI, and several field agents had arrived before Ethan was finishing up his statement.

"Genna Snow would like to hear from you when you're finished here," a handsome young black agent took Leah aside and said. "She saw the news this morning and called our office first thing, figuring that we'd be sent over, being the closest. She said if you were still here when we arrived, that she'd like you to call."

He handed her his cell phone after punching in the number.

"Genna's an ace. We went through the academy together," he told her. "Any friend of hers is a friend of mine."

"Genna? It's Leah."

"Leah! For heaven's sake, girl, what is going on up there? I saw the story on the news first thing this morning."

"What did they say?"

"That someone left your sister's wallet in a box on your kitchen table, then went down the road and murdered two of your neighbors. Or maybe it was the other way around."

"I guess that pretty well sums it up, though it hasn't been proven that the same person did both."

"Rich just told me the fingerprints were a match in both places. In your place and the place where they found the bodies."

"Rich?"

"My buddy there, the one who made this call for you."

"The prints matched?"

"Apparently. Leah, do you have someone to stay with, someplace to go?"

"I could go home. My cousin is there."

"I don't know how safe that would be."

"Why not?"

"Well, I'm thinking that you should be someplace where no one knows how to find you. Obviously whoever brought you that present knows where you live. As remote as the news made the cabin sound, chances are he followed you from the city. I don't know how else he could have found it."

A chill ran through Leah.

"Leah?"

"I'm here."

"Think about it, will you? About someplace safe? And let me know where that is. I'm not assigned to this investigation, but I am interested, and I'll do whatever I can to help out."

"I appreciate that, Genna. Thank you." Leah bit her bottom lip. "Genna, Ethan and I were thinking that there must be a connection between this person . . . this killer . . . and Raymond Lambert. That maybe he told Lambert about Missy and Lambert came after the reward on behalf of this other person."

"Did you mention that to Rich?"

"No, actually, I didn't have a chance to do that."

"Tell him everything. Everything you can think of. In the meantime, I'll see what I can come up with from here regarding any possible associates of Lambert's who might still be on the outside, though a loner like him probably didn't have too many friends. Tell Rich everything and he'll take it from there."

"Okay. Thank you."

"And Leah, think about what I said. You need to be very careful right now. We don't know who this person is or what he's after." Genna paused, then added, "I'm hoping it isn't you."

"Why would anyone be after me?" Leah asked, recalling her conversation with Ethan the night before.

"I don't know. Hopefully we'll figure it out before this goes any farther. Keep in touch."

"I will." Leah hit the end button and handed the phone back to Rich.

"So what advice did she give you?" the agent said as he tucked the phone back into his jacket pocket.

"She suggested I talk to you about some . . . things."

He took her elbow and steered her to an empty desk at the back of the room. "Well, if Genna thinks we should talk, then go right ahead. Start talking. I'm all ears . . ."

Leah had gotten less than three sentences out when Rich motioned to another agent and called him over.

"Leah McDevitt, meet Dave Wilcox. Dave, I think you need to hear this . . ."

By the time Leah and Ethan had finished telling their

stories for the last time, they were both hoarse, tired, and hungry.

"I'm sorry to put you through this, but we need to get as much information up front as we can," Chief Hunter told them.

"Let's just get it all over with today, because as soon as we're finished, we're leaving for Maine," Ethan told him.

Chief Hunter frowned.

"I don't know about leaving—"

"Are either of us suspects?" Ethan asked.

"No." Hunter shook his head.

"Then we're free to go. I live in Maine. I'm going home. I'm taking Leah with me." He watched Leah out of the corner of one eye, waiting for a reaction. When none came, he told the police chief, "I'll leave my phone number with you. If anything comes up, you can call us."

Chief Hunter hesitated, then called over the FBI agent they'd been talking to earlier.

"He wants to leave for Maine." Hunter nodded in Ethan's direction.

"May be a bit premature. We're still not sure how Ms. McDevitt fits into all this. I'd feel better if she was someplace where we could keep an eye on her."

"You don't have to worry about Leah," Ethan told him as he stood up. "Anyone trying to get to Leah will have to go through me first."

"Very gallant, Mr. Sanger. But it well may be that the person we're looking for could do just that. I'd hate to see that happen." He tapped his pen against the palm of his hand. "Give us a few more days before you take off."

"I want to stick around a little longer anyway," Leah spoke up for the first time. "Chief Hunter said that the Calhouns' bodies might be released tomorrow. There will be a service for them the following morning at the cemetery. I'd like to attend."

She looked over at Ethan and added, "After that, a few days in Maine would be most welcome."

"I'll call my dad and let him know that we'll be back in a few days. If he's seen the news, he's probably crazy with worry by now," Ethan said.

"Catherine, too, I'm sure." Leah turned to the agent who seemed to be in charge and asked, "We're done, aren't we?"

"You're free to go." He nodded. "You might want to let Chief Hunter know where you'll be while you're in town, though."

"We're at the Roadside Inn on Main Street. Room number 128."

"Good. We'll have someone keep an eye on you."

"I've never been under the watchful eye of the FBI before," Leah told Ethan as they returned to their room after a very late lunch. "It's kind of creepy, in a way."

"Be grateful they're there," Ethan told her as he turned on the light. "Because we don't know who else is watching."

"You know, you're all going to make me crazy, talking as if someone is hiding under the bed, just waiting to pounce out and get me. You, Genna, the chief, that other agent—"

"Wilcox."

"Yes. Wilcox." Leah sat on the edge of the bed and toed off her shoes. "You know, I always thought that if someone was after you, you'd know it. That you'd sense it. Now I'm not so sure. Maybe that's only true in books."

She drew her legs up under her and leaned back

against the pillows. Rearranging them behind her, she reached for the phone.

"I have to call Catherine. I'm sure she's been frantic." She dialed the number for Catherine's line and waited for her assistant to answer. "Shelly? Leah. Is Catherine around? Yes, I'm all right . . . thank you, no, no need to worry. I'm sure the news overdid it, you know how reporters are. Yes, I'll wait for Catherine . . ."

She put her hand over the receiver and told Ethan, "Everyone in New York must have heard about this by now. It's been on all the news channels and . . . Catherine? Yes, I'm fine. Really . . ."

Ethan turned away to give her privacy. He lay down across the other bed and picked up the remote control for the television. He scanned the channels before settling for a show about deep-sea fishing. He'd never gone, but watching that marlin put up a fight made him wish he had.

The room was dark except for the white light from the television screen when Ethan woke up. He stretched his arms over his head, trying to work out the kinks that had settled in his shoulders and his neck while he had slept at such an odd angle.

"Ah, he rises," Leah said from the other bed. "I was wondering if you'd sleep right through the night."

"I feel as if I have. What time is it?"

"Close to ten."

"Are you hungry?" he asked.

"A little. How 'bout you?"

"So-so." He flexed his back against the stiffness.

"What's wrong?" she asked.

"I slept at an angle. My shoulders feel as if they're twisted inside out."

"Come sit over here and I'll work it out for you," she told him. "I owe you a massage, anyway."

He moved to the edge of her bed and sat down, and Leah moved behind him.

"How's this?" she asked, kneading the muscles in his neck.

"Great. You've got great hands." He closed his eyes and relaxed.

"That's a new one," she said, smiling.

"Well, you have great legs, too," he told her. "From what I've seen of them, anyway. Which hasn't been much, come to think of it."

She laughed softly behind him.

"How's this?" she asked, strong fingers moving down his spine.

"Great," he murmured.

Leah continued to work on his back for a few minutes, before sitting up on her knees to better reach his shoulders again. Ethan felt the brush of her breasts against his back, felt her soft breath against his neck, and the sensation rippled through him like a shot.

"Leah," he said hoarsely, when he could catch his breath.

"Hmmmm?" She leaned close to his ear, her body so close and snug against his back that he was almost afraid to move.

She rubbed her face against the side of his head, her hands slipping around his chest to caress the taut muscles under his shirt.

"Leah . . ."

She turned him to her and, taking his face in her hands, kissed his mouth, softly at first, as if waiting for his response. His arms wrapped around her, and it was then that he realized she was wearing little else but a long T-shirt. His tongue found the corners of her mouth in flickering waves and she opened her mouth to him, urging him inside. She took his hands and brought them to her breasts and when his fingers began to move over her skin, she lay back against the pillows, bringing him with her, holding him so that his mouth never left her own. Her heart was about to beat its way through her ribs and out of her chest, she was certain, and her legs had surely lost their ability to stand. Her bones had seemed to turn limp, and her body responded mindlessly to his touch, as if instinct had taken over and reason had been lost.

"Ethan," she whispered between increasingly urgent kisses.

She moved against him unconsciously, seeking him, and when his mouth began a trail the length of her neck, a soft moan escaped her lips. She arched against him and he slid up the shirt so that his mouth could find an aching nipple and take it between his hungry lips.

"More," she demanded, and he gave her more.

Her hands sought his belt and unfastened it, urging him out of his jeans. Her legs wrapped around his, drawing him closer to her center, and his mouth tortured her flesh in a hundred places, until there was no place that his lips had not been, no place that his mouth had not tasted. When she drew him inside, completion was swift and sure and wonderful. So wonderful that they made love again, more slowly this time, and then once again before morning.

By the time they realized they'd missed dinner, the sun was beginning to rise over the Connecticut hills behind the motel, and finally, they slept.

And somewhere, close by, someone waited.

$\mathcal{I}$n the end, it had actually taken three more days for the medical examiner to complete his work, another for Reverend Tillitson of the First Presbyterian Church of Bannock to prepare the service for the departed members of his congregation. Never having been called upon to memorialize victims of so brutal a crime before, Reverend Tillitson wanted to make certain that he covered all the appropriate bases in his eulogy.

Early on the evening before the service, Leah and Ethan sat in the comfortable dining room of the Bannock Inn, sipping chardonnay and sharing a seafood appetizer. It had been an exhausting week, a week of profound emotions and intense soul searching, a week where the worst in man as well as the best had been exposed to Leah's eyes. Having learned the details of the Calhouns' murders from Chief Hunter once the autopsies were completed, Leah had gagged at the revelation of what those dear and gentle people had been forced to endure in the final moments of their lives. The horror of it had rocked her soul.

And at the farthest end of the emotional spectrum, Ethan Sanger had rocked her heart.

If the past four days had been hell, the nights had been sheer heaven. If it was true that for every soul there was a mate, Leah was convinced that she had found hers. Ethan was a gentle and commanding lover whose touch set her being on fire, whose kisses reached places inside her she had not known existed. Where they would go and what they would do once they left Bannock was a question Leah refused to entertain. What they had right now was all she'd ever dreamed of finding, and more, and she would not look beyond it.

Cherish these days for what they are, she told herself, and so she memorized the curve of Ethan's jaw, the way his hair just brushed his shirt collar, the feel of his muscled back beneath her searching hands, the shape of his mouth, and kept it all stored away someplace inside, like favorite photographs, against the time when he would return to Maine and she to New York.

Leah was thinking exactly this thought as she stirred her coffee, and it sparked a memory that had been eluding her for days. She frowned.

"What's wrong?" Ethan asked.

"I was thinking about the photographs on the piano."

"And?"

"And I want to go back and look at them again."

"Why?"

"Because I think something is missing." She stirred uneasily in her chair. "I keep seeing the top of the piano in my mind, and it's not right."

"Well, you did say that you had removed a picture of your sister. You brought it with you to White Bear Springs, remember?"

"Not that picture," she said, shaking her head. "A picture of me."

Ethan put his fork down and stared across the table at her.

"There was a photo that someone took of me a few years ago at a dude ranch in Wyoming where I'd gone for an article," she told him. "I was leaning over a fence, wearing a big white cowboy hat. I'd forgotten all about it, but then Carolyn, my secretary, found it not too long ago and had it enlarged and framed for me. I brought it up with me one weekend and put it on the piano, but I don't think it's there now."

"How long ago was that?" Ethan asked.

"Two months or so."

"And you're sure that photo is missing?"

"No, I'm not sure. I just don't remember seeing it. I could be wrong."

"We'll talk to Chief Hunter about that first thing in the morning. If everyone has finished their investigation, maybe they'll let us go back inside."

"I don't know how I feel about that place now." Leah put her fork down. "Knowing that he was there. Whoever he is—"

"We'll talk to Chief Hunter in the morning," Ethan repeated more firmly, rattled by the reminder of just how close the killer might have come to Leah without her even being aware of his proximity. "We'll call him, first thing, before we leave the motel for the funeral."

"I wish I'd thought of it sooner," she said. "I saw the chief this afternoon when I stopped to grab a sandwich between errands."

"I thought you only went to the dress shop."

"Well, after the dress shop, I stopped in at Scott's Pharmacy for some makeup, since I left mine at the cabin and didn't know when I'd be able to go back in to get it," she explained. "Then, while I was there, I saw Chief Hunter having lunch at the counter with one of the FBI agents, so I joined them."

"Did they have anything new to report?"

"Only that they thought they might have a lead on a suspect. That maybe they'd know by tomorrow."

Ethan put down his fork.

"I'd say that's significant. Why didn't you tell me?"

"I would have told you as soon as I got back to the room, but immediately upon entering, I was set upon and ravished until I was barely capable of babble, let alone coherent speech." Leah grinned. "If you expect me to report hard facts, then at least let me get past the door before you assault me."

"I couldn't help it. I missed you. You were gone all afternoon," Ethan told her, surprised by how much he had, in fact, missed her presence.

"It was less than three hours," Leah said with a laugh, refusing to think about how much she would be missing him in another week.

"Well, it seemed like all afternoon. Anyway, tell me about this suspect."

"I don't know anything, except they think they have a lead on someone they traced through a post-office box that Raymond Lambert had sent correspondence to. That's all Wilcox had to tell me today. Maybe by tomorrow morning they'll have some more information."

But they wouldn't have to wait that long. Before they'd finished dessert, Agent Wilcox appeared in the dining room and, finding their table in the corner, apologized for the intrusion even as he invited himself to join them.

"Rich said he thought he'd seen you come in a while ago," Wilcox said.

"Not much you can hide in a small town, is there?" Leah smiled.

"I don't want to spoil your dinner, but there're some things we need to talk about."

"We don't mind," Ethan told him. "What's going on?"

"Well, as I told Leah this afternoon, we got a lead on someone Raymond Lambert had been corresponding with from prison. A post-office box in a town outside of Pittsburgh."

"That's in western Pennsylvania." Leah put down her fork.

"Exactly," Wilcox said, ignoring the *Thank you for not smoking* sign and lighting up a cigarette from a pack he pulled from his shirt pocket. "West Newton is the name of the town, by the way."

He inhaled quickly, then exhaled as sharply.

"Anyway, your buddy, Snow, has an old friend who works for the prison where Lambert was incarcerated."

Leah nodded. "Genna had contacted someone down there for me when I wanted to visit him."

"Right. She mentioned that. Anyway, she talked to this friend off the record, asked about who Lambert hung out with, who his buds were."

"And?" Ethan asked.

"And it turns out that he didn't have any. But in talking with the guards, this friend of Snow's mentioned that Lambert had a very active correspondence going with someone from PA. Got mail at least once a week, wrote back as often."

"Great. Did they find the letters?" Ethan asked.

"Nope. The guards said that Lambert always destroyed them the same day he got them. Ripped them into little, tiny pieces and flushed them down the john as soon as he read them. Strange, no?" The agent took a long drag from his cigarette. "Here you have this guy on death row, who nobody talks to, who has one contact outside those walls. He gets these letters, reads them once, then rips them to shreds. Now, if that was you, what would you do with those letters?"

"I'd save them, to read over and over," Leah responded without thinking.

"That's what I'd do, too." Wilcox nodded.

"Didn't anyone at the prison look over the letters before Lambert received them?" Leah asked. "Isn't prison mail subject to scrutiny?"

"Yes. At least, the incoming mail may be read, and everything is scanned electronically to make sure there's no contraband or weapons being sent in. The guard said that, for the most part, the letters were all mostly about this other guy's social life. Who he had dates with and where they went, that type of thing."

"You mean this friend of Lambert's wrote to him about his lady friends?" Ethan asked.

"That's what the guard said, though he did say that he didn't read them all. A model prisoner like Lambert was, whose mail had always been clean, they wouldn't spend a lot of time looking at his mail. Oh, they'd spot-check it once in a while, maybe every fifth letter or so, just to make sure that someone from the outside wasn't sending him information on escaping or some means of creating havoc within the prison. Chances are if the guards were used to seeing the same return address over a long period of time, they wouldn't bother with him."

"But you have to wonder what it was that Lambert didn't want anyone else to see," Leah said.

The three sat in silence, each of them doing exactly that.

"We'll never know, will we?" Ethan said at last.

"It all depends," Wilcox told them, "on whether or not his counterpart destroyed the letters he received from Lambert."

"Lambert wrote back?"

"From what the guard said, he mailed several letters each week to this post-office box."

"So all you have to do is find out who the correspondent was, who rents the box—"

"Done that," Wilcox told them. "William John 'Billy' Briggs. Forty-seven years old, once married, once divorced, no children. Currently unemployed. He quit his job as a truck driver for a chain of convenience stores about two months ago. Told his boss he was coming into some money and he wouldn't have to work for a while. No one's seen him since."

"I assume you've searched his house?" Ethan asked.

"We're waiting on getting a warrant signed. Apparently he's lived in the same house all his life, inherited it from his parents. I expect we should have the warrant within twenty-four hours."

"The company he worked for?"

"Hasn't heard from him since the day he left. He had no friends that anyone knew of, his next-door neighbors said they rarely saw him. The woman across the street said she hasn't seen him in five weeks."

Leah frowned.

"So he could be—"

"Anywhere." Wilcox nodded. "He could be sitting there at the next table. He could have been the guy you smiled at when you left the drugstore today."

"Stop it," Ethan said, watching Leah's face go white. "You're scaring her."

"She should be scared." Wilcox punched out his cigarette. "We don't know who this guy is. Shit, we don't even know if this guy is *the* guy. He has no record, no previous arrests. By tomorrow morning, however, we should have a copy of his driver's license photo, so at least we'll have a face."

"If you could get fingerprints from his house, then you could compare them to the ones you took from the Calhouns' and from my cabin," Leah said.

"That's the plan. In the meantime, Chief Hunter is having one of his men keep an eye on your room."

"You think he's still here, in Bannock?" Leah asked.

"It depends on whether or not he feels his work here is complete." The agent lit another cigarette.

"You think he's after Leah?"

"Right now, we don't really *know* anything. We're trying to come up with a reasonable scenario. Let's suppose this Billy Briggs is our man. Here we have a guy who, as far as we know, hasn't worked in a couple of months, hasn't been seen in weeks."

"Roughly since the time of Lambert's death," Leah murmured.

"Exactly. Since Lambert's death. Then suddenly he disappears. Then the next thing we know, we have a break-in at your cabin and two dead bodies down the road. What ties it all together?" Wilcox's cigarette punctuated the air.

"You don't even know if Billy Briggs is even remotely connected," Ethan pointed out. "Maybe it's someone else."

"Maybe. But you have to admit it's a damned odd string of circumstantials. *Damned* odd." Wilcox shook his head. "Anyway, what we're thinking is this. Supposing Briggs is our man. Suppose he's still in the area. Maybe he's wondering what his old friend Ray would do."

"Meaning?" Ethan asked.

"Meaning maybe he'll be at the funeral," Leah answered. "That's what Lambert used to do, remember? You told me that yourself. He used to stick around for his victims' funerals."

"Right. Now, we've already alerted Reverend Tillitson to let us know if there's anyone who stands out in the crowd as an obvious outsider."

"How hard could it be to spot a stranger in a small town like this?" Ethan asked.

"Maybe harder than you think. It turns out that Mrs. Calhoun had a number of cousins. Any number of them could show up tomorrow. With their spouses, their children." He held up his hands in a gesture of futility. "We won't know who's who."

"Wouldn't they introduce themselves to Reverend Tillitson?"

"Maybe. Even if they did, would he know if they're real relatives or not?" Wilcox asked. "And then there's the press. And there will be the curious. I just want you to keep your eyes open, Leah."

"Agent Wilcox, I don't know as many of the town people now as I did when I was younger. There're hundreds of people here whom I've never seen before. I'm afraid I won't be much help in picking out a stranger."

"True. But you'll know if someone is maybe getting too close to you or staring too long, making you uneasy. It'll be worth checking out."

"You don't expect him to try anything at the funeral?" Ethan asked.

"I don't know what to expect, to tell you the truth. But forewarned is forearmed, as they say." Wilcox took a last drag from the cigarette and stubbed it out in the ashtray the appalled waiter had brought over after he'd put out his last smoke on Ethan's dessert plate. "So go on back to your room and get a good night's sleep. Tomorrow could turn out to be a very long day."

Leah donned the new black dress and leather pumps she'd picked up the day before in Bannock and, with Ethan, set out for the church a little before ten. They'd been up earlier and had a quiet breakfast where they were joined by Rich. It seemed, Leah thought, that every time she turned around, there was another FBI agent standing behind her. Considering the alternative, she really didn't mind.

The eulogy was duly respectful of the deceased, sincerely delivered by the minister who had known the Calhouns for so many years. Hymns were sung by the same choir with which Mrs. Calhoun had sung for much of her adult life, and memorials were offered by several members of the congregation. Leah's mind was wandering, contemplating the events of the last week, thinking back to her life before she and Ethan had opened the door of the cabin and she had found the box containing her sister's wallet.

No traces of grass or dirt had been found on the wallet, Genna Snow had told her late the night before when she called to express her concern for Leah's safety. The results of the fingerprint comparisons had come in, and Genna felt that Leah should know. To no one's real surprise, the prints in the cabin matched the prints found at the Calhouns'. Which matched the prints found in Billy Briggs's house. Which matched the prints on Melissa's wallet and the box it had been found in.

Leah had the feeling there was more that Genna wasn't sharing, but she wasn't about to push. If there was other information Genna thought Leah should have, she'd share it with her. Till then . . .

The hairs on the back of Leah's neck pricked.

Her eyes made a sweep of the church, searching for

someone whose eyes would avert when hers met theirs. But none did. *Your imagination is working overtime*, she chided herself.

Still, from time to time throughout the service, she imagined that she felt eyes watching. She sat back in the pew, her head down but her eyes going over the crowd. The church was packed with townspeople and curiosity seekers. And FBI agents, she reminded herself. Wilcox had mentioned that they'd brought several new agents in for the day, sprinkled them through the crowd. Maybe the eyes she felt had been those newly arrived members of Wilcox's field staff.

Like that man there, in the dark blue suit. He looked like he could be an FBI agent. Or that one, there, in the dark gray . . .

There must be a hundred men in this church, she reminded herself, and I only recognize maybe thirty or forty of them. That leaves a lot of strangers. Best to stick with Ethan and let Wilcox worry about who's here and why.

Others in the church rose, and she followed, a reflex action, her hands resting on the back of the pew in front of her. The prickling at the back of her neck began again, and she glanced up quickly to see a man two rows up on the other side of the aisle turn away. He could be anyone, she told herself. Anyone. One of Wilcox's men. One of Mrs. Calhoun's cousins.

No point in getting too paranoid.

She tucked her arm through Ethan's and, without looking down, he covered her hand with his own, giving her a squeeze, comforting and reassuring her. She breathed easier at his very touch. She held on to his hand, slipping her fingers through his, grateful for his presence in the church and in her life.

Overhead, the organ began to play sonorously, signaling the end of the service. One by one the pews began to empty, the occupants filing slowly toward the back of the church. With Ethan's arm around her, Leah drifted along with the crowd, which, once outside, followed the brick path to the churchyard and the cemetery that spread out over the adjacent hill. The pallbearers carried their burdens from the wide front doors of the church to the freshly dug graves that marked the hillside like open wounds. The congregation clustered in little groups, and Leah watched to see who stood where.

The members of the choir, she realized, stood together, as did the members of Mrs. Calhoun's Friday afternoon card club. The small group holding flowers to the right of the coffins must be the relatives, Leah thought, and those just behind the minister would be the church elders. And so she categorized this group or that, until she realized that there were few who appeared to have come alone. That woman in the black coat standing near the choir. And that one there, by the pharmacist. And that man, there, in the brown coat . . .

Her eyes traveled past him, then back to his face. In that second her eyes connected with his, then widened with recognition. She had seen him before. But where?

Reverend Tillitson was just finishing up his prayer, so Leah quietly touched Ethan's arm to get his attention, but when she looked back, the man in the brown coat was gone. She turned to see which way he had gone, but by then, he had vanished.

"Can you remember where you saw him before?" Agent Wilcox asked her when the service had ended and she had sought him out to tell him about the stranger.

"No. I just can't . . . no." She shook her head.

"Leah, think," Ethan urged her. "Was it here, in Bannock?"

"I don't know," she told him. "And I'm trying to think. I just don't know. It will come back to me. Just like the thing with the photograph."

"What thing with the photograph?" Wilcox asked.

Leah told him about the photo of herself that had stood on the piano.

"I just can't remember if it was there when we were at the cabin last weekend. I have the feeling that it was not. But it's one of those things, there must be twenty photos on the piano. You just don't always look at every one of them. So I don't know if it was there or not. I thought we'd ask permission to stop back out at the cabin to take a look."

"I can save you the trip," Wilcox told her. "We ran fingerprints on every one of those photos, and I can tell you there was no picture of you in a cowboy hat."

"Why would someone have taken a picture of me?" she asked.

"So he'd know what you look like," Ethan said.

"But why?" She turned to him. "Why would he want to know who I am?"

"That's what we're working on," Wilcox assured her. "And as soon as we know, you'll know. But until then, you're going to have to be extremely careful. As a matter of fact, if we could spirit you out of town this minute, I'd be all for it."

"Actually, I thought I'd take Leah home with me until this is over," Ethan suggested.

"Tell me again where 'home' is."

"Northwest of Bangor, Maine."

"What's it near?"

"Not much." Ethan told him about White Bear Springs.

"That could be just the right place, as long as you don't tell anyone you're going." Wilcox nodded agreeably. "And I suggest you leave your car at the motel right where it is. I'll arrange for you to drive something else. If he's watching your room, it's best that he not see you leave."

"That's fine with me." Ethan turned to Leah and asked, "What do you think?"

"Yes. Yes, I'll go with you. Anything to get away from this feeling that someone is watching every move I make. Just let me call Catherine—"

"No one," Wilcox repeated.

"But she's my cousin," Leah said.

"Whose phone could be bugged. We don't know how sophisticated our Mr. Briggs is. It's better that no one knows where you are. We'll certainly contact her and let her know that you're all right, but your whereabouts need to remain secret for the next few days."

They had arrived at Agent Wilcox's black Taurus, and they waited while he unlocked the passenger side door, then reached inside for the tan envelope that lay on the front seat. He removed a fax copy of a photograph and handed it to her.

"Here's a blowup of Briggs's driver's license photograph. Does he look familiar?"

Leah inspected the photo.

"This is him. There's no doubt in my mind."

"Now all we have to do is have you remember where you saw him before."

"It will come back to me," she told him. "It may take a while, but I'll remember."

"And you'll let me know the minute you do. In the meantime, let's head back to the Bannock Inn for lunch. I'll have a car delivered to the back. You can sneak out through the rear and be on your way, hopefully before anyone realizes that you're gone. My guess is that if he's watching you, he's watching your room, expecting you to come back this afternoon. It will take a while for him to realize that you're not coming back, and a while longer before it occurs to him that you've left town. By that time, you should be long gone."

"Do you think he's staying at the motel?" Leah asked.

"It's possible. But if he thinks you saw him—that you knew him—this morning, my guess is that he'll be watching from someplace nearby. With the right pair of field glasses, you can be a half a block away and still have a damned good view of what's going on. And with the motel being right there on Main Street, well, he could be watching from anywhere. My advice is to go on over to the inn with me and several of the others, and just quietly slip away as soon as we can get the car there for you. Then head on up to Maine and keep your head down until we can get our hands on this guy."

Wilcox appeared to think this through for a long moment, then added, "In the meantime, I'll call the closest field office and have someone keep an eye on things up there. And I'll have a car follow you until you get there."

"I hate to upset Ethan's daughter. It might scare her to have the FBI swarming all over the place," Leah thought aloud.

"No danger of that," Wilcox assured her. "For one thing, we don't swarm. You won't even know anyone's there. And for another, we want to keep the focus of this thing down here. I don't want anyone to know that you've left the area until we've caught him."

"Do you think you will?" Leah asked.

"Half the field agents on the East Coast are on their way up here. There's no way he'll be able to slip past all of us." Wilcox lit a cigarette and forced a grin. "And hey, we're the FBI. We always get our man."

And with luck, you'll get this one, Ethan thought. *Hopefully, long before he figures out where Leah is.*

Chapter 18

*W*here was she?

He adjusted the focus of his binoculars for about the tenth time. He'd been watching all day, since he'd left the graveside service after catching her gaze. He'd been tingling all over since meeting her eyes across the gentle rise of the cemetery. Even now, he could still see her face, the one eyebrow raised, as if in question, *Do I know you?*

He chuckled to himself.

She was still probably trying to figure out where she'd seen him. Well, it just goes to show you that people aren't always as observant as they should be. He wondered what that FBI fellow would say if he realized that it had been he, Briggs, who had offered to move down a seat at the counter in the drugstore just the day before. That it had been he, Briggs, who had given Leah his seat.

She hadn't remembered this morning, but oh, soon enough, she'd know him. She'd know him damn well.

"And I'll know you," he said aloud to the picture, "better than any man has ever known you . . ."

With a long finger, he traced the outline of her face on

the photo before him, touching the tip of the finger to her mouth, letting himself dream, just for a minute, what it was going to feel like to have that mouth on him. Wherever and whenever he wanted. He groaned softly, just thinking about it.

A car pulled into the motel lot and he licked his lips in anticipation. Was it her? But no. The sedan merely turned around and drove off. It was frustrating, not knowing what to watch for, since Leah had left the motel that morning and walked the three blocks to the church.

With Ethan Sanger.

He'd known about Ethan. Because of the tapes. He closed his eyes and the memory of the voice on the tapes swelled through him.

Ray. His friend. His only friend. Oh, to hear that voice again! Having the tapes fall into his hands was like receiving a gift from the gods. He was grateful enough to Ethan Sanger that he'd almost considered letting him live.

His spirit, however, wasn't quite that magnanimous.

He tried to imagine what Ethan and Leah had been doing behind the locked door of their motel room. Speculation made him angry, and he cursed aloud, an ugly slur to foul the air of a beautiful late afternoon.

Where was she?

He shifted his weight and tried to think things through.

He'd been close enough to know that she was the one.

And hadn't she been promised to him? To make up for having cheated him?

Leah McDevitt had a lot to make up for. She had kept what rightfully belonged to him, and she would have to pay it back.

And paybacks, as everyone knew, could be a bitch.

Chapter 19

*D*addy, you brought Leah!" Holly called happily from the top step of the front porch.

Leah smiled, touched by the warm and spontaneous welcome.

"We've been so worried about you. All this craziness going on . . ." Tom called from the doorway, paused, then asked, "What exactly is going on?"

"Dad, I told you just about everything that I know when we were on the phone." Ethan stopped to kiss his daughter's cheek, then held the door open for Leah to step inside.

The foyer was chilled, since the heat had been turned down during the daytime hours and no fire had yet been made to chase the cooler air of early evening.

"That someone broke into Leah's cabin, stole the tapes of your conversations with Raymond Lambert out of your car, then went down the road and killed some folks. What the hell is going on? Why would someone be after Leah?"

Leah kneeled down to pet Dieter, who, oblivious to the drama around him, rolled onto his back for a tummy rub.

"We don't know." Leah looked up. "We don't know that someone still is after me. For all we know, all he really wanted was the tapes."

"He wouldn't have had to kill your neighbors for them," Tom said.

"He didn't." Ethan shook his head. "The FBI is pretty much convinced that the Calhouns just happened to be at the wrong place at the wrong time. They think the killer may have gone to Leah's cabin to break in to leave her sister's wallet, but then saw the Calhouns, realized they had a key, and just took advantage of the opportunity to have a little sport with them."

"That's sick, Ethan," his father snapped.

"It's not my game, Dad," Ethan said wearily.

Holly's eyes shifted from her father to her grandfather, then back again.

"Holly, your dad told me you made some great spice cookies last week. I sure could use a snack," Leah said, sensing that perhaps Holly had already heard more than enough, and that the conversation was about to turn in a direction that Ethan might rather his daughter not overhear.

"The spice wafers are gone, but I made peanut butter cookies yesterday morning," Holly told her.

"My all-time favorite." Leah smiled and reached a hand to Holly, who took it and pulled Leah to a standing position. "Come on, Dieter. Maybe we can find a treat for you, too."

"Why do they think he left the wallet?" Tom asked when the kitchen door had closed.

"It's all speculation right now, but the FBI thinks that he wanted her to know that her sister's killer was still out there. And that he could get close to her if he wanted to. That he was just playing with her for a while."

"Do you think he went there for another reason?" Tom could not bring himself to voice the possibilities.

"I honestly don't know. What would he have done had she been there alone?" Ethan shook his head. "I don't even want to consider the options, Dad."

"Do they know who he is?"

"Billy Briggs, an unemployed truck driver from some small town in western Pennsylvania that just happens to be about a four-hour drive from where Melissa McDevitt disappeared. He'd worked for a chain of convenience stores for years. His travels took him from Ohio through Pennsylvania to New York State, and south through West Virginia and western Maryland. The FBI is contacting all the local police departments in all those areas to track any unsolved murders or disappearances over the past ten to fifteen years."

"Ten to fifteen years!" Tom exclaimed. "And they never caught him?"

"Caught him?" Ethan's eyebrows raised. "They'd never even heard of him. He has no police record. His fingerprints weren't even on record anywhere. The FBI had to lift prints from his house and compare them to prints taken from the crime scenes in Connecticut."

"He must be very smart," Tom observed quietly.

"Or very lucky," Ethan told him. "We're hoping his luck runs out before he figures out where Leah is."

"You really think she's in danger, son?"

"I think she will be, before too long, if they don't catch him soon."

"Maybe we ought to spend a little time cleaning up some of those hunting rifles." Tom nodded to the gun cupboard that hung on the far wall. "You never know when you might need one."

"Not a bad idea. Though Leah has made friends with

an FBI agent named Genna Snow, who is a friend of John Mancini's. You may remember him from Lambert's trial."

"I do. Big man, tall, broad through the shoulders. Dark hair—"

"Yes. Anyway, Mancini had left the agency for a while, though Leah tells me he's on his way back. Apparently, he's kept up with this case through Genna Snow. He handled the Lambert investigation and may end up working on this one as well. Genna mentioned to Leah last night that he may be coming up to spend a little time here. Just to keep an eye on things from the inside."

"I'd feel better with a platoon of agents looking after her."

"I don't know that there won't be, especially if Briggs can't be located elsewhere. But Mancini will be staying at the lodge, and he'll be very visible."

"Think that'll be enough to scare off this fellow?"

Ethan considered, then shook his head and said, "I doubt it, Dad. Maybe the most we can hope for is that they manage to find him before he figures out where Leah is."

"How likely is that?"

"I honestly don't know. They just don't know enough about Briggs to have a read on him."

"Billy Briggs," Tom repeated softly. "Sounds more like the name for one of those Hollywood pretty boys, doesn't it?" Without waiting for Ethan's response he asked, "Why did you bring her here, Ethan?"

"Because she's safer here than she'd be anyplace else. Because I need to keep her safe. I'd kill him with my bare hands if I had to, Dad."

"It's like that, then, between you and Leah—"

"Yes," Ethan told his father. "It's like that."

Tom mulled over this news for a few minutes.

"I guess the time is right to get on with your life."

"It's only right because of her, Dad. Because *she's* right."

"Well, son, here's hoping that the authorities find this Billy Briggs and put this whole thing to rest, that he doesn't get any closer to her than he already has. How soon will this friend of a friend be here?"

"I'm not certain. Maybe the beginning of next week."

"I hope it's soon enough."

"Yes," Ethan said, looking out the window at the sun setting over the lake. "Here's hoping . . ."

In spite of the tragedy of the past week, Leah could not help but feel secure and safe, for this moment, anyway, seated as she was in a snug chair in a cozy room warmed by a lovely fire, Ethan less than three feet away. For just this time, she could almost pretend that there was no danger anywhere, no reason to feel anything but sheltered in such tranquil surroundings.

She watched Ethan from the corner of one eye and her heart swelled within her. How had it happened that this wonderful man had come into her life so quickly and taken her heart so completely? Had there ever been such a man in her life, a man so caring and selfless, a man who would sacrifice his own peace of mind on her behalf and walk through fire for her? *Had* walked through fire for her, she told herself, recalling the hours they'd spent in the cabin listening to Lambert's tapes. And hadn't Ethan spirited her away from the danger that threatened her, bringing her to this place where, even in the midst of all that was going on, the threat seemed so remote.

Leah concentrated on the job at hand, that of braiding

Holly's hair, only half-listening to Tom and Ethan talk about hunting rifles. Remingtons and Colts. Brownings and Winchesters. Distance and velocity. Bear and moose and elk.

When she was a little girl, Leah's favorite "let's pretend" always found her cast as a princess locked in a tower. She'd lean out the window like Rapunzel and wait for her hero to come and rescue her. He'd ride a white horse and wear yellow silk breeches like the picture in her fairy tale book. Leah almost laughed out loud at the thought of Ethan—who favored jeans and flannel shirts—in yellow silk knee-high breeches. In her daydreams, her hero had to find some creative way to save her because, even in her dreams, she couldn't imagine hair long enough to reach the ground like Rapunzel's had been. So sometimes he'd bring a rope to swing, lasso-style, onto the parapet so she could climb down. Sometimes he'd bring a ladder. Sometimes a dragon would come and he'd slay it with his bow and arrow. But he always saved her . . .

"Leah, I said, will you be here on Saturday for the big dance? Dad's going to chaperone. You could come with us." Holly had turned around and tugged on Leah's hands to get her attention.

"Oh. If I'm here, yes, I would love to come to your dance." Leah nodded, pulling herself back to the present.

"Great! I can't wait for you to meet Chrissie." Holly grinned and headed for the nearest phone.

"Where did you go?" Ethan teased. "You looked like you were a million miles away for a minute."

Leah grinned. "I was thinking about archery."

"Archery?"

"Yes. I took it one semester in college."

"Were you any good?"

"Yes, actually, I was."

"We get a lot of bow hunters up here in the fall," Tom commented.

"What do you hunt up here?" Leah asked.

"Depends on the time of the year."

"I could never shoot anything for real," Leah shook her head, "but I used to enjoy target practice."

"If a big, snarling bear—or something worse—was coming after you, you'd better be able to make the pull and let that arrow fly," Ethan told her.

"Well, I haven't picked up a bow in years," Leah shrugged, "so I don't know that I could."

"We have bows here," Tom said, looking across Leah to Ethan. "Maybe not a bad idea to let her practice some. Brush up on her skills. Never know when she'll need to bring down a bear. Or something worse."

The air in the room seemed to chill, and Leah looked from Tom to Ethan.

"A gun would be more effective," Ethan said.

"No." Leah shook her head. "Uh-uh."

"Why not?"

"Because guns are so . . . so . . . *lethal*."

"So's an arrow, properly aimed," Ethan noted.

"That's different. If I had to shoot someone with an arrow, I could shoot them in the leg."

Ethan and Tom looked at each other from across the room.

Ethan sat down on the spot Holly had vacated.

"Leah, if someone is trying to kill you, you don't shoot them in the leg."

"It would give me time to try to get away."

"So he could shoot you in the back."

"Ethan, I don't think I could aim a gun at anyone and pull the trigger."

"Could you aim at a target?"

"I don't know."

"Maybe we should find out."

"Maybe so," she said softly.

"Maybe tomorrow," Ethan replied.

"Tomorrow might be good," she agreed. "But only the bow and arrow."

Ethan wanted to protest that a bow and arrow would be useless unless she had plenty of time to load the bow and line up a damned good shot. But getting her used to the idea of defending herself was the first step. If she was only willing to consider a bow for now, that was okay. Perhaps once she became comfortable with the idea, she'd become more amenable to learning how to use a handgun. Walk before you run, he reminded himself.

The next morning, with Ethan's help, Leah managed to find a bow with an appropriate pull for her strength in the bow cabinet in the study, and surprised herself by remembering more of the sport than she had given herself credit for. By the end of the practice session she was able to hit the target, though not necessarily the bull's-eye in the center.

"That will come," Ethan promised. "You have a good eye, and good upper-body strength. By the end of the week, we'll have you ready for competition."

"That's overly optimistic, but I appreciate the sentiment. It's nice to know you have faith in me. I have to admit that I've surprised even myself. Of course, no victory is complete without sacrifice," she told him. "I seem to have awakened a lot of sleeping muscles."

Ethan's hands reached for her and caressed the back of her neck. "Like these?"

"Yes." She nodded.

"And these?" His hands moved down her back.

"Definitely those."

"Any others?"

"Lots."

"And where might they be?" He nuzzled the side of her face.

"Everywhere. Too many to even talk about now. But if you come to my room later, I could show you. And maybe you could give me a massage."

"I might have to do that," he told her, his voice growing husky. "A full-body massage might be in order."

"I may turn in early tonight," she said, holding his eyes with hers and touching his face with the fingers of one hand.

"Yes. Early would be good." Ethan kissed her. "Early would be very, very good."

As things turned out, early wasn't possible. Holly had to try on her dress for the dance and get Leah's opinion of the length and nail polish color and shoes before going to bed. Then at ten o'clock, Genna called, to let them know that John Mancini had called while on his way to Miami, where he'd gone to attend a family funeral. He figured he would be a few more days, but then he'd be on his way to White Bear Springs. If it turned out to be necessary, that is. There had been rumored sightings of Briggs in New York. That, combined with the knowledge that Briggs would have no reason to look for Leah elsewhere, went a long way toward putting everyone's mind at ease as far as Leah's safety was concerned.

Leah had spoken with Genna first before handing the phone over to Ethan, and taking the opportunity to say good night, pleaded fatigue after all the archery practice she'd had that afternoon.

Shortly thereafter, Ethan excused himself as well, and followed the well-worn carpet to the very end of the hall and the room overlooking the lake and the lumber trail that rose behind it.

"I just thought I'd stop in to see if you're still interested in that massage," he said, stepping into her room and turning the key in the lock behind him.

"I thought you'd never ask," she said, and held her arms open to him.

"Want to show me where it hurts?"

"Well, here," she said, guiding his hands. "Oh, and here."

"Here?"

"Oh, yes, there. Definitely there . . ."

"Hmmmm. This could take longer than I thought. This could take all night."

"Then you'd better get started," she drew him down with her to rest against the pillows, "because by my calculations, the sun will rise in, oh, roughly seven hours . . ."

Ethan rose with the sun, tucking the blanket under Leah's chin and tiptoeing toward the door.

"Not so fast, buddy," Leah stage-whispered from beneath three layers of blankets. "Where are you sneaking off to in the middle of the night?"

"It's hardly the middle of the night. It's almost six in the morning." Ethan came back to the bed and leaned over to kiss her forehead. "And I thought I'd get back to my own room before Holly wakes up. I don't think it would set a good example for her to find me here, if she decides to come in and see if you're awake yet."

"I agree, that would be awkward." Leah yawned. "And she did come in yesterday morning." She snuggled back into the warmth of flannel sheets and quilts. "Maybe I'll just catch a few more winks . . ."

Ethan smiled and watched her close her eyes and sink

back into blissful sleep. She looked so peaceful and so contented, and Ethan knew in that moment that he wanted nothing as much as he wanted to see her just so, every morning for the rest of his life.

He tucked the blankets around her as she drifted back off. First, he reminded himself, there would be dragons to be slain. Maybe today. Maybe tomorrow.

It made him uneasy to know that Billy Briggs had not been seen since the Calhouns' funeral. There had been rumors, but to Ethan's mind, rumors didn't count for fact, and that meant that, theoretically, Briggs could be anywhere. The chances of him having followed them to White Bear Springs were remote. More likely than not, he was in fact still in New York, where he could watch Leah's home and her office. Catherine had been warned, of course. The FBI had already sent agents there to talk with her, so that she would be on her guard, and both the brownstone and the office building were being watched day and night, as was Catherine. Genna had told Ethan that she was planning to stop in to see Leah's cousin later in the day, just to see for herself that all was well.

But until Briggs was caught, Ethan had no intention of letting his guard down.

Later, after she was rested and had her first cup of Tom's good coffee, Ethan would again suggest that the situation called for lessons in self-defense that went beyond a bow and arrow. While it was good that Leah was willing to defend herself, if the need arose, she could be dead by the time she pulled an arrow from the quiver.

But for now, Ethan thought as he quietly closed the bedroom door behind him, he'd let her sleep in peace. Later would be soon enough to deal with the idea that perhaps one day she might be called upon to shoot at something livelier than a bull's-eye painted on a sheet of newspaper and nailed to the side of a tree. And with something she could aim and fire a little more quickly than a bow and arrow.

"What exactly did Genna tell you?" Leah asked Ethan over breakfast.

"Probably the same thing she told you. Just that they still don't know for sure where Briggs is, though they're fairly certain he's still in New York and that that's where he'd look for you, if in fact he's looking for you. He has no reason to suspect you'd go anyplace but to your home."

"But if he knows about you, wouldn't it occur to him sooner or later that I might be with you?" she pointed out.

What would they do if Billy Briggs arrived unannounced at the camp? The thought of him getting his hands on Leah or on Holly made Ethan weak at the knees.

"I guess that's possible. But right now, they believe he's hunkered down in New York. Genna said they planted a story with the news media that that's where you've gone."

"Oh, my God. Catherine." Leah blanched. "I have to warn Catherine. What if he goes to the house? If Catherine's there . . ."

With shaking hands, Leah reached for the phone. Ethan stopped her, taking her hands in his.

"Leah, your cousin is fine. There are agents watching the house, watching the office building. Catherine will be under constant surveillance until this is over. It's all under control."

"It is?"

Ethan handed Leah the phone.

"Go ahead. Call Catherine and set your mind at ease. Just don't tell her where you are."

"Why not?" Leah frowned. "You think she's going to tell someone?"

"No, of course not. But we don't know that Briggs hasn't somehow managed to tap into the phone line. We don't know enough about him to know what he's capable of."

"But Catherine will want to know."

"All she needs to know for now is that you are safe."

"It will make me feel better, just to hear Catherine's voice. I guess you're right. It doesn't really matter where I am, as long as I am safe. As long as she is safe."

The phone in the brownstone was picked up on the third ring.

"Cat?"

"Oh, Leah," Catherine exclaimed. "I've been frantic, sweetie, wondering where you are." She paused for a second, then asked, "Where are you?"

"I'm not supposed to tell anyone that. But you know about . . . about—" Leah stammered.

"Everything, yes. That horrible man . . . oh, sweetie, I was so worried about you. Of course, they've been assuring me that you're all right, but still, it isn't quite the same as hearing your voice. And why can't you tell me where you are?"

"They're afraid that maybe Briggs has found a way to tap into the phone line."

"I see. Well, then, give me a hint. You're not in Connecticut, we already know that."

"I'm with a friend," Leah said. "I don't think I can say anything else."

"All right, then, we'll let it go for now. And I do feel so

much better, now that I've heard from you. I've been so worried, Leah."

"Well, it's my turn to worry about you. They think he—Briggs, that is—might be in New York."

"Sweetie, it would take an army to get around the number of FBI agents they have around here," Catherine told her.

"They said they were watching the house. And the office."

"They are. I doubt there are more than half a dozen agents on the East Coast who are not watching this house." Catherine paused, then asked, "There are agents there with you, too, aren't there?"

"I guess, though I haven't seen anyone. I do know that someone will be here in a few days."

"Just one?"

"I don't really know."

"Do you have any idea how long you'll be there? When you'll be home?"

"None. Though I would expect to be here at least through next week. If for no other reason, than because Holly has a dance to go to on Saturday night—"

"Holly?" Catherine said softly. "Oh, of course. She's the daughter—"

"I shouldn't have said that," Leah muttered once she realized that she'd given away her location.

"Don't worry, sweetie, who am I going to tell?" Catherine reassured her. "But at least now I know you're in good hands. That someone is taking good care of you."

"The best."

"That's lovely, Leah. I do feel so much better now."

"Make sure that the FBI calls me if anything happens, anything at all. Although you could probably figure out how to call me, if you needed to."

"You keep in touch, too, sweetie. And thank you for calling. You'll never know how you've set my mind at ease."

Ethan came into the room behind her as she hung up the phone.

"Do you feel better now?"

"I do. I knew she'd be worried, all that's happened and not knowing where I am—"

"You didn't tell her, did you?"

"Well, I didn't name it, but I'm afraid that I let Holly's name slip out—"

"Leah, no one is supposed to know where you are."

"This is *Catherine* we're talking about. *Catherine*, Ethan. What if she needed to get in touch with me?"

"She could go through the FBI."

"But—"

"No buts, Leah. The FBI said no one should know where you are."

"Catherine is all the family I have in this world," Leah protested.

"Then let's keep her safe by not giving her information that someone else might feel is worth hurting her to get."

"No one can get to Catherine. She said that there are agents all over the place."

"But why take a chance?"

"She loves me, Ethan. She was worried about me. I had to let her know that I was in good hands."

"I understand. Let's just not make any other little slips, okay? After all, we don't know who's tapping into whose phone, do we?" Ethan held her to him for a long moment.

"No, I suppose we don't. But there isn't anyone else I'd call, anyway. Catherine is really the only person I'm that close to that I'd want them to know." Leah held him close, then leaned back and looked up into his face and asked, "Hey, isn't it just about time for my archery practice?"

"Well, I was thinking about that this morning. I really think I'd feel better if you had a few lessons with a handgun."

"Uh-uh. No way. I told you. No guns." Leah shook her head. "I hate guns. There's no reason why I have to learn to shoot a gun."

"Under normal circumstances, I'd agree with you, since I suspect you're not inclined to go hunting. But these aren't normal circumstances."

"Ethan, I don't—"

"I don't want a time to come when you wish you had learned when you had the opportunity. Chances are you'll never need to use it. But why take that chance, Leah? It won't hurt to know what to do . . . if you needed to . . ."

She stared at Ethan for a long time, then nodded slowly and went off to the back hall to get her jacket as the phone began to ring and Holly hopped to answer it. Maybe it wouldn't hurt her to know what to do with a gun. How to load it. How to aim. How to shoot . . .

After all, Ethan was right. These weren't ordinary times.

Chapter 20

*W*here was she?

How could she have vanished?

Rage tore at his throat and he roared over the sound of the traffic rushing past, like some great wounded beast.

Where was she?

He smashed his hand down on the side of the pickup truck he'd stolen. That first night, when he'd realized she was gone, he'd just walked right out of town, taking to the fields, and was two towns away by morning. He stole a car from a driveway and later left it in front of a car wash in Hartford, where he'd stolen the pickup he was driving now. He'd switched license plates with a truck parked in a parking lot in Wethersfield and, after removing the women's lacrosse sticker from the back bumper, drove toward I-95 while he contemplated his next move.

The fury inside him had been building for three days, since he had realized that somehow, Leah had been spirited away. The news on the television in the dim bar where he'd stopped the night before said that Leah was under guard at her home in New York. Well, that was okay. He'd gotten close to her once before in New York. He could do it again.

But he had to wait. He'd promised.

He growled in frustration.

Then came the calming thought that he only had to wait for Leah. There were others . . .

The voices had been still these past few days, but then again, he reminded himself, he had been totally focused on something else. Perhaps if he relaxed and cleared his head, they'd speak to him once again.

Smiling, he got back into the pickup and headed toward the nearest exit. It was already night. He would pick a spot, then watch, and wait for the voices—those other, more familiar voices—to guide him. And then, once they'd led him, once he'd found her—once he got close enough to make sure that she was the one—he would figure out a way to make her his own.

He always did.

Chapter 21

$\mathcal{T}$he first thing you need to know," Ethan said, "is how to find out if the gun is loaded. Because the first thing you will do every time you pick it up is check to see if it is. Every time. Without fail."

Ethan stood before Leah, the .38 caliber Colt in his hands. It looked like a benign enough instrument, Leah thought, if one didn't consider what it was capable of doing.

"Ethan, I really think this is unnecessary. You heard what Genna just told us. They know that Briggs is in Connecticut, they found that body, they lifted his prints from that poor woman's car. The FBI has already started tracking him."

"Yes, well, they don't have him yet. Now, while you're checking, before you know for a certainty that the chamber is empty, you point the muzzle facing the ground and you push the cylinder latch, which is here."

Ethan demonstrated, pressing the latch so that the cylinder slid out to the left side.

"It is, as you can see, empty. Now," he said, closing it back up again, "you do it. Show me how to open the cylinder."

Ethan handed the Colt to her, muzzle down, handle first, then folded his arms to watch as she did exactly as he had done.

"Fine. Don't forget. Every time. First thing, got it?"

"Got it." Leah nodded.

"Okay, then, let's show you how to hold it." Ethan stood to her left side. "Use both hands, to keep it steady."

Leah gripped the handle with a hand on each side.

"Which finger do I put on the trigger?" she asked.

"Neither of them, right now." He straightened out her arms. "Elbows straight."

"Like you see on TV."

"Right."

"Okay, so I'm holding the gun out in front of me with both hands. What next?"

"Step up with your left foot for balance, since you're right handed. Now line the gun up with the center of your body. The more centered the gun is, the better your chances of hitting your target."

"I think this is as centered as it's going to get. These suckers are heavier than they look, you know?"

"Now you'll learn to sight. There are two sights on the barrel. The front sight, which is here," he pointed, "and the back sight, which is this rectangular thing right here."

"So you focus the target through the sight."

"Actually, you don't focus on the target. You focus on the front sight."

"Then how do you hit the target?" She frowned.

"You point the barrel at the target, which you line up with the front sight. Here, look here." Ethan took the gun from her hands. "Hold out your left hand."

She did.

"Hold up your index finger. Now, make a peace sign with your right hand and hold that up in front of your nose so that you can see through the middle of the V. Hold your left hand so that your extended middle finger appears in the center of the V."

"I have to close one eye to see it."

"That's right. And that's exactly how you line up your sights. Your right hand is the back sight, and the left hand is the front. Once you line that front sight up on your target, that's when you start thinking about firing." Ethan handed the gun back to her. "You asked me when you put your finger on the trigger? Not until the front sight is lined up with where the bullet is going to go. That's when you pull the trigger. Now, sight on the trunk of that maple tree."

"Okay." Leah was squinting, trying to line up the front sight. She lowered the gun and said, "This isn't as easy as it looks."

"You'll get used to it. Try it again. Try closing the other eye."

"That's better."

"Okay, lower the gun to the ground." Ethan walked to the tree trunk and drew a circle on the trunk with a piece of colored chalk. He walked back to stand beside her and said, "Now aim at the circle."

"When do I get to shoot?"

"When I put some bullets in it. You think you're ready to try that?"

Leah nodded. "I might as well. Isn't that the point?"

"The point is for you to know how to defend yourself. You never load the gun unless you intend to fire it. You never point the gun at anything that isn't a target, and then, only when you intend to hit it. If you have picked up this gun, and you have loaded it, assume that you will fire it. Understand?"

"Yes. I understand."

"Give me the gun, and I'll load a bullet into the cylinder. Now, this is a six cylinder. That means it has room for six bullets." He slid a bullet into the chamber and closed it, then looked up and smiled at her as he handed the loaded gun to her. "We'll go bullet by bullet."

"I'm still not so sure I like this."

"You don't have to like it," he told her. "You just have to be able to use it. Now, sight on that circle again. When you think you have it lined up, lock on to that front sight."

Leah raised the gun as she'd been shown and stared at the sight for a long minute.

"I have it," she said at last. "At least, I think I have it."

"Squeeze the trigger smoothly, don't jerk it. You can take your time, squeeze slowly. When the gun goes off—"

"Oh!" Leah exclaimed as the bullet seemed to explode from the muzzle, and the gun seemed to explode in her hands.

"That's great! Good!" Ethan told her.

"It scared me near to death!" Leah looked stunned.

"You did exactly right," he told her. "What I started to say, was that when the gun goes off, it should surprise you, because if you're locked on your sight, you're concentrating on your sight, not the trigger."

"It surprised me, all right." Leah looked annoyed. "I had no idea it would be that loud."

"Ready to try it again?"

"Did I hit the target?"

"We'll check in a minute."

Ethan took the gun from her hands and loaded another bullet into the cylinder, then handed it back to her.

Leah shifted her feet for balance and raised the gun, focused, concentrated, locked in, and fired.

"Oh!" she cried again.

"Good." Ethan grinned. "Now let's go take a look at that tree."

"When do you stop being surprised?" Leah grumbled as they walked to the tree.

"Never," he told her, touching the rough bark with searching fingers. "Looks like you might have nicked it once. Want to try a full round?"

Leah hesitated, then nodded. Last night she'd shuddered to think about what could happen to Holly, to her, if Billy Briggs came calling. She prayed she'd never have to use a weapon such as the Colt, but having come this far, she might as well become as skilled as she could. She might never in her life have to pick up a gun and use it, but if the day ever came that she needed to, she might as well know how to hit her target.

"Yes. Let's do it. Let me load it, this time, though." Leah pulled the cylinder latch and held her hand out. "Let's do all six this time . . ."

"Are you sure this dress looks okay?" Holly bit her bottom lip and turned worried eyes in Leah's direction.

"I think it's great. Perfect," Leah told her honestly. "Now, let's finish getting your things packed so that we're not late getting you to Chrissie's."

"It's so cool that you are coming to the dance with Dad," Holly said as she wiggled out of the short blue dress and held it up for Leah to hang on the padded hanger.

"It's so cool that you asked me." Leah grinned.

If someone had told Leah even two weeks ago that she'd be chaperoning a school dance, she'd have laughed at the notion. Now, here she was, getting ready to do exactly that. Whistling softly on her way to her room to put on the black dress she'd bought for the Calhouns' funeral, the only dress she had with her, she realized she was looking forward to the evening. She and Ethan would dress at the lodge, but Holly would be dropped off at her friend Chrissie's house to dress, lest her skirt wrinkle on the hour's drive from the lodge. They would all meet up at the dance, which Ethan had agreed to chaperone.

I guess if my dress wrinkles, it's of no consequence, Leah grinned wryly as she slipped her own dress over her head, *since it apparently doesn't matter how I look. I wonder if this means I've been relegated to the rank of "old fogey."*

Actually, Leah was grateful for some time alone with Ethan away from the lodge. They'd spent so much of the week on a tightrope that it would be a relief to get away, if only for a few hours, and have dinner at a restaurant, just the two of them, while Holly dressed at Chrissie's along with the two other girls who had been invited to the predance soiree where they would admire one another's dresses and experiment with one another's makeup. Leah remembered the days when she had done exactly that and knew that Holly would have as much fun before the dance as she would once she arrived at the school gymnasium.

It would be lovely, Leah thought as she put on her favorite gold earrings and brushed out her long dark hair, *to sit and sip a glass of wine in a quiet place, as we did in Bannock before the nightmare had begun. Hard to believe that had only been weeks ago.*

Everything had happened so quickly, so intensely, since that day in February when she arrived home from Turkey and found that first note of Lambert's. Her whole life had changed, in so many ways and on so many different levels. It truly was the very best of times, the very worst of times.

"Leah?" Ethan tapped lightly on her door.

"Come on in." Leah stood and brushed off her skirt.

"You look beautiful." Ethan took her hands and bent to kiss them, then laughed. "Even down to the callus on your trigger finger."

"Excuse me, but I earned that callus, having spent the last several days aiming and firing, aiming and firing."

"Well, you should feel confident in knowing that if you ever had to use it—"

"I would feel more confident if I knew I would never have to, Ethan." She looked up at him solemnly. "That's what would make me feel truly confident."

"I know that, sweetheart." Ethan tucked a dark curl behind her left ear. "And if there was anything I could do to guarantee that, God knows I'd do it. Unfortunately, we're not at that point yet, so the best thing I can do for you is to make certain that you can protect yourself, in the event that for whatever reason I'm not there to protect you."

A dark wash of emotion clouded his eyes.

"Did Libby know how to shoot a gun?" Leah asked softly.

"No," he told her. "And I never insisted that she learn. It never occurred to her that she'd ever be called upon to save herself. I wish I'd encouraged her to do something, karate, at the very least. It still bothers me that she had no self-defense training at all."

"I see," Leah said, nodding, and she did.

Ethan had insisted that Leah learn to save herself, in case she had to. In case he wasn't there to save her. He hadn't insisted that Libby learn how to protect herself, neither had he been there where she'd needed him. He obviously wasn't going to run the risk of having history repeat itself.

"Do you think you could pull the trigger if the target was a man instead of a tree?"

"I don't know, Ethan. I'd like to think I could, if the target was Briggs. I just don't know for sure, though, and hope I don't have to find out."

"Daddy, Leah, we're late," Holly called from the bottom of the steps.

"We're coming," Ethan called over his shoulder, then leaned down to kiss the corner of Leah's mouth. "John Mancini called about twenty minutes ago. He apologized for the delay, but thinks he'll be here sometime tomorrow."

"Didn't he talk to Genna? Doesn't he know about the woman in Connecticut? That the FBI believes that Briggs is somewhere between New York and Connecticut?"

"Yes, well, maybe John isn't as confident that they're that close to Briggs. Or maybe he just wants a few days in the Maine woods. Either way, he'll be here tomorrow."

Leah stepped to the door and Ethan followed, snapping off the overhead light.

"You know that Mancini's back with FBI, don't you?" Ethan told her.

"That should make Genna happy."

"You think?" He raised both eyebrows.

"I think—" Leah nodded.

"You are so slow, Dad. Come on. I'm going to miss pizza at Chrissie's." Holly stood at the bottom of the steps, impatiently tapping one foot, her jacket already on, her dress in a plastic bag held over one arm.

"Then you'd have to go to dinner with us," Ethan told her as he and Leah came down the steps.

Holly rolled her eyes, and Ethan laughed.

"Kiss your grandfather goodnight," Ethan reminded her.

"I already did."

"Dad," Ethan called into the den, "we should be back by midnight or so."

"Have fun. I'll probably still be sittin' here, reading this mystery that I got from my book club. It's a corker," Tom called back.

Ethan paused on the front porch after they had stepped outside, then whistled for Dieter, who'd been out since his dinner an hour ago.

"In you go, boy," he said to the dog. "Go stay with Dad."

And for the first time in as long as he could remember, Ethan locked the front door behind him.

"You look as if you're a million miles away." Ethan leaned closer across the table in the small restaurant—the only restaurant—on the main street of Arlenville.

"I guess I am." Leah nodded. "I was thinking about Melissa. About how all this started with Melissa."

She toyed with her fork.

"Do you think I'll ever find out what really happened?" she asked him, her eyes clouding with tears. "Do you think I'll ever find her?"

"If they catch Briggs alive, it's possible. Then again, there's always the chance that he could be killed while they're trying to apprehend him."

"Then I'll never know the truth," she murmured.

Ethan took her hands in his.

"For your sake, I hope that before this is over, you at least find out what happened to your sister. I would hate for you to have gone through all this and have nothing to show for it."

"Oh, but I do have something to show for it." Her eyes brightened and she played with his fingers. "As terrible as this has been, I don't regret what's happened."

"It's not over yet, Leah," Ethan reminded her. "It can't be over, for any of us, as long as Briggs is still out there."

"I know that. But if Raymond Lambert hadn't written that letter to me, I'd have never come looking for you. I'd have never found you. I'd still be looking . . ." She hesitated. She'd never been good at this type of thing.

"Looking for what?" he whispered.

She took a deep breath and said, "There's something I feel I should tell you."

"What's that?"

"I'm afraid I'm dangerously close to falling in love with you."

"And why would that be such a bad thing?"

"Well, it's not necessarily a bad thing—"

"You said you were afraid."

"Figure of speech," she told him.

"I see. But the use of the word 'dangerously'—"

"Also a figure of speech," she said, nodding.

"And the part about falling in love?"

"That you can take literally."

He kissed her fingertips, each and every one, then kissed the palm of each hand.

"I cannot tell you what it means to me, to hear you say those words." Ethan held her hands tightly in his own. "I never thought that anyone would. I never thought it would matter much, either way. I figured I'd be spending the rest of my life just sort of drifting along, watching Holly grow, by myself. Loving someone hasn't been much of a priority these past few years. It's actually come as somewhat of a surprise." He cleared his throat. "A very beautiful, very wonderful surprise. I thought that part of me had curled up and died a long time ago."

"You mean when Libby died."

"I mean when I became swallowed up in the aftermath. You know, Libby's been dead for ten years, and it's taken almost all that time to get beyond it. She'd been missing for a full three years before Lambert was caught and confessed. Then it was another few years until the trial was over and he contacted me about writing his book. It seemed that every time things started to settle down, something got it all stirred up again. I never thought I'd be able to put that behind me. I never thought I'd want to."

"Do you? Want to?"

"Oh, I think I already have. It wasn't a conscious decision. I never sat back and thought, Well, I think today I'll fall in love with Leah. It just happened."

"Sort of sneaked up on you when you weren't looking, did it?"

"Yes."

"Aren't you going to tell me when? A woman likes to know these things, you know."

"I think it was the first day I met you."

"Really?"

Ethan nodded.

"I never would have had you pegged as the 'love at first sight' kind of guy."

"Neither would I."

"Is that why you agreed to help me?"

"I'd say it probably had something to do with it. But I think I would have helped you anyway. I don't know that I could have turned anyone away, given those same circumstances. You'd already gone through so much. Having gone through so much of the same, I knew exactly how it felt to wonder." A slow smile tugged at the corners of his mouth. "At least, that's what I told myself. The fact that I couldn't get you out of my mind probably had nothing whatsoever to do with it."

"I'm glad you did. And for the record, I think I felt the same way."

"Instant attraction?"

Leah nodded. "That, and instant recognition."

"Of—?"

"Of another soul that had known sorrow."

Leah freed one hand and poured wine into their glasses. Handing a glass to Ethan, she said, "Let's drink a toast."

"What shall we drink to?"

"To the life that begins where the nightmare ends."

"Gladly," he said, touching the lip of his glass to hers. "Gladly . . ."

Some things never change, Leah mused as she watched from the sidelines as the young girls in short dresses danced with each other in clusters, while the boys stood on the opposite side of the room trying their best not to watch. Or at the very least—and even worse—not to be *caught* watching. Overhead, a silver ball spun, and here and there throughout the room, blue and green streamers anchored blue and green balloons to the back of the chairs. The music was obnoxious and loud, certainly nothing she could dance to, though the girls on the dance floor didn't seem to be having a problem with it.

"Feeling old?" Ethan whispered in her ear, and she laughed out loud.

"I never thought I'd see the day arrive when I'd admit that the most popular of popular music wasn't music at all. Just like my father used to say about the music I listened to as a kid."

"Ah, but that's part of the eternal generation gap. I somehow suspect it's meant to be so. I recall feeling a bit smug that my father didn't know who Genesis was. I detect the same trace of smugness when I catch Holly watching MTV and I make some comment about the videos. It's the old *But you're not supposed to understand what I like* syndrome. Each generation likes to set itself apart. One way to do that is through its music."

"I guess that's a thing that parents need to know."

"Among a million other things." Ethan tilted his head, and narrowed his eyes. "Wait. What is that I hear?"

". . . for all you chaperones," the DJ was announcing, "here's a little something for you to dance to. Enjoy it folks, I'm only playing it once."

Ethan took Leah's hand and led her to the dance floor that was filling with parents eager to do something besides stand around. He pulled her close, and she wrapped her arms around his neck and rested her head next to his. His lips moved near her ear, singing along softly.

Something in the way she moves . . .

Leah sighed her contentment. The days ahead might be as trying as the days passed—and could well be worse—but there was something life affirming about dancing with your man to a favorite old love song at a high school dance in a gymnasium decorated with crepe paper flowers and balloons and tiny white lights. She smiled to herself as he sung the words in her ear, singing for only her to hear.

Somewhere out there, in the world beyond the high school walls, an evil man roamed. No one knew where, no one knew what he wanted or to what lengths he would go to get it. But inside the gym, the music was too loud, the punch too sweet, the air too close. And the love of her life sung a sweet song in her ear.

For Leah, at that moment, it was enough.

Chapter 22

*L*eah turned over beneath the down comforter and opened her eyes. It was past dawn, the light outside the window was glowing from either side of the shade that had been pulled all the way down before they'd gone to bed the night before. She wished that Ethan was still there with her, to love her into this new day. Leah stretched her arms over her head, then sat up.

The room wasn't as chilled this morning as it had been over the past week. Maybe spring was coming to Maine, after all.

She all but laughed out loud remembering having jumped nearly out of her skin their first night back, when she'd heard the deep cracking sound from somewhere beyond the trees. Ethan assured her that no natural disaster was about to occur, nor were they under siege. It was just the ice cracking in the lake, he'd told her. The surest sign of spring in their neck of the woods.

Later in the day they'd walked down to the lake, and she'd seen for herself that the ice had begun to melt and to move. By the end of the week, he'd promised, most of it would be gone, and at least on this side of the lake, where no dense line of trees shaded the ice from the warming sun as on the far side, he had been right.

Ethan had taken the opportunity to inspect the docks for repairs that might be necessary, while Leah explored the boathouse that stood just off the lake. Made of logs, it was one of the original buildings, and it housed the rowboats and canoes used by the campers in the summer. Holly had come down later and stood on the end of the dock and said that by Thursday, she'd be able to take a rowboat out for what she called her first float of the year. Leah had watched her maneuver the small craft as far as she could go before she reached the area where the ice still stood firm. When she'd rowed back to the dock, Holly had announced that by the following week there'd be little ice left to impede her progress to the other side of the lake. The ice was thinner than she'd expected, she told Leah, and it would melt quickly if the temperatures stayed in the forties as they'd been that week.

And the temperatures had remained surprisingly benign. If winter defined life in the Maine woods, then the first days of spring had to be more welcome here than in other, more temperate parts of the country. The ground was beginning its thaw, and the days were growing longer, slowly but certainly, though the trees had yet to show any signs of budding. The streams had started to swell, a sure sign that the snow in the hills above and beyond the camp had started to melt. Leah had noticed the sure green spikes around the front porch of the lodge, the promise of daffodils to come in May. Yesterday, she'd noticed that the snow on the hillside overlooking the lake had melted and that hundreds of snowdrops and crocuses had emerged as if overnight. She'd asked Tom if he'd planted them, and he'd shaken his head.

"That was the wife that planted them there," Tom had

told her. "That hill is the first place at camp where the snow melts completely, every year. The hill on the opposite side, that's the last. The wife wanted to be able to watch the new season come to camp each year, so she planted the earliest blooming plants there, every year adding more. Seems they spread themselves."

"It's a beautiful sight," Leah had said.

"More beautiful, still, once you'd spent a whole winter or two up here," Tom chuckled. "That bit of color on the landscape is more welcome than you could imagine."

Leah tugged on the bottom of the shade to raise it, opening to view the lake and the hillside on the other side. From here, the colorful crocuses looked like confetti sprinkled over the hill. Leah raised the other shades to welcome the new season, then pulled the comforter down to straighten the sheets. She'd just finished making the bed when Holly knocked on the door.

"Come in," Leah told her.

"Oh, I'm glad you're up." Holly, in a red, white, and blue plaid robe, peeked into the room before entering it. "It's such a gorgeous day, the weather report said it might go up to fifty today."

"A true heat wave," Leah laughed.

"It is," Holly told her. "And it makes me feel like doing things."

"Like what?"

"Like hiking and playing with my goats and going for a row on the lake."

"You've been doing all those things all week," Leah reminded her.

"Yes, but today I won't have to wear as many clothes, because it won't be so cold. It's a nice change, to put away the parka and be able to go outside in only a sweater."

"Well, fifty is still chilly."

"Not so much when the sun is out." Holly looked out the window. "This room has one of my favorite views. From here you can see both sides of the lake and the hillside and the old logging road, though that still has a lot of snow left to melt off. The trees keep it from melting early. Don't you love the hill over there? I always thought it was magical, the way the flowers seem to come from nowhere. When I was little, I used to pretend that mischievous fairies had danced in the moonlight the night before, and the flowers had sprung up in all the places where their little feet had touched the earth."

Leah laughed. "Mischievous fairies dancing on the hillside in the moonlight, eh? Sounds like you have the makings of a fine children's story."

Holly draped herself across Leah's bed and, lying on her stomach, seemed to be considering this.

"It would make a fun story, wouldn't it? I think I'll work on that. I like to make up stories. I do it all the time." She colored slightly at the admission she'd obviously not intended to make. "It helps pass the time, sometimes."

"I guess it can get a little lonely here at times for a young girl."

Holly nodded, then added, "But it's been more fun with you here."

She traced the pattern on a square of the quilt that lay across the bottom of Leah's bed.

"Do you think you'll stay for a while?" Holly asked, without looking up.

"A little while."

"How long is a little while?"

"It all depends."

"On whether or not they catch the killer?" Holly's finger trailed from one square to the next. "I hope they don't catch him for a long time. Then you'll stay longer."

"Well, as much as I'd like to stay, I do have a job, back in New York. I'm going to have to get back to it soon." Leah sat down behind Holly and tucked a few loose strands of hair that had come loose back into the braid. "And remember that this is a very dangerous man. The longer it takes for him to be captured, the greater the risk that he'll hurt someone. Maybe a lot of someones."

"You mean kill them."

"Yes."

"I wouldn't want anyone to get killed. I just want you to stay." Holly turned around to face Leah. "Didn't you have fun at the dance last night?"

"Yes, I did."

"My dad did, too. I could tell. I never saw him dance before last night. He's different now that you're here. He doesn't seem so . . . so . . . ." Holly searched for a word. "So somber."

She paused and, her face brightening, said, "Isn't that a great word? *Somber?* It was one of my vocabulary words last week. Grampa gives me a list of words to learn every week and I have to use them during the week. *Somber* is one of the last words I had to use. It just occurred to me that it was a good word to describe my dad. Before you came, anyway. He laughs a lot more now than he did before. He likes you a lot. I can tell. And you like him, too, don't you?"

Leah smiled. "Yes. I do like your dad a lot, too. And I like your granddad, and I like you. Very much."

"Then you should think about staying for a long time," Holly said, smiling back. "It's nicer here with you than it is without you."

"Thank you, Holly. That's a lovely thing to say. I actually feel . . . well, a little less somber myself, now that I've been here for a week or so."

"There you go," Holly repeated one of Tom's favorite phrases. "That proves that you should stay."

"Well, I'll stay for a while. A few more days, I would suspect." Leah stood up. "Now, how about if you and I go downstairs and make breakfast? I heard about that maple syrup that you and your dad made a few months ago, and it seems to me that we should try it out with some waffles or French toast or something equally good."

"Oh, yum! I love French toast!"

"Why don't you go on down and get the ingredients out for me, and I'll be down in a few minutes and we'll get started."

"We can surprise Dad and Grampa." Holly slid her feet back into her slippers, which she'd left on the floor when she'd climbed onto Leah's bed. "I'll run down right now and put the coffee on."

"Good idea."

Leah closed the door behind Holly and leaned on it.

She did feel less somber here at White Bear Springs. She also laughed more and found herself humming at odd times.

She pulled her nightgown over her head and began to get dressed. The day had begun in so lovely a fashion that she had to remind herself that there was a killer out there somewhere, maybe wondering where she was, even as she wondered about him.

A sobering thought, if not a somber one.

Maybe if I was in New York or Connecticut, I'd be more frightened, she rationalized as she dressed. *That's where they say Briggs is. Regardless, I can't ignore the other things that are happening in my life because of Briggs.*

Leah went to the window and looked out, knowing she was in no hurry to leave White Bear Springs. In spite of the threat, she felt safe here in a way she'd never felt safe before. Here, there was sanctuary, there was strength. Here, there was a man who loved her, a man who had made a place in her life that no man had occupied before. A man who would fight for her life if he had to.

If Briggs came for her here, she thought she could survive. Because she would not be alone. Because Ethan would be there to protect her. And because she knew how to defend herself if she had to.

Mischievous fairies dancing in the moonlight, she mused as she looked out the window onto a tranquil morning. With luck, that will be the only mischief we'll have to worry about.

Leah finished dressing and whistled as she closed the door behind her, leaving the dark thoughts behind.

It was easy enough to believe that all could be well, while making breakfast for people you care about, there in the Maine woods, wrapped in the peace of an early spring morning. Easy enough to believe it could always be so.

"Do you realize that there's a hockey game on television this afternoon?" Ethan said as he and Holly finished cleaning up the breakfast dishes.

"Oh, be still my heart," Leah murmured.

"Who's playing?" Tom asked.

"The Bruins and the Flyers."

"That should be a great game. Both teams have been tough this year." Tom nodded. "Might be worth watchin'."

"That's what I thought," Ethan agreed. "I thought I'd maybe finish fixing that dock, then call it an early day so I could watch the game."

"Sounds like a good plan to me, son. I'll be needin' to spend a little time looking over the résumés I received from would-be counselors for the new season. I can't believe that we'll be opening in another six weeks. And Mrs. Beaumont has already sent me her suggested menus and her shopping list."

"Who's Mrs. Beaumont?" Leah asked.

"She's the lady who comes here to cook for camp. She has the hots for Grampa."

"Holly . . ." Tom grumbled.

"Well, she does, Grampa. 'Oh, Tom, were you able to try one of my potpies? No? Lucky for you I saved one,'" Holly mimicked.

"That'll be enough, miss." Tom tried to appear stern but laughed in spite of himself. "Mrs. Beaumont is a fine lady and a very fine cook. We're lucky to have her here at White Bear Springs every year."

"Oh, she is a great cook. And she does make great potpies, Leah," Holly assured her. "And wild blueberry buckle, and blackberry pies. Of course, the kids have to pick the berries, because the bugs get too fierce for the grown-ups to go outside," she added dramatically.

"A budding thespian." Tom nodded in Holly's direction.

"I think I will let my goats out into their pen today," Holly announced as she dried the last plate.

"I think we should check those side rails first," Ethan told her. "You don't want to take the chance of them getting out and getting lost in the woods."

"No, I would not." Holly shook her head, then looked at Leah and said with a shiver, "The bears are usually waking up around this time."

"I'll take a look at the pen before I do anything else today," Ethan promised, "and then you can let the goats out for a while this afternoon."

"And don't forget you have a history test tomorrow," Tom reminded Holly. "I heard it was going to be a tough one."

Holly rolled her eyes.

"Grampa! Why do I have to have a test on a Monday morning?"

"Because you have more time to study over the weekend. And because if you're going to go to high school next year down in Arlenville, you'd better get used to spending Sunday afternoons doing something other than floating around the lake, daydreaming."

"I'm not daydreaming. I'm being *contemplative*," Holly told him smugly, then grinned at Leah. "Also a vocabulary word for the week."

"And a good word it is," Tom laughed. "Leah, thank you for taking over the breakfast chores today. That was a fine surprise, first thing in the morning."

"My pleasure." Leah smiled.

"I'm going to run up and change and then we can check the goat pen, okay, Dad?" Holly asked as she folded her dish towel and hung it over the oven door to dry.

"Okay." Ethan nodded.

"And I'm going to go look over those resumes," Tom said as he followed Holly through the swinging door into the hallway.

"Well, I guess that leaves just the two of us," Leah mused.

"I guess it does." Ethan took her in his arms and nuzzled the side of her face. "How shall we spend the few minutes we've been allotted?"

Leah took his face in her hands and brought it down to hers, reaching her lips to his and kissing him soundly, tasting both the sweetness of the maple syrup and the last trace of strong coffee.

"Breakfast was great, by the way. That was very thoughtful of you."

"Well, I figured you needed some nourishment to rebuild your strength after being up most of the night," she said with a grin. "And since there's a good chance you'll be up half the night again tonight—"

"There's a very good chance of that." Ethan pulled her closer, savoring the sense of normalcy that had pervaded the morning.

"Good. I'll hold you to that."

"Now, tell me what you're going to do today."

"Maybe I'll give you and Holly a hand with the goat pen."

"It's not that much of a project."

"Then maybe I'll be a bit of a contemplative myself and take one of the rowboats out on the lake." The thought appealed to her. Just an hour or so of floating along, as she had watched Holly do the day before, might be just the thing.

"Just don't go too close to the shore on the west side there," Ethan cautioned. "You don't want to run into a momma moose with a baby. Mommas tend to be protective."

"I've never seen a moose."

"You will if you spend enough time up here," Ethan told her. "Henry David Thoreau once described moose as 'great frightened rabbits, with their long ears and half-inquisitive, half frightened looks.' Sooner or later, you're likely to cross paths with one."

And later that day, she had.

Leah had watched Ethan and Holly repair a small patch of fence around the goat pen, then had watched Holly frolic with her goats. Later, she'd watched the opening few minutes of the hockey game with Ethan and Tom, then, spying Holly out on the lake in a rowboat, decided to walk down to the lake and sit on the dock in the sun. Trading her parka—too heavy for so warm a day—for an old red sweatshirt of Ethan's, Leah walked the well-worn path from the lodge to the boathouse.

The sun had melted almost all of the snow on this side of the lake, making the ground oozy and slick. Leah was glad she'd opted for heavy rubber hiking boots that kept her from landing butt first in the mud. As she approached the lake, a clatter overhead caught her attention, and she stopped to watch as a dozen or so large crows swooped down angrily on a nest at the top of a nearby tree. A large dark head poked out of the nest, and Leah raised her hand to shield her eyes from the sun to watch.

"It's a great horned owl," Holly called from the lake where she sat in the rowboat, oars resting on her knees. "The crows know it will raid their nests and steal their young, so they don't want it moving into their neighborhood."

"Doesn't it already live close by?" Leah called back.

"Yes, but probably back in the woods someplace. That nest that it's in, the ospreys nested there last year. The owl would like to take up residence closer to its prey. Which is just about anything it can get ahold of." Holly rowed a little closer to the shore. "Want to come out with me? I can row over to the dock and pick you up."

"No, that's okay. I think I'll just sit out there," Leah pointed to the end of the dock, "and just watch the lake for a while."

Holly nodded, understanding. She liked to just sit and watch the lake sometimes, too.

Leah walked to the end of the short dock and sat

down, dangling her legs over the side. The lake was a rich, true blue in color, brought to life by the dazzling sun that reflected off it in sparkling gold rays. She leaned back against one of the pilings and stretched her legs out before her and let the sun sparkle on her, too. Closing her eyes, she relaxed, letting the warmth seep through her, welcoming its tranquilizing power. A splashing sound close by startled her, and she sat up and leaned over the side of the dock. Below, in the water, fish darted through the grass on the lake's bottom. A little farther out from the dock, a fish broke the plane of the water and danced upon it for a second or two before disappearing beneath the surface again. Leah sat, content to watch and to listen, until Holly drifted toward her.

"I'm going to have to go put my goats back into the barn," Holly was saying. "And then I have to study for my history test. Do you want to take the boat out on the lake for a while?"

"Sure," Leah responded without hesitation. "That would be fun."

Holly rowed closer and tossed a line to Leah, who caught it and held it taut while Holly got out of the boat and pulled herself up to the dock. Then she held on to the rope while Leah dropped down into the boat.

"When you come back, and you're by yourself, just tie the rope onto one of the pilings. There's a wooden ladder on the other side, too, if you'd rather use that."

"Thanks." Leah caught the rope that Holly tossed to her. "I probably won't be out here very long."

"There's no hurry. Dad and Grampa will be watching the hockey game for a while longer, and I'll be studying most of the afternoon. Take your time. It's real nice out there today. Not windy or anything."

Leah held the oars and stroked smoothly, if not

exactly gliding, then at the very least making her way from the dock toward the middle of the lake in a fairly straight line. Once there, she did as Holly had done, drew the oars in to rest on her knees, and sat back and let the sun soak into her winter-weary skin. It was lovely to be alone, to be adrift on a placid lake in the middle of nowhere and welcome spring under open skies, to let your thoughts drift as aimlessly as the clouds overhead. If the lake—indeed the entire camp—was this peaceful in April, how beautiful, how wonderful it must be in the summer, when the trees had filled out and greened up, when the windowboxes and flower beds up at the lodge would spill over with color. And in autumn, when those same leaves would turn red and orange and yellow to ring the lake with fire.

So hard to believe that only two months ago, she'd never even heard of White Bear Springs or Ethan Sanger, that in so short a time the camp had come to feel like home, that Ethan had become the most important person in her life.

Then again, she reminded herself, two months ago, she hadn't heard of Billy Briggs, either. And right now he was a pretty important person in her life, too.

A *whoosh* from off to one side drew Leah out of her reverie, and she found that she'd not only drifted to one side of the lake, but that the *whoosh* was the sound of the head of a large moose emerging from the lake with a mouthful of vegetation it had pulled loose from the lake floor.

"Ohmigod," Leah whispered, eyes wide, and hearing her, the moose stopped chewing and looked directly at her.

His nostrils flared, and he snorted at her from less than twelve feet away.

That was all it took for Leah to grab onto the oars and

row like crazy toward deeper waters. She glanced back to shore and, seeing that the great beast had immediately dismissed her, began to laugh. What had Thoreau called moose? Great frightened rabbits?

We know who the real frightened rabbit is here, don't we? Leah grinned as she sat at a safe distance and watched the moose as it continued to chomp away, never bothering to look up at her again. It was a surprisingly tall animal, maybe seven feet at the shoulder, and had a handsome rack of antlers that bobbed as it moved along the shoreline. And it seemed docile enough, at least now that she was far enough away from his dining table.

Leah laughed out loud again, this time laughing at herself. What a sight she must have made, scurrying to grab the oars, floundering around in the water, trying to get out of Dodge as quickly as possible, while the moose had decided that she was worthy of absolutely no notice. She couldn't wait to get back to camp and tell Ethan she'd had her first moose sighting.

Rowing evenly back to the dock, she opted for the side where Holly had told her the steps could be found. Maneuvering the small craft, she was pleased to see how neatly she came alongside the wooden pilings. She stood carefully in the boat, sliding the rope through one of the metal rings attached to the side of the dock, to keep the boat steady until she could secure it.

The last things Leah would recall would be climbing the ladder.

Leaning over to tie the boat to the ring.

Hearing the hushed and hurried footsteps behind her.

Trying to rise.

And the colors.

The red pain that shot through the back of her head. The black darkness that swallowed her whole.

Chapter 23

*I*t had been cool in the shadow of the boat-house, and he had a perfect view of the lake. He'd leaned against the rough-hewn logs and lit a cigarette, took only a few long, sharp drags before realizing that the smell of the smoke might drift out across the lake and alert her to his presence.

That was the trouble with these scenic, pristine places, he had grumbled to himself. A guy couldn't have a smoke without worrying about giving himself away.

She had been halfway across the lake when he'd gotten to the boathouse, and he'd watched her drift farther and farther away. He'd wished she'd get on with it and just bring the damned boat back. They were wasting time. He had started to fret over having let the girl get away. By now, wouldn't she have told someone that he was here? Would someone soon be on their way down to take her away from him?

I'd like to see someone try, he snorted, even as he had looked over his shoulder to see if someone might be headed down to the lake.

But the path had been clear all the way up to the

lodge. And he had known he could take the girl later. After he'd taken care of Ethan. Ethan, who thought he was so smart, bringing her here. Thinking he could keep her safe from him.

He had shaken his head, barely able to understand their stupidity.

They just didn't understand who they were dealing with.

Doing that woman in Connecticut had turned out to be a stroke of genius. Where before the FBI had scattered their search, they now had narrowed it considerably as they "closed in on him."

Hearing that on last night's news had made him laugh out loud.

And while all the ladies in Connecticut were padlocking their doors, and every law enforcement agency in southern New England launched a massive manhunt, he'd slipped right through their fingers and headed north.

Damn, I am good, he had told himself, wishing that Ray could have been there to appreciate the beauty of it.

The thought of Ray having been done in by some penny-ante goon in the prison infirmary never failed to infuriate him. He missed Ray, missed his letters, his counsel. No one in his life had ever understood him the way Ray had. There was nothing he hadn't been able to tell Ray, and Ray had always understood.

Even about Momma.

And Dolores.

Both of them, taunting and humiliating him until he had snapped.

He squeezed his eyes shut to push them back into the far recesses of his mind. If he could squeeze them out, he would win and he would not have to hear them and the terrible things that came out of their mean mouths.

Not Momma, who had made her living on her back and who was not above selling her little boy if the price was right.

Come here, Billy. Mr. Byers has something for you . . .

And if he didn't run real fast, he'd find out sure enough just what it was that Mr. Byers had.

Not Dolores, who had humiliated him, taken another man into his bed and laughed in his face, told everyone in West Newton what a failure he was as a man.

Maybe you oughta watch sometime, Billy. Maybe you oughta see how a real man does it.

Beads of sweat had begun to form on his forehead then, and he wiped them away with the sleeve of his shirt and tried not to listen. Tried not to remember how their brown eyes had laughed at him.

He should have taken care of Dolores right then and there. He shouldn't have run away like he had, shaking and bawling like the baby she'd said he was. By the time he'd gotten himself pulled together, she was gone. He'd been looking for her ever since. He knew she was out there, but she was so clever. She had so many disguises.

Just like Momma. Sometimes in a yellow wig, sometimes in a black one, Momma never seemed to hit the same corner wearing the same getup.

Gotta keep 'em guessing, Billy-boy. Gotta make 'em think there's something new.

Who knew how many disguises Dolores might have?

But the eyes—her brown eyes—had always given her away.

He pushed it all away, back into those little holes inside where he kept them, kept their voices and their faces and the rage they inspired. Separate, of course, from those other voices. The ones that guided him and told him what to do.

He had heard the splash of oars as Leah rowed rapidly toward the shore as if she was being pursued. Crouching in the shadows, he had watched her row up to the dock. For a minute he had been afraid that she'd get out of the boat facing him, and then what would he do, the element of surprise being so vital here.

Turn around. Turn the boat around, damn it, he'd silently commanded.

And she had.

He had sighed, knowing it was a sign. A sign from Ray that he was there, watching him, giving him strength, letting him know that all would go as planned.

As soon as the boat turned, he'd started stealthily toward the dock, the canoe paddle he'd taken from the boathouse in his hands.

Wasn't it perfect, the way she had played right into his hands? Hoisting herself onto the dock and leaning over with her back to him? It had been so easy. He had known that it would be. She had been promised to him.

And now she was his.

$\mathcal{D}$ad." Holly stood in the doorway of the den where her father and grandfather were busy yelling at the television.

"Wait a minute—where's the call for spearing?" Ethan was yelling at the referee in the black-and-white striped shirt who skated across the television screen. "That was spearing, for cripe's sake!"

"Dad!" Holly tapped him on the shoulder. "You have a telephone call."

"Who'd call in the middle of a hockey game?" he muttered.

"Genna Snow."

"Oh." Ethan rose quickly, the game forgotten, and walked briskly into the hallway and picked up the receiver.

"This is Ethan," he said.

"Genna Snow here. I was actually looking for Leah. I'm hoping she's still there."

"Yes. I think she's upstairs," Ethan told her, not really sure where Leah had disappeared to. "Would you like me to run up and get her?"

"No, I can tell you what's going on and you can relay the message, if you would."

"Dad . . ." Holly whispered.

"Not now, Hol. Go ahead, Genna. What's going on?"

"Well, we have a much more complete picture of Briggs. The agents searching his house found boxes filled with letters from Raymond Lambert. Briggs apparently saved them all. They go back several years. We've been able to piece together a portrait of Briggs that is anything but pretty, I'm afraid. I thought that you folks should know what we're dealing with here."

"Go on."

"For starters—and remember, we're having to infer some of this because all we have are Lambert's responses to what we're assuming Briggs told him. Briggs was a real fan of Lambert's. In the first letter, Lambert thanks Briggs for contacting him and sharing with him. It looks like Briggs wrote to Lambert with details of a murder he'd committed, details that he wanted to share with Lambert."

"How could he do that? Wouldn't the prison guards who read the incoming mail have swooped down on something like that?"

"The letters merely substituted words. All of Lambert's letters comment on the details of the 'dates' with 'girlfriends' that Briggs shared with him. 'Dates' were obviously killings, 'girlfriends' were the victims. He had different euphemisms to describe the various things he did to them, but I'll spare you the specifics. But he did refer to some of his 'dates' by first name and the letters are dated. We've already started to contact local police departments across his old driving route to see if any of the names and dates match up with missing women from these areas. We're betting they will. Several bits of information that are significant to the present situation have surfaced, however." Genna cleared her throat. "Lambert makes reference to something that Briggs had told him about a 'date' he'd had with a young woman outside of Meadville, Pennsylvania, in late May of nineteen ninety-three. Something about her made Briggs extremely angry, because Lambert says he knows how it feels to be deprived of his game, that once, he too had 'taken his date home' earlier than he'd planned because something had happened to ruin the mood."

"Oh, man," Ethan muttered.

"And it seems our man Briggs has a fondness for brown-eyed women."

"What?"

"Briggs only went after women with brown eyes. One of Lambert's letters made a reference to it."

"Leah told me that when she met with Lambert, he asked her about her sister's eyes. Apparently, when Briggs first saw Melissa, he thought she had brown eyes. Because of the contact lenses."

"The fatal choice Lambert spoke of to Leah."

"Why? Why brown eyes?"

"Let me share with you what we learned from the neighbors." Genna paused, then began, as if reading from notes, "Briggs was married very briefly some years ago. His wife, Dolores, was openly carrying on with another man while Briggs was on the road. Briggs caught them together in the house. The wife bragged at the local bar about how she had taunted him, about how she offered to let him watch, so he could learn how a real man made love to a woman. She and her boyfriend left town pretty quickly after that. At least, that's what Briggs told everyone, that they'd run off to New Mexico together."

"You think he might have killed them?" Ethan asked. "And could one event like that be enough to cause someone to murder over and over again?"

"I spoke with one of our profilers. He thinks that the wife could possibly have been Briggs's first victim, but the act of killing her did not satisfy his rage. So he has to keep killing her over and over. Mind you, this is speculation. Sometimes we never learn what sets these guys off, Ethan. Most of the time, in fact, we never do find out what goes on inside their heads. It's more likely that something happened to him when he was very young, at the hands of a woman—probably his mother, because that's who it usually is—that unbalanced him. Somehow, through the years, he'd managed to keep his emotions in check. The incident with his wife may have just unleashed something that had been lurking beneath the surface for a long time. The only way we'll ever really know for certain is if we catch him, and if he chooses to talk to us. Many of them don't. But one thing we do know for a fact is that his wife had brown eyes."

"How do you know that?"

"They found an old driver's license of hers when they searched the house."

"Didn't anyone question that these two people just disappeared?"

"All the neighbors said that they really thought that they'd run away together. Neither the wife nor the boyfriend were from the town originally, so I guess no one knew either of them well enough to care to track them down. And maybe they did leave the state, Ethan. Maybe he's killing these other women as substitutes, because he couldn't get to her—he didn't kill her then and he can't find her now. We are, however, trying to trace them in New Mexico. If they're there, we're hoping to find them."

There was silence on the line.

"I'm afraid there's more," Genna said softly. "After Lambert saw Leah on *Newsline*, he wrote to Briggs, telling him that he had thought of a way that he, Lambert, could help Briggs get his hands on something that he needed. That Briggs wouldn't have to worry about his job anymore—he'd apparently been having problems with a new supervisor—and that Briggs should telephone him upon receipt of the letter and they'd talk about it."

Ethan could hear papers shuffling on the other end of the line.

"Lambert later told Briggs all about Leah's visit to the prison. How pretty she was. How she had the prettiest big brown eyes he'd ever seen—"

"That son of a bitch," Ethan cursed.

"And that he'd found the perfect way to make Leah pay for that 'date that he'd had to cut short.' Lambert told Briggs that a friend had come to see him, someone who could help him, that he'd given this friend both Briggs's post-office box number and his phone number. That Briggs would be hearing from this friend soon."

"Friend? What friend? You mean there are *two* of them?"

"I don't know, Ethan. All he said was that Briggs would be hearing from the friend. That was the last letter. The same one in which Lambert tells Briggs that he was expecting the first half of what had been promised to him and that he'd already arranged to have it sent to the post-office box."

"Has anyone spoken to Lambert's lawyer about this?"

"Yes. We've learned that Lambert notified the attorney that he'd be receiving money via wire and instructed him to send the full amount, less the attorney's handling fee, to Briggs's post office box in cash in a padded envelope."

"Where did the attorney think the money was coming from?"

"He said that Lambert told him that it was part of his grandmother's estate, and he was her only living relative so it was coming to him. He said he was passing it on to an old friend who had fallen on hard times. All obviously lies."

"Leah canceled the transfer after Lambert's death—"

"That's right. And chances are Briggs is none too happy about being cheated out of his windfall. Ethan, I think maybe it's time to bring Leah in to a safe house. I've already arranged it. John Mancini is on his way up there to pick her up."

"You know, all along, I really thought she'd be safer here than she'd be anyplace else. Now I'm not so sure. I'll go upstairs and get her right away and we'll . . ." Ethan said. Noticing Holly's hand signals, he put his hand over the receiver and said, "What, Holly? This is an important call and—"

"Dad, Leah's not upstairs."

"She's not? Where is she?"

"I've been trying to tell you. She took a rowboat out onto the lake."

"How long ago?"

"Maybe an hour or so."

"Leah's out boating, Genna. I'll run down and find her. What time do you think Mancini will get here?"

"Probably within the next half hour," Genna said, at the same time that Holly said, "He's already here."

"Who is already here?" Ethan asked.

"The FBI agent. I saw him down by the boathouse. When I was coming back to the barn to put the goats in. There was a man going down toward the lake, and I asked him if he was with the FBI and he said he was." Holly sipped at her can of soda. "And he said not to worry. He'd take care of everything. And then he asked if I knew where Leah was."

"What did you tell him?" Ethan stood on legs that suddenly had no feeling.

"I told him that Leah was down on the lake, that she'd gone row—" Holly stopped, her father's face having gone ashen. "Dad, what's the matter?"

"What did he look like?"

"He was real tall and thin and had a beard. A short beard. Kinda blond. Why?"

"That doesn't sound like John Mancini," Ethan said. "Genna, did you hear—?"

"Yes, and you're right. That wasn't John. I'll get him on his car phone and tell him to get there as quickly as he can. In the meantime—"

"In the meantime, I'm going for Leah." Ethan hung up the phone, pushing past Holly as he fled to the stairwell.

Taking the steps two at a time, Ethan rushed down the hall to Leah's room. He pushed open the door and went to the windows, leaning forward until his forehead was resting on the glass. From where he stood, he could see the lake—and the lone rowboat adrift from the mooring that had not been secured, the oar floating several feet from the bow. His frantic eyes scanned the stark landscape, searching for a spot of red.

And then he found it, halfway up the old logging road on the opposite side of the lake, moving slowly up the hill. The red sweatshirt Leah had borrowed from him earlier in the day. Ethan ran to his room for his binoculars, then back to Leah's window and trained them on the red speck. With shaking hands, he adjusted the focus and cursed his frustration, his anger, his despair.

Billy Briggs had Leah and, like some evil beast of prey, was dragging her to his lair, the white pickup truck that sat at the top of the hill. It was hardly noticeable against the last vestiges of snow that had yet to melt.

Ethan ran back down the steps and into the den, grabbing ammunition and the Colt from the gun cabinet.

"You and Dieter stay inside," Ethan said as he brushed past his daughter. "Help Grampa lock all the doors and the windows. Dad, call the state police. And no one goes out, hear me? And no one gets in until I come back. I don't care if he says he's from the FBI or the state police. Until you see my face—or John Mancini's, Dad, you remember what he looks like?—you don't open the door for anyone."

Ethan ran from the front of the house, down the path toward the clearing where he'd parked the Jeep the night before. He hopped in and started the engine. He would approach the old logging road by driving straight up the hill on this side, then make his way to the other by going through the woods on foot. With luck, he'd get there before Briggs reached his pickup truck.

The Jeep slipped and slid up the side of the hill where no vehicle had gone in months. There was no real road here, and the surface was slick with mud. Ethan was unaware that he was sweating until it rolled from his face in large droplets that he brushed away with the back of his hand.

"*Shit!*" he exclaimed when he'd gotten three-quarters of the way from the crest of the hill.

A fallen tree blocked his path. There was nothing he could do but to run the rest of the way. Ethan jumped out of the car and, leaving the door open, ran for the trees that separated one side of the hill from the other. The woods were dense and filled with fallen branches that he had to dodge or jump over. Here were vestiges of the last winter storms and twice, in his haste, he slipped on the icy remains. By the time he reached the old logging road, he was out of breath, and almost, he thought as he crouched behind a large tree, almost out of time.

But not quite.

Briggs was ten feet away from the white pickup truck, carrying Leah over his shoulder like a sack of potatoes. Ethan leaned against the tree and slid the .38 from his pocket. He opened the cylinder latch and dropped the bullets in, one by one, until all six chambers had been filled. He'd have to wait until Briggs put Leah down before he could take a shot. Ethan snapped the cylinder shut and quietly made his way closer, slipping from behind one tree to the next, until he was almost parallel to the pickup. There he crouched, and he waited.

Briggs was dragging Leah now, her heels making soft furrows in the snow, her form lifeless as a ragdoll. Rivers of fear shot through Ethan with devastating force as the thought occurred to him for the first time that Leah might already be dead. He stood next to the tree, raised the .38, and locked his sight on Billy Briggs.

The minute Briggs laid Leah on the ground, Ethan squeezed the trigger. He stood to watch as Briggs staggered, then fell in a heap next to his truck.

The crows exploded from the trees overhead as the bullet blasted forth and Ethan began to run. He set the .38 on the ground as he picked Leah up cautiously, looking to see if she had been hurt, if there was a sign of blood.

None but that which was oozing from the front of Billy Briggs's shirt.

Ethan sought and found her pulse, and thanked God that he'd gotten to her before Briggs had a chance to do anything other than render her unconscious. He ripped the tape from her mouth and began to untie her hands.

"Leah! Leah!" Ethan called her name, over and over. "Leah, can you hear me, sweetheart?"

"Ummmmm," escaped through her lips.

"Leah, can you hear me?"

"Yes." Her head lolled to one side.

"Are you all right?" Ethan asked anxiously, his heart in his mouth.

"I think so." She tried to sit up. "I'm so glad to see you. Both of you."

"Both of who?"

"Both of you. I think I'm seeing double." She blinked, then looked behind him. She raised her hand to the back of her head, then flinched. "Ouch!"

Ethan tilted her head forward and gently parted the hair at the back of her head.

"You're going to have quite a lump back there. Let's get you down to the lodge and get some ice on your head. Can you stand?"

"With a little help," she told him, and he helped her up from the ground.

Once on her feet, she peered around him and said, "That's Briggs—"

"Yes, sweetheart, I believe it is."

"He crept up on me while I was tying up the boat. That's the last thing I remember. I couldn't wait to get back to the lodge to tell you that I'd seen a moose. I rowed over to the dock and was tying up the rowboat, and then I was hit from behind."

"Leah, you'll never know how scared I was," Ethan told her as he helped her to her feet. "I couldn't even think about what he might do to you. All I could think of was getting here in time."

"And you did," she said simply. "You saved me, and God only knows how many other women after me that he might have . . ."

The force came from nowhere, hitting Ethan square in

the back and sending him propelling forward into the remnants of snow. A shocked Leah was thrown to the side as Briggs attacked with a fallen branch that he used as a spear.

Ethan staggered to his knees, shaking his head to clear it from the blow, then struggled to stand, circling slightly to buy precious seconds. When Briggs attacked the second time, Ethan was ready for him, wrestling him to the ground and pinning him there with the branch until Briggs, summoning up all his strength, pushed the branch and Ethan off and over to one side. They wrestled and they punched and they rolled in the snow and in the mud, the blood dripping from Briggs's shoulder marking their passage across the hillside.

Leah scrambled in the snow, searching for the Colt. She had seen it somewhere, somewhere around the truck where Ethan had placed it when he picked her up. Where . . . where . . . ? She circled the area where they'd stood and caught the glint of sunlight off the barrel, there, right next to the back tire. With desperate hands, she grabbed it, raised it, sighted it, but could not get a clean shot.

The two men were rolling down the side of the hill, almost indistinguishable in their frenzied pas de deux. Leah moved to her right, trying to position herself so that the sun would be at her back, raised the gun again, and waited for her shot. And as she waited, the thought occurred to her that, if she hit her target, she could lose her last chance of ever finding out where her sister's body had lain, forgotten, all these years.

Briggs pushed Ethan back with a kick to the chest, then raised the tree branch over his head.

Never raise the gun unless you intend to use it.

Never aim unless you intend to pull the trigger.

Lock on to the sight, then squeeze smoothly . . .

"Oh!" she exclaimed, the blast startling her, some voice inside reminding her that she'd done it right if she was surprised that the gun had gone off.

She watched the branch drop from Briggs's hands, watched Briggs himself drop into the dirty snow. Leah held the gun out in front of her and walked to within five feet of where he lay.

"I shot him," she said as if very surprised. "Is he dead?"

Ethan raised himself onto his knees and, completely out of breath, managed to reach the fallen Briggs and checked for a pulse.

"Yes. He's dead." Ethan looked up at her.

Wide-eyed, Leah looked down and said, "Ethan, I killed him."

"Yes. Yes, you did." Ethan pulled himself up and took the gun from her hands.

"Good," she said. "Good."

And then she began to cry.

Ethan was still holding her, rocking her silently, when John Mancini appeared at the crest of the hill. Walking slowly toward them, he stopped at the motionless body and looked at Ethan and observed, "You got him."

"She did," Ethan said softly.

Mancini knelt beside the body and patted the pockets of the dead man's jacket. From an inside pocket, he withdrew a cell phone. Standing, he hit the last number dialed button and stared at the number that flashed on the small digital readout. He held the number up for Ethan to see.

"Do you recognize this number?" Mancini asked.

Ethan stared at the phone, then nodded.

"Yes," he told the agent, holding Leah just a little tighter, wondering how they would tell her. "Yes, I know the number."

 $\mathscr{T}$ he brownstone was dark when Leah arrived, the lights on the timers not having come on just yet. She snapped on the lamp that sat on a small marble table just inside the front door and paused as she did so. She had never liked that table. Catherine had purchased it years ago at a sale at Sotheby's of the contents of some famous person's home. Leah couldn't remember just who the famous person was, though she had known at the time. It certainly didn't matter now.

The red light was blinking furiously on the answering machine as she passed by, and she paused to listen to the messages, all for Catherine. When the last finished playing out, she continued on her way, her jaw set, her eyes dull with pain.

Leah walked to the kitchen through the dining room, where Uncle Harry's china stood so proudly in the handsome antique cupboard at one end of the room. The Wedgwood had belonged to Leah's grandmother. The Waterford crystal had been purchased by Uncle Harry on a trip to Ireland the year after Leah's Aunt Anna—Catherine's mother—had died. Uncle Harry had taken Catherine along and let her pick out the crystal pattern she liked the best. Catherine said she'd chosen this one—Powerscourt was the name of the pattern—because she liked the big crystal ball at the base of the cup part of the glass.

It was all Leah could do to keep from throwing a chair through the glass doors.

On into the kitchen, as if passing through a foreign land of furniture and artwork she no longer recognized, plants that had been nurtured by someone else's hand. She turned on the big overhead light and went straight to the stove, not bothering to look around, and put the water on for tea. Catherine, a creature of habit, should be walking through the door within minutes. Leah unlocked the back door, then rummaged through the cabinet to find Catherine's favorite chamomile tea.

Leah opened the refrigerator and checked to see if there were lemons. She took one out and sliced it on the counter, moving methodically. When the water boiled, she poured it into the two cups she'd set out, then carried both to the living room, where she sat, and waited, a stranger in the house she had, for so long, called home. There was nothing of her here, Leah realized, and nothing of Missy, as if they had both been erased with a big, soft cloth.

Well, almost.

The house was quiet, and the ticking of the clock on the mantel was starting to get on her nerves. She was wondering if perhaps there wasn't a way to still that *tick tick ticking* away of the seconds when she heard the key turn in the front door. High heels clicked sharply, confidently, across the tile floor. A pause at the answering machine. The message from Catherine's hairdresser reminding her of an appointment the next day. An old friend with tickets for a show that Catherine had wanted to see. And then the last.

"I'm here. I have her. Consider it done."

A soft sigh from the hallway, a long pause, then the sound of heels clicking once again, then stopping in midstride. Tentatively coming toward the small sitting room where Leah sat in the dimly lit room, the candles on the tea table the only light.

Catherine paused in the doorway as if momentarily confused.

"Why, Leah, you're home."

Catherine let her briefcase and her purse drop as she approached Leah with open arms.

"Don't, Catherine." Leah's voice was husky, almost gruff. "Don't come near me."

"Why, Leah . . ." The smile froze on her lovely face.

"Stop it. It's over. Except for knowing why."

Catherine stood very still for a very long time, then crossed the room slowly, unbuttoning the jacket of her crisp navy suit. She sat on the edge of the loveseat opposite the chair in which Leah sat and picked up the cup nearest her.

"Is this mine?" She sipped at it slowly. "It's very good, as always, Leah. Thank you. You know how much I look forward to a nice cup of tea at the end of the day. Just like Uncle Harry, remember?"

"Why, Catherine?" Leah whispered hoarsely. "Why?"

"Sweetie, you didn't really think I was going to let you take *Trends* from me, did you? After all I had gone through to get it?"

"Catherine, I never wanted the magazine. I never would have wanted to take anything from you. *Trends* was always yours to run. It always would be."

"True enough, as long as Melissa was missing." Catherine sipped at her tea, as if this was normal conversation on a normal day.

"What are you talking about?"

"While Melissa was *missing*, things could remain the same. I had the majority of the stock, you and Missy split the rest. My share was larger than yours, individually, but yours and Melissa's together was the greater share. If Melissa was declared legally dead . . . well, you inherit her shares." Catherine paused and looked Leah in the eyes calmly. "I think you can understand where we're going here."

"No. I don't understand a thing."

"When Raymond Lambert contacted you and said he knew where Melissa's body was, I knew that you would do whatever it took to find her. Well, once you found her, Leah, she'd be officially dead, and you'd inherit her share of the magazine, which would give you control."

"Catherine, it wouldn't have mattered. I never wanted control of *Trends*. You were the one who took over when Uncle Harry died, you built the magazine up to what it is. You deserved—"

"You're goddamned right I *deserved*," Catherine's voice rose shrilly, unexpectedly. "For all the years I had to put up with Harry in my bed, all that I had endured—"

"What . . . ?" Leah asked, certain she had misunderstood.

"Dear, sweet old Uncle Harry had been abusing me from the time I was ten years old. He was hardly the grieving brother when my mother's will named him my guardian. He couldn't wait to get me under this roof, every day and every night." Catherine's hands were shaking and she tried unsuccessfully to set the cup and saucer down on the tray without clatter.

"Catherine, you could have gone to my mother. You could have stayed with us—"

"Oh, and what a wonderful life that would have been. Living with perfect Aunt Sally and even more perfect little Melissa. The only reason I could tolerate being around you was knowing that you weren't as perfect as Missy, either. God, she was nauseating. I hated her. I hated all of you."

"Catherine—"

"I did. I still do. All I cared about was *Trends*. He promised it to me. All I had to do was keep our little secret. And I did. Always. I never told anyone. Imagine my shock when his will was read, and I only received forty percent of the stock and you and Missy each received thirty percent." Catherine opened the drawer in the front of the tea table and took out a leather pouch. She unsnapped the flap and took out a cigarette and a small silver lighter. She lit the cigarette and inhaled deeply.

"I'll never forgive that bloody son of a bitch for doing that. He took everything I had, for more years than I can bear to think about, then left me forty goddamned percent of the magazine. It should have all been mine, Leah. I shouldn't have had to share anything with either of you. I paid dearly for everything I have."

"Catherine, did you have anything to do with Missy's murder?"

"Are you crazy?" Catherine exploded. "Didn't you hear a word that I said? As long as you were both alive and well, I still held the majority of the cards. It wasn't until after you started to try to prove that Melissa was dead that I had to do something."

"How did you find Billy Briggs?" Leah asked.

"Through Raymond Lambert." Catherine flicked an ash off the end of her cigarette.

"How did you get to him?"

"Your own Genna Snow was kind enough to leave a step-by-step on how to contact him on the answering machine, if you recall."

"You went to visit him?"

"Three days before you did. I needed to know if he really had killed Melissa. If there was anything I needed to do to protect myself. Well, that Ray was quite astute, I must say. He understood the situation perfectly, understood exactly what I needed. And since I could help him in return . . . well, his plan really was quite clever, Leah. We could kill all the birds with just one stone. Pun intended."

"Explain it to me."

"Ray had this friend—"

"Billy Briggs."

"Yes. Billy Briggs. Ray was a little worried about how Billy was going to get along once Ray had been removed from the scene, what with the execution looming and no hope for an appeal. Billy, it appears, wasn't the brightest bulb on the chandelier, if you get my drift. But he had talents that Ray admired, talents that Ray had even helped Billy to cultivate." Catherine stubbed out her cigarette, then immediately lit another. "It seemed that Billy was in need of some quick cash, since he was having some problem or other at his job. Ray proposed a simple enough quid pro quo solution. I would help Billy, Billy would help me."

"By killing me."

"Yes. Sorry, sweetie."

"The twenty-five thousand dollars I wired to Lambert—"

"Was supposed to be sent to Billy. Unfortunately, Ray went to his eternal reward before the money got to him, since you canceled the wire. But by then, Ray had already written to Billy about me. Once Ray was dead, of course, I had to regroup slightly, but I had Billy's phone number. I called him. At first all he did was wail about Ray. Honestly, Leah, how that man did carry on. You'd have thought that Ray had been his father or something. It was truly pathetic."

"And after that, you dealt directly with Briggs."

"Yes. I really had no choice at that point. I mean, I'd trusted Ray to work this all out, and then there I was, Ray was dead and I had this homicidal maniac at my beck and call. I figured I might as well take advantage of the situation."

"You sent him to my cabin."

"Yes, only, unfortunately, he was a few days early. He was supposed to just take care of you, but, no. He had to play with you a little first. Had to see if he could spook you a little. Stupid bastard."

"You mean, the hang-up calls and moving things around in the cabin."

"Silly immature stuff like that." Catherine rolled her eyes.

"So he got to the cabin in the middle of the week and ran into the Calhouns."

"And he just couldn't resist. He got into the backseat of their car and they just took him right home with them. Never knew what hit them. Or so he said. I didn't ask for details."

"They knew what hit them," Leah said softly.

"Oh? Well, that was Billy's thing." Catherine shrugged. "That had nothing to do with me."

"How can you say that, that it had nothing to do with you?" Leah's well-controlled demeanor was beginning to crack. "It had everything to do with you."

"No, Leah. That was a little sideline of Briggs's. All he was supposed to do was take care of you, then leave, and I'd send him the rest of the reward money. I had already sent him the first installment, which he thought was already his anyway, since you had promised it to Ray, and Ray had promised it to Billy. He felt you owed him. He really did feel bitter toward you, you know, for reneging on the reward."

Catherine stood up and began to pace.

"And then when you finally did get up to the cabin and Ethan was with you . . . well, Billy wasn't sure what to do. Taking on old Mr. Calhoun was one thing, but he said that Ethan looked strong. But once I told Billy just what you had there, you and Ethan, well, he would have walked through hell to get them. Fortunately for you and Ethan both, he didn't have to do that. Unfortunately for me, they proved to be a greater distraction than I'd bargained for."

"What are you talking about?"

"The tapes. Briggs was ecstatic, being able to hear the voice of his mentor talking about his own killings. There was nothing in the world that meant more to him. Well, after they were in his possession, he was a little more difficult to control. All he wanted was to go off someplace and listen to those damned tapes. I had to remind him on several occasions that Ray had promised me that he'd take care of my problem for me and that he wouldn't be paid the second twenty-five thousand dollars until he had."

"Your problem," Leah repeated flatly.

"Yes, sweetie. And you are still just a big problem, more so now than ever. Damn that Billy Briggs for not finishing the job." Catherine rose and walked nonchalantly to the small antique chest near the door and quietly slid open the top drawer.

"If it's any consolation to you, Briggs did try to 'finish the job.'"

"Oh?" Catherine raised one eyebrow. "What happened?"

"I killed him." Leah faced her cousin's gaze levelly, wanting to see her reaction.

"You . . ." Catherine's jaw dropped. "*You* killed *Briggs?*"

"Yes."

"How in the world did you do that?" Catherine appeared stunned.

"She shot him through the heart." John Mancini entered the room through the dining room door and encircled Catherine's left wrist with his hand. "I'll take that. Thank you."

Catherine watched the small handgun disappear from her hand into his, then calmly turned to inspect the stranger from head to toe before saying, "I'm assuming you're with some law enforcement agency."

He nodded.

Catherine turned to Leah and said matter-of-factly, "You know, I always knew that the magazine was going to end up in your hands, though it never occurred to me that it would happen quite this way."

Leah sat back on the chair and unbuttoned her blouse just far enough to remove the microphone that was taped to her chest. Without saying a word, she handed it to one of the agents who, along with several members of the NYPD, had followed Mancini into the room.

"I'm so sorry, Leah," John said as Catherine's rights were read to her and her wrists were secured behind her back. "I can't even begin to imagine what you were going through the whole time . . ."

Leah shook her head, watching as Catherine, who was asking for her lawyer, was led out through the door into the foyer.

"I loved her very, very much. She was all the family I had left. I thought she loved me, too," Leah said in the very small, wooden voice of one who was stunned.

"Genna . . ." Leah heard John say from behind her.

"Come on, Leah." Genna came forward and gently put an arm around Leah's shoulder. "Let's go out through the back. Ethan is waiting for you."

"$\mathcal{D}$o you think we should take a few more sweaters?" Leah tucked two boxes into the back of the Jeep. They'd drop them off at the Mattersons' house while on the way to school to watch Holly's first soccer game of the season.

"She's only an hour away," Ethan reminded her. "She can always call again if she needs them."

Leah frowned.

"I think I'll just run back upstairs and get her heavy gray sweater. Just in case it gets cool this week."

Ethan chuckled as he watched Leah hustle back up the path. She had turned into such a mother hen where Holly was concerned, and no one, apparently, was more surprised than Leah.

Ethan stepped to the edge of the path and looked down on the baseball field on the other side of the tree-line. In another month or two, it would be under a foot or more of snow. It was time to take the nets down from the tennis courts and put the rest of the lawn chairs away. Except for a few hunting parties and groups of old-timers who enjoyed an autumn getaway, White Bear Springs was officially closed for the season.

"I think I'll take this one, too," Leah was saying as she came back down the path, holding up a cornflower blue sweater she'd bought for Holly the previous week in New York.

"I thought that was supposed to be a Christmas present."

"Well, it was. But she might need it now."

"You're spoiling her," Ethan observed.

"But it's practical, see? She can wear it as a jacket. And the blue will match her eyes."

"I repeat, you're spoiling her." Ethan slung an arm over Leah's shoulders as they walked to the Jeep.

As he slid in behind the wheel, he said, "You know, you haven't said much about your trip to New York."

Leah shrugged. "I don't know that there's all that much to say. I met with my lawyers. There are a lot of decisions to be made."

"Anything you want to talk about?"

"There's just so much, Ethan. The brownstone and the magazine . . . I just want to rid myself of all of it, but it just isn't that easy. The good news was that the headhunter I contacted found a wonderful candidate for the editor's job at *Trends*. I met with her on Wednesday. The magazine needs someone with heavy experience to keep it on top."

"And you're certain that you don't want to be that someone?"

"Positive. I never did. I never had any interest in running *Trends*. It still astounds me that Catherine ever thought that I did. I never loved it the way she did. I loved my piece of it. I loved what I did. But I never felt the way she did about the magazine. Certainly not enough to kill someone over it."

"Maybe she assumed that if she loved it that much, it somehow followed that you did, too," Ethan offered.

Leah looked out the window and shook her head. A few minutes later, she said, "I also told the headhunter to look for a new features editor."

"I thought that was your job."

"It is. Was," Leah said pointedly.

"Leah, are you sure?"

She nodded emphatically.

"Leah, I know that traveling the world to exotic locales can't hold a candle to the exciting work you did here this summer. Making French toast for the campers, leading the kids on forays into the woods to pick wild blueberries—"

"And don't you forget the children's theater group I put together, and the musical we wrote," Leah reminded him archly.

"Oh, how could I—how could anyone—forget that original play . . . what was the name of it again? 'The Little Bear'?"

" 'The Little Brown Bear,' " she corrected him. "And I want you to know that I loved doing that. I'd forgotten just how much I enjoyed doing plays."

Leah's voice softened. "Acting was one of the few things that I did really well when I was younger. I belonged to a children's theater group, and I was in so many plays while I was in school. Working with the kids here at camp this summer made me happy in a way I hadn't been in years. It has since occurred to me that if I played up to the boss, perhaps he'd let me do it again next year."

"I hear he's open to bribes." Ethan nodded. "I also heard that he's easy."

"That's good to know. I'm sure I can come up with something."

"I'm counting on it." Ethan reached across the seat and took Leah's hand. "Now, tell me what's bothering you."

"I couldn't even bear to go back into that building," Leah said softly.

"You mean, the magazine offices?"

Leah nodded.

"Sweetheart, you own it. The magazine, the building—"

"Only until we can cut through the legalities and sell it. I hate it, Ethan. I hate what it did to Catherine. I hate what she did to get her hands on it and I hate what she did to try to keep it. I want no part of it. As soon as I can sell it, I will. Until then, if I can stay here with you and Tom and Holly, I'd be very grateful."

"Leah, you can stay here forever if you want. You know that. As a matter of fact, I'm hoping you'll want to do exactly that. I just don't want you to *hide* here. I did it for years, and I know the symptoms." He hesitated, then added, "If you stay, I'd like it to be for all the right reasons."

"I want to be able to work, Ethan, and I want to be with you. I just don't know how I'll work it all out."

They rode in silence, Ethan wondering what would happen when she finally did know. After having spent the entire summer working side by side with her every day, lying down beside her every night, Ethan wasn't sure he was in much of a hurry to find out.

A week later, however, Leah stretched alongside of him in her bed, and said, "I think I want to start doing some writing again."

"What kind of writing?" Ethan asked.

"Magazine articles. The kind I did for *Trends* these last few years. I loved doing that, Ethan. I miss it."

Ethan's heart sank.

"Well, I'm sure that any magazine would be happy to have you."

"I don't want to work for any particular magazine." Leah shook her head. "But I am thinking about freelancing."

"What would that involve?" he asked.

"Traveling, certainly, but I'd always come back here, if you wanted me."

"I want you." He took her face in his hands. "I want you every day, Leah. Every night. There's not a second of my life that goes by that I don't want you."

"Good," she said, and grinned. "There's something so satisfying in knowing that I can have my cake and eat it, too."

Ethan laughed.

"Well, it's sort of like the way you feel about doing your arson work. You like doing it, you enjoy the people you meet, and the people you work with. But you come back here because it's home. It's where you belong. That's how I'm starting to feel, too, Ethan."

"Even if you get put to work in the kitchen from time to time?"

"A little KP never hurt anyone." She pulled him back down to her and he stroked her bare arm.

"I love you, Leah," he told her, covering her body with his. "If you want to go back to work, then do that. But you're right about one thing. This is where you belong. This is your home now."

"That's pretty much what I was thinking," Leah whispered as she drew his mouth to hers and moved against him with the slow rhythm of their love. She knew that it was true. She was, at long last, home.

"Leah, telephone," Tom stood on the back porch and called from his cupped hands, hoping that she would hear so that he would not have to go traipsing down to the playground area to get her.

Leah appeared from behind the jungle gym that she and Ethan were attempting to cover with thick plastic for the winter, and she waved to let Tom know she had heard. She trotted up the path and called to him, "Who is it?"

"Your buddy from the FBI."

"Genna?" she asked, and when he nodded, she quickened her step.

Leah took the nearest phone, that being in the kitchen.

"Hi, Genna."

"How are you?"

"Great. Never better. How about you?"

"Fine. Terrific."

"What's going on?" Leah asked.

"I have something to tell you, but you might want to sit down."

"I'm sitting. What's up?"

"Remember that a few months back I had contacted several law enforcement agencies in northwestern Pennsylvania about possible missing persons or unidentified bodies?"

"Yes," Leah replied.

"Well, we've had a callback from one."

"What do you mean, a callback?"

"I mean, hunters up above Cook State Forest found a partial skeleton last week. It's obviously been there for a long time. The local state police barracks still had my flyer, and they called me this morning."

"Missy?" Leah whispered, barely daring to speak the name aloud.

"Or someone who met a similar fate," Genna said gently. "I thought you should know."

"What happens now?"

"We check Missy's dental records against the remains that we found. It either is or isn't her. But either way—"

"Someone's quest will be over." Leah could not stop the tears that flowed down her face. "You'll call me—"

"Of course. Immediately."

Leah stood and looked out the window, the news flooding through her like an electrical current. She'd all but given up on ever finding her sister since that split second she decided that killing Briggs—knowing for certain he could never hurt anyone again—was more important than locating the remains of one person, even if that one person was her own sister. It was the choice she had made, and she had made her peace with herself, with apologies to Melissa.

The thought that Missy might have been found left Leah breathless, and when Ethan and Tom came into the kitchen, all she could do was repeat over and over, "They found someone. They found someone . . ."

It had taken two days for Leah to have Melissa's dental records located, then transferred into Genna's hands, and then several days more before they got the call. The records matched.

Leah sat on the back porch and cried, and that was where Ethan found her when he came back up from the boathouse.

Sitting down beside her and taking her in his arms, he let her cry it out, knowing that what Leah felt was a jumble of relief and gratitude and grief all at the same time. He knew, because he remembered how it felt when they found Libby, how it felt to know that the search was, at long last, over. That that last bit of doubt could be put to rest.

"Where would you like us to send her?" Genna asked

once the medical examiner had completed his task and released the remains.

"I don't know. I guess . . . I don't know," Leah had answered. "I always used to think that she would be buried next to our parents, but somehow, that doesn't seem to feel right."

"Where do you think she would have liked to be?" Genna asked.

Leah remembered her dream and Melissa's request that Leah "bring me back here."

"At the cabin," Leah had replied without hesitation.

"Then perhaps you could have her cremated and you could scatter her ashes there."

"Yes. That feels right. That's where she wants to be."

Leah had Melissa's remains sent to a funeral home in Bannock, where arrangements for the cremation could be made. A memorial service was planned for the following week. That Ethan would accompany Leah was a given. That both Tom and Holly insisted on coming as well filled Leah's heart. Even Mrs. Beaumont, the camp cook who had grown so fond of Leah over the summer, asked to come along as well.

Genna Snow met them at the cabin, and John Mancini apparently had caught a ride with her. From a front window, Leah watched the duo approach. Genna, looking perturbed, walked briskly along the side of the road, three or four feet in front of John, who strolled along at an easy pace, looking mildly amused. How, Leah wondered, could Genna act so . . . so *nonchalant*, as if she didn't notice this big, hulking, handsome guy who appeared for all the world content to follow along behind her? What was the story there? Leah knew there had to be one . . .

She'd have to have a little chat with Genna one of these days.

Leah had called Melissa's college roommate, Diane, to let her know that, at long last, her friend had been found and would finally be at peace. Of course, Diane wanted to be there. And of course, she told Leah, some of Missy's other friends—classmates and sorority sisters—would want to be there as well.

And so it was that the narrow road that wound past the old McDevitt cabin was lined with cars that October morning. Leah stood on the back deck, the cloisonné urn holding Melissa's ashes clutched tightly in her arms, and watched them gather in the backyard. Young women, Missy's peers, stood along the creek and remembered the talented, beautiful young girl they had called friend. They shed tears and shared hugs and memories. It was with a lump in her throat that Leah joined them. With Ethan by her side, Leah stood on a large, flat rock near the creek bed, and with the sun rising behind her over the trees that had already changed from summer green into autumn golds and reds, she thanked them all for coming.

"That we are all here today to remember Melissa is nothing short of a miracle. A miracle brought about largely by Genna Snow of the FBI, who never gave up. I can never thank her enough for everything that she has done." Leah swallowed, trying to clear her throat, but the lump was a stubborn one and refused to move. She went on in spite of it. "When I lost my sister, I lost so much of what was dearest to me. She was the last of my immediate family, and family is, as I'm sure you all know, the anchor that holds you steady and keeps your life balanced. I have missed her every day that she's been gone. I will never stop missing her. But I am very grateful to have been able to bring her home. And I am grateful to each one of you who took the time to be here with me—with her—to say goodbye."

Leah turned and opened the urn and shook some of the ashes over the water. The swift current immediately carried them downstream. Leah turned and said to the others, "Somehow, I think I expected them to come out sparkling like fairy dust or something, not gray ash."

Leah heard polite laughter behind her, then Holly pointed to the stream.

"Leah, I see sparkles. See, right there . . ."

Leah leaned forward in time to see a small shiny fish dart under a rock.

"Not exactly fairy dust, but it will do."

The laughter was more genuine.

"Holly, you can scatter your wildflower seeds now, if you like."

"Okay."

Holly opened a large tin container that had been sitting at her feet. She took a fistful of seeds and walked along the stream, letting the seeds fall through her open fingers. When she came back to the tin, she looked around at the adults who'd been watching her, and said, "Leah told me that Melissa liked flowers. I thought we should plant some, right where she could see them. You're welcome to plant some, too, if you like."

She gathered a second handful and followed the rocks to the other side of the stream to scatter them there, as well.

One by one, the other mourners went to the tin and took a handful of seeds, then scattered them all along the stream until the tin was empty. Then, in small groups, they came to Leah to say goodbye and thank her for including them in the memorial.

"There will be lots of flowers next summer, Leah," Holly told Leah after everyone left.

"Then we will be able to sit on the deck and admire

them, and we'll have lots to pick for bouquets to put around in the cabin."

"We can put some on Melissa's piano," Holly suggested.

"It sounds as if you've decided to hold on to the cabin," Ethan said, taking Leah's arm and walking with her to the deck.

"I could never sell the cabin. It's been in my family for generations. I want it to be here for the next generation. I want to bring my children here."

"No lingering vestiges of Briggs?"

"Somehow, I feel that having a part of Missy here has, I don't know, *cleansed* it somehow. Does that make sense?"

"Absolutely," Ethan said, nodding.

"It's sort of like the way I feel about the camp. I'll never forget what happened there. But it hasn't gotten inside me. I will never forget that I killed a man, Ethan, but I'd do it again if I had to."

"Taking another life is not something that anyone could forget. But God knows you were justified."

"I really didn't have a choice, Ethan. It was him or you. There was no choice to be made." Leah leaned back against the deck. "What Catherine did—well, that got inside me. As soon as the lawyers can get her to agree, I want the brownstone and the Dean Building and the magazine sold. Looking back, they've brought nothing but sorrow to this family. Uncle Harry held it all over Catherine's head from the time she was a child so that he could use her. And she let him do it in order to get what she wanted. Sorrow and betrayal—that's all I see when I look back."

Ethan put his arms around her and held her so that her head rested on his shoulder.

"And besides, Ethan, I'm tired of looking back. I want

to start looking ahead. I want to see what the future holds."

"I have a few thoughts about that."

"You do?"

"For starters, there's a great old house in Arlenville that just came up for sale. It's about two blocks from the center of town."

"Near the lake?"

"Well within walking distance," he told her. "It has a pretty yard and a small building in the back that someone could use as an office. Maybe even have a darkroom out there, if someone was inclined to develop their own photos. Someone who took a lot of photos, that is."

"Walking distance to the high school, too?"

"Well, you know, all the schools are just a stone's throw from each other, so yes, one could walk to the high school. And to the kindergarten, too, for that matter."

"If one had a wee one."

"Right. Or if one planned on having wee ones." Ethan nodded. "And it's close enough to camp that I can be there for my dad. Close enough to the road into Bangor that someone who needed to fly off to some exotic place for a week or whatever could do so quite easily."

"When might one see this house?" she asked. "If one was interested, that is."

"I suppose I could arrange for a little tour on our way back to White Bear Springs."

"Why don't you do just that while I go down to the stream to get Holly?" Leah took her cell phone out of her purse and tossed it to him. "But what about your dad? What would he do if you moved from camp?"

"He'd be welcome, of course, but I doubt he'd ever leave the lodge."

Leah frowned.

"I would hate to think about him there all alone, all winter long."

"I doubt that he will be." Ethan nodded his head toward the ancient maple, where Mrs. Beaumont had seated herself on the old wooden swing that still hung from a branch on heavy chains. Tom was just about to give her a push. "She's been chasing him for years. Maybe he's slowing down just enough for her to catch him."

Leah laughed. "Call the Realtor, Ethan."

Ethan started looking through his wallet for the phone number of the Realtor who had listed the house.

"Do you think that old branch will hold?" he asked.

"I don't know. I think I'd better warn your dad not to push too hard or too high. We may end up having to pull Mrs. Beaumont out of the stream."

Leah started walking across the grass, then turned and looked up to where Ethan stood on the deck and said, "It's funny, isn't it, how it has all come full circle? How I searched for Missy, and in the end, I not only found her, but I found you, too?"

"Maybe there are some things that were just meant to be." He leaned over the side of the deck.

"Like bringing home a lost soul. Or finding the love of your life when you least expect it." She stopped and looked back at him, her heart swelling within her.

"Yes. To both," he said with a nod.

"Make that call," she told him. "We have a lot to celebrate when we get home."

Leah turned and took a step toward the stream when something shiny in the grass caught her eye. She bent down and lifted the penny that someone must have dropped earlier in the day, since it looked newly minted and bore no trace of dirt.

With a smile, she recalled the children's rhyme that

her mother had taught her, and that she, in turn, had taught Melissa.

See a penny, pick it up.

All your days, you'll have good luck.

Leah grinned and looked over her shoulder at the man she loved, the man who had brought so much good into her life. At that moment, that very man was pacing across the deck, chatting away to the Realtor who would show them the house Ethan wanted to share with Leah, with the family they would make together.

All your days, you'll have good luck.

Leah pocketed the coin. She was counting on it.

She figured they were due.